DEATH BLOW

Loretta Jackson & Vickie Britton

The Fiction Works

1-26-06

Death Blow is a work of fiction. Names, characters and incidents are products of the author's imagination or are used fictitiously. Any resemblance to actual events or locales or persons, living or dead, is entirely coincidental.

Published 2004 by
The Fiction Works
Corvallis, Oregon
fictionworks.com

Copyright © 2002
A novel by
Loretta Jackson & Vickie Britton

ISBN 1-58124-797-4
Printed in the
United States of America

To our parents,

Edwin and Veda Sallman,

with love

Chapter One

Mommy said they would move soon, but Karma liked the old house near the river, the huge rooms, the open back yard that led to big rocks and shady trees along the riverbank.

"Dinner is almost ready, Dolly." Karma's long, dark hair had escaped its careful bow. "Oh-oh!" Mud splattered across her clean, white T-shirt as she carefully shaped and patted a mud pancake into one of the chipped saucers. She offered it to the smiling doll, who waited patiently by cups of water filled from the outside hose at the end of the lawn. The make-believe party made Karma's stomach rumble and she glanced toward the distant porch, wishing Mommy would call her in for supper.

She had been outside a long time. Mommy had sent her out to play while she finished her sculpture. Karma thought of the scary mountain lion with its menacing, yellow eyes emerging from the stone.

The sun was sinking low in the sky. Frogs and crickets called from the river's edge. Soon it would be dark. Karma slapped at a mosquito, which circled the bare skin of her legs. It was time to go in. Why hadn't her mother called? A while ago, she thought she had heard voices. Had someone come to visit?

Karma glanced down at her soiled shirt and hoped Mommy wouldn't be angry. She rose, wiped grimy fingers on the back of her shorts and moved toward the house.

The child peered in through the sagging screen door, stopping when she did not see what she expected to see . . . her mother at the worktable of the screened-in porch, putting the last touches on the mountain lion. The first thing that caught her eye was the blood.

Karma's wide eyes followed the spattering trail into the kitchen. Mommy lay sprawled upon the floor like a great broken doll, her eyes staring, her black hair soaked in a pool of darkness.

"Mommy?" Karma tried to whisper but the words stuck in her throat like a piece of swallowed glass.

In the flash of an instant, through the screen door, she saw a shadowy form bend over her mother's still body. Blood dripped from the jagged object clenched in his hand.

Heart pounding in fear, Karma turned and ran. She felt the sting of thorny branches whipping her legs as she fled the yard and stumbled toward the river.

Her secret place! If only she could reach it, she would be safe!

Imagined footsteps pursuing made Karma lose her footing and trip upon an upturned root. She put out her hands to catch herself, felt the sting of dirt and pebbles graze her palms, the searing pain as her forehead struck hard against a sharp rock.

Dazed, she scrambled frantically to her feet again.

Near the river, she found her secret place, an overhanging shelf of rock with an opening just large enough for her small body to fit inside. She shrank into it and for a long time crouched motionless.

Karma's forehead throbbed. Dampness matted her hair. She touched the sore place; her hand came away wet and sticky.

Darkness was falling. How long had she been there? Karma was afraid of the dark. Tears blinded her eyes. She wanted to go back, but she was afraid. She began to rock back and forth.

She knew something very bad had happened to Mommy. She whimpered into the darkness. Her own sounds frightened her, like the strange mewlings of some terrified animal.

She was still rocking, arms clasped tightly together, when they found her.

Karma was barely aware of the eyes invading her terrible solitude. In spite of the darkness, the eyes seemed to reflect the surrounding green. They were nice, kindly eyes in a pretty face encircled by tangled tresses of blonde. Mommy's friend. Lara!

"Over here!" Lara gasped. "She's bleeding!"

More footsteps. Karma heard a man's deep, anxious voice, felt gentle hands reach out to her, coaxing her from her hiding place. Strong arms lifted her. She remembered the feel of those arms, the pleasant scent of him, like leather and spice. Karma stifled a sob and clung to the man's broad shoulders, feeling the warmth of him, the safety.

Whispering soothing words of comfort, he carefully inspected her forehead. It stung where his large hand pressed against Karma's feverish skin.

Karma drew in a shuddering breath and began to cry. "I want Mommy! Where is my mommy?"

The woman broke the stillness, but not to answer her question. "Are you all right, Karma? Did you fall?"

"Were you in the house?" the man demanded.

Karma buried her face against his shoulder. She could not answer—but a scream sounded that she hadn't intended to make.

"This is very important," Lara spoke. "Was someone there with your mother?"

In her mind, Karma pictured the shattered mountain lion. She saw the gleaming eyes, the snarling lips, and the jagged edge where part of it had broken away.

The man's grip on her loosened. Eyes, almost black, seared into hers. "Who was in there? Did you see him?"

The dark figure she had seen clutching the lion

wavered before her mind. Through the screen door Karma had momentarily glimpsed his face as he bent over her mother's body . . . distorted lips, cold eyes, angry like the mountain lion's.

With cheek pressed hard against the man's shirt, Karma struggled to remember. But a protective shield rose up in her mind, blocking his image. She could see his form crouched over her mother's body. But as he raised his head toward her his features melted into a dark, gaping void. The emptiness slowly filled with the snarling lips and the glittering eyes of the shattered mountain lion.

And the killer had no face.

Lara Radburn slowed her gray Taurus near the narrow iron bridge that hung suspended over the sluggish Quachita River. Through the gathering dusk she could see the fork in the road ahead and catch glimpses of the stark whiteness of the weathered, two-story house, the "river property" that Crystal had leased some time ago. Ghostlike branches stirred in a breeze that smelled strongly of earth and river.

Now that her father's estate had been settled, Lara could only hope for a quick sale of the remaining property, especially of this house and the old, abandoned hotel, which sat back on wooded acreage a few miles from the bridge. She wanted very much to accept the only offer received so far, one on the house, made by the adjoining landowner. Still, she didn't want to make a hardship for Crystal.

Lara idled the engine a moment and debated whether or not she should discuss this offer with Crystal tonight. The meeting with Joan, her Realtor, had kept her longer than she had intended. Although Crystal had given her a standing invitation to drop by anytime, a glance at her watch told her it was almost seven. Crystal, as always, would still be engrossed in her work, so much so, that she probably hadn't bothered to fix the evening meal for her four-year-old daughter, Karma.

Lara wondered if Crystal had finished the stone lion. When she had stopped by several days ago, the sculpture had been taking shape. Lara, with her artist's eye, had recognized already that it was a masterpiece—the huge, obsidian pupils set into the amber glass of the animal's eyes, the wide-open mouth, with the stark-white teeth and powerful, threatening jaws. A sudden eagerness to see the mountain lion's progress made Lara decide to turn down the rough, unpaved road.

The road, so overhung with trees and so deserted, had always made her uneasy; despite this, each time she found herself looking forward to her visits. Crystal's overtures at friendship had taken the edge from the loneliness when her temporary stay in Quachita Springs had dragged on from June into late August. If they had not yet eaten, Lara thought, she would, as she often did, prepare supper for Crystal and her little girl, whom she feared often went hungry during her mother's zealous work phases. Lara usually brought a treat of some kind for the child. This evening she had picked up two Hershey bars without almonds—Karma's undisputed favorite.

Lara smiled in anticipation of the way Karma would run toward her. She had just had her fourth birthday but still had the chubby legs of a baby. She would be all dimples and smiles and glowing dark eyes. Lara had not been around children much, and the immediate fondness she had developed for Crystal's bright and precocious four-year-old had taken her totally by surprise. Lara often worried about Crystal and her daughter. Lately Crystal, usually so zestful, had been immersed in gloom and heaviness. Was it short money causing the change in her? Although Crystal was never behind on the rent, Lara knew how hard it must be for a single woman to be raising a child alone on a freelance artist's wages. Lara wanted to speak to Crystal about doing a feature on her stonework and bronzes. That would be sure to help her. Maybe she would even buy the latest sculpture when it was finished. Though cramped for space, surely Lara could find a place for the magnificent mountain lion in her small apartment once she finished business here in Arkansas and returned to New York. She wondered if the crouching lion, about two feet in length, would fit upon the fireplace mantel.

Lara was anxious to get back to the city and the job she loved: interviewing and featuring various artists in the "Entries on Art" section of the well-renowned City Square magazine. She had worked day and night since she had received the news of her brother Mark's accident; it filled up the empty spaces, kept her from brooding about the senselessness of his death. Lara suppressed a shudder. She knew it was foolish and irrational to blame the town, but beginning with her parent's divorce when she was only five, Quachita Springs was a place she had come to associate only with unpleasant memories.

Her father had died three years ago and her brother Mark eight months later. Her brother's death had severed Lara's final emotional tie to Quachita Springs. She had shrunk from the idea of seeing the town again. But Charles, who had been running the business since Mark's death, was anxious to retire and Lara, the only family left, had no choice but to return and take care of the remaining property. At least one bid had been made on the house by the river. But Lara knew the old, isolated hotel on its wooded acres, that Mark had once envisioned renovating into an artist's retreat, would be her major challenge.

As Lara maneuvered a sharp curve, memories of Mark

rose up to haunt her. She knew she must be within miles of the place where the accident had happened. A hit-and-run, the sheriff had told her. It happened late at night, at a point beyond the bridge on the country road leading through the woods to the old hotel.

The thought of the ancient hotel, the huge, sprawling stone landmark surrounded by dark hills and shadowed trees, made her shiver. Lara was grateful to have the hotel property rented, for since her return, she had not been able to bring herself to cross the bridge and follow that winding road past the spot where her brother had so tragically met his death.

Lara slowed in front of the white house near the river, noticing how still and empty it seemed. Clouds were gathering overhead, bringing a premature darkness. Lara frowned. Usually, by now, Karma came running out to greet her; eager to see what little gift she had brought. A glance to the side where the old station wagon was parked reassured Lara the little family must be home. Was it the feel of the impending rain or the emptiness of the yard that made the first stirrings of warning brush over her?

Trying to bolster her spirits, Lara reached for the candy bars upon the seat beside her and slipped them into her pocket. A sweeping wind tousled Lara's shoulder-length blonde hair as she left the car. She loosened the blue silk scarf about her neck she had worn to brighten her linen dress for the business appointment earlier with Joan. Now it threatened to strangle her.

Lara smelled rain in the air. She glanced up at the darkening sky. Still not quite acclimatized to the sultry heat of an Arkansas summer, she usually found herself welcoming the promised coolness of a summer rainstorm. But this evening, the thought of the approaching cloudburst made her feel anxious.

As Lara crossed the gust-blown yard and stepped up on the wooden porch of the property her father had purchased years ago, she noticed the chipped and peeling paint, the sagging porch roof. She would not need to worry about the serious need for repairs if Joan could manage to close the deal.

Lara didn't really like the thought of Crystal and Karma living here. Too isolated. No place to raise a child. When Lara had first begun to feel a fondness for her tenants, she had discussed this with Joan and asked her to try to locate some nice place for Crystal to rent closer to town.

Lara crossed the porch. She raised her hand to knock, felt puzzled when the front door gave to her touch and creaked slightly ajar. She sensed the emptiness within. She pushed the door open a crack and called, "Anyone home?"

Layers of silence settled at the fading of her voice. Dusk had not quite fallen; coming here Lara had been able to see the road without turning on her car headlights. So why did the absence of light at the windows cause such an eerie feeling, like some horrible premonition?

Cautiously, tension forming a tight band across her chest, Lara stepped into the center of the living room. "It's Lara!" she called, then again, "Anyone home?" She waited expectantly, hearing only the crazed buzzing of a bluebottle caught between a screen and window glass; the slow ticking of a shelf clock.

Lara's gaze skirted the sparse furnishings—the second-hand Herculean chair and sofa, a cold fireplace in the corner, dark drapes, looking oppressively heavy and dingy, hanging from the old-fashioned windows. She paused to locate the clock on the mantle as it chimed the half-hour.

Even the quick tap of her heels on the wooden floor of the hallway sounded unnaturally loud. "Crystal? Karma?"

The hall connected to the kitchen and screened-in back

porch converted into a workroom where Crystal spent a good part of her time. Lara relaxed a little, comforted by the thought that at this very moment her friend was probably so absorbed in her sculpting she hadn't even heard her calls. And Karma was surely in the back yard playing.

An image of Crystal sprang to mind, trim and strikingly attractive even in worn T-shirt and baggy jeans, even with her straight, dark mane of hair tied carelessly back from delicate, oval face. She would be humming a little to herself as she worked, long-lashed eyes lowered, intent only upon her sculpting.

Lara listened intently; by now she should hear the humming, the hollow clink of chisel against stone.

Her own voice sounded dry and frightened. "Crystal?" At the threshold to the kitchen Lara halted. Time seemed to hang before her, suspended. Her numb senses refused to admit the invading horror of the scene before her. The image of Crystal happily working hung juxtaposed over the reality of her motionless body sprawled across the tiled floor, black hair tangled around a deep wound, the broken body of her sculpture, the stone lion, beside her covered with blood.

"Crystal! Oh, no!" The words escaped Lara's lips as a heart-rending moan. She attempted to step forward, but found it necessary to grip the doorway for support as strength drained from her. When she at last was able to bend over Crystal and caught her first glimpse of the eyes focused unblinkingly upon the ceiling, she knew Crystal was beyond her help.

Lara's heart seemed to stop beating. Crystal had obviously been killed by a blow from the stone sculpture. The blood had not dried, was, in fact, still flowing. Lara heard only her own ragged breathing as she rose and recoiled back toward the hallway. That meant the killer might still be in the house!

Where was Karma? Voices in her mind warned her to call the police, to summon help. But her concern for the child blotted out all else. Had Karma been abducted? Or would she find the little girl's body, too?

Panic overruled her fear. She rushed from room to room calling "Karma! Karma!" She searched until she was certain the downstairs was empty. Heart pounding wildly, Lara's gaze fastened to the stairway. Was it possible that Karma had seen, had heard, the struggle that must have taken place between her mother and the intruder and had fled up to her room to hide?

A weird, misshapen shadow, like devil's horns, fell across the darkness of the stairwell, making Lara cry out, her hand frozen upon the banister. When she realized it was only one of Crystal's bronzes, she exhaled a shaky breath, and continued up the steep stairs.

Because Crystal's room was the first one along the hall, she entered it first. A white lace comforter lay smoothed across the bed—the entire room was all rose and white and undisturbed. A smiling photo of Crystal and her daughter set on the nightstand. She couldn't think of Crystal now, downstairs, dead. She must think only of Karma! "Please, God," she prayed silently as she looked under the bed, opened the closet, then moved on to Karma's room. "Just let me find her alive!"

The first item she saw was the teddy bear she had given Karma for her fourth birthday. Brown and shaggy, it watched her from its place of honor on the child's small bed. She looked every conceivable place large enough to conceal a small girl. When she found no trace of the child, she returned downstairs and with aching heart dialed 911.

A numbed part of her listened to the calm, formal voice of the dispatcher. She managed to spill out to him what she had discovered and added tearfully, "Crystal Mar's daughter, just a little girl, is missing! I can't find her anywhere!"

The voice, as if it were not talking to a real person, responded, "Help is already on the way."

"I'm going to continue looking for her!"

"No! Stay on the phone. How did you . . ."

Without ever hearing the ending of the question, Lara dropped the receiver into place. Immediately it rang again, but she was already hurrying outside. She searched the front of the house, then moved along to the side. At the far edge of the lawn she stopped. The sight of a ragged doll propped against a tree as if waiting for a tea party filled her eyes with tears.

She looked down the empty, isolated road she had taken from town, then raised her face to the fast-darkening sky. Waiting for the sheriff to arrive would be endless. She must find the child while there was still enough light to guide her. Karma's very life might hinge on what she did now!

It was evident the child had been playing outside in the yard while her mother worked. Had she been frightened away by the intruder? Or had the killer slipped silently in through the front entrance, attacked Crystal, then fled, leaving the child to discover her mother's body? Lara's throat tightened as she imagined Karma peering in, seeing her mother's body, running away into the night.

Lara examined the ground and found small, scuffed prints leading down the path toward the river. Lara thought of the old boathouse. The two of them, waiting for Crystal to complete some work, had often walked there together. Would the child have run there for protection?

The trail, encroached upon with pines and overhung with the branches of mingling hardwoods, encircled Lara in eerie semi-darkness. A sudden twist in the path made her lose sight of the looming white house and caused her to falter.

Motionlessly, she stopped to listen. An unfamiliar

sound caught her attention. Could it be the parting of branches, a footfall against underbrush? Drawing on what small reserve of courage she had left, Lara strayed from the path into the thick trees.

Lara hadn't realized how closely the trail followed the river. She stopped as she reached the edge and saw the filmy haze rise into the wooded ridges surrounding the bank. Lara gazed down at river water, olive-green, deep and still. Moss and lichens clung to the rocks around it. Further down, where the riverbed sloped, the water moved at a swifter pace, sweeping around boulders in the shallower areas. She felt a momentary relief believing this must have been the noise she had heard.

The gathering darkness made furtive shadows. Poor Karma! If she had run into the woods to hide, how terrified she must be!

Lara returned to the path she had left. She remembered that just ahead, it would widen and fork. Karma and Lara had always taken the adjacent trail, but she suspected that both of them would end at the old makeshift boathouse.

Her eye caught a sudden motion from the north fork of the trail. Lara tensed as the looming form of a man headed directly toward her. Her eyes strained, but she could not see his face, only a tall, taunt outline.

Suddenly, the man ceased walking. The tilt of his head spoke of awareness, alertness. She knew he had spotted her. Even as she instinctively ducked back into the cover of the trees, she realized the uselessness of trying to hide.

Heart pounding, Lara emerged from the shadows and without looking behind her began running back toward the house.

She could hear footsteps thudding swiftly, cat-like, on the path behind her. She knew he was overtaking her. Desperation increased her speed, but the steel-like grip of hands caught her shoulders and forced her to slow and face him.

She stifled a scream.

A very deep and gentle voice said, "Don't be afraid."

Lara gazed up into dark, melancholy eyes. The steady voice continued, "Please. I'm not going to harm you. I am only trying to find the child." The tight grip upon her shoulder blades loosened, and she struggled away, shaken, regarding him warily.

"Who are you?" Lara demanded. "Where did you come from?" In the gathering darkness Lara studied him, the deep, brooding eyes, sensitive mouth, the waves of black hair with slight touches of silver.

"I had a business appointment with Crystal this evening. I was still some distance from the house when I heard Karma screaming and saw her running into the woods. Ever since, I've been trying to find her."

A shiver passed through Lara. Should she believe him? "You don't know . . . why?"

He nodded grimly. "Yes, I know why. We must find the child without delay! I know she's out here somewhere, hiding, terrified."

Lara felt suddenly faint, and pressed a hand to her temple to ward away waves of dizzying blackness that threatened to engulf her. She saw the look of anxious concern as the stranger leaned closer, saying, "I'm sorry if I've frightened you. All you all right?"

This time she felt grateful for the strong arms that reached out to steady her. For a moment she lingered in his supporting embrace, aware of his distinguished appearance, the dark, well-cut suit jacket, the faint scent of pipe tobacco, which put her vaguely in mind of the art professors she so often had interviewed. The sense of familiarity reassured her, drew her to him. He seemed solid, strong, and responsible.

In spite of her fears and the prompting of common sense, she felt compelled to trust him.

"I'm all right." Lara said, gaining control. "We must find Karma! Do you think she went this way?"

"I'm not sure. I lost her in the woods."

As they approached the place the path branched off in two directions, Lara asked, "Where did the path you were just on lead?"

The stranger frowned. "I didn't follow it very far. I had just started down it when I saw you."

"I'm sure both trails lead to the old boathouse. Why don't you search that path and I'll follow this one. We can meet at the old boathouse."

"I think we should stay together," he said, his brow darkening.

"We need to cover as much area as we can before the storm breaks," Lara insisted.

He glanced up at the threatening sky. Then, with reluctance he turned down the other path and disappeared into the darkness. Once again alone, encompassed by trees, Lara wished he were still beside her. Fearfully, she quickened her steps, pausing now and then to call out: Karma!

The farther she went the rockier the narrow path became. On several occasions in her haste Lara stumbled upon sharp fragments hidden by overgrown weeds. This time, looking down, she gasped at the sight of fresh blood spilled across a large, loose stone.

Lara drew away from it aghast. Karma's blood! A wave of horror swept over her. Surely this rock was evidence that whoever had killed Crystal had caught up with the fleeing child! The monster! How could he strike out at a helpless four-year-old?

Aware of tears blinding her eyes, Lara forced herself to step around the bloody stone and stagger on down the gloomy path. She felt her aloneness and wished she had heeded the stranger's advice about staying together. The bloodstains remained vividly in her mind as she moved quickly through the stillness, anxious to reach their meeting place. Her heart became faint. She no longer called out to the child.

A weak shaft of light broke through the sky as Lara left the grove of trees. Through drifting clouds a ghostly white moon illuminated the hills and winding river. The old boathouse loomed as a frightening shadow, which leaned precariously toward the water. Lara's gaze wandered from it to locate the path dropping from high ridges, from which she expected the man she had left a short time ago to emerge.

Instead, her eye caught his silhouette beyond the boathouse. His head was lifted as he scanned a sheer drop of rock above the river. She stopped, scarcely breathing, her eyes holding to his straight back, wide shoulders in dark jacket, outlined against the rough outcropping of buff-colored boulders. He stood perfectly still and silent, alert, listening, like some wary beast of prey.

Who was he? Why had she ever trusted him?

She had wanted to find him; now she held her breath, wavering whether or not she wanted to call out to him. She felt a strong urge to step back into the obscurity of the trees and then to race back toward the house and hope the sheriff had arrived.

Before she could dart out of sight, he turned and saw her. With what light remained in the threatening sky, she got a clear glimpse of his face, of glittering eyes, rough-hewn cheekbones, windswept, coal-black hair touched with silver.

With lithe grace he moved steadily toward her, an intent expression upon his face. "What's wrong?"

"I know she's hurt!" Lara burst out. "I saw blood back on the path!"

"Did you check inside the boathouse?"

A wintry chill swept across Lara's heart. "I couldn't."

"Then we must do so now." The unquestionable authority in his tone, the air of strength again reassured her. Lara followed his lead as they returned to the weathered boathouse, apprehensive of what they might find. Lara clung to the hope that Karma might be hiding within, injured but still alive.

Through the spaces in the bare boards, dim light filtered into the small room as they entered. Life jackets hung from pegs on the wall. An ancient rowboat, tilted to one side, set in the center. Other than that, it was vacant.

"She isn't here!" Lara's statement was a cry of despair. "Where else can we look? We'll never find her!"

The stranger moved outside. Lara remained near the boathouse, as he began to explore the rock-covered slope just beyond the building where she had seen him earlier. She watched his gaze skim the entire hillside where tall oaks towered above the conformity of native pines. Then his attention settled again upon the boulders.

"What is it?" Lara called out. "Do you see or hear anything?"

"Listen. Over there by the rocks."

This time she heard it, too, although the sound was not clear enough to identify. After a short period of total stillness she recognized what she thought was a distinct whimpering. It seemed to come from within the rocks themselves.

"Karma!" Lara dashed forward and began scrambling from one huge rock to another.

The plaintive noise did not stop, nor was there any change in volume, just a steady, low wailing that led her to a small, dark crevice. How could Karma have squeezed through such a tight opening? Maybe she was unable to get out by herself.

Lara peered inside. As her eyes grew accustomed to the darkness of the cave-like gap, she saw Karma huddled into a fetal position. The girl rocked back and forth, eyes closed. Lara could see only long, dark strands of hair, straight, like Crystal's. A floodgate of emotion filled Lara . . . Karma was alive!

"Karma, it's me. It's Lara." She reached out her hands to her. " Honey, are you all right?"

When the little girl did raise her head, Lara gasped at the sight of blood streaming down her forehead. Her first instinct had been to attempt to pull the child from the opening, but her fear concerning Karma's injury caused her to look back at the man, who had followed close behind her.

Within seconds the stranger took her place at the narrow opening and ever so gently spoke to the child. Lara heard in his voice a stirring compassion. Little by little, he coaxed the frightened girl to accept his outstretched hands and move into the soothing circle of his strong arms. "You're all right, Darling. No one is going to harm you."

"She's hurt!" Lara whispered.

"Only a surface wound," he reassured her. "But it's bleeding badly."

The way he held Karma, so protectively, led Lara to believe he knew both Crystal and her daughter very well.

Karma's safety assured, they returned with the child to level ground. Lara pushed back her wet, matted hair to uncover the deep gash beneath the bangs.

Karma's wailing increased causing Lara to flinch.

"We'll need something to staunch the flow of blood," the man said.

Lara's fingers fumbled at the scarf around her neck. Karma struggled as the stranger pressed it against her forehead. Gradually, the child's protests weakened. Drawing in a shuddering sob, she cried, "I want Mommy! Where is my mommy?"

Lara and the man exchanged shadowed glances. How much had the child seen? Had she been a witness to the murder? Lara gently touched her shoulder. "Karma, did you go into the house?"

The child did not answer, only turned and buried her face deeper against the stranger's broad chest. But for a moment, the long-lashed eyes, so much like her mother's, had been filled with some unfathomable fear. Dear God, what had she seen?

"Karma, was someone in there with your mother?" The man's grip upon the child's shoulders tightened as he shifted her around, moving her so that she faced him. Surely, it was concern for Karma, a desire to know the truth, that made his voice seem to thicken and become resolute. "Did you see anyone besides your mother?"

As they waited, Lara noticed that the stranger's eyes were almost opaque. When they widened, rims of white seemed to encircle the pupils. He looked suddenly dangerous, like a trapped and threatened animal. Crystal's sculpture of the mountain lion—the weapon that had struck the death blow—leapt to Lara's mind.

"She didn't see anything," Lara intervened quickly. "She heard the struggle between Crystal and . . . the intruder. It caused her to run away."

"Is that right, Karma?" he demanded as if not entirely convinced. "Karma, you must tell me exactly what you saw!"

Instead of answering, Karma raised her hands to her face and began to scream. The man stroked her tangled hair, but was unable to calm her. "I want my mommy!" Karma reached out to Lara, and she took the child, holding her until gradually her crying subsided. For a moment, they stood in silence.

The small hands clung to her with desperation. Then

Karma began yelling her name, like a moan, "Lara, Lara!"

"It's all right, baby," she said. "It's all right." The little girl went limp in her arms. Lara felt the trembling of her own hand as she placed it to Karma's burning cheek. "She's feverish. We must get help!"

"Wait." The man, suddenly tense and alert, placed a warning hand upon her shoulder. "Someone's coming."

They stared toward the path Lara had intended to take. She caught the sweep of a flashlight, then heard a harsh voice calling, "Lara! Lara Radburn!"

Lara, startled and frightened, answered, "Who's there?"

"Scott Tyler. The sheriff! We've looked everywhere for you!"

Clutching Karma closer, Lara stepped toward the angry voice, but instead of feeling relief, she steeled herself for confrontation. She was aware of the tenseness of the broad jaw, the coldness of ice-blue eyes, although she could not actually make out the sheriff's stern features behind the gleam of light.

"I have the child!" she cried, meeting him in the pathway.

The sheriff allowed the beam of light to fall first upon the pale, frightened child.

"God!" he burst out before he was able to stop himself.

"It's only a gash on the forehead. I think she must have fallen," Lara quickly explained.

The sheriff looked closer. "It's not deep, but it may need stitches." He spoke to the child in gruff, kinder tone. "It'll be all right, young lady. We'll fix you up in no time." Then, to Lara, "Where did you find her?"

"We found her hiding in the rocks above the boathouse."

"We?" The sheriff stiffened as he peered into the darkness behind Lara. "Who was with you?"

Lara looked back, too. The scene, still and deserted, filled her with a frightened emptiness. "He was just behind me. This man, I met him out here while I was searching for Karma."

"What man? What are you talking about?" Scott Tyler, half-dragging Lara and the child with him, proceeded into the clearing and demanded again. "Where is he?"

Where could he have gone? Lara felt stunned, almost betrayed, by the stranger's sudden disappearance. Her heart dropped with the acknowledgment of what that might mean. She had trusted him instinctively. Surely he wasn't . . . he couldn't be the murderer! She drew Karma closer.

Scott Tyler, with drawn gun, entered the boathouse. Lara waited. Heavy clouds once more concealed the face of the moon, blotting out the last traces of light. After what seemed a long time the sheriff came out again. He moved cautiously around the vacant area, playing his light in every direction. "There's no way I'm going to find him in the dark. Did you see a car?"

"I met him walking on the path. I didn't see one. If there was a car, he probably had it well-hidden from the main road." Lara thought of the many back roads, seldom used, that wound into the hills beyond the bridge, of the one in particular that led past the old hotel, the one in particular where Mark had been struck down. "He's long gone by now, but if the rain holds off we might find tire tracks." As Scott Tyler lowered the flashlight, she could see the look of condemnation on his face, as if he believed the whole business were somehow her fault.

Lara tried to explain. "I don't think he had anything to do with . . . the murder. He said he was here to keep an appointment with Crystal. When he came up to the door, he discovered the body, just as I did. Then he saw Karma crying and running into the woods and followed her."

"And, of course, you believed him! You knew a killer was on the loose! Didn't you once think that it might be him?"

The sheriff's words made her feel naive and gullible. How could she explain her instinctive trust of the man, the concern and compassion that convinced her he meant no harm? Scott Tyler would mock these intuitive feelings, say they had no basis in reality. "No, that's not possible," she maintained. "He helped me find Karma!"

Lara could not see, but could feel the burning of Scott Tyler's eyes as he faced her. "Or were you helping him find the child? What in the hell is wrong with you, Lara Radburn?"

With one hand roughly on her shoulder and one on his gun, he begin leading them back toward the house, saying under his breath, "It's damned lucky for the both of you that I showed up when I did!"

Chapter Two

The rain Lara had sensed in the air all day broke through the clouds with unexpected suddenness. The light mist turned into a blinding downpour as they started back down the path to the house. Strong wind shifted the branches, and in a matter of minutes puddles formed, which Lara no longer even attempted to avoid.

Karma made no sound or movement. She was a dead weight against Lara's rain-soaked body. Lara stopped and attempted to switch positions to relieve her aching right arm.

"Here, let me carry her," Scott Tyler offered once again.

"No! No! No!" Karma cried out. Chubby, but strong hands, encircled Lara's neck and clung as if she were hanging on to life itself. When Scott insisted, Karma's words changed into short, gasping screams.

"She's all right," Lara said. "It can't be much farther now."

A twist in the path allowed them to see the old house, rising two stories like a setting from another century. Light diffused from every window and from a yard light outside. Police vehicles with whirling lights parked so close to the porch caused Lara to shiver, less from the drenching than from the image that arose of Crystal's lifeless form. Lara saw again in her mind the spattering of blood that led from the porch to the kitchen. Crystal must have been hit once at the table where she was working. Trying to get away from the madman, she had staggered into the kitchen, where he had followed and struck again. Would she still be as Lara had left her, blood-soaked hair spread across worn linoleum, dark eyes, pupils widened in death, staring up at the ceiling?

Lara wasn't aware of having drawn to a halt until Scott

placed a reassuring hand on her back. "We won't wait for an ambulance," he said. "I'll have one of my deputies take Karma directly to the hospital. Wait here just a minute!"

The sheriff went into to the house. Lara, her hand pressed tightly to the back of Karma's head so the child would not look up and see the doorway, stepped back into to the shelter of the big oak. She could heard the blare of a police radio from one of the cars, see the lights of the sheriff's men combing the area.

As she waited, Lara's gaze fell to Karma's doll, fallen face down from where it had been propped against the trunk. Thinking the child would find comfort in some familiar object, Lara drew forward. She bent to lift the doll, but with a startled intake of breath, let it drop back quickly into the puddle of water. The porcelain face, which some careless foot had crushed against mud and stone, was shattered beyond repair.

Scott Tyler returned with a thin, uniformed man, and steered Lara around several cars toward one marked Quachita County Sheriff. Lara worked Karma's hands loose from her neck and struggled to set her inside the patrol car. She started to slip in beside her but was stopped by Scott's restraining hand.

"You will have to go to the hospital later. We have need of you right now. There are questions you must answer."

"But she can't go all by herself!"

"My deputy will see to everything. He'll admit her to emergency. Our business won't take too long."

"But Karma . . ."

Lara glimpsed Karma's tear-swollen face looking back at her as the car swished away, sliding a little in the mud, straightening out, then heading to the highway. The sound of the siren had already grown dimmer before she angrily faced the sheriff. "She needs me! Whatever you have to say to me can certainly wait! I'm going to follow her in my own car!"

The big form blocked her way. She stared defiantly up at the squarish face, disliking him even more than she had upon their first meeting, when she had confronted him with what she had considered his inept investigation of her brother's hit-and-run accident. Scott, uniform sagging with rainwater, managed to look determined; the way his jaw tilted upward assured her of his total inflexibility.

Lara pushed by him and slid into her car.

"Let me drive." Was he agreeing, then, to follow Karma to the hospital? Reluctantly she moved over and he climbed in beside her, but he did not speak again until they had crossed the iron bridge and turned on the high- way leading to Quachita Springs. "Our talk can't wait," he said staring directly ahead. "But it won't take long if you cooperate."

"You think your investigation is more important than Karma's welfare?"

"She's not in any danger. Not from that small wound."

"But she will be afraid all by herself! Do you know if she has relatives close by?"

"We'll check on that. Until someone arrives, my deputy will stay with her."

Feeling defeated and utterly exhausted, Lara turned away from him. The back and forth, back and forth, swish of windshield wipers sounded loud and harsh in the stillness.

"I want you to tell me all about the man you saw at tonight. Let's start with a simple description."

She stared from the side window, at the rain pounding against tree-covered hillsides. "He was tall, six foot, trim, well-dressed in a dark blue suit. In his late thirties, proba- bly. Very black hair and eyes. Distinguished looking. Some gray at his temples."

"That's just what I thought." Scott settled back in the car seat with satisfaction. "The man I'm thinking of just got out of prison. No doubt he headed right back to his old girl friend, found out she had been stepping out on him, and . . . bamm!" Scott hit his large fist against the steering wheel.

"This man didn't look like a criminal," Lara exclaimed. "In fact he looked . . . cultured . . . professional."

"For every genuine person there are at least two thousand frauds," the sheriff answered shortly. "And here's one of them! All I need is for you to make an identification. I have photos for you to look at."

"But why can't I go to the hospital first? Then I'll stop by your office."

"No, my dear, this comes first."

She did not like the way he called her "dear" without any kindness or without even the slightest indication of affection. She fell silent again, her thoughts turning to the man she must soon identify. This stranger, who she believed had come to her aid, had seemed so concerned about Karma. How could he have just murdered Crystal and have been intending to kill both the child and her? She just couldn't accept his guilt. His image arose vividly in her mind, his features as they had looked illuminated by the last rays of fading sunlight. She had read in him some quality that had caused her to trust him. Could she have been so totally wrong? "Why are you so certain he's guilty?" she asked tonelessly.

"His running away when I appeared does give me some faint indication," Scott answered with sarcasm. "What you want me to do is give him the advantage of time. But I'm getting an APB out for him immediately, before he runs so far away we have no chance of finding him!"

As his harsh words ended, he pressed his foot harder on

the gas. For a time, tires splashing water in every direction, they sped along at breakneck speed. When the lights of Quachita Springs came into view, he slowed the car again, and casting Lara an oblique glance, that took in her muddy dress and disheveled hair, stated, "I'm going to stop by your place. See how fast you can change into dry clothes."

The sheriff's office was dominated by a huge, marred desk, where haphazard stacks of papers set among the jumble of candy wrappers and empty coffee cups. Scott struggled free of his wet jacket and gave it a careless toss toward a vacant chair.

When he turned, his blue eyes fastened on Lara's. His face in the brilliant light seemed even more square, defined by prominent cheekbones and jutting jawline. His brownish-red hair would probably always appear more crumpled than combed.

Old feelings of resentment flooded over Lara. How had this bungling man, who had failed so miserably to investigate the hit-and-run death of her brother a little over two years ago, have ever managed to win reelection? Despite Lara's promptings and pleadings during Mark's investigation, Scott had not acted at all.

"No one could make a case out of what little information I have," he had told her. "I'm sorry, Miss Radburn, I have done everything I can."

Inefficient, apathetic—but why didn't he look so now? He seemed just the opposite, eager to prosecute, ready to convict the stranger who had helped her hunt for Karma without even asking him a single question. Was it because he had some special feeling for Crystal Mar himself? Or was he looking for a quick conclusion to appease the people who had put him in office and to satisfy what she believed to be an enormous ego?

Creases deepened around Scott's eyes, as if he were reading in her face her low opinion of him. "Sit down," he said. He moved toward the coffee urn and returned to hand her a paper cup. "After you make an identification, I'll get things moving. We'll have him back in custody before dawn."

Lara took a long drink. The coffee had a bitter taste, as if it had been heated and reheated all afternoon. "You seem so very certain that he's guilty," she said doubtfully.

"The man's a convicted criminal."

"Convicted of what?"

"Of armed robbery. I sent him up myself." Scott spoke over his shoulder as he shuffled through files. "A violent man. The type that murderers are made of."

He placed a bundle of loose photographs on the desk in front of her. After an accusatory silence, he demanded, "Why are you so certain that he's innocent?"

Lara felt ridiculous trying to explain to him why she had believed that the stranger had been as concerned as she was over Crystal's death.

The mug shorts were grouped in a series of five. She spread several of them in front of her on the desk. Under each face was a number, a description, and a name. Lara skimmed the row after row of faces, hard, cold, unsmiling. She was aware of Scott's watching her, his lips very thin and bloodless, pressed as they were into a harsh, tight line.

Lara restacked these shots and laid out another group. As she did, her eyes locked immediately upon one picture. Her breath caught—6'1", 189 lbs., 38, Dane Lanford.

Lara could not take her eyes from the photo. The inner-fire she had first noticed appeared even in his printed likeness, plainly captured in the large, black eyes. His brow had an aristocratic curve; the nose and lips followed the same distinguished pattern.

She began to feel slightly dizzy. The features in the picture became vague and indistinct. Lara brought a hand to her face and pushed aside the lank, damp locks of hair falling across her cheeks. Was it merely fatigue that made her feel such an unreasonable impulse to protect him, to place his picture with the rejects, and to identify no one?

Why would she have such a crazy desire to trust a total stranger? Particularly one just out of prison? What if he were a cold-blooded killer and she, because of some inane instinct, failed to perform her duty? For Crystal's sake, she must identify him. She had no other choice.

As if Scott were afraid Lara was going to bypass the Lanford photograph, he stepped closer, asking, "Do you see anyone that looks like the man you saw tonight?"

Lara hesitated. "That's him, the third from the top."

"You're sure?"

"Yes, I'm sure."

The sheriff—past experience had made her consider him incapable of action—lost no time. She listened to the sharp, quick sound of his footsteps as he crossed to the door. He raised a hand in summons and several men entered the room, which became loud with voices and commotion.

Her eyes strayed again to the photograph, then raised to find Charles Cade, her father's best friend, standing squarely in the doorway. She had seen him earlier today at her office, where he since his retirement from the police force had helped Dad, and had continued after her father's death three years ago, to look after the Radburn's once vast business interests.

Lara rose, wanting as she had many years ago, a child, like Karma, to rush into Charles' protective arms.

Charles approached her in his slow, calm way. He asked no questions, but she could tell by the way he placed a reassuring arm around her shoulder that he knew everything that had taken place.

"Stumbling into something like this," he said. "You poor kid."

She looked up at his large, blunt features, into the usually humorous, gray eyes that dropped down at the corners, at his gray hair, wet from the rain. He liked to laugh, to tease, and his face looked strange to Lara in its seriousness.

Charles Cade listened to the deputies' voice on the scanner. "Male, Caucasian, 38, 6' 1", 189 lbs, black hair, black eyes, last seen wearing a dark blue suit."

Lara, watching Charles, had the strong impression that he had never fully given up his job as police chief. Slow and cautious by nature, he looked as if he were still in charge, calm and steady, amid the frenzy of activity.

Scott spotted him. "Glad you're here, Charles. I was going to call you the first chance I got."

"I never need calls. You know me," Charles answered. "I've got a sixth sense when it comes to trouble in Quachita."

"Our own John Wayne," Scott observed, flashing a grin toward Lara. "But he's ridden in too late on this one. I've got our killer nailed already. Just a matter of time." He pointed at the photo. "Dane Lanford just got out of prison. He beat it back here to get even with Crystal for being unfaithful to him. My men are going over every inch of the house now. We're bound to find fingerprints, hair samples, some clue, to establish a bonafide case against him."

"I hope it's going to be that easy," Charles replied.

In the quietness of the narrow, hospital room, Lara listened to the sound of Karma's breathing, regular and steady.

Her face, so much like a baby's, looked very pale, framed by tangled, dark hair.

The doctor must have given the child a sedative; she was

sleeping so peacefully. The only sign of trauma visible, other than the pallor, was the white bandage on her forehead.

Very soon, Scott would contact her grandparents, an aunt or uncle—surely someone must exist. Even though the nurse said Karma would no doubt sleep undisturbed throughout the night, Lara couldn't bear to leave her so totally alone.

Aloneness rang hollowly around Lara. It was, after all, her own life's story. Upon the separation of her parents, Mark had stayed in Quachita Springs with Dad; Lara had gone to New York with Mother. Mom had left her with one sitter and another while she worked, while she filled her spare time with her own entertainment that did not include Lara.

Where was Mother now? After Dad's death three years ago, she ran off with a salesman half her age. Lara had seen her only briefly at Mark's funeral, although she had diligently traced her first to one place then another—to Seattle, to San Diego—the correspondence all being one-sided. No matter that Lara was of age, she still rankled from the stink of total abandonment, the horror of being all alone in a world where no one really cared.

She looked down at Karma again, unable to resist the desire to smooth the child's hair. Poor little girl, no one would love her the way she knew her friend Crystal had.

Overwhelmed by fatigue, by a desire to sit down and cry, Lara abruptly left the room. The corridor opened into a vast lobby fronted with a mass of glass. She sank down into one of the chairs and watched the drizzling rain, the occasional glimpse of car lights from the distant highway.

Of all times to think of Mark, to miss him! Of course, when she longed for the support of family, it was Mark who came to mind. Dad had always been immensely busy. Lara had admired his cleverness, how he had out of limited capital built up a small empire. But she suspected that in the end, the content of his heart was a filing cabinet filled with statements of financial profit and loss.

Only Mark had stood by her, had visited her whenever he could, had made long, confiding phone calls and written endless letters. She and her brother had looked and acted so much alike, no wonder people often thought of them as twins. They were both of a slender build, with the same sun-lightened hair and faint sprinkling of freckles across the high bridge of nose, with identical brown eyes that showed a tinge of green.

Between them had existed an uncanny meeting of the minds, a primitive form of telepathy that often allowed them to complete each other's sentences or share each other's thoughts. When he was hurt or in trouble, somehow Lara instinctively knew, just as she had known the night he had died. Mark's death had left such a deep and empty void. She had not and would probably never fully recover from his accident.

She must not think of his death tonight, not when her spirits were already totally downcast by the tragedy of Crystal and Karma. Lara rested her head against the hard back of the chair and closed her eyes. They felt gritty and dry, despite the constant sting of tears. She simply would drive out all thoughts of darkness and death, would refuse to admit images of Mark's body crushed by a fast-moving vehicle, or see Crystal lying dead in the isolated house that Charles, acting as her agent, had rented her.

The void she had momentarily succeeded in capturing and that she was determined to hold began to fill slowly with a sense of gnawing fear. Her startled eyes opened. Was someone watching her?

Lara's gaze darted toward a nurse, who dispassionately read from a clipboard, skimmed to an elderly woman, moving slowly toward the elevator. Her heart seemed to stop in panic. She was fully conscious of an evil presence, hidden, perhaps, in some dark recess very close to her.

A flash of lightning lit up the dark, eerie sky that the great, glass panel brought so close into the room. Could the killer, a maniac, be stalking her, be lurking just outside the lobby? Or was her mounting fear only a product of the terrifying happenings of tonight? Lara stared through the sea of glass, whose reflections were distorted by the pelting rain. Forms seemed to emerge from each shadow.

She stood up abruptly. She could not allow herself to fall apart. If there were danger, it existed for Karma, an eyewitness to murder, not for herself. The thought made her hasten toward the child's room.

Lara felt steadied by Karma's closed eyes, by the calm sounds of her breathing. She seated herself in the chair by the child's bed. She sat rigidly and wondered how much of the crime the little girl had actually seen. She was so very young—even if the killer knew the child had seen him, would he believe he would have anything to fear from her testimony? Common sense would say no, but in his violent, deranged state, the murderer might not be willing to take the chance! A shiver of fear ran over her.

"The child is not in any danger," a nurse's voice, motherly and kindly, sounded from the doorway. "You should just go home and get a good night's sleep."

"I think I'll just stay right here . . . if you don't mind."

"We keep the rooms cool. You'll be chilly. I'll bring you a blanket." She disappeared down the corridor.

Kept awake by coffee from the visitor's lounge nearby, Lara for most of the night maintained an alert vigil.

She now twisted in the unrelenting straightness of the chair beside Karma's bed and tried to settle back into the short, but deep slumber of the last hour.

Without ever opening her eyes, she felt aware of the gray brightness of the room. Morning had come at last! Karma had awakened only twice during the night. Lara had told her fairy tales until she had drifted back to sleep. And, thankfully, Lara noticed that she still slept.

Groggily Lara tried again to return to the comforting confines of her dream. Mark was seated on the ground beside a battered fish box smeared with his messy collection of paints.

Deftly his brush moved across the canvas in his lap. Lara's feet were dangling in the icy water of the Quachita River. Mark, absorbed in his own vision of the autumn hillside that stretched before them with color and beauty, only half-listened to her constant chatter.

It took a long time for the vivid impression of Mark, of a time long past when they had been happy children, to begin to fade.

A nurse, one less agreeable than the one who had allowed her to stay the night, appeared at the doorway and announced with a sharp frown. "If you're Lara Radburn, there's a gentleman in the lobby waiting to talk to you."

Lara, stiff from the uncomfortable chair, rose and attempted to straighten her clothing and hair. It would probably be Scott Tyler with some news for her about the case. If it were Charles, he would simply have bounded into Karma's room.

She was surprised to find another of her father's friend, Whitney Jordan, waiting beside the lobby desk. He was in his late forties, tall and rangy, with dark skin, lined as if he had spent much of his time squinting against brilliant sunlight instead of occupying a small, modest attorney's office just off main street.

Whitney's look of alertness, his gauntness, had always captured Lara's artist's eye; she always thought of him as attractive despite the dominating, hooked nose and the chin that tended to recede into the thin, leathery neck. Part of his overall appeal centered on his fastidious neatness. He now wore a rich tweed suit that contrasted with the color of his blue eyes, one that fit with an exact perfection.

He extended both hands to her, his grip conveying a great a concern. "I've been talking to Scott," he said.

Lara, unsure of whether or not she wanted to hear any news from the sheriff, remained silent.

"Lara, you look so tired. Are you all right?"

Whitney Jordan, his wife Nancy hovering, as always, in the background, had met her at the airport when she had flown in for Dad's funeral. Together they had embraced and cried, for Dad had always referred to Whitney as family, and despite the fact that they were unrelated, there was no doubt that Whitney had considered himself Lawrence Radburn's favorite son.

"How is the little girl?" He did not wait for her to respond, "What a ghastly ordeal for you, Lara." As he spoke he guided her toward the cafeteria. "We need to talk. Let's have a cup of coffee."

The cafeteria, except for employees, was totally empty. "Why don't you find a seat." Whitney, with the great assertiveness that characterized him, left her to fill a tray with coffee and glazed donuts. He didn't speak again until they both had sampled the coffee.

"After what Scott told me, I thought I should come right up and talk to you," he said. In the silence he put on his rimless glasses, which drew attention to the shrewdness of his eyes. He took a paper from his vest pocket, and looking at it instead of at her, said in his deep, serious voice, "Scott brought this copy to me. It's Crystal Mar's will, which he found locked in a box inside the house. No doubt the original is filed with her attorney at Hot Springs."

Lara's eyes fell to the document then rose questioningly to his. "Why would it concern me?"

Whitney didn't answer her question. "It was made out the 23rd of last month."

"Living as she did in my old house by the river, I don't she would have had enough money to warrant her making out a will."

"According to this," Whitney responded, "she does have substantial holdings. Her sculptures must have been selling well. But I'm not here to discuss her financial condition, Lara. Scott wanted me to talk to you because I'm a lawyer, because I have given you as well as your father all of your legal advice. Crystal has done something very much out of the ordinary." As he spoke, he unfolded the paper. "Scott thought it best that I discuss this . . . very unusual matter with you."

Whitney's deep, penetrating eyes held to hers. "Crystal Mar has named you as executrix of her estate."

Relief flooded Lara. "We didn't know each other very well. But in the short time since my return here, we did become close friends. Probably our mutual love for art made that possible. I helped her with several projects and she probably trusted my judgment. Even though she never mentioned any of this to me, I don't find it that unusual."

"If it were only business," Whitney said, "it would be simple enough."

The steadiness of his gaze, that usually inspired her confidence, caused her to shrink away from him. What did he know that she didn't? Why didn't he simply tell her? "There's more to it than being the executrix of her will?" she prompted.

"Crystal Mar has named you as guardian of Karma."

"What? Named me guardian? How could she do that?"

"Didn't you know about this? Didn't she ever discuss it

with you?"

"I've only been back here three months. Sure, we became friends in that time but . . ." Lara's voice died away, then she added with a moan. "To write out a will at her age, to be thinking that Karma would need a guardian! Crystal must have known someone was going to kill her!"

"She's known for some time that Lanford was getting out of prison," Whitney replied.

Lara, so he would not notice that her hand was shaking, set down her coffee cup. "Have they found him?"

"Not yet."

The stillness lay thick around them, like layers of mist over the Quachita River. Whitney's face was dark and placid. He did not once take his eyes from hers.

"Being named in a will as Karma's guardian, doesn't necessarily mean what you're thinking it means," he said at last. "In fact, it is in no way legally binding. Since there was no meeting of the minds between Crystal and you, no contract on your part to serve in any capacity whatsoever, there is therefore no responsibility on your part to accept any position at all."

"Was it really necessary for Crystal to appoint an almost stranger to . . ." Lara's protesting voice drifted away. "Doesn't she have any relatives?"

"Crystal grew up in first one foster home, then another. She was an abandoned child, never adopted. Karma . . ." he tried to put it delicately, "has no father on record."

It was easy for Lara to ask him—she had done so many times before. "Whitney, what so you think I should do?"

"I would simply decline to act as either executrix or guardian. If you get tied up with all of this, you'll never get back to New York City. And I know how much that job as art editor means to you."

"But what will happen to Karma?"

"Orphaned children are a very ordinary occurrence. The social system will place her in a foster home . . ."

"That seems so cold-hearted," Lara interrupted. "To be left with strangers after all she's been through."

Whitney lifted a donut from the paper plate and matter-of-factly, as if he had grown immune to other people's pain, began to eat.

"Of course, even if the court did appoint you as legal guardian fulfilling the wishes of Crystal's will, that still doesn't mean that you would have to take the child to raise. You could oversee her welfare, make sure that she is adequately provided for and that Crystal's assets are used to Karma's advantage."

Whitney continued to speak, his words sounding like excerpts from some legal textbook in his office. She had ceased listening to him. Poor little Karma—was Lara the only one who really cared what happened to her? She soon broke in with a question, "Legally, would I have any trouble getting custody of Karma? Maybe not custody, but I would like to take her home with me. Temporarily."

"I'll see what can be done." Whitney stood up, his eyes squinting, making tight crinkles elongate into his fleshless checks. "But, again, I would advise against doing this. You have your own future to think of. You don't know who the father of the child is. You don't know what might happen next. There is no sense in getting involved in such a messy situation."

Whitney smiled a little as if in attempt to alleviate the coldness of his words. "We've always been good friends, Lara, square with each other. I won't hesitate to tell you straight out: this matter with Karma can only bring you heartache." His light blue eyes darkened. "Maybe worse. This is an extremely dangerous situation—one that is very likely to bring you harm."

Chapter Three

Lara felt the pressure of Karma's small hand in hers as they stepped from the sterile hospital corridor into the parking lot's warming sunlight. The kindly doctor, satisfied with Karma's progress, released her to Lara's care a few hours earlier than scheduled on Friday afternoon. A wide bandage barely visible beneath dark bangs still covered the stitches upon Karma's forehead. Lara was grateful the injury was not expected to leave more than the faintest traces of a scar.

Lara bundled Karma into the car, then tucked the teddy bear she had asked Scott to bring her into the child's arms. At the stoplight, she paused to glance at Karma, who sat quietly beside her, teddy clutched tightly, staring vacantly from the window of the Taurus. Lara studied her forlorn expression, the way her dark lashes cast shadows upon her pale cheeks. Memories of the happy child who had talked a mile a minute haunted her. Physically, Karma would heal. But Lara knew sometimes the worst scars lay buried deep, somewhere within the soul.

They rode in silence. Lara wanted to reach out to touch her, say something comforting, but words and gestures seemed ineffective. What could she do to ease the little girl's terrible loss?

"We're home." Lara forced herself to sound cheerful as, ten minutes later, she slowed in front of the sprawling split-level house that had belonged to her father. As she pulled into the circular drive, she noticed Joan Sommer's car, the "Ozark Reality" upon its side, which matched the one staked in the front lawn of the natural wood house with its wide deck, sliding glass patio doors and many windows.

Because she felt the child needed rest and quiet, Lara

suppressed a feeling of annoyance as Joan poked her head out to call, "Welcome home!" As they crossed the hedge and approached the open front door, she added, "I hope you don't mind, Lara. I used my Realtor's key to get in."

Wiping frosting from her fingers with a paper towel, Joan stepped back and proudly ushered them into a room brightly decorated with balloons and paper streamers.

"Is it my birthday?" Karma asked solemnly. She looked bewildered, Lara thought, as if uncertain how to react. Something in her eyes made her seem sad and old beyond her years.

"It's sort of an in-between birthday," Joan explained. "To celebrate your getting out of the hospital and coming home with Lara."

Attracted by the drifting balloons, Karma wandered further into the room to explore.

Lara felt apprehensive when Joan drew her aside to whisper, "Poor little thing! She's been through so much. I thought a little welcoming party might cheer her. Anyway, it's just Charles and me. And Whitney might drop by later."

"She tires very easily." Lara's worried gaze followed the child, who had wandered from the spacious living room into the open, L-shaped kitchen area where gifts and a half-frosted cake waited.

"Is it chocolate cake?" Karma asked. No smile appeared on her face, only sober curiosity.

"Yes, sweetheart," Joan called.

"Good." Karma made prompt response. "That's the kind Mommy always makes." She sat down quietly at the table and folded her hands in her lap.

Lara and Joan exchanged cautious looks. Lara had read somewhere that children were unable to grasp the concept of death in the same way adults did. Still, Karma's innocent words made a chill invade the festive room.

The doorbell rang. "There's Charles!" Joan said. Lara moved quickly to answer the door.

"I hope I'm not late. Had a little stop to make." He gave Lara one of his endearing smiles. Lara's mouth flew open. Squirming in Charles' arms was a puppy. Well, not exactly a puppy, but an awkward, half-grown brown and white creature with enormous paws. "Thought the kid might be able to use a pet."

"My God, Charles!" Joan cried, taking a step toward them. "A dog? I wouldn't blame Lara if she slammed the door shut right in your face!"

"He'll make a good watchdog," Charles explained sheepishly. "Friendly as hell, but very alert."

Lara moved forward and scratched the pup behind the ears. "Judging from the size of those paws, I'm afraid he's going to turn into an awfully big dog!"

"A good part German Shepherd," Charles boasted.

"And the better part mutt from the looks of him," Joan commented wryly. "Is he good with children?"

As soon as Charles set the pup down, Karma strayed timidly forward. She reached a hand out toward the puppy, then drew back and glanced up at Charles for permission.

"Go ahead," he encouraged, squatting down beside her. "He likes to be petted."

Experimentally she stroked the pup's shaggy head and gave an unexpected laugh at his delighted wriggling. The rare smile deepened in Karma's dark eyes as the puppy lunged forward to lick her face.

"He's telling you he likes you," Charles said.

"Are you sure he'll make a good watchdog?" Joan questioned. "If you ask me, he looks too high-strung to be very responsible."

"High strung is exactly what you look for in a watch dog. You should hear his bark." Charles, smile quickly drooping, gazed from the puppy to Lara. "I can return him, if you want."

But, of course, it was too late for any such notion. When Lara watched Karma place an arm around the dog's ruffled neck and hug him close, she knew the dog was here to stay.

"He's used to being outside." Once more, Charles looked hopeful.

Lara knew when she was defeated. "There's old shed out back."

"Come help me get him settled in, then" Charles said to Karma. "You can call me Uncle Charles if you like. Now, what shall we name him? Sebastian's a good name. Or Beauregard."

"Spot," Karma replied quickly. She looked up at Charles for approval. "He's got spots."

Charles chuckled good-naturedly, "So he does! Then to the dog, "By the powers vested in me, I hereby christen thee Spot!"

"How do you like that?" Joan commented as they watched Charles set the dog down in the back yard. He began foolishly romping around Karma. Joan's dry voice sing-songed, "See Spot. See Spot run."

Lara's problems seemed to be quickly multiplying. First a child, and now a half-grown puppy. She knew owning a pet would only complicate things more when it was time to return to New York.

Lara continued to watch from the patio window. Charles' and Karma's voices rose happily above the excited yips of the pup. For a while, her thoughts brightened. The shaggy brown and white dog would give Karma something to think about, to love, and this diversion would certainly make Lara's task easier. Still, she wished Charles had consulted her before bringing them a pet.

"I've got to finishing frosting the cake." As Joan moved

back toward the kitchen table, Lara noticed she wore a dress beneath the candy-striped canvas apron, and that she still had on heels, as if she had rushed over directly from work.

"Thank you, Joan, for going to all this trouble." From the hall closet Lara took a gift she had also been saving for Karma's homecoming, and placed the plain, rectangular box with the other brightly-wrapped packages.

"You're the saint," Joan insisted. She cast Lara an admiring look as she put the finishing touches on the cake. "Taking in that poor, homeless child!"

"I just couldn't bear the thought of her being shuffled around from stranger to stranger." Lara felt pangs of self-doubt. "I hope bringing her home to stay with me was the right decision." She glanced out at the "For Sale" sign in the yard. "Right now, my own life is so unsettled."

"If you ask me, coming home with you is the best thing that has ever happened to that little girl." Joan scraped frosting from the bowl and smoothed it expertly along the edges of the cake.

"Whitney keeps telling me she would be well off with foster parents, some people he knows," Lara said. Maybe it was her own sense of emotional abandonment at an early age that had made Lara so reluctant to let go of the child. "Crystal trusted me to watch out for her. If the court does appoint me legal guardian, I'm seriously considering taking her back to New York with me. I just don't know if she'd be happy. I want to do what's best for the child."

Lara felt a little awkward confiding in Joan. She was several years older, Mark's age, and tended to control Lara, as she would have a younger sister.

"I think it's really odd how Crystal chose to make you, a total outsider, guardian of her child."

"I wish I had known more about Crystal," Lara

responded. Her friend of just a few months had volunteered only bare facts about her past. Lara knew she had spent time in Little Rock, where she must have attended the University, that she had lived around Quachita Springs since that time, that she had rented the old house by the river about two years ago.

Joan's words burst into Lara's thoughts, "I always thought she was a little weird. What kind of a mother would name a child Karma? You know what that means, 'fate?'"

"Fate is defined as destiny. It can be good."

Yet it was obvious that Crystal, an artist, a drifter, a woman with secrets, hadn't been a traditional person, certainly not anyone's idea of a typical mother. Still Lara knew she had loved her daughter more than anything in the world. And Crystal had placed that child's future, Karma's destiny, in Lara's hands. Not even Lara could understand how this responsibility frightened her.

"Crystal must have known she was going to die."

Lara fought against the eerie sensation left by Joan's veiled gaze, by the ambivalent tone of her voice.

"Maybe she got mixed up with the wrong kind of people. Do you think she could have been into something illegal?

"I'm sure Crystal wasn't involved in drugs, if that's what you're thinking."

"Then she must have been hiding from something, or someone. Maybe it was a jealous lover. Did she ever say anything about the child's father?"

"No." An image of the mysterious man Lara had encountered in the woods came back to her. She remembered his deep concern for Karma, the gentleness in his voice as he had comforted the injured child. No doubt he was Karma's father.

In a hushed voice, Joan asked, "Do you think Karma . . . might have seen something?"

"The sheriff talked to her in the hospital. Since she couldn't describe anyone, Scott is convinced Karma didn't witness the murder or see . . . the killer."

"Thank God for that. Then I guess she's in no danger. Still, the thought of a murderer running around loose in Quachita Springs gives me the chills. I hope they capture him soon."

Charles and Karma's entering the room put an end to the disturbing conversation. "Mmm—that smells delicious," Charles said, eyeing the cake. "I hope we're not waiting on Whitney."

"He told me not to count on him," Joan said. "You know how hard it is for him to get away."

Charles helped Karma wash her hands at the kitchen sink. Then, turning back to Joan, he teased, "Aren't you a little overdressed for the occasion?" Joan had removed the apron to reveal a very chic, basic black dress.

"I have an important meeting at eight," Joan explained. "Austin Graham is picking me up here."

Charles raised a bushy eyebrow. "Am I hearing you right? *The* Austin Graham? The richest guy in the state?"

"He may be Austin Graham III, but everyone knows there's only one!" Joan smiled, flipping back chin-length ash-colored hair. "I hate to disappoint you, Charles, but it's not really a date."

Lara, glad that the atmosphere had lightened, began to cut slices of cake and place them on plates. She poured punch and wished she had thought to brew a pot of coffee.

"Not really a date," Charles mused, a sparkle in his eyes, as he took a sample bite.

"We're going to a land development meeting at the new convention center. That's all. Did you know he's thinking about putting one of his Graham Manors right here in Quachita Springs?"

"Then maybe I should invest in a new set of golf clubs."

"Can I open my presents now?" Karma asked quietly, picking crumbs from her plate with her fingers. Even though she lacked the expected eagerness, her plump, child's face was no longer marked by tragedy.

"Of course, sweetheart." Joan handed her one of the brightly-wrapped packages. "Open this one first."

Karma undid the wrappings to reveal a colorful kit. "Have you ever used finger paints?" Charles asked. "I'll bet you can make a pretty picture with that!"

"I can." With an amiable lift of small shoulders, she added, "Mommy taught me how to be an artist. I'll paint a picture for Lara." She put the paint set aside and reached for another gift. She fumbled with the wrappings and drew out a ruffled pink dress and a small assortment of bracelets and bows.

"I have a feeling you'll look very pretty in that," Joan said. Karma smiled up at her as Joan reached out to wipe a bit of chocolate from her chin. "Just like a little princess."

Lara found herself touched by both Joan and Charles' efforts. She was grateful for their company now, thought about how lonely it would have been coming home with the child to a quiet, empty house. She didn't even mind so much about the puppy anymore. Not if it would help Karma adjust.

Putting the dress aside, Karma reached for the plain, rectangular box Lara had added to the others. Lara drew in her breath, hoping Karma would like her gift.

She saw the pleasure in Karma's eyes as she lifted the new doll with its long, shiny black hair and smiling face from its box. Lara had tried very hard to find a close replacement for the doll that had been ruined, which she knew had been special. She felt a tug at her heart as Karma hugged the doll close.

The doorbell rang. "That must be Whitney now," Charles said. But when Lara crossed into the living room to answer the door, she found instead of her father's friend, his wife Nancy. "Whitney asked me to drop by," she said. Her voice was thin and breathless, almost a whisper.

"Come right on in and join us."

"Oh, I can't stay!" Nancy Jordan hovered uncertainly just outside the doorway. Although the evening was warm, Whitney's wife wore a loose sweater over her thin, sloping shoulders. Wisps of limp, brown hair spilled from its careless clip as if it had been put up hastily for this errand. "I just wanted the little girl to have this." Long, delicate fingers offered Lara a small ceramic figure.

Lara accepted the wide-eyed ceramic squirrel with its curled, bushy tail from her outstretched hand, saying, "Won't you come in for a few minutes and meet Karma?"

"No, I can't!" Nancy stepped back, seeming as wide-eyed and startled as the little creature she had made for Karma. "I really have to get home."

Before she could say more, Nancy scurried with rapid steps down the walkway and out to her car.

"Who was that?" Charles called, craning his neck to see into the living room.

"Nancy."

"Why didn't she come in?"

"You know Nancy. She couldn't wait to get back home." Lara moved back into the bright kitchen. "A nice lady made this for you, Karma." Karma examined the gift and smiled at the amusing face, the large ears and bushy tail.

"Whitney's wife is such a mouse," Joan said. "I often wonder how Whit puts up with her. He's so dynamic, so involved! I've been trying to persuade him to run for county attorney. Of course, Nancy doesn't want him to."

"As long as my family had been acquainted with

Whitney, I've never really gotten to know his wife. But," Lara added, "It was thoughtful of her to stop by."

"Whitney made her do it. She's a real homebody. Doesn't work, never turns up at any of the social functions." With a glance at the ceramic squirrel, Joan said, "She spends most of her time with her ceramics."

Lara's eyes fell to the comic, amateurish squirrel, and with a flash of pain she was reminded of Crystal's beautiful stonework and bronzes.

"She wasn't always so standoffish," Charles said. "I remember when Nan and Whitney were first married; they went everywhere together. After she lost the baby a few years back, she just seemed to let herself go."

"She always looks so pathetic," Joan said. "Whitney really should get her some help."

"I'll make coffee," Lara said, wishing to put an end to Joan's sharp criticism. She couldn't help feeling sorry for the poor shadow of a woman, who had seemed too shy to even come in and meet the little girl.

"I've got an idea," Charles said to Karma. "Let's see who can paint the best picture." Lara's fond gaze followed the man and child as they slipped off to the living room to experiment with the finger painting kit.

"I hope to get Austin interested in your hotel property," Joan said. Her words captured Lara's attention as she began measuring coffee into the brewer. "The land out there would be a perfect setting for one of his resorts. The main drawback is the bridge. It would cost quite a bit of money to widen the passage and, of course, he would insist on paved roads."

"I've been meaning to drive out there and look around," Lara said. "Do you know I've never even met my tenant?"

"Jim Bearle's a shiftless sort, according to Charles. He has a lot of people coming and going out there. You know, wannabe artists, mostly riffraff."

"But his checks have been good and that's a plus." Lara countered. "I guess I feel lucky to have the place rented. The hotel's probably gotten pretty dilapidated. Since I came back, I must admit, I've put off going out there."

Joan sadly patted Lara's hand. "I know. Since Mark's accident, it's hard for me, too, to cross that bridge."

There had been a time, long ago, when Lara had thought Joan might become part of the family. Joan and Mark had been childhood sweethearts, but had eventually gone their separate ways.

"I think you might be surprised at what's been done out there. Mark must have sunk a lot of money into renovation that last year before . . ." Joan's voice trailed off, then she added, "Still, developers are mostly interested in the land."

"I suppose eventually the hotel will have to be torn down," Lara said. Lara thought of the "Graham Manors" brochure she had seen, sand-pink facades rising like garish blights along the Texas coasts, in Colorado mountains, along scenic rivers. Maybe because Mark had put so much of his dream into the idea of an artist's retreat, the thought of a "Graham Manors" standing in place of the stately old stone building depressed her.

Lara heard the puppy barking.

"In three day's time you have a child and a dog named Spot. And you're living in a beautiful house paid for, free and clear." Joan arched her brow. "I shouldn't say anything to jeopardize my commission, but maybe you should forget about returning to New York. Let me take down that "For Sale" sign. We'll find you a husband and you can settle down right here in Quachita Springs."

"Joan!" Lara protested, always astonished by her friend's bluntness. Joan would always be Joan, she guessed, pragmatic, down to earth, always speaking her mind.

"Quachita Springs isn't really such a bad place. It's

unfair you've had such a bad view of it. Since your parents divorced, you've come back here only for funerals." She shook her head. "And now this. It's no wonder you have the place associated with bad memories."

After Dad had died and Mother had left, Lara had even considered returning to Quachita Springs to be near Mark. But at that time she had just been offered the job as art editor for City Square, which influenced her to stay in New York City.

Now regretful over her decision, Lara looked in on Charles and Karma, who had spread newspapers out on the coffee table and were busy on their pictures. Lara noticed how Karma kept her new doll close by her side as she worked, and she felt pleased that the child liked her gift so much.

"Charles is so good with kids," Joan said, coming up beside her. I really wish you'd think about staying. "We could both help you out with Karma." Lara had forgotten how people in small towns tended to stick together. "I'm getting sort of used to having you around."

"Thank you, Joan. I really appreciate your being here for me."

"If things had been different, we might have ended up as sisters in law." A wistful look came over Joan's face, one crossed with pain. "You know, I never really got over losing Mark. But it seemed that after he came back from the university, he was like a stranger. Some professor had filled his head full of ideas about making that artist's retreat. He convinced Mark it would be a way to supplement his income while he worked on his oil paintings. The more involved he got in renovating that hotel, the more time he spent out there. Your dad had always hoped he'd show more interest in the real estate business, but after your father died, he turned most of the responsibility over to Charles."

Joan remained silent for a while, then asked sadly, "When people make new friends, why do they shut out the old? It got so Mark didn't even want to see me. And when we did meet, I couldn't even talk to him. I couldn't understand him anymore."

When her brother had been alive, Lara had never encouraged his relationship with Joan. Lara had told herself Joan was too superficial, that her desire for material possessions would get in the way of his dreams, of his plans of becoming an artist. The thought that she might have been over-protective of her only brother, resentful of anyone who might step in the way of their special closeness, made Lara feel she might have misjudged Joan. Because of Mark's shining idealism, his splendid talent, it had been hard for her to fathom anyone as good enough for him.

"I can understand Austin Graham," Joan said. "When he sees a scenic landscape, he wants to buy it, not paint it." She gave a significant pause. "Real estate and money. Realities a pragmatic mind like mine can grasp."

"Something tells me Charles was on the right track about Austin being more than just a business acquaintance."

"Maybe I'm hoping our relationship will develop into something more."

"You deserve to get exactly what you want."

"So do you, kid." Lara sensed a softness beneath Joan's hard edge that had never noticed before. Maybe losing Mark had matured both of them.

The sound of car wheels crunching on the gravel driveway made Joan nervously smooth her hair. "Oh, dear, Austin must be here already! Do I look all right?" She took a quick glance at her reflection in the glass cabinet, saying, "I'm so anxious for you to meet him."

Joan hurried forward, but Charles had already reached

the door. "So you must be Austin Graham," he boomed, sounding impressed. Around Quachita Springs, and throughout the Ozarks, Graham and his ambitious developments were already a legend. "Come right in!"

"I can't stay long." Declining the offer of a chair, Austin Graham, silver-haired, dressed in a finely tailored suit stepped forward to greet Joan.

"Austin, I'd like you to meet my good friends, Lara Radburn and Charles Cade."

Austin nodded in polite acknowledgment. "So pleased to meet you."

"And this is Karma, who is staying with Lara."

Austin smiled down at the child. "What a nice picture you are making."

As the adults exchanged pleasantries about the weather, Lara noticed Austin's gaze wander about the room, as if admiring the rich damask draperies and tasteful, heavy oak furniture Lara's father had favored.

"Joan tells me you are speaking at the new convention center tonight," Charles said. He leaned back in his chair and studied the successful entrepreneur as a father might size up a daughter's date for the prom.

Lara, too, subtly studied the man behind "Graham Manors." She would have recognized without introduction his thin, arched brows and aristocratic features from the pages of the local paper. He possessed a larger than life quality that the *Quachita Times* had time and again successfully captured. He was stouter than she had imagined him and only of average height, but fit, as if he made working out a daily part of his regime. Only the steel-gray hair betrayed his age, at least twenty years older than Joan.

"Is it true you are considering locating one of your resorts here?" Charles inquired.

Austin's cool gray eyes sparked with sudden interest. "Quachita Springs is booming! And I'd like to be a part of that growth and development."

Joan looked uneasy, as if she expected Charles to inquire about free golfing. "Don't you think we should be going," she urged.

"It was nice meeting all of you," Austin said as he gallantly ushered Joan toward the door. Joan looked especially striking tonight, the picture of understated glamour in the black above the knee dress that accentuated the shapely curve of her slender legs. Lara was reminded of the news photos she had seen of Austin, attending charity balls and ribbon-cutting ceremonies, always in the company of some attractive, younger woman who seemed eager to impress.

Joan collected her purse and turning back to smile and say, "Goodnight all," left the house.

"He's got my vote!" Charles said. "He gets old Uncle Charles' stamp of approval. Joan needs someone like him, older, solid."

"Rich," Lara added lightly. Try as she would, she could not share Charles' enthusiasm. Deep inside she felt misgivings. Maybe it was the rumors of Austin's womanizing that made warning notes go off in her head. At any rate, she knew Austin Graham was way out of Joan's league, and she didn't want to see her get hurt. She knew that beneath the pretense of sophistication, Joan was just a simple, hometown girl. And, as always, when Lara was fond of someone, she felt the terrible burden of protectiveness.

Since his wife Marie had passed on, Charles was always the last to leave any function. He sank down again on the recliner and accepted a cup of coffee.

"Here's your picture," Karma, rubbing sleepily at her eyes, held up the painting she had just finished.

"It's simply beautiful. Is it Spot?"

"Yes. But he shouldn't be blue, should he?"

"You have just taken artistic license," Lara smiled, reaching for the little girl and drawing her into her lap. Karma rested her head contentedly against Lara's shoulder.

"It's getting late," Charles said. "Guess it's time I was going. Then, still reluctant to leave, he added, "Unless you have another cup of coffee."

The house seemed quiet, too quiet now that everyone had gone, Lara thought, as she half-carried Karma up to her room and helped her wash and change into pink pajamas. When she tucked her in, Karma asked for her doll.

Shadows filled the room as Lara went back downstairs and located the doll lying near the finger painting kit.

Automatically straightening the room a little, Lara gathered up the paints, the new dress, and the ceramic squirrel and carried them all up to Karma's room.

Karma, her teddy cuddled on one side, the doll on the other, gazed sleepily up at Lara. "Will Spot be O.K? He's all alone out there."

Lara paused to sit on the edge of the bed. "He has a nice blanket and he's got water and a bowl of dog chow. I'm sure he's very happy."

Karma smiled. "I like him."

"And I like you." She felt small arms cling to her neck as she bent to kiss Karma good night. As Lara held her, she smelled the scent of her skin, sweet and freshly scrubbed with soap.

"I miss Mommy." Karma said softly as she settled down in bed. "Will Mommy be here tomorrow?"

Lara reached out to smooth dark hair away from the child's pale forehead. Her fingers lightly touched the bandage on her temple and all the horror of Crystal's death slammed back to her. "Your mommy wants you here with me a while," Lara said carefully, a catch in her throat.

"Then will you stay with me until I go to sleep?"

"Of course I will, honey," Lara said.

"Tell me the story you told me last time, about the princess." Soon Karma nodded and closed her eyes. As Lara sat in the darkness, gazing down at her, she wondered what the child was feeling. A part of Karma must know that her mother was never coming home. Yet, another part of her wanted to deny the reality of her death. Grief would come in time. Lara knew she would have to help Karma through the steps of understanding, accepting, and letting go.

Lara sat with Karma until her eyelids stopped fluttering and her calm and even breathing told her she was had gone to sleep. Then she crept back downstairs.

Alone, the silence seemed deep and pervasive. Even the dog had quieted down and was probably curled up on his blanket asleep. Lara thought about turning on the television, then instead chose to settle down on the sofa with a book. Sleepless nights at the hospital had made her drowsy and a time or two she found herself nodding off.

Lara awakened to the frantic barking of the puppy and Karma's screams. Jolted into awareness, she sat bolt upright on the sofa. Frightened cries broke through her disorientation. Karma! The child must be having a nightmare! Hysterical sobbing guided her steps as Lara stumbled up the pitch darkness of the stairs to the child's room to comfort her.

"Darling, what's wrong?" Lara switched on the light, blinked against its blinding brightness.

Karma sat huddled upon the bed, knees drawn together, her face covered in her hands. Lara rushed over and gathered her into her arms. "What's wrong, Karma? Did you have a nightmare?"

"A monster!" she gasped. "The monster was in my room!"

"Calm down, honey." Lara held her and stroked her long locks of hair. "It was only a nightmare. Just a bad dream. She eased the trembling child back down on the bed and handed her the teddy bear that had fallen to the floor.

"My doll! I want my doll!"

Lara glanced around the room and found the doll lying beneath the window. As she reached for it, Lara felt a stab of shock go through her. Surely it was only a trick of moonlight, her own overwrought nerves, that made it seem to be lying in the exact position Crystal's body had lain when she had found her. Lara felt a chill creep up her spine. Why hadn't she noticed before how much the doll resembled Crystal? As she lifted the doll, Lara drew in a horrified gasp. A smear of red paint slashed across the plastic head, matting the shining dark hair. A smear that looked like blood!

Behind her, she heard the child's terrified shrieking. "A monster was in my room!" she cried. "A monster killed my doll! A monster killed my mommy!"

Chapter Four

The sharp, spirited barking of the puppy had ceased, leaving only disquieting stillness. Hazy blackness shadowed Lara's vision, remained before her eyes even as she turned back from the night to the sheriff. "This window was closed when I left Karma's room."

"But it wasn't latched?"

"Apparently not. You can see for yourself that it hasn't been broken." A mental picture flashed to her mind of the intruder climbing up the iron latticework that linked the deck with the garage. She could hear the scrape of the window as it opened and picture how stealthily he eased himself into the room. She could imagine his hunched shadow, with eyes straining to locate the sleeping child.

Blackness again blotched her vision, intermingled with the sheriff's blue-clad form, with the unyielding set of his features. "I've never been responsible for a young child before," Lara spoke uncertainly. "I hate to think what could have happened if Karma hadn't awakened! If I hadn't heard her!"

The sheriff strode to the window and stared, as Lara had a moment ago, into the empty darkness outside. His vigilance increased Lara's anxiety. After what seemed a long time, he turned back to her. "The little girl," he said quietly, "had a nightmare. No more than that."

"Of course that's possible. But isn't it also possible that he could have been right here in this room?"

"Who, Lara?" His asking seemed only a gesture, an attempt to prove himself right. "Did you actually see anyone?"

"No, but . . ." Why did he totally refuse to confront her doubts? Anger and terror seemed to surge within her simultaneously, one as strong as the other.

"I don't believe anyone was here tonight, Lara." His words were calm and measured, intending to reassure. "The little girl must have opened the window herself."

"What about the doll?"

Lara felt an inward shudder as Scott knelt down to inspect the doll, to study the horrifying glob of red paint that looked so much like blood. "Karma painted the doll herself," he said finally.

The badge on Scott's jacket caught the light, seemed out of place on the rumpled uniform as he rose. Lara did not meet his gaze, but she knew it would be tolerant, even pitying. "You've been through so much," he said. "I can't really blame you for jumping to conclusions." Then, as if to appease her, the sheriff added. "Of course, you did the right thing calling me. No use taking chances."

Lara had never resented the sheriff as much as she did at this moment. She had never met anyone so blind to anything but his own opinion. With a toss of her head, she confronted him. "After what happened to Crystal, how could you possibly rule out . . ."

"We went over every inch of this ground," he interrupted. "but we found no sign of any trespasser. No car tracks, no footprints. Nothing."

"How do you account for the barking dog?"

Scott shrugged. "Dogs bark. At cars. At other animals."

Scott continued in his own line of thought, "I'm no psychiatrist, but I'd say smearing paint on that doll is this little girl's way of acting out what she is far too young to face. Tonight she was reliving the shock of discovering her mother's body, of seeing the blood."

"Maybe and maybe not!"

Lara attempted to move away from him, but firm hands stopped her. "If Crystal's murderer had been in this room tonight, Karma would not be alive now! And if you had tried to stop him, or even interrupted him, neither would you."

Her gaze caught the paint-smeared doll and she felt overwhelmed by renewed waves of fear. "He could have left this as some kind of . . . warning."

Scott's voice increased in volume, as if this alone would stand for positive proof. "To think Crystal's murderer would crawl in the window and dab red paint on a doll's face is nothing but damned foolishness!" His strong hands clasped her shoulders as if he might shake her. "Please, Lara. Try to be logical."

"What if he isn't logical? Look at the way Crystal was killed!"

"We haven't caught up with Dane Lanford yet. But I don't believe for a minute he was here in this room tonight. Oh, don't get me wrong. If he thought the girl had seen anything, he'd have no qualms about harming her."

Scott's large hands dropped to his side. She watched him pace around the room. "We were hoping that Karma would be able to testify against him. But the police psychologist who examined her at the hospital is certain Karma didn't witness the actual murder. Lanford watches the news. He must know the child is able to tell us nothing. So what reason would he have to come back and terrorize her now?"

"What if Dane Lanford . . . isn't guilty? Lara felt her stomach knot. "What if we are dealing with . . . some madman?"

"Oh, Lanford's guilty all right! And probably about as far away from Quachita Springs as he can get!" She saw Scott's features harden, as if he bore some kind of personal grudge against the man. "But don't worry, I'll find him! And when I bring him in for questioning, I'm going to hold him, some way, until I get a case against him. One that will put him away for good!"

Lara chilled at the reminder that the man she had encountered in the woods the night of Crystal's murder was a convicted felon. She envisioned the enigmatic stranger and recalled how she had been instinctively drawn to him, compelled to trust him. "You mentioned this Lanford had just been released from prison."

"Ever since he came to town, there's been nothing but trouble out at that artist's retreat!" Scott said vehemently. "He uses that 'charm' of his to attract followers. He's surrounded himself with riffraff and he's fooled them into believing themselves great artists. I knew right from the first his being here meant disaster!"

"Why was Dane Lanford in prison?"

"For some time, Lanford had been trying to purchase some original paintings from an affluent, elderly couple here in town. But they weren't interested in selling. Then one night, these priceless paintings were stolen."

Lara had mentally prepared herself to hear some crime of passion or brutal violence and felt something akin to relief. "He was convicted of theft, then?"

"Grand larceny. You don't know how hard I worked to get that conviction! Lanford's an expert at winning people's confidences. And, damn it, people are taken in by him. Even the Baxter's weren't fully convinced of his guilt!"

Lara remembered John and Martha Baxter. Mr. Baxter was a retired banker, and the couple lived in one of Quachita's finest homes along the north side of the river.

"It was an open and shut case. I found the paintings in the trunk of Lanford's car," Scott went on hurriedly. "We also had a very reliable witness that placed his vehicle near the Baxter's home at the time of the robbery. You would think that would be enough proof to convince anyone!"

"Who was the witness?"

Scott hesitated. "A neighbor." He appeared not to want

to discuss it further for he turned away, grumbling, as he did, "I pick these criminals up and what happens? They're turned lose in a few months and I have it all to do again! Lanford didn't serve much more than a year! And now look what he's done!"

Scott's attention came to rest once more upon the painted doll. He picked it up and studied it. "Too bad we couldn't get any identifiable prints. Then you'd know I'm right about Karma." His voice was slow and definite. "Discovering her mother's body brought on this severe trauma. She can't contain it, so it has taken this form." His blue eyes raised to hers, as if he were for her own good determined to go on. "Maybe Karma will get over this, maybe she won't. If I were you, I'd let the social workers take over. They are experienced. You're not." He placed the doll upon the dresser, dismissing it, then turned and said in summation, "This whole evening proves one thing: Karma needs therapy."

"The therapy she needs is patience and love!"

Scott Tyler leveled a challenging look at her. "Do you have enough of that for someone else's child?"

His mind had been closed to all of her concerns during the investigation of Mark's death and was just as closed now. The stone wall of resentment in Lara's mind rose a little higher. "You can be certain of it!"

Scott continued to gaze at her steadily. "Let's go back downstairs," he said.

Scott waited for Lara at the doorway. As she approached, he stepped in front of her, blocking her way. As if sensing the disapproving censure of her thoughts, he said bluntly, "We got off to a wrong start a long time ago. I know you blame me for not finding the driver involved in Mark's accident. But let's not let this affect our relationship now."

She hadn't realized how transparent her feelings were.

"Did I ever say I blamed you?"

"You don't have to. I can see it in your eyes, hear it in everything you say to me. Listen, I knocked myself out to find that car. I worked day after day, long after everyone else had given up. It was one of those impossible, dead-end cases. No one could have solved it. But, Lara, I'm still trying."

For an instant she wondered if because of her own grief over her brother, she had judged him too harshly. Maybe it was unfair of her to harbor resentments because he had been unable to find a hit-and-run driver who had vanished into the night, leaving behind no clue.

Scott could also be entirely right about what had just happened here. The sheriff would surely be competent enough to detect signs of an outside entry. And Lara of all people could not deny the fact that Karma was experiencing extreme emotional shock, that might, if she didn't counteract it, become permanent.

Lara's eyes raised to Scott's. Surely, she had been overreacting to Karma's nightmares and to the bizarre, unexpected sight of the paint-smeared doll that looked so very much like Crystal.

Scott's voice softened as he searched her face. "Even though I know it's not returned, Lara, I have always had a very special feeling for you."

Lara followed Scott down the stairway. Over the square frame of his shoulder she could see Charles, whom she had called even before she had called the sheriff. He was seated on the couch, with Karma in one arm and Spot, wiggling and waggling, in the other. Charles' presence restored some sense of normalcy and stability.

His gray eyes met hers and he nodded reassuringly as if he had everything under control.

Lara felt a rush of gratitude. Charles had no children of

his own, which had brought him closer to Mark and her. He had been around at every crisis in her life and how glad she was that he was here for her now. Karma had taken to Charles instantly, and Lara knew his comforting appearance tonight provided for her the same sense of warmth and security it had for Lara long ago.

"Did Karma tell you anything?" Scott demanded.

Charles frowned slightly, then shook his head. "Nothing that makes sense."

"Let's not upset her anymore tonight," Lara interceded, with a worried glance toward Karma.

The child, withdrawing a chubby hand from the puppy's squirming head, looked directly at Lara. Her tragic, dark brown eyes became liquid, and her voice so imitative of Lara's, announced, "My Dolly's gone. I won't see Dolly anymore."

Lara felt her heart wrench. "Of course you will."

"No. No, I won't!"

"She just needs washing off. Why, she'll be as good as new."

"No! No! No! I don't want to see her anymore!" Karma burrowed her face against Charles' jacket.

As he relaxed his grasp on the puppy, the dog leaped up and began licking his face. Pushing Spot away and attempting to quiet the child, he said, "I like rag dolls better myself. I think I'll buy you one of them."

Karma's face remained tightly pressed against Charles' shoulder, as if his offer did not even tempt her.

The puppy, reacting playfully to Charles' shove, leaped forward again.

"Put him outside, will you, Scott?"

Scott lifted the romping dog. "You're being evicted," he said good-humoredly. Holding the puppy made him seem less insensitive, even, Lara thought, quite likable. The sheriff shuffled Spot outside, closed the screen door between them, and stood surveying the dark yard.

When he turned back to them, a grimness had overcast his features. He drew closer until he towered in front of Charles and Karma, saying in his brusque manner, "I could leave a deputy here until daylight."

At the sound of his voice, Karma raised her head. She looked up timidly, first at Lara. Then her eyes shifted to the sheriff and she cowered back. At the same instant a shrill, piercing scream tore from her lips.

Scott's voice, his tendency to abruptness, must have frightened her. Still Lara felt her legs weaken as Karma, in desperation, clung frantically to Charles. "Sweetheart, what's wrong?" Lara gasped.

"There's nothing to be afraid of!" Charles soothed. Worried gray eyes over the child's head met Scott's.

Scott's tall form became even straighter. "She's remembering that she saw me that night Crystal . . ." the sheriff's sentence faded off, but the tempo of his voice increased as he continued to explain. "It's just like I told you, Lara. She definitely is reacting, having what we called in the army, flashbacks."

Charles rocked the child back and forth, saying, "It's OK, Dimples. Everything's all right." Karma's screams had subsided, were slowly giving way to short, choked sobs.

Scott leaned over her. "I'm not going to harm you, Karma."

The child shrank at the touch of his hand on her shoulder.

The image returned to Lara's mind of Dane Lanford gently coaxing Karma from her hiding place in the rocks, of a terrified and bleeding child extending trusting arms to him. Karma had not been in the least bit frightened of Dane Lanford; yet she remembered now how Karma had refused to allow Scott to carry her that night. Why was she so afraid of him?

"It's the gun," Charles said, as if he had tuned in to her thoughts. "Almost all young children are afraid of guns. And uniforms."

"Right." Scott Tyler moved the holster until it was out of Karma's sight. Then he squatted in front of the couch. "Come on, Honey," he encouraged, holding out his arms, attempting to win her away from Charles. "Cops are the good guys." He tried to interest her in his shiny badge. "Don't you know, I'm here to protect you?"

Karma turned tear-stained face away from him and huddled closer to Charles.

"I'll just take her into the kitchen," Charles said. "We'll see if we can find some ice cream."

"No! No, I don't want ice cream!"

Scott, solemn in the face of Karma's rejection, said, "You might as well stay where you are. I'm going now, anyway." He brushed past Lara, saying, "I'll be as close as the phone if you need me."

Lara followed Scott to the front door. There he faced her, steady, blue eyes looking deeply into hers. "I know a good psychiatrist, Dr. Meg Warner. We often call her in when young children are involved. I can get Karma an appointment with her right away."

"If you think it will help her," Lara answered.

"She's a very disturbed little girl," Scott said emphatically.

"Who wouldn't be?" Charles boomed an indignant retort toward the door the sheriff had just closed. "Poor little kid!"

Karma, fears slowly ebbing, crawled from the couch into Lara's lap. The steady, creaking sound of the rocker soon began to soothe both her and the child. Very slowly

Karma began to relax and the sound of her breathing became deep and easy.

Lara smoothed the strands of tear-damp hair that fell across the smooth, baby face. Scott was probably right about tonight; still, after what had happened to Crystal, she could feel no assurance concerning the child's safety. Perhaps it was wrong to want to keep Karma with her. If someone meant to harm the child, Lara might not be able to protect her! Maybe she would be safer in police custody, with foster parents. But would they want her, love her, the way Lara did?"

No, Lara thought fiercely. Crystal had trusted Karma to her and she wouldn't let her down! As she cuddled the child now sleeping so peacefully in her arms, she knew she could never bear to trust her to anyone else's care. Nor would she even consider giving her up permanently. Maybe Karma and she could leave Quachita Springs soon. Once in New York, they would be free and safe!

Charles, as if sensing her troubled thoughts, said, "I don't see any reason why you and Karma couldn't go back to New York very soon. I was talking with Whitney. He seems to think he can speed up this court work so your appointment as guardian will be approved. Then there will be nothing to keep you here."

"What about your wanting to retire?" Lara asked. "I came back here to sell out, to settle all the business affairs. So far I've accomplished nothing."

"I can stay on for a while. We'll get Joan busy selling what holdings you have left. You don't have too much at stake here anyway. Your father sold all the good property before he died. And as for Mark, he sank all of his assets and all the cash he could drain from your old man, into that blasted hotel. Why, I don't know. It's a white elephant if there ever was one."

"Mark had such hopes for the place. Have you ever been out there?"

"Once or twice. Each time I saw Dane Lanford, surrounded by his lively little colony of artists he called his students." Charles chuckled. "Scott thinks he is some kind of demon, that he mesmerizes his blind followers and exploits them."

"And you? What do you think?"

"Definitely the man has a kind of charisma. Frankly, at first I thought Mark was lucky to have persuaded someone of his stature to join him in such a shaky venture. In the beginning, things seemed to be going so well. Mark's paintings were starting to sell faster than he could finish them."

After a period of silence, Charles went on, "Lanford always called Mark his protégé. Crystal Mar was another of Lanford's successes. You know how popular "Crystal Mar" sculptures were becoming. Before she studied under Lanford, she had never sold one single work."

"Does anyone actually stay out at the hotel now? I mean, besides this Jim Bearle, who pays the rent."

"It used to be packed full. After Mark's accident things began to fall apart. When Lanford began serving time, most of his students scattered. Except for a handful of drifters." Charles paused. "Jim Bearle, there's a cutthroat for you. He looks like a Mafia hit man instead of a painter. And Hallie Parker still hangs around out there, they say. She has herself quite a reputation here in Quachita Springs." He smiled a little. "But not as an artist."

Charles leaned back on the couch. The lines around his eyes and mouth had tightened as if he were deep in some deliberation. After a while, he said, "There's something I should have told you on your last visit, Lara, but you were so upset. And I didn't know what good it would do."

Lara felt her body grow tense. Her arms tightened

around the sleeping child. She knew that what Charles was going to say would concern Mark and would support her own view of what had happened to him.

"Right before Mark was killed, one day in the office, Mark confided in me, 'I've trusted the wrong person.' I'd never seen Mark like that, so hurt and shocked. He went on to say, 'I've suspected for a long time that I'm being cheated, now I have definite proof.'" Charles ran a hand thoughtfully though his gray hair. His brow remained furrowed, as if he were trying hard to recall Mark's exact words, "'I've gathered all the evidence I need and very soon these documents will be in the right hands.'" Charles, who had been avoiding her gaze, now looked at her. "I keep thinking of that."

"Did he say who was cheating him?"

"No. Whenever I tried to question him about it, he clammed up. Wouldn't say another word. But . . . I have a feeling a woman was involved."

"Why?"

"A woman kept calling the office and asking for Mark. This caller would never say who she was, but would just hang up when she found out Mark wasn't there."

"Did you recognize the voice?"

"No, but I believe I've heard it before. It did sound . . . vaguely familiar."

"Do you know what kind of incriminating papers Mark could have been talking about?"

"Something to do with the sale of his paintings, maybe. By then, he was spending most of his time out at the hotel. When he did come into the office, he would be quiet and moody. I got the impression a lot of money must have been involved. I really don't know. But I do know one thing: Mark was crushed. This person that betrayed him must have been someone very close to him. I keep thinking whoever this was could have killed Mark to keep from being exposed."

"If this evidence, this proof Mark had, could only be found . . ." Lara began excitedly.

"Now, don't get your hopes up, Lara. You just leave all the investigations up to the sheriff. And me," Charles added with confidence. "Scott and I make a good team. We always have, during all my years in law enforcement. He still contacts me on practically every case."

"I don't see how you can work with him. I find him very, very narrow."

Once again Charles sprang to the sheriff's defense. "You just don't know him. Oh, he can be pigheaded at times. But Scott's a good, solid man to have on your side."

"I've always had this feeling there was more to Mark's accident than was ever revealed. But I never could convince Scott of that. And you never once let on that you had the same suspicions I did."

"Deep inside, I think Scott also believes there was more to Mark's death than a hit and run. But what could he do without proof?"

"Do you think this Dane Lanford is guilty?"

"Mark brought Dane back from Little Rock and within six months he was dead. Now Dane gets out of prison and immediately Crystal is murdered. It certainly looks suspicious." Charles' frown deepened. "But that woman who kept calling the office bothers me. I have a gut feeling that a woman is behind this or at least is in some way involved."

Lara fell to her own thoughts. If Mark had papers that proved he was being defrauded, and if that was the reason he was the victim of the hit-and-run, she must immediately make an attempt to find them. She hadn't been able to bring herself to go out to Mark's room at the hotel, but that seemed the most likely place to start.

They remained talking for a long time. Charles spoke of

Mark and laughed at the memory of his childhood antics. He talked in length of Lara's father. She hadn't quite realized how very much Charles missed him.

"Your dad always wanted Mark to become a partner in his real estate investments. If only Mark had listened to him, he would probably still be alive."

"My brother would never have been happy sitting behind a desk," Lara said. She felt the familiar sting of unshed tears burn her eyes. "He had to follow his dreams."

Charles sighed. "We're not getting anywhere with this morbid reminiscing." He rose heavily to his feet. "Why don't you go on up to bed? I'll catch a few winks here on the couch."

"You don't need to stay, Charles. "I'll just take Karma into my room for the rest of the night. We'll be perfectly all right."

"Tomorrow's Saturday," Charles said. "I have this idea. How do you feel about my picking Karma up early, then, and taking her to my sister's at Eureka Springs? Donna works with puppets, you know. Kids always get such a big kick out of the show she puts on for the tourists. It might be just what Karma needs."

Lara hesitated. She glanced down at the sleeping child in her arms. The idea of parting with Karma, even for a brief period of time, was difficult. But Charles was like family! Lara trusted his judgment and after the trauma of tonight she knew a brief change of scene would be good for Karma.

"Shall I pick her up about eight?"

Lara nodded. She said goodbye to Charles and he started out to his car. When she had returned from carrying Karma into her bedroom, he was back at the doorway.

"I'm going to leave you a mind-easer," he said, extending a revolver, polished a gleaming black.

At the sight of the gun, Lara's eyes widened. "I wouldn't know how . . ."

"Don't give me that. I trained you myself."

Lara lifted the revolver by the wooden handle and pointed the long barrel toward the carpet. The weapon felt heavy and awkward. Lara drew in a shaky breath. The offer of the gun told her Charles had not completely dismissed, as Scott had done, the possibility that an intruder had been in the house tonight!

"You know how to load it. Here are the bullets."

"Surely I won't need this."

"If I can't stay, then I insist on leaving my best friend," Charles said, "my Smith and Weston 22." He smiled a little and gave the flippant warning, "Don't shoot at shadows," before he disappeared into the darkness.

When Mommy had been making the stone lion, Karma would sometimes stop and stare at it in fascination. The sculpture gave her the goose bumps because it looked so real. Sometimes, when she walked by, its menacing eyes seemed to follow her every movement, as if it were watching her.

Once, when she had been alone in the room, she had imagined that the lion was about to spring to life. She thought she saw the cruel mouth drawing back in a snarl, the claws extending like those of a cat ready to pounce. In terror, she had fled. After that, she had been careful not to go into the room where the lion was alone.

Snuggled next to Lara in the big, warm bed, Karma did not want to think about the lion. She did not want to remember that terrible night when the lion had come to life. And she had looked through the screen door and had seen the streaks of blood and Mommy . . . Mommy lying so still!

Karma had felt bad about running away. But she had been so frightened! She thought she had heard the swift padding of paws rushing after her as she had run away through the woods, but when she had looked behind her nothing had been there. The lion hadn't been real.

Or had he?

And then she remembered the bad man.

Beside Lara, Karma tossed and turned restlessly. The bad man had come in to her room tonight. She had seen him crawl into the window and he had painted her doll and then he had leaned over her while she lay very still, pretending to be asleep. She had tried to tell them how she had seen him. She had even told Charles about his not having a face. Why didn't anyone believe her?

Snuggled next to Lara, feeling her warmth next to her, Karma once more began to feel comforted. Maybe it had all been just a terrible dream. Maybe there was no bad man. And if there was no bad man, then it made sense that there also was no lion. Karma would close her eyes and when she woke up in the morning Mommy would be there. Then she would know it had all been a nightmare. And everything would be all right.

Chapter Five

Karma, scrubbed and groomed, peered from the window of Charles' car, her huge, dark eyes wide and revealing of the fact that she did not like the idea of leaving Lara even for events that promised fun. Karma continued to wave, watching expectantly for Lara's response, as if Lara were the most important person in the world.

Even after Charles and she were out of sight, Lara remained on the step, a cool, damp breeze whipping her hair. Forested hills spread with hazy light. A battered van crept along the highway. How different this was from the bustle of New York City!

Lara thought of the view from her luxurious New York apartment, the giant windows filled with skyscrapers, fog, and bay. She thought of high-heeled shoes, smart business suits, and days crammed with phone calls and meetings. The isolation of Quachita Springs transported her into another world—a world whose center was a little girl, whose safety had begun to mean everything to her.

Inside she stopped in the kitchen to fill a cup with coffee, which she carried from room to room. At the door to the basement, she stopped and thought of Mark. All during his growing up years, the basement had been strictly Mark's domain—a jumble of paint and canvas, an ancient couch that he pulled out into a bed.

During her summer visits when Mark was in high school, Lara would anxiously sprint down these steps—little sister, not so welcome, with too much talk and an eye that could immediately spot flaws in his work.

In those days she had known all of Mark's secrets, about the cigarettes he kept in his paint box hidden from Dad, about Joan's love notes passed to him between classes at school. These letters, because he couldn't bring himself to throw them away and because they were too private to be viewed by as scrutinizing and critical an audience as "little sis", he often concealed behind the back of his homemade wooden frames.

Mark was fond of leather and he had always painstakingly backed each of his wooden frames with the material. This procedure of stretching rawhide across the back of each completed canvas was peculiar to her brother and became his own individual trademark. It was here, behind frame and backing, that he often concealed Joan's letters. Although Lara had known exactly of their whereabouts, she had never allowed herself to go near them. Because she hadn't, Joan Sommers' and Mark's budding romance had been enshrouded with mystery and glamour. Even though her maturing years brought with them the opinion that Joan and Mark were not well-matched, when the news reached her that they had broken up, she had felt poignant disillusionment, for in her mind Joan and Mark were linked with Anthony and Cleopatra, with Romeo and Juliet. What had made these great lovers all of a sudden quit loving one another?

Lara took a tentative step or two downward. The best days of her life had been spent here with Mark, on summer vacations. Through him, she had formed her devotion to art, where she had learned to assess and judge form and style and appreciate beauty.

She could see the huge room below her, bare and empty. Even the battered couch had been removed, as had the sloshes of paint and the disorder that had always lined the shelves. When Mark and her father had argued and he had moved out, obviously he had taken every shred of himself with him.

Convinced that all of Mark's belongings would be in his room at the artist's retreat, she knew what she must do next.

The thought of going out to that deserted hotel filled her with dread. She had put off dealing with Mark's personal things, as a final task to be performed before she went back to New York City. But after what Charles had told her last night, she must steel herself and go out there today.

Her expectations prompted her. It wasn't likely that Mark would have had the papers Charles had spoken of with him the night he was killed. Whoever had silenced him must believe the papers would be of no significance to anyone but Mark.

Lara's sense of dread increased once she was headed down the highway away from Quachita Springs. She glanced toward a truck stop whose weather-beaten sign read, "Last Stop Cafe". The restaurant was open twenty-four hours a day, a hangout for rough, hard-working men. It made her think of bitter coffee, loud, laughing wait-resses, and an over-abundance of cheap food. From the restaurant she could see the Quachita Bridge.

Her heart pounded as she turned from the highway and glimpsed the fork in the road that led to her river proper-ty. She passed it, averting her eyes to avoid catching a glimpse of the white house that now held such terrible memories.

Once across the rusted iron bridge she must pass the exact spot where the mysterious hit-and-run had occurred. For some reason, Mark had been walking back to the hotel very late that fateful night. The bridge was narrow, not meant for two cars to pass. She drove slowly, aware that the water below, around the iron frame of bridge, settled into stagnant depth. Once on the other side she increased her speed. She did not want to wonder again and again, "Was this the spot? Was this the very place where Mark died?"

She was looking for a sign that would read "Lost Pines

Hotel". Noticing an unmarked road, she stopped the car and backed up. Even though there was no longer a sign, this had to be the turn-off. She recognized the steep, upward incline that led through wild, thick growths of trees.

Her car chugged along slowly until she reached the clearing at the top of the hill. A gazebo, made of age-darkened, crudely cut native stone like the hotel itself, set in the direct center of an ivy-choked lawn, around which looped a wide driveway. She drove around it and stopped in line with the entrance, but remained in her car, leaning forward to get a full view of the hotel. Huge rounded towers smoothed back into the long, flat-roofed mid-structure, leaving the false impression that the building itself was circular.

Her eyes skimmed the huge row of windows at the top, empty, hollow windows, a few boarded over, as if restoration had not been carried to the third floor. Overall, the place looked abandoned, neglected, even somewhat sinister.

She could imagine Austin Graham looking at it with disdain, his mind already full of plans for its demolition. If she were lucky enough for him to even make an offer. Of her remaining property, this hotel, built around the turn of the century, would be by far the hardest to sell. For a moment, she wasn't even certain she wanted to let it go. This aged, weathered monstrosity had become linked in her mind with all of Mark's dreams. The building, towering, enduring, was all she really had left of him.

And yet it frightened her. She had to force herself to cross the semi-circular flagstone entrance that led to wide, double doors.

Original drapes of dark blue velvet increased the dimness of the lobby. She paused, her eyes adjusting to the change of light, and felt awed by what she saw. How wonderfully the room had been restored! It looked perfect in every detail, the gleaming crystal chandelier which hung in the center of the room, the polished desk, the great, stone fireplace around which set finely carved furniture, that no doubt dated back to the hotel's first opening. And oil paintings! She was drawing closer to the one that hung above the fireplace, when the sound of footsteps stopped her.

A figure in a soiled T-shirt and faded jeans that bagged across his long legs, emerged from an adjoining room. His face, deeply lined, struck her as mean, even brutal. This must be Jim Bearle—how had Charles described him?— as looking like a Mafia hit man. The description was in every way apt.

He came toward her, then stopped, glaring with open hostility. In the brief instant that followed, she took in his crude appearance and braced herself for an unpleasant confrontation. His hair, sparse on top, straggled in varying lengths around his neck; his bottom lip jutted heavily from his face, but the upper one was thin and tense. He would have fit in well with the hard-eyed men she had often seen idling around the New York City streets.

"What the hell are you doing in here?"

Lara, in spite of herself, retreated a little toward the door. "I'm Lara Radburn. I own this hotel."

"That don't give you any right to trespass!" he said. A spark of anger brought a strange, unstable glow into his eyes.

"My brother was Mark Radburn. I've come for his belongings."

Jim Bearle advanced a step or two toward her. "Nobody's welcome to come and go here as they please! We pay the rent. That makes these premises ours!"

"You surely can't object . . ."

"I can! I do! Now get yourself out of here! If you want anything, you can call for an appointment, like anyone else!" The volume of his voice fell to a threatening rumble.

"You rich bitches think you can do anything you like. We've got rights, too. We pay our rent on this place!"

"Only if I continue to rent it to you!" Lara retorted angrily. "It takes only a thirty-day notice for termination. And you have one, as of now!"

"I would like to apologize for Jim's rudeness," a deep, cultured voice said. Dane Lanford appeared in the arched doorway that Jim Bearle had a moment ago passed through. He paused, his tall, muscular form very straight, as if he were awaiting her response. Then he moved forward, slowly, purposefully, the light from the open doorway falling across the lean, handsome contours of his face.

Lara drew in her breath as he came toward her. What was he doing here? His unexpected presence intensified her apprehension. She glanced from one man to the other. Compared to Jim, Dane Lanford seemed totally civilized, refined in every detail, from the tailored fit of cream-colored linen jacket to the sophisticated touches of silver at the temples of his deep, black hair.

Jim continued to glower at her like some eager guard dog awaiting the master's order to attack.

"It's all right, Jim." As Dane Lanford stepped casually between Jim and her, she could not help but feel gratitude for his intervention. Lara did not miss the look that passed between them; Dane's, that of a reprimanding teacher to an errant student. "I'll show you to Mark's room now," Dane said to her.

Jim with a sullen scowl bypassed Lara and pushed through the front door. With long strides, shoulders hunched, head toward the ground, he hurried past the gazebo and into the thick trees beyond the circular driveway.

"Jim is a very loyal friend. He gets a little over-zealous trying to protect me," Dane said.

"From what? The police?" Lara knew she had reason to

fear him. Why, instead, did she have the desire to warn him that he shouldn't be here? The thought kept entering her mind that he should have left town, that Scott Tyler would most certainly be looking for him here.

Sensing her misgivings, Dane said, "I intend to talk to the sheriff soon, just as soon as I am able to complete some necessary business."

"What were you doing at Crystal's place that night?"

"She called me that evening. She was very upset. And I intend to find out why."

His words either reassured her . . . or Lara wanted very much to believe him. "Why did you disappear so suddenly?"

"If I had remained, I would be in jail this very minute."

"Scott only wants to question you, not convict you."

Dane's lips tightened into a slight smile. "I've dealt with your sheriff before. Scott Tyler's methods are totally familiar to me."

They faced each other in a moment of silence. The smile had moved into his eyes, a smile that threatened to erase the last of her doubts.

"Here." The sudden touch of his hand on her bare arm bought an unexpected tingle to her skin. "Let me show you around the hotel."

He steered her toward the painting above the fireplace, the one she had started to view before Jim had interrupted her. She stood squarely before—what was it?—a boat wreck? From a distance she had thought it only an angry, frothing sea. Every line swirled with some despairing emotion. Whoever had painted it was very skilled in the use of color. Although it suggested a thousand emotions, it rang of one—total emptiness.

"This is one of Jim Bearle's first works."

Lara was startled to find him to be the creator, that such depth could be portrayed by someone who looked and acted like a common street thug.

"Jim may not talk or dress like your ideal artist, but he is in fact talented. I find so many of my gifted students are total nonconformists. They find it difficult to fit into society's constricting roles."

"I must admit he does have a super-abundance of the artistic temperament," Lara commented wryly.

A smile again touched Dane's lips. "If it's any consolation, Jim becomes less frightening when you get to know him. By the way, he is not renting this place from you. I am. I hope this eviction notice does not extend to me."

"But Charles has been collecting the rent from him."

"Jim paid the rent for me. While I was . . . away."

He put everything so delicately. Why didn't he simply say, "while I was in prison?"

Dane, dark eyes skimming the lobby, stepped away from her. The pride evident in his expression became tinged with worry. "I wouldn't want to lose this," he said emphatically. His expression, the fire beneath his words, reminded her of Mark, of his love and loyalty to this place.

"I have been considering putting this property up for sale," she told him quietly.

"I could buy it in time," he said with conviction. "But I couldn't afford it now." He paused, and added ruefully, "I can't afford to lose it either. I've sunk all my dreams as well as all of my savings into this venture."

"Did you loan my brother money?" Lara asked, surprised.

"Mark and I were partners. I invested mostly in promotions and advertising. All the work and what little investment I've put into the hotel itself, I would not even try to claim. But, come along. I want to show you some more of the restoration work."

They passed through the arched doorway where Dane

had overheard her sharp encounter with Jim Bearle. "This room and the one on the other side of the lobby, we will eventually use to display the students' best works."

The walls were completely empty. The room itself was bare except for benches that set back-to-back in the center. The vast length of the room glowed a pale beige, and the ceiling above with its intricate design had been perfectly restored.

"The track lighting was Mark's idea," Dane said. "Good lighting is so important to showing the work to its best advantage."

"This is an ideal setting for an exhibition!" Lara exclaimed.

Upon leaving this room, they passed into a great hallway that ended with a flight of stairs that twisted at the top reminding her of a scene from *Gone With the Wind.* Straight across from them was a closed door. "This opens to the north tower," Dane said, "which at the present time Hallie claims as her private studio. She should be here now." He tapped on the door. "Hallie?"

"Door's unlocked!" a high, shrill-pitched voice called.

Lara made out the hunched form of a girl seated on the floor before a canvas. Around her a series of candles gleamed. The room, flickering with candlelight and without the dimension of square walls, seemed profoundly eerie.

"We're going to have to turn on the lights." Dane's deep laugh sounded as he pulled a switch near the door. "We're not like you. We have no eyes to see in darkness."

The sudden light flooding the room disclosed the fact that she was not a girl, but a woman nearing forty. Lara looked down into a plump, shiny face topped by a wild array of blondish hair. She wore cut-off jeans, that revealed heavy legs, and a tight sweatshirt smeared with paint.

"Hallie, this is Mark's sister, Lara."

Hallie wiped her hands against her shirt. "Hello, there, Lara." She nodded to the candles. "I suppose you think this is weird, but for the things I do, I need mood, atmosphere. Look, Dane." She rose clumsily and gestured toward the canvas she had been working on, anxious for his approval.

Lara stepped forward to see it. The enormous head glaring from the canvas had slits for eyes and a mouth distorted in an expression of anguish. Scarlet accent lines crossed the top of the mouth and colored the hollows beneath the eyes.

The sight of the red paint brought a sickness to Lara's stomach, the identical feeling she had experienced last night when she had stood staring down at Karma's doll.

She forced her eyes to remain on the canvas. Hallie had captured a deadly monotony of form. The body was set in rigid blocks, which freed it from actual, human shape. Overall, Lara found the work revolting.

Hallie waited expectantly.

"It's reminiscent of primitive art," Dane's deep voice stated, "in its desire to harness the power of the spiritual world."

"Spiritual?" Lara had not intended to speak the word with such challenging disagreement.

"I meant by that, not the actual world, but any world that goes beyond our knowledge, like the occult."

"You like it, then?" Hallie asked anxiously.

"I find it very powerful," Dane answered. "And you, Lara?"

Lara, not able to summon a verbal answer, did manage to nod. The word occult rang loudly in he mind. She recalled uneasily the vague rumors she had heard since arriving in town, rumors about the old hotel becoming a home for some sort of cult, particularly rumors of Dane

Lanford, as the cult's despotic leader.

Jim Bearle's dogged protectiveness, this unearthly painting of Hallie's gave credence to the whispers. What was it Charles had told her? Scott Tyler believed Dane Lanford mesmerized people, used his charm to prey upon the weak and rootless. Was Dane Lanford using his unfailing charisma to establish himself here as all-powerful, as demagogue over blind followers?

Lara's gaze roamed around the room as if she expected to see some sign . . . strange markings, pentagrams. She felt Dane watching her.

"You have to be a student of this certain art form to appreciate it," he explained, meeting her eyes. He looked so refined, so rational. Lara suddenly felt profoundly foolish for letting such ridiculous notions about him creep into her mind. She remembered Dane's telling her how many promising artists were unconventional people. Certainly, both Hallie and Jim fit that description. Dane was only encouraging freedom of expression and creativity; of such concepts her brother Mark would have wholeheartedly approved.

"I'm sorry we disturbed you, Hallie, but I did want you to meet Lara."

"A friend of Mark's is a friend of mine," Hallie chirped. "I'll always miss Mark. We all do." She cast Lara a look of sympathy, which seemed undeniably earnest. As they left, Lara paused thoughtfully before closing the door.

"Mark's room is up these stairs," Dane directed.

Lara moved woodenly upward, gripped again with the dread of coming face to face with her brother's personal belongings. They would be certain to flood her with all those memories of Mark she had for her own good tried to put aside.

"How's Karma?" Dane's voice sounded from behind

her. "And where is she?"

Lara stopped on the stairway and turned back to him. Common sense prompted her to fear him. She was at a loss to know why she did not, why she trusted his concern for the child. She even felt close to him as if, through Karma, they shared some common bond. She was beginning to feel an undeniable attraction to Dane Lanford. This realization did frighten her, for hadn't Scott warned her about how easily Dane drew people to him?

"In her will," she said forthrightly, "Crystal specified me as Karma's guardian."

His hand tightened on the railing. "That's strange. I didn't think you knew her all that well."

"I didn't, but we had formed a special friendship and she did trust me."

"What do you intend to do?"

"Karma's staying with me now." Lara went on quickly, "I've been thinking of adopting her."

Dane's hand moved from the railing to cover hers. "I'm glad."

She liked the sincerity in his deep voice, the warm, strong feel of his fingers. She allowed his grasp to linger a moment before she slipped away and continued up the steps.

"Mark's room is the first door on the right. It's the same as he left it that night."

Again Dane had carefully selected his words, not saying the night of the accident. Was it possible he shared her own suspicions concerning Mark's death?

"Were you living here at the hotel at that time?"

"Yes." A murkiness filled his dark eyes. "I was investigating Mark's death, when a criminal charge was trumped up against me. I spent the next sixteen months in the state prison."

"Had you . . . a prior record?"

Dane shook his head absently, as if he were not thinking

of her question. "I received no justice here," he said. "Scott Tyler had spread rumors around town about this place, so the jury had preconceived opinions of me. Besides that, the Baxters are very influential people." As he spoke, he reached around her and opened the door.

Mark's furniture was arranged exactly as it had been in his basement room at home. Tears stung Lara's eyes. It was as if he had just left—a jacket slung over a chair, his battered paint box left open, his old couch unfolded to make a bed. "Could you . . . could you leave me alone here?"

His quick glance toward the phone beside Mark's bed did not escape Lara's notice. Was he thinking that she would call the police the minute he was out of sight? She had no intention of doing that. The police could do their own work and she would do hers.

"I'll be just across the hall," he said before he closed the door.

Lara had come here mainly to look behind Mark's canvasses for hidden papers, but where were the vast number of paintings he always had on hand? A few unfinished canvases void of Mark's special carved frames and special leather backings lay against the shelves near the desk where he had worked. Lara took her time, shifting through the contents of drawers, looking into the pockets of his clothes.

Nothing. She felt an overpowering disappointment. How had she ever have believed she would actually find proof that he had been murdered? If her brother had been killed, the killer had no doubt destroyed the evidence with him!

When she finally stepped into the hallway again, the door across the corridor immediately opened, as if Dane had been waiting for her to finish.

"Mark always had a number of finished paintings around. I wonder where they are?"

"Mark's art was starting to bring top prices. Although I

tried to discourage him, I'm afraid he sold all of his finished paintings at auction. To finance his work here at the hotel."

Lara could not conceal from him her deep regret.

After a brief silence, Dane said. "There is one left. I couldn't quite allow him to part it. I bought it myself." He gestured for her to follow as he crossed back and opened the door to the room he had emerged from a short time ago. "Come in. I'll show it to you."

Behind Dane, Lara glimpsed the masculine bed with thick posters that looked like Doric columns and realized they were entering his private bedroom. Feeling foolish for her hesitation, she quickly stepped inside after him. The south wall was dominated by a fireplace as large as the one in the lobby. Around it set two cushioned velvet arm-chairs, the legs carved with lion heads. To Lara, used to forming quick judgments concerning taste, the room, like Dane's urbane appearance, was flawless, nothing seemed capable of being added or deleted.

"That's Mark's painting above the fireplace. It's called, "The Healing Water".

Mark's themes were easily identifiable, for her brother had been enthralled by the Quachita Indians, and he often set his paintings back in time and based them upon scenes from their abundant legends. She also readily recognized his dramatic use of color and dashing brush strokes, the flare of life and immediacy that had been his trademark.

Lara drew nearer to study the raised head, the slightly open mouth, the straight half-naked form of the Indian poised upon the rocks. So many touches to note in detail! Bubbling water, so very hot, mist, so wonderfully real. The painting left her breathless, as if she herself were caught up on some grand, worshipful moment.

"How adept Mark was at blending realism with fantasy." Lara mused.

"I recognize those cliffs in the painting. Mark told me he had found a place not far from here that gave him inspiration. He used to go there and set up his easel." As he spoke, Lara's attention was drawn to an unusual, mushroom-shaped boulder that made up part of the hazy, almost surreal background. "I don't know the exact location," Dane told her. "But someday maybe you and I will go looking for it."

You and I—the words were spoken so casually. But there was nothing casual about the way he was looking at her. His eyes burned intensely, intimately, as if he were looking into her very soul.

Dane's brilliant gaze held her captive and she felt suddenly breathless, as she had been a moment ago when under the spell of Mark's painting. Her eyes remained locked to Dane's. Desperately she tried to heed the warnings that flashed through her mind: Dane had just been released from prison. He could be dangerous, a ruthless killer! Lara couldn't just wait, unresisting, for him to take her in his arms!

Lara thought this was his intention, but she was wrong. He broke the enchantment by lifting the painting from its place above the fireplace. "This is Mark's finest work, his masterpiece," Dane said. "And I think it should belong to you instead of me."

"Mark's paintings are worth so much," Lara said. "Please, let me pay you . . ."

Once again Dane's large, dark eyes returned to hers. "No," he answered almost reverently, "This is my gift to you."

Chapter Six

Suddenly reluctant to be leaving the vast, quiet coolness of the old hotel, Lara glanced back at the wide doors Dane and she had just passed through. She had been impressed with the renovations. Through Dane, she had today caught a glimpse of Mark's dream. "You didn't show me any of your own paintings."

"I will," Dane met her gaze with an appealing flash of white teeth. "Next time. And then, we'll go exploring. The Arkansas hills are full of so many lovely places, places to stop and set up an easel."

Lara had not worked on any of her own art projects since Mark had died. She thought of bringing her watercolors and trying once more to capture the perfect, Arkansas sunset. Lara stopped herself, realizing with a start that she had already been looking forward to the possibility of a "next time", imagining pleasant walks through the surrounding woods with Dane Lanford. Lara quickly reminded herself that he was almost a total stranger, a man intricately tied to Crystal Mar and the dreadful night of her death.

Dane placed the painting he had given her in the Taurus and returned to stand in the shade of the Magnolia tree. Hot, humid air settled around them, and from bushes growing close to the high stone walls of the hotel the cloying scent of honeysuckle drifted.

Dane's low, even voice broke the stillness. "I never once believed your brother's death was an accident, Lara," he said. "The road across the bridge to this hotel is seldom used, least of all, by Saturday night drunks. Whoever ran Mark down purposefully followed him from town." She heard sadness in his voice, sadness darkened by anger. "His death was carefully planned by someone. It was cold-blooded murder!"

How often these same thoughts had swirled though Lara's mind! Their shared beliefs seemed to bring them closer.

"I was not willing to let his death go down on record as an accident then," he said, "and I'm not now."

His determination strengthened the bond that was beginning to form between them. "Someone wanted to get you out of the way," Lara said, surprised that her voice had no unsureness in it, that she believed this as firmly as she believed what he had just said about her brother's death. "so you wouldn't be able to continue searching for Mark's killer!"

"My investigation was only delayed," he said, "not stopped."

"Then we'll work together. We'll find out . . ." Lara's words were interrupted by a rush of noise and confusion. The screech of wheels against gravel, the uneven blast of a siren made her spin around quickly. For a moment she stood frozen, startled by the intrusion. A white car marked Quachita County Sheriff sped around the circular driveway. Behind this car, another vehicle recklessly turned and approached from the opposite direction.

Scott Tyler sprang from the driver's seat. As if closing in on a gang of dangerous criminals, he crouched behind his open car door for a few tense seconds.

When he cautiously drew forward, both hands held his revolver, pointed upward, but ready to focus in and fire.

Astounded, Lara cried out, "Scott!"

"Get out of the way, Lara! All right, Lanford, keep your hands in full sight! Step forward slowly! I mean slowly!"

The second car had pulled into a position to block the exit of her own vehicle. Two deputies, also holding guns with both hands as Lara had seen them do in movies, eased behind Dane.

Dane made no motion besides a sudden tensing of his

form. But she could sense, beneath the surface, his quiet rage.

Lara, too, seethed with indignation. How long had Scott been concealed outside the hotel, waiting for the right moment to close in? No doubt he had followed her here, had watched though binoculars as she and Dane had stood talking in the front doorway. He had gone back to his car and called for backup.

"Are you arresting me?" Dane asked, calmly facing the sheriff.

"You are wanted for questioning in connection with the death of Crystal Mar." Scott's voice, cold and mechanical, told him, "I am asking you to accompany me to the sheriff's department. If you are unwilling . . ."

"I'll come with you," Dane responded with dignity. Still he remained where he was. Eyes, grown black and opaque, moved from Scott Tyler to Lara. Lara paled. Surely, Dane didn't think she had called the sheriff!

But what else could he think? Lara felt the impact of his accusation, felt, rather than saw, the evidence of deep hurt, surprising him, alarming, like the thrust of a knife blade. "Dane, I . . ." Lara faltered.

Scott lost no time. Before Lara could further explain, he drew forward and with professional briskness searched Dane for a weapon. Dane, unresisting, allowed his wrists to be forced behind him and snapped with handcuffs. She saw the look in his eyes, sadness mingled with the pain of betrayal.

"There's no need for that!" Lara cried.

Scott's answer was clipped, "I let him slip away once!" Lara resented the look of triumph on the sheriff's face. "I've gone to a lot of trouble finding him. He's not getting away again!"

Dane avoided Lara's eyes. His lips, that had smiled at her with such warmth minutes ago, became tightly drawn, silent.

The two deputies hurried forward and led Dane to the sheriff's car. Lara followed, wanting to speak to Dane, but the sheriff's heavy hand on her arm, stopped her. "Frankly, I think you have some explaining to do, Lara," Scott Tyler admonished, his blue eyes cold. He began leading her back toward her own car.

"There's nothing to explain," Lara responded flatly. "Dane fully intended to go to your office and talk to you. He certainly wouldn't come near this hotel if he were trying to hide from you."

"Maybe he's using reverse psychology."

"Maybe you are on the wrong track thinking he's guilty."

Scott's eyes narrowed. "I would like to know what are you doing out here . . . with him?"

"This is my property. Our meeting was purely a coincidence."

Scott drew to a stop. His eyes flickered briefly, but with interest, over Mark's painting, propped behind the seat of her car. His gaze lifted doubtfully to hers. But whatever remanding words he had for her were interrupted by the deputy's voice calling his name. "We'll talk later," he assured her gruffly.

Lara remained staring after him, hoping Dane would look her way. Scott slipped into the driver's seat and she watched the squad cars move in solemn line around the driveway toward the dusty road leading to Quachita Springs.

Anger at Scott filled her. She tried hard to control it by reminding herself that Scott did have every right to pick Dane up for questioning. Dane Lanford was the prime suspect in Crystal's murder! As much as she believed in his innocence, she could not let her personal feelings, her vulnerability to him.

Anyway, Dane Lanford would not be held in jail. They

had no solid evidence against him. He would merely be questioned and released. There would be time enough to explain to Dane she had played no part in his apprehension.

Lara caught a final glimpse of Dane. Through the barrier of the car window she saw his grim profile, the rigid set of his shoulders. She wished that he would look at her, but his gaze remained fixed straight ahead. Why did he refuse to glance her way? If he would, perhaps she could assure him by a look or a gesture that she had not called the sheriff when he had left her alone in Mark's room, that she had not betrayed him!

The squad cars disappeared into the shield of trees, leaving in their wake total stillness. Dane's being taken away in handcuffs made her feel so strange and empty.

The scent of honeysuckle and wildflowers mingled with the damp, weedy smells of old growth and underbrush. Just a short time ago, these August, mountain fragrances had been refreshing, now they closed around her, oppressive and suffocating.

Lara faced the hotel where Hallie, no doubt oblivious to the outside world, still painted, then glanced uneasily toward the path Jim Bearle had taken. How would Jim Bearle react to Dane's plight, if he knew? She had no desire to stay around and find out.

Fingers tense on the wheel, Lara hurried toward home. She prayed that Mark had hidden the papers she had been looking for behind the frame of "The Healing Water"—papers that would somehow miraculously provide the key to what had happened to Mark and Crystal!

Once inside the house, Lara placed the painting face down on the dining room table. She stared down at the unique, rawhide backing that Mark meticulously placed upon each of his finished canvases. Lara gently removed the backing, then anxiously checked the space between leather and canvas. Empty! No papers were tucked inside or stapled to the wood.

Disappointment brought tears to her eyes. Lara thought she had known her brother so well! She had been certain that if he had hidden important information, she would find it here, concealed behind his final painting!

Lara, overcome by her discouragement, replaced the backing with tiny brads she found in the nearby drawer. As she worked, her fingers lingered upon a torn place, as if the rawhide backing had been taken apart before. Lara tried to dismiss her uneasy feelings by telling herself that if the backing had been tampered with, Mark had probably removed it himself.

Lara carried the painting to her bedroom where she found a spot for it above the white oak nightstand. For a moment, she stepped back to view "The Healing Water."

Again captivated, Lara studied the contemplative pose of the lone figure upon the rocks, the beauty of the surrounding landscape. She had watched Mark work his magic before, knew well the unbound imagination that could transcend space and time, that could transform a single tree into a forest, a rock into a cave.

Lara gazed at the searching, yet peaceful face of the Indian, barely visible through the layers of mist. She could almost feel the warm, healing waters from the legendary spring of the Quachitas rise to envelop his silent, pensive form. Lara found the scene comforting and knew she would always draw strength from its presence.

The solace of the painting did not last. Before she had returned downstairs, Dane's image returned to haunt her, his frozen expression, beneath which she had sensed his pain. She felt almost guilty, as if she really had called the police, as if she had scorned the gift of his trust. If Scott hadn't prevented it, she would have had a chance to speak to Dane, to explain!

But Scott could not hold Dane more than forty-eight hours without some solid evidence to link him with the crime—evidence Lara knew he did not have. After questioning him, Scott would have no choice but to release him. In the meantime, Lara would continue to search for the papers Charles had told her about, papers that would lead her to Mark and Crystal's killer—that would prove Dane's innocence.

As Lara drove across town to her father's office, her hopes resurfaced; she had not been able to find hidden papers at the hotel, maybe she would at the Radburn office. For a short time, before Mark had hired Charles to take over for him so he could resume his work at the old hotel, she knew Mark had attempted to take over the family business. Maybe her brother had left behind some personal files Charles had not found or had overlooked.

The huge glass-fronted building rose, sleek and modern, for all of its twenty-five years. Dad had built it, but his venture had failed and the bank had repossessed it. "I decided to keep my office here," he had chuckled. "It keeps me humble."

Joan Summer's thriving real estate offices dominated the bottom floor. Joan wasn't there. Lara passed a travel bureau and a corner coffee shop named "Gino's", and took the elevator up to the second floor. Her father's office was the first of a row of nearly identical offices, all closed for the weekend.

Below the frosted-glass window of the door, a brass plate lettered "Lawrence Radburn, Radburn Investments" remained unchanged. Lara searched her purse for the spare key Charles had given her, turned the lock, and peered into the shadowy darkness. Leaving the door to the quiet hallway ajar, she stepped inside and switched on the overhead lights.

Memories of her father assailed her. She almost expected to see him sitting in the leather chair behind the huge desk, intent upon finishing some last piece of paperwork, to smell the ever-present scent of cigar smoke mingled with Old Spice or English Leather.

As a child, she had often watched him work, waiting patiently sometimes for what seemed like hours, for the promised treat of ice cream or lunch with Dad. Eventually, he would glance up, seeming surprised to see her, as if he had totally forgotten her presence. She remembered how Charles would usually drop by and volunteer to take her out instead, how he would drive her to across town to Baskin Robbins, where she could choose between the thirty-one delicious flavors. When they returned, her father would say wearily, "Sorry, Pumpkin. Business always seems to take longer than I think it will. But you did have fun, didn't you?" and give Charles a grateful look for having relieved him of the chore.

Now, glancing around, she noticed a few personal touches of Charles' appeared about the room. A picture of the wife he had loved so dearly had been added beside the one and only existing portrait of the entire Radburn family . . . Lara at age seven, a twelve-year-old Mark, a smiling Mom and Dad. Before the divorce. Before all the tragedy. Happier times.

She quickly averted her eyes to the cluster of plants, in desperate need of watering, upon the window ledge. A stack of legal pads covered with Charles' scribbling rested near the phone near a marmalade jar crammed with pens and pencils.

The quiet Saturday afternoon gave her the opportunity

to go through the files undisturbed. Lara slipped into her father's chair and pulled open one of the filing cabinet drawers beside the desk. She flipped through the files, glancing at the worn labels: Deeds and Titles, Tax Reports, Rental Contracts. Nothing out of the ordinary.

After a while, Lara rose and stretched her legs. She longed for a strong cup of coffee. She glanced wistfully at the empty percolator in the corner, but feeling a lack of energy, decided against brewing a pot just for herself.

She wandered over to the window. She raised the blinds and allowed sunlight to pour into the room. This reminded her that it was still early afternoon. Lara stood for a minute taking in the scene before her, the panorama of the town with its crooked, winding streets against backdrop of hazy, ridged mountains.

She remembered when Quachita Springs had consisted of only a main street of solemn, rock buildings. Thanks to an energetic advertising campaign by the new mayor, the area prospered from an influx of tourist trade. The entire town seemed to be shifting, changing, outgrowing its boundaries. What had once been the hub of activity was now only a quaint little section of older stone buildings dwarfed by larger, more modern complexes, which accommodated the rise in summer population with hotels, small tourist shops, and fast food restaurants.

Despite the bad memories it held for her, in weak moments, Lara still thought of Quachita Springs as home. She remembered it through a child's eyes, and perhaps because only her early life had been filled with stability, found the changes a little frightening. It seemed that each time she returned some new concrete giant had broken through the earth, rising up out of nowhere, seemingly overnight. Quachita Springs was evolving from a sleepy little town into a fast-growing metropolis, and she wasn't sure she welcomed the change.

Lara noticed the huge crane and bulldozer that rested upon the vacant tract of land adjoining the new, round-domed convention center across the street. She was curious about what project was going up there, on the undeveloped land that had for so many years belonged to her father.

Lara turned from the window and resumed opening and closing files. After she had scanned several more burgeoning drawers, it began to dawn upon her that her task was useless, hopeless. Like hunting for a needle in a haystack. Except, she thought, the person searching for the needle at least knew what he was looking for. Lara realized she must take a different approach. She must delve into Mark's personal life and try to discover who might have had reason to profit from his death and why.

Once more, her thoughts strayed to Dane Lanford. Dane could help her. Dane had been his friend and partner: he would know more about Mark's business than anyone else.

Footsteps echoed from the corridor. Lara glimpsed Whitney Jordan, briefcase in hand, as he proceeded toward his attorney's office just down the hallway. The familiar sight of him cheered her and she called to him.

"Lara, it's you." Whitney said, stepping into her father's office, as he had done so often in the past. "I might have known. I've yet to catch Charles working on Saturday."

"He's taken Karma to a puppet show in Eureka Springs,"

Whitney wore a sports jacket of light blue exactly the color of his eyes. Because of the darkness of his skin and hair, one expected his eyes to be of the same hue instead of so robin-egg blue. The contrast gave Whitney's face an alert attractiveness.

"Charles will enjoy the show more than she will,"

Whitney commented.

Lara hesitated and decided against telling Whitney about the events of last night, the real reason Charles had volunteered to take Karma away for the weekend. She didn't want Whitney to worry about her, and he, with the over-protectiveness of a big brother, certainly would if he knew.

"How is the little girl?" Whitney asked with concern.

"Fine," Lara replied. "I thought spending time with Charles might be good for her. I remember how much I used to look forward to his little outings when I was a child." Fondly, she added, "Some people never lose their sense of fun. They make the world a more pleasant place."

"And more work for the rest of us," Whitney said good-naturedly. "You know how much time I spent with your father. I know this office as well as my own. Is there something I can help you find?"

In her rummaging Lara had come across the contract for the vacant land, which her father had sold to the Evergreen Corporation. Realizing she still held the contract in her hands, she let it drop back into the files. "No, I was just sorting through some paperwork, seeing what needs to be done before I leave for New York." Turning back to him she asked, "Do you often come in to your office on the weekends?"

"Nan calls me a workaholic," Whitney confessed with a short laugh that seemed oddly without mirth. "Maybe she's right. Your father was my mentor. What he taught me was never to enjoy life." Whitney went on quickly as if he feared she would take offense from his off-hand remark. "Seriously, I'd much rather be working than fishing or chasing some little white ball around a golf course."

"And, as Dad used to say, you can buy fish cheaper than you can catch them." Lara grew suddenly serious as she recalled the many important occasions in her and Mark's life, where her father had been conspicuously absent. "I can't help but think he missed out entirely on what's really important," she said. Right then, she vowed silently that she would always make time for Karma. Just the thought of her returning from Eureka Springs filled Lara's heart with warmth and anticipation.

"I guess if Nancy and I had children, I might feel obligated to spend more time at home. But as it is, she has her hobbies and I have my work." He paused and rested his briefcase on top of the desk. "We've come to comfortable terms."

Lara thought of Nancy Jordan, her careless appearance, her flighty, unfocused mannerisms. She thought of the pathetic way she had presented to Lara the ceramic squirrel she had made for Karma. Lara wondered if Whitney ever noticed how lost and lonely his wife often looked. Was his legal practice really so demanding, or was he becoming one of those men who spent long hours at work to avoid unpleasantness at home? Because she had always thought of Whitney as one would think of an older brother, the question disturbed her.

Lara rose and wandered back over to the window.

Whitney joined her. They gazed at the vacant lot that had once belonged to her father. A bulldozer and crane waited in the large, vacant tract. Monday morning the site would be buzzing with activity.

"It's changed, hasn't it?"

"The whole town is slowly moving out this way," Lara said. "What are they building now?"

"Word has it Quachita Springs is finally getting its own bona fide shopping mall."

"A shopping mall?" Lara reacted with surprise. "Then Dad definitely should have hung on to that property."

"So I advised him."

"He sold it for under $200,000."

Whitney hesitated before he responded, "A fair price for undeveloped land. He didn't know at the time, I suppose, that the town was going to boom like this."

"Someone made a fortune overnight!"

Whitney's gaze rose to the mountains beyond the rising concrete. She felt supported by him, glad for the familiarity of his presence.

"Father was such an astute businessman. You would have thought he'd seen it coming."

"Your father was very ill at the time."

"Still, it's surprising that he sold it. Dad so often spoke of hanging on to this particular piece of property. In fact, he considered it his best investment. By the way, who is this Evergreen Corporation that bought the land?"

Whitney rubbed a hand across his forehead as if to ward off the beginnings of a headache, a gesture common to people who need glasses but seldom wear them. "Big developers, outsiders like Austin Graham, have been moving in here, taking over everything."

Lara felt a sense of dismay. "Father was so against dealing with large corporations."

"Yes, but toward the end Lawrence became very anxious to sell out. He confided in me that he wanted to discontinue his business, to rid himself of all responsibility." As Whitney spoke, Lara watched his hawkish profile, bathed in light from the window, the prominent nose and slightly receding chin. "After he had that falling out with Charles, he seemed to lose heart."

"Charles and Father fought?" The knowledge surprised Lara. "Charlie has never mentioned any trouble between Dad and him."

"I thought you knew all about it," Whitney said, turning to look at her with raised eyebrows. "For months they never spoke a word to one another. Charles didn't even come near the hospital when Lawrence had that last heart attack. He wasn't even there the night your father passed on." After a long pause, Whitney added, "It's regrettable, but those things happen. Even to good friends. It probably hurts Charles to even think about it."

"Dad depended so much on Charles." Lara said sadly. She remembered how distraught Charles had looked at her father's funeral, realized now the burden of guilt he must have carried along with his grief. She thought of how good he had been to her, how he had postponed his retirement to look after the business, and wondered if he weren't still trying somehow to make it up to Lawrence.

"I know it disappointed Father that Mark never had much interest in the business. I was always so grateful Dad had you and Charles to count on."

"He came to accept that both of his children were destined for other things," Whitney said in an effort to be supportive. "Secretly, he was proud of Mark's talent. And he always boasted about his New York daughter's exciting career in the publishing world. That's why your father became determined to sell off as much of the business as he could, so it wouldn't be an encumbrance after his death."

"Do you know what caused the rift between Charles and him?"

"Not really," Whitney responded shortly. "If I had to guess, I'd say it had to do with Mark and all the money he was spending on that foolish retreat of his."

"I must admit, I was a little shocked when Charles showed me the financial statements on the business. Father made so many cash withdrawals right before his death. I suppose they all went to Mark. To be honest," Lara confided, "there isn't much of the money left from that land sale."

"I'm afraid Mark convinced your father to sink a small

fortune into the hotel." Whitney cast her a sympathetic look. "I guess that didn't leave much capital for you. But when you sell the family home, you'll end up with a substantial amount."

"And then there's the hotel and the house near the river," Lara said, trying to be optimistic. "A lot of land goes with the hotel, it should bring a fair price, enough to pay Dad's debts. I would like to at least break even."

"Joan can sell those places, if anyone can," Whitney said with admiration.

"She's been trying to interest Austin Graham in the hotel."

"Graham," he said, disapproval clear in his tone. "I don't trust that man! Greedy people like him are rushing in here like prospectors to a gold strike! They have no real interest in our community."

"I may have no choice but to sell to him . . . if Joan can even get him to make an offer. I'm not worried about the family home. Joan can easily find a buyer for that. But I am really anxious to sell these not-so-desirable places."

A car pulled into the parking lot directly below them. Lara could see the "Ozark Reality" sign upon the side of the white vehicle, which quickly identified it as Joan's. As Joan Sommers stepped from the car, she glanced up, saw them standing in the window, and waved enthusiastically. Then, tottering on very high heels, she briskly disappeared into her own ground-floor office.

"I wouldn't get your hopes up, Lara," Whitney said. "I've heard Austin Graham's been looking at property along the north side of the river, near the country club."

"Joan can sell the hotel, if anyone can," Lara responded. But an ancient hotel and a house where a murder had been committed . . . not even a Realtor as persistent and convincing as Joan would be likely to have much success. Lara prepared herself to accept the fact that she might have to stay in Quachita Springs much longer than she had expected in order to complete all necessary business transactions.

"I know you want to get back to New York right away. And I don't blame you. You've got a first-rate job waiting there, and they don't wait forever." Whitney gave her a considering look. "If you don't get an acceptable offer by the time you are ready to leave, maybe the two of us can come up with a satisfactory figure."

Surprised, Lara faced him. "You mean, you would consider buying? But, Whitney, what would you do with a white elephant like that old hotel? And you know the house where Crystal lived will be impossible to rent."

"Since I'm settled here, the property would be much easier for me to manage, than for you. The hotel has tenants." He shrugged. "And rumors fade. Eventually, Crystal's house will rent again, especially if I spend a little time fixing it up."

Lara felt touched by his offer. "I can't imagine you'd really want to be burdened with this. I can't let you do it just to help me."

Whitney's blue eyes deepened as they met hers. "Your Dad was just like a father to me. He would have wanted me to step in and take over for him."

Taking advantage of Whitney's long-time friendship had little appeal for her, but if Austin Graham didn't come through, she knew Whitney would insist on making the purchases. She was grateful for Whitney's considerate proposal, and if it did come to her accepting it, she would be sure to make him a bargain price.

Whitney waited while Lara locked up, and together they headed to the elevator. When they reached the "Ozark Reality" office downstairs, Joan motioned to them from behind the glass enclosure.

"Lara thinks I'm the only one who works weekends,"

Whitney said, giving Joan one of his rare smiles.

"When's the last time I had a Saturday off? Why, it's my best day for showing houses. And what a hectic day it's been! Have you ever tried to convince a family of two they need four bathrooms and eight-bedrooms?" She touched Whitney's arm as she breezed by him to the filing cabinet. "I'm starved! Are we still going for quiche?"

Noticing Lara's quick glance toward Whitney, Joan hurried to explain, "Whitney and I often meet for lunch. Since we're always here, laboring day and night, it's become a habit." Her voice lowered in pretended seriousness. "Don't tell Nancy. You know how jealous she is of this gorgeous male!"

Lara glanced back to Whitney. How suited they seemed to each other, Joan, so buoyant, Whitney so severe. They even looked as if they should be a couple, Joan, pert and trim in her chic, yellow suit; Whitney, tall, slender, and correct in every detail. Lara found herself wondering if Joan were really joking or if her lightness concealed some very deep feeling for Whitney Jordan.

A little ashamed for her run-away thoughts, Lara said, "I must be going."

Whitney's polite voice followed after her. "Why don't you join us for lunch, Lara?"

"Of course she will!" Joan spoke in a comradely fashion. "I've just heard the most exciting news. I'm anxious to tell you and Whitney all about it!"

Chapter Seven

"Scott has caught up with Crystal's killer!" Joan shared her news breathlessly after they had settled into a corner booth at "Gino's". "This very minute he has Dane Lanford locked in the county jail! And Scott told me that's right where he's going to stay!"

Dane couldn't have been arrested for Crystal's murder! There just wasn't enough evidence against him! Lara's fingers tightened around her coffee cup. She tried to sound indifferent. "I thought Dane Lanford was only wanted for questioning."

"And for leaving a crime scene! And now for resisting officers of the law!" Joan said. "Lanford's finally met up with someone he can't manipulate. Scott will show him who's who!"

A picture of Dane rose hauntingly to Lara's mind— Dane, seated dejectedly on a hard bunk in a cold, narrow cell. The image affected Lara deeply, evoked in her ardent and tender feelings of compassion. She didn't understand this strong reaction toward a man she barely knew, but it was present none the less.

"Guilty! Guilty! Guilty!" Joan sing-songed.

Whitney, stirring sugar into his coffee, said evenly. "Now, Joan, you don't know that." Whitney's perceptive, light blue eyes looked into Lara's. She, head bent, turned full attention to the coffee, but she was thinking of Scott Tyler, and the deep, personal hatred he showed for Dane. She remained silent and immobile, deeply troubled by Dane's plight. Would he ever be able to prove his innocence, or would he again be railroaded? This time for murder!

Whitney, leaning forward, fastidious even in his casual sports clothing, interrupted her thoughts. "Are you going to have the quiche, too?"

"That sounds fine."

After the waitress left, Joan, her voice low and confidential, said, "Everyone knows Dane and Crystal were lovers!" She leaned back allowing her audience time to savor her news. "I didn't know Crystal very well, but I remember her telling me once, 'I have this great fear of permanent ties!' You can be sure someone like that wouldn't wait for a boyfriend to get out of prison. When Dane Lanford was released, he came right back here and got even! Jealousy is one of the major causes for murder, isn't it, Whitney?"

"I don't know much about crime," Whitney said, "My practice deals with the more mundane side of the legal system."

"Poor Crystal!" Joan exclaimed. "Bludgeoned to death by one of her own sculptures." Joan finished with a delicate little shiver, "What a horrible way to die!"

When the food was placed before them, Lara felt no appetite for the rich spinach and bacon quiche.

"Remember, Whitney, how hard Scott worked to put Lanford away on that robbery a while back?" Joan paused to sample her quiche. "He was so worried when the Baxters maintained doubts of his guilt."

"The Baxters' have always been art patrons," Whitney informed Lara. "They're probably the only ones in Quachita Springs who supported Lanford's idea of this artist's retreat. John Baxter had a very high regard for Lanford's talent and they became solid friends. He felt sorry for Lanford; the way he struggled to keep the place together after Mark died. He had even talked about making a big donation before this robbery occurred. Of course, the evidence against Dane Lanford was mostly circumstantial."

"I'd think those paintings in the trunk of Lanford's car were pretty convincing evidence," Joan chirped, casting an arch glance toward Whitney. "It doesn't take a lawyer to figure that out!"

Lara suddenly recalled Scott's reluctance to discuss the case and an uneasy feeling gripped her. "Scott told me there was a witness, a neighbor, who placed Dane's car near the Baxters' house the night the Baxters were robbed."

Joan looked puzzled. "Whit, do you remember anything about a witness?"

"I'm sure there was one, but I don't recall who," Whitney responded, a deep frown cutting between his brows. He pushed back his plate as if he, too, lacked appetite, and said, "As I said before, I don't try to keep up with criminal cases. Drawing up wills and settling divorces is more my territory. But I'm convinced Scott would never have succeeded in sending Lanford up if he hadn't had a pretty strong case against him."

"It was simply unbelievable, the way Scott Tyler caught him!" Joan said, beaming as she leaned back in the booth. "Scott Tyler is the greatest thing that ever happened to Quachita Springs! And, besides Whitney here, he's the cutest!"

"He is a fine sheriff," Whitney agreed, embarrassed over Joan's off-hand flattery. "Scott's definitely the best law officer we've ever elected. And I'm not just saying that just because he's one of my close friends."

Lara had grave doubts concerning their unqualified praise for the sheriff. She believed, as Dane had told her, in the possibility that Scott had trumped up charges against him in order to keep Dane from investigating Mark's death. But that would mean that Scott himself was involved in Mark's murder, and in her heart, she did not really believe that. Scott could have been protecting someone. Or, more likely, Scott had been fully convinced that Dane had murdered Mark and could get him on no other charge.

Once she left the cafe, Lara decided she would stop at the library where back issues of the Quachita Times were stored on microfilm. There, she could read for herself the details of the crime for which Dane Lanford had been sent to prison and form her own opinion.

"Where's Karma?" Joan asked.

Lara explained how she had gone with Charles to Eureka Springs.

"Charles absolutely dotes on that girl. He should have had a dozen grandchildren!"

"I'm anxious to get my guardianship approved. My boss has been pressing me for a return date."

"Crystal's appointing you as guardian makes the whole process much less complicated." Whitney's voice inspired confidence, and she knew why her father and so many others had relied on him so completely. "Since she has no living relatives and no father was named on Karma's birth certificate, I don't foresee any problems. I'm trying to get the court date pushed up so you can get back to that job you love so much! By the way, I contacted Crystal's lawyer. I'm afraid there isn't very much in that trust fund that Crystal had just started for Karma. Only around twenty thousand."

Joan broke into Whitney's talk of business. "I keep wondering who Karma's father is," she said. A worried look clouded her face as she asked, "Do you think Dane Lanford is her father?"

"Karma is the very picture of her mother," Lara said. "I was so fond of Crystal. And I don't care who Karma's father is." But a vision of the little girl with her jet-black hair and wide, dark eyes arose in Lara's mind; alongside of it appeared the image of Dane. Dane was so especially protective of Karma; he was, like Lara herself, intensely drawn to the child. The thought that Dane was her father was not a new one for her, but it now added immense weight to her already overwhelming worries.

"We'll probably never know for sure who the other parent is," Whitney responded. "And believe me, it's better that way. If he did come forth now, we'd have a tough legal battle on our hands."

Lara shrank from the thought of Dane or some unknown person fighting Lara for custody of the child.

"Lara, I've got good news for you," Joan said brightly. "It took some smooth talking on my part, but I've finally persuaded Austin to take a serious look at your hotel property. I'm driving him out there the first of the week."

"You know he'll never make a decent offer, Joan." Whitney said almost caustically. "First, he'll make a big fuss over that unpaved road and try to stick Lara with the cost of making improvements. Then he'll want her to pay for the demolition of the hotel itself. All he ever wants is land for those big-shot projects of his."

"Whitney, the great, gloomy pessimist!" Joan turned to Lara. "He'd never make it in the real estate business!"

"A vast amount of good timber land goes with that hotel. Don't forget that. He'll try to cheat you. My advice," Whitney said wryly, "is to be very careful with any dealings you have with him!"

As a close friend of her father's, Lara knew Whitney felt protective of her interests. Usually, as in this case, she fully agreed with him. She had her own reservations concerning the powerful entrepreneur, and had from the very minute Joan had introduced them.

"Don't you worry, Lara," Joan said, undaunted. "I have Austin Graham right in the palm of my hands!" A confident glow caused her pretty hazel eyes to shine. "You can be sure I'll discuss our little deal with him over dinner tonight at the country club!"

Whitney rose abruptly. "Graham's just leading you on,

Joan," he said dourly, "In more ways than one."

Joan's injured look told Lara he had struck a nerve.

"Leaving, Whitney?" Joan shot back acidly. "How we'll miss you! You're so pleasant and charming today!"

Ignoring her sarcasm, Whitney said politely, "I promised Nancy I'd find someone to fix that kiln of hers. She's working on those blasted ceramics of hers all the time and that damned thing is always breaking down."

Lara watched Whitney leave and wondered what was really at the heart of Whitney's dislike for Austin Graham. Lara knew Whitney was a man who firmly followed his instincts, but in this case, perhaps there was a little more to it than that. He could be jealous of the man's afflu-ence—or of his relationship with Joan Sommers!

As soon as Whitney was out of ear range, Joan com-mented, "Always at that pitiful woman's beck and call." She gave a little sigh. "Whitney's so sharp and ambitious. Imagine what it must be like for him, tied to that poor, washed-out little creature."

"I feel sorry for Nancy," Lara said, a little astonished at Joan's hostility. "She seems so lost, so much in a world of her own."

"Do you know that in all the time I've been acquainted with Whitney and Nan, I've never once set foot inside their house?" Joan responded. "And I'll bet you haven't either!"

"No one accepts Nancy. Whitney knows that. I've often wished I could find some way to befriend her."

"Not me! You're wasting your time pitying that poor undeserving specimen! If you have so much pity, pity Whitney!"

Joan, with a glance at her watch, rose. "I guess Whit saw to the check," she said, as she placed tip money on the table. "He really is a dear, after all. Now I've got to run."

*   *   *

Once in the library, Lara patiently scanned reels of the Quachita Times on microfilm, searching for some mention of the robbery that had taken place almost two years ago.

A caption caught her eye as it whirred past, and she slowed the machine to view the article beneath the dark heading, "Local Man Sentenced in Art Theft".

"Dane Lanford of Quachita Springs was convicted and sentenced today on the charge of burglary in connection with two valuable paintings which were taken from the home of John and Martha Baxter, 1004 Riverside Drive.

Richard Norville, attorney for Lanford's defense, maintained his client's innocence on the grounds that most of the evidence against him was circumstantial, and is seeking an appeal.

Sheriff Scott Tyler testified that while making his rounds at 12.00 p.m., he positively identified Lanford's vehicle, a late model, maroon Pontiac parked near the Baxter residence.

Immediately upon hearing the robbery reported, Sheriff Tyler apprehended Dane Lanford at his artist's retreat, formerly the "Lost Pines" hotel. The paintings were recovered from the trunk of the Lanford car.

Since he had no previous record, Judge Carl Henry handed down a sentence of two to five years.

As Lara scanned the printed words, she felt the first stirrings of alarm. Frowning in concentration, she carefully re-read the entire article. She had made no mistake! Scott had clearly told her that a witness, a neighbor, had seen Dane's vehicle in the vicinity of the Baxter home the night of the robbery. But according to the newspaper account, Scott

Tyler was the only witness who had testified against him.

Lara felt stunned. Why would the sheriff have deliberately lied to her? For some reason, Scott had not wanted her to know that Dane Lanford had been convicted solely on his testimony!

The idea that the sheriff might have purposefully set Dane up that night to keep him from investigating her brother's death was becoming a very real possibility.

What should she do? Lara's frightened indecision seemed magnified by the quiet coolness of the library. Barely aware of people moving noiselessly all around her, Lara wandered over to a desk and sat, staring out of the window, trying to make some sense of what she had just discovered.

She had caught Scott Tyler in one lie. How many more had he told her? She had felt all along that he had failed to properly investigate Mark's death. Would he fail again to investigate Crystal's, to look into the possibility of a link between the two crimes? Lara felt absolutely certain that another of Scott's lies was responsible for Dane's being detained in the county jail.

Her thoughts leaped back to the days just before Crystal's brutal murder. She had noticed that her friend had been tense, edgy, not quite herself. Once, Lara had felt Crystal had been on the verge of confiding in her, and that she would have if Lara had in any way encouraged her.

Lara regretted now that she had failed to do so. At the time she had believed that Crystal's problem was simply a disagreement with some boyfriend and she hadn't wished to pry, but now she knew that she could have obtained vital information. According to Dane Lanford, Crystal had called him out to the house shortly before she was murdered. She had no doubt intended to confide her problems to him. Lara knew now she must talk to Dane Lanford and try to find out why.

*   *   *

Approaching the sprawling, brick building on the out-skirts of Quachita Springs, where the sheriff had taken her the night of Crystal's death, Lara's apprehension mounted. She stopped at the door, almost deciding to turn back.

She told herself sternly that she must go on inside, she must face Scott Tyler and ask to talk to Dane Lanford. If she did not, she might never find out who killed Mark and Crystal.

She almost wished she had not identified the photo of Dane Lanford as the man she had encountered in the woods behind Crystal's house. If she had not singled Dane out for him, then Scott would not have him locked up now.

Lara entered a hallway where a thin, dour-faced deputy peered out at her from behind an open wooden-frame window. She could see beyond where he stood a cluttered room and a closed door marked, Scott Tyler, Quachita County Sheriff. The deputy waited for her to speak.

"Is Scott Tyler in?"

"No. I am in charge."

Feeling relief at Scott's absence, she said more confi-dently, "I'd like to see Dane Lanford."

A little unwillingly the deputy came around the parti-tion that separated them, and, jangling keys, gestured for her to follow. The door he unlocked led into another hall-way, this one much longer. It struck her as cold, dreary, oppressive. On either side were bar-enclosed cubicles, most of them empty.

The deputy said, "He's down at the end. The last cell on the right. Press this buzzer when you want out."

Lara had never visited anyone in jail before. Maybe this was what made her so terribly nervous. She was aware that Dane had noticed her arrival and stood waiting as she reluctantly drew closer.

When she was near enough to see his features clearly, she read in his expression no anger, only a very evident surprise.

She was aware of his distinguished handsomeness, the sensitive mouth and strong features, the waves of black hair winged with silver.

He looked so out of place! His eyes were so darkly intelligent, his wide shoulders proudly set. She had expected to find him sunk into despair or hopelessness, but he seemed only impatient with his confinement, but not defeated by it. This surprising reserve of strength gave her courage.

"I wanted to tell you," Lara said, "that I had nothing to do with your arrest."

"I'm sure you wouldn't be here if you had," he responded gently. His lean hand reached between the bars and warm fingers pressed hers.

When he let go of her hand and turned away, Lara noticed that a bruise darkened the hollow of his cheekbone.

Startled, she asked, "Dane, what happened? How did you get hurt?"

"This is only some more of Scott Tyler's kind of evidence."

"Did you try to get away again?"

"I had on handcuffs, Lara, if you remember. They weren't taken off until I was in this cell."

Lara's sense of shock deepened, as did her resentment of Scott Tyler and his unlawful tactics! "I'll get you a lawyer," she said. "You can't let him get away with this."

"No one is going to believe that I didn't resist being brought in for questioning. This town is prone to think the worst of me. But all that seems relatively unimportant compared to what else I'm facing."

"You didn't kill Crystal! There's no way you can be

arrested for her murder!"

"I'm not so sure."

"There's so much we need to talk about," Lara said. "This morning you told me Crystal called you out to the house the night she was murdered."

Dane nodded gravely. "I was very worried about her. She sounded so upset and frightened."

"Do you know what she wanted to tell you?"

"She refused to discuss it over the phone. But I think she was being threatened."

"Threatened? Do you know who would threaten her? Or why?"

"I believe she intended to share this with me." He spoke in a lowered tone, "I had been her art instructor for many years." His voice became more emphatic, as if he wanted his next words to be perfectly clear. "Crystal and I were very good friends—nothing more. I was used to her asking my advice, confiding in me. I told her I would be out right away. She must not have thought she was in any immediate danger, for she asked me to give her a while to finish her sculpture. I started from the hotel around dusk." He stopped speaking. Shadows of pain moved into his eyes. "If only I had left sooner!" Another long pause. "When I got there, she was dead."

In the silence that followed, Lara realized with disappointment that she had been grasping at straws. Dane wasn't going to be able to tell her anything.

"I don't have any idea what this might mean," Dane said slowly, as if carefully measuring his words, "But from our conversation I gathered that Crystal had hidden something within the house. I got the impression it might have been important papers, documents, something of that nature." He paused reflectively before adding, "I've been thinking whoever murdered Crystal might have been after this information."

Was it the same papers Lara had been looking for, involving some unknown person who had betrayed Mark? Mark had been only in the process of collecting evidence, waiting for final proof before going to the authorities. Realization stole over her: Mark must have given these papers to Crystal to keep for him.

"I had plans to go and search the house tonight," Dane said. His voice was calm, purposeful, the way it had been the dreadful night of the murder when he had helped her search for the lost child. She studied him, his jaw set, his eyes serious, and again she felt that instinctive trust of him.

"Do you think Mark might have given Crystal something for safekeeping?" she asked carefully.

Dane considered this a moment. "It's possible. Mark trusted Crystal implicitly. Everyone who knew her did."

Of course Mark and Crystal had been acquainted through the artist's retreat. But Lara hadn't realized the two of them had been good friends. Did Crystal know, then, who had killed Mark? A shiver crept up Lara's spine. Could this knowledge have led to Crystal's own murder?

"The police have already gone over every inch of the house," Lara reminded him.

"They wouldn't know where to look or what to look for."

"If this has to do with Mark, chances are I would be able to recognize it," Lara said. "But I wouldn't know where to begin to search."

"If Crystal did hide something," Dane told her quietly, "I have an idea just where it might be. She had a secret hiding place in the house where she used to keep valuables."

"Tell me where! I'll go back to the house now."

"No," he spoke determinedly. "It would be far to dangerous for you to return to that house alone." She saw his fingers tighten around the bars that separated them. "If you go back there, I must be with you!"

"How long can Scott keep you here?"

Dane turned from her with a futile gesture. She watched him pace the confines of the cell. Their talk seemed to have changed him. Dane no longer seemed in control, in terms with his being locked up here. He now seemed angered by his confinement. Lara watched him pace around the small cell like some magnificent, trapped lion.

Lion! She thought of the murder weapon that had been used to kill Crystal! Dane's voice called her back to the present. "Fleeing the scene of a crime, resisting arrest. He'll try to find one charge and another to keep me here until he can think of some way to indict me with Crystal's murder. But he's not going to get by with it. Hallie and Jim are posting bond. I will be out of here by late afternoon."

Did she dare trust him? Scott Tyler's deception, his eagerness for a conviction, made Lara more and more inclined to accept Dane's story as truth. Besides, Lara told herself, she needed his help! Dane Lanford was the only person she knew willing to investigate the link she was convinced existed between her brother's death and Crystal's. The knowledge forged a strong bond between them.

"Then meet me tonight. We'll go out to Crystal's house and see what we can uncover."

Dane came back to stand in front of her. Cold, steel bars separated them, but he once again reached through them, softly touching her hair, smoothing it. His dark eyes lit. "As much as I would like to have you along, it's far too dangerous."

Dane wasn't guilty! She must help him find Crystal's killer. He mustn't go free, as free as the driver of the death car that had struck Mark!

"I'm going to investigate this whether you are with me or not!"

Warmth, such approval lit in his eyes. From the first time she had looked into them, she had felt so unique, so important. Was that the secret of Dane's charm? Had numerous other people, had Crystal Mar, felt the same way?

Once again feeling uncertain, Lara spoke. "If you want to join me, I'll meet you tonight at seven."

He hesitated, then said, "At the Last Stop Cafe, where it's well lighted and safe. From there, we'll go together and search the house."

When Lara reached the door, she glanced back at Dane. He stood watching her, his hands still tight on the bars.

She was glad the deputy and not Scott Tyler responded to the sound of the buzzer. At least she was spared having to face him! How furious the sheriff would be when he found out she had been here!

Chapter Eight

Once back home, doubts began to surface. What if she was wrong about Dane Lanford? In Lara's mind an image of him arose, the elegantly handsome face, the black, smoldering eyes. Was Dane too polished, too practiced? Was that fascinating balance of perceptiveness and sensitivity only part of an overall deception?

Dane might have been the one cheating her brother, either through the sale of Mark's artwork or in the plans for the artist's retreat. The gift of Mark's painting could have been a carefully designed move on his part to gain her trust!

Doubts grew as Lara recalled how certain she was that someone had tampered with the back of "The Healing Waters". Had incriminating evidence been hidden within the painting's framework, evidence Dane had already removed and destroyed?

Lara's thoughts drifted back to the moment Dane had given her the painting, remembering the closeness she had felt to him. The grief for Mark that had shone in Dane's dark eyes had been convincingly real.

Lara clung to the hope that what Crystal had intended to show Dane was the papers Mark had given her for safekeeping, and this thought renewed some trust in him.

With time to wait before their meeting, the house seemed unusually still and quiet. She changed into jeans and a comfortable sweater. After preparing a solitary dinner of canned soup and crackers, she almost placed two bowls on the table. She missed Karma. How quickly the little girl with the tragic eyes had worked her way into Lara's heart.

The phone on the stand jangled noisily and Lara, sinking into the nearby recliner, answered in a hushed tone, "Lara

Radburn."

"Lara." Charles said jovially, "someone here wants to talk to you."

The baby-like words, filled with hesitation, rattled off breathless sentences that ended with, "Lara, we're going to another show tomorrow!"

"Tell me more about the show you saw today."

"I saw a bird with purple wings and long, long legs. He could dance, too!"

Charles, laughing, took the phone again. "Donna is spoiling her. She's going to take her back stage now and let her look at all the puppets." He paused. "You're all right, aren't you, Lara?"

"Of course."

"We'll be back Sunday. Look for us after supper. Now, Karma wants to say goodbye."

"I miss you and I miss Spot."

"We miss you, too, Karma."

"Goodbye, Mommy."

Feeling a chill, Lara replaced the receiver. Her spirits, which had risen by the call, plummeted to a new low. For a moment the child had forgotten and thought she was Crystal.

Lara closed her eyes against the rush of pain. For a long time she leaned back in the recliner, her thoughts turning ever so slowly from Karma to Crystal, to wonder again why Crystal had selected her, a person she had known such a brief time, to be guardian of her child. Who was Karma's father? Why hadn't she named him as guardian?

Why, in fact, hadn't Crystal married him? From the first Lara had believed that Crystal had herself selected the option of remaining single. Lara had understood Crystal's fierce independence, her total commitment to her art, which was the single ambition that ruled her life. Karma had been a mistake; one Crystal wouldn't let force her into an unwanted role as wife.

But other reasons could exist for Crystal's not acknowledging Karma's father. He could have rejected her. He could have been married, or totally unfit to be a husband and father. He might have seduced her, used her, until finally Crystal had felt nothing toward him except loathing and fear.

Once again, Lara's thoughts turned to Dane Lanford. She became increasingly apprehensive as it drew nearer and nearer to the time she was to join him at the truck-stop cafe. She found that she was frightened both of meeting Dane and of the idea of searching the river property where Crystal had been so brutally murdered.

Reluctantly, Lara rose, checked in her purse to make sure she had the key to Crystal's house. The whole plan, which had once seemed the natural unfolding of logic, now seemed a deadly mistake.

The feeling increased as she turned north on the highway, leaving the small scattering of houses for the isolation of the forested hillsides crowned with darkness.

She did not allow herself to linger outside the truck-stop cafe, but hastened inside. Crammed with truckers, the room rang loudly with talk and laughter. Above the noise Hallie noticed her and called, "Hi, ya, Larie! Take a seat over here. My breaks coming up and I'll take it with you!"

A burly man on the stool said something to Hallie Lara couldn't hear and Hallie gave him a playful swat as she joined Lara in the booth.

Hallie wore white slacks and low-cut blouse that looked as dingy as the wall behind her. Blondish strands of hair clung to her broad forehead, damp from her exertion.

"Have you seen Dane?"

"Not since we got him out of jail. That was around

three o'clock." She leaned back against the plastic cushion. "They are going to wait on me, now," she said with satisfaction. "A chicken-fry," she called to the girl behind the counter. "And what do you want?"

"Just coffee."

"Two coffees! What you brings you here? You must have known I wanted to talk to you." Her blue eyes widened sincerely, "I can send messages to people. Mental ones, you know!"

Lara did not feel up to pursuing her physic powers. "What did you want to talk to me about?"

"The auction in Hot Springs. This Wednesday at the Rasswell Gallery." Hallie stopped. She enjoyed creating interest and wasn't anxious to satisfy Lara's sudden curiosity.

"I'm interested in art, of course. That's my job. But I am not a collector."

Their order arrived. Lara took a sip of the black, bitter coffee.

"You'll want these painting! I'll wager that!"

Again Lara had to prompt her. "Why would I? Are some of Mark's works going to be sold?"

"Bingo!" she cried. "Two of them, in fact! And you know why?" She straightened up self-importantly. "Because I am the owner! I bought them from him!" Her voice dropped to a tone of regret. "I can't afford to keep them, though. I'd like to, but my own work hasn't been doing so well and this," she waved her hand, "this job pays peanuts!"

"I would like to purchase them," Lara said. "I have a lot of Mark's early work, but only one of his recent paintings."

"Oh, he was ambitious! Just like Dane! And a brain, as well," Hallie paused, then added significantly, "Just like Dane!"

"Crystal Mar was talented, also. Did you know her well?"

"Even though Crystal called the place she lived her studio,

she still worked a lot at our retreat. God, that old hotel was some place at one time! Mark and Dane would have made a fortune! But it all fell through, unless Dane can bring it back. And every day he gets a little more discouraged."

"I understand that Crystal was one of Dane's students."

"Oh, yes! Dane took a lot of stock in her. You should have seen the two of them together! They had a special— what do they call it?—rapport? I just loved to watch them work. They spent hours together, sculpting, painting. They were so happy, never quitting until they were all covered with dust and paint."

Lara responded with sudden resentment to the picture of Dane and Crystal that sprang to her mind. She saw clearly the intimacy that had existed between them, which made a certainty of all of her suspicions.

"The damned coffee isn't even hot," Hallie said, as if blaming this for Lara's rapid change of mood. "I'll get you some more."

"The coffee's fine." Lara reached for the cup again, her swift motion caused the thick, black liquid to swirl. Even after she had finished the drink, she felt locked in deep silence, distrusting Dane, wishing she had listened to Scott Tyler and had never allowed herself to become involved.

Hallie continued her chatter, but Lara had long ago lost the content of her words. Even if Dane and Crystal had been lovers, that didn't automatically make the sheriff's assessment correct—that Dane had murdered Crystal in a jealous rage because she had not waited for him to be released from prison.

Lara glanced at her watch—seven-twenty. "I was supposed to meet Dane here at seven," she said.

"Oh, I didn't know you and Dane . . ."

"Nothing like that. Business."

Hallie craned her neck toward the huge glass windows

that lined the restaurant front. "I'll swear I saw him go by just a mite before you got here. He turned off the highway, and I think he turned again, for I never did see him cross the bridge." She laughed loudly. "Dane says I see everything—day and night! Everything! I guess I do!"

Dane must have gone directly to Crystal's house by the river. But, why? Hadn't he clearly stated he would meet her here?

Lara paid for the coffee at the cash register at the end of the counter, then returned to Hallie to say, "I'll be at the auction in Hot Springs Wednesday. Thanks for telling me about it."

Lara had intended merely to drive to the house and see if Dane were waiting for her there, but once in the empty expanse of front yard, she clicked off the engine.

The sheriff had completed his investigation, not even the mark of yellow ribbon remained. No longer a crime scene, just a slightly dilapidated, two-story farm home, one that, sooner or later, she must enter.

Lara had never driven to the house at night without seeing patches of light spilling across the yard. She had often wondered: had Crystal ever slept? The scene before her now loomed dark and abandoned, yet at the same time, strangely occupied, as if Crystal's abundant life's energy seethed beneath the surface of quietness and night.

Her mind, retreating from such thoughts, snapped back to reality. As Karma's guardian, the task of disposing of Crystal's personal effects would fall to Lara. No use being squeamish about facing the house or its contents. In fact, why shouldn't she go in now and try to find the clue Dane had been so positive must be hidden inside?

Seated behind the wheel of the Taurus, her fears had been abstract, but as she proceeded to the house, they steadily intensified. Clouds had drifted across the full moon. The momentary darkening seemed purposeful, like a forewarning of doom. The sudden rising of wind against the blackness of encroaching trees added a chaotic sense of menace.

She stopped to listen, but heard only the rustle of branches. She glanced around, assured that she was totally alone. The panic receded a little as she hurried toward the whitewashed front porch.

Her nervous fingers worked with the security lock, that she had insisted Crystal install upon the front door, a lock Crystal had probably rarely gone to the trouble to latch. Then, as if she had won a race and triumphed, she reached inside, her hand groping for the light switch.

The glow of the overhead chandelier magnified the emptiness of the living room. She clicked the lock behind her and stood immobile near the doorway grappling with memories of her last visit. In spite of promptings not to do so, she found her gaze shifting to the hallway that would lead to the kitchen where Crystal had died. She shuddered as the vivid image of Crystal formed in her mind, of Crystal, her long, black hair moist and bright with blood.

Why had she ever entered this house tonight? She could flee now, return in the daytime, when she would feel less vulnerable, perhaps with the support of someone she totally trusted, someone like Joan Sommers or Charles Cade.

But she was now safely locked inside. She must not think, just plunge into her search and blot out her fears.

Lara drew in a deep breath and headed toward the walnut corner cabinet built into the wall. Neat stacks of sketches, papers, and photographs overflowed from the shelves. Her heartbeat quickened at the thought that she might recognize as important some paper the sheriff and his men would have tossed aside as insignificant.

The hope began to diminish as she moved more and more papers from the cabinet to the floor beside her. At the bottom of the first stack, she found a large photograph taken in front of the hotel. Dane, in the center of a group of about twenty people, stood out from the others, looking debonair, as if he were accustomed to a central position. She spotted Mark on the far right, between Crystal and a gray-haired man. Who was he?

Lara carried the photograph closer to the light. Charles! Charles had told her he had only been at the hotel once or twice. What would he be doing in this photograph? Instead of looking at the camera, merry, gray eyes regarded Crystal, joining her in carefree laughter.

For some reason, the image of Charles and Crystal bothered her. There must be some logical reason he would appear in a photograph with Dane's students. He must have merely been out there at the time and had been politely asked to participate in the photo-session.

But the imprint of Charles' face remained as she returned to the cabinet and undid another bunch of photographs clipped with a rubber band. Most of them were of art shows. She recognized the room just off the hotel lobby that Dane had shown her. In this picture, however, the room was not bare, but flagrant with displays of paintings and sculptures.

Anxiously Lara unfolded advertisements of shows and other papers that made up the history of Crystal's life. She found nothing of great importance, only the scattered mementos that people are inclined to keep.

The next bundle consisted of bank statements. Lara opened the top one. Crystal had made a six thousand dollar cash deposit on the third of the month. She opened the next one, then checked the others. Periodic deposits of substantial amounts—what would that mean? Even if Crystal were receiving such large sums for her sculptures, would she have sold them with such uniform regularity?

She would ask Scott. As an investigator, he would surely have checked into her business interests.

Lara replaced the contents of the cabinet, rose and skimmed the room. A sculpture of a long beaked bird in a cage set on the fireplace mantel. Lara could easily identify the work as Crystal's—those special, very feminine touches of detail were as clear as her signature would have been. Even the wooden stand used for a base carried out the same airy design and complimented the unpainted, brownish-orange terra cotta.

She recalled other times she had stood before this fireplace, how the mantle had been jammed with Crystal's numerous projects. It seemed odd that only one remained.

Maybe there would be more of her work upstairs. As Lara climbed the stairway, she caught sight of the bronze stag's head mounted upon the wall that had so startled her the night she had searched for Karma. Some of that uneasiness returned as Lara, as if somehow reenacting that terrible night, moved silently across the hall to Crystal's bedroom.

This room, too, was bare of Crystal's finished works. Still, Lara could not say for sure that anything was actually missing. Since Crystal's sculptures were selling well, she might have consigned the bulk of them to some local gallery. Or, remembering the bank statements, Lara wondered if it was possible Crystal had sold them all. Strange she hadn't come across any receipts.

No longer having any expectation of finding anything significant, Lara nevertheless continued her search in the same, thorough manner, looking in dresser drawers, jewel boxes, and in the great old closet Crystal herself must have remodeled to hold her grand assortment of garments.

Nothing. She stopped in the center of the room for one final survey. In this close scrutiny Lara noted the space beneath the oriole window. Usually in these old houses, a door was present under a circular window, behind which were shelves used for storage. This one had been paneled over. She crossed the room to take a closer look. The paneling didn't look solidly attached, as if it had been removed and replaced. A perfect hiding place!

As Lara leaned over for a closer look, she glimpsed a movement in the yard below, near her car. Lara settled flat against the wall beside the window. Terror pressed down upon her, caused the strength to melt from her body. She ventured another look. Hunched beside her car, the form was only a dark shadow. She could see that something black or darkish blue, maybe a stocking cap, covered the top of his head. What was he doing?

She must try to identify him! One more quick look. Was he still there?

The figure rose and she shrank back against the wall again, aghast, the image remaining before her eyes. Because he had stepped back into the full moonlight, for a moment she had caught a clear glimpse of him. But his face had been covered by a dark ski mask!

When she looked again, he was gone.

Lara moved quickly away. Her trembling hands groped for the phone on Crystal's nightstand. Her heart sank at the stillness of the line. Had he cut the phone wires or had Crystal failed to pay the last bill?

What would she do now? With pounding heart, hand clutching the stair railing, she moved cautiously down the steps. A madman! A maniac! He must have been watching her, stalking her, just as he had Crystal. He now planned to kill her in exactly the same way!

She had one advantage. He did not know she had seen him. Did he intend to lurk in the shadows beside her car waiting for her to come out? Or was it his intention to break into the house? She looked around desperately for something to use for a weapon. If only she had brought along the gun Charles had given her!

Lara, frozen in indecision, heard a sudden crash coming from the direction of the kitchen. She interpreted it as foot kicking soundly against the door on the screened-in back porch. The door creaked, another bang, and a shattering sounded as if the wood had broken loose from around the latch.

Lara dashed toward the front door. She fumbled with the lock with cold, stiff fingers that scarcely obeyed her commands. If she were fast enough, she might get to her car while he was still breaking into the house!

She fled, gasping, toward the Taurus. Before she reached it, she froze, appalled. Both tires on this side were flat! That's what she had observed from the upstairs window, his bent form busy with the destruction.

Should she try to drive away on the rims? No! He could have done other things to the car. She couldn't take the chance of being trapped inside, helpless.

Giving way to panic, Lara raced toward the closest cover of trees, toward the path behind the back of the house. She was aware that the door stood ajar, aware of a form drawing forward and standing, a huge, hunched shadow. By another fleeting glimpse caught over her shoulder, she saw him, saw the dark ski mask pulled over his face. With the agility of a lion, the form sprang into action, running after her, gaining on her with those frightening, lunging steps!

Chapter Nine

Lara fled into the darkness beneath the trees. Visions of Karma swam around her, of Karma, running, running, without destination or hope. The child's terror merged with her own, spurred her to a higher panic that manifested itself in unfathomable speed.

He followed relentlessly. His gait had changed, no longer jerky, springing, but steady, methodical. She sensed the tension of his body, the power of his limbs. Did he clutch some weapon? Would he strike her down, as he had done to Crystal?

The trail turned sharply. He could no longer see her. Just ahead the path would fork. She must make a split-second decision. She quickly chose the trail along the river. Maybe she could manage to hide from him in the dark tangle of undergrowth that grew along the bank!

Without hesitation, she veered to the left. His not knowing for certain which way she would go would serve to slow him. She must work this to her advantage. She pushed herself to put greater distance between them. After a hard, five-minute run, Lara left the path and tore, half-sliding, down the steep embankment. She could not see and did not expect the great drop-off. She found herself stumbling and falling to the bottom. The impact of the fall twisted her right leg and struck full-force on her shoulder, sending immobilizing fingers of pain throughout her body. With agonizing slowness Lara dragged herself into the high grass and lay still. The pain, the labored breathing, seemed to belong to someone else. She tried to force herself to stifle all movement, all sound.

It took all her effort and what seemed like hours before quietness settled around her. Through the layers of silence, she visualized Karma's face. The child was extending her arms in trust and love. Thank goodness she was safe with Charles! Charles had been a loyal and staunch friend, faithful to her father and Mark, faithful to her. If she didn't come back tonight, she knew she could count on him. He would personally see to Karma's welfare.

The possibility of her own death for the first time in her life seemed imminent. She felt in her heart that the killer could stay here, all night if necessary, stalking her. Even if he weren't a good tracker, eventually, he would be sure to find her.

She listened, every sense alert. Sounds she hadn't noticed before, the croaking of a frog and the rippling motion of the river, now seemed intensely loud.

A long time passed. Because of the pain, she found she could no longer maintain her taut position. Aware of her muddy jeans, she moved slightly, allowing the injured leg to stretch.

Lara raised her head. A breeze, scented with earth and vegetation, rose up from the edges of riverbank, tousled her strands of hair, damp with sweat. Did she detect the crunch of a footfall against twigs? She ducked down again, and holding her breath, waited.

He must have stepped off the path. Just above her, she detected the faint rustle of legs against undergrowth.

Lara eased her hand forward. It closed over a large rock, which she drew noiselessly toward her. If he came down here, she would surprise him. She would jump up and strike out at him with all of her strength.

She waited tensely. No more sounds. Had he moved on or was he still there watching? She couldn't judge how much time had passed, but her fingers locked around the stone begin to feel numb and cold.

Still she remained. Time no longer had any meaning.

She had no idea whether she had stayed motionless for fifteen minutes or a half-hour. But only her time perception was muddled. She was relieved that her thoughts were clear, calmly weighing her options, intent on saving her.

The cafe was at least a mile and a half from here. But heading in that direction meant backtracking to the house. The killer, if he wasn't still out here somewhere, must have returned that way himself.

No, she must try to reach the hotel. It couldn't be more than a fourth mile. Before the iron bridge was built, the forested trail that wound past Crystal's house had been the only road. The wooden bridge across the Quachita, so seldom used, still stood intact. She had only to continue south following the river to find it.

Her best chance, probably her only chance, was to make her way to the hotel, to a phone, and call the sheriff.

Lara's whole being rebelled at having the hotel for a destination. Even in daylight, it loomed ominous and threatening. Would she be able to slip into the building without Jim Bearle spotting her? Was it even sensible to go there, thinking as she did, that Dane Lanford himself might have set her up, might be stalking her this very minute? Even though it seemed her only choice, she might well be walking directly into Dane's final trap.

She wasn't thinking clearly after all. Dane was not the one to fear. She would be safe with him! She couldn't misjudge someone so completely.

After another long wait, she attempted to rise. Tentatively she bore her weight upon her right leg, relieved that she could stand, could step ahead and find the fiery pain somehow bearable.

The trail that wound just a few yards overhead would be much faster, yet she could not risk leaving the cover of cave-like rocks that made up the bank. Soundlessly she groped her way along. At every twist of the embankment, her heart pounded in fear of coming face to face with the man, whose features were concealed by the dark ski mask.

He might be hiding anywhere, ready to attack. She could almost feel the blow of stone or steel against her temple and feel herself sinking into the swirling darkness of death.

Life had never seemed so dear, her affairs so all-important. There was so much she needed to do, to accomplish!

The moon appeared from behind clouds and lighted the clearing where the boathouse stood. She must pass into the vast opening of trees if she were to continue to follow the river and find the wooden bridge.

As if poising before a death-defying dive, she took one look around. The area seemed totally empty. Still she must hurry, must try to run from this shelter of trees to the ones just beyond the boathouse.

Her gaze fell to the gaping doorway of the boathouse, half-expecting the killer to emerge from the black depths inside. She darted past it. Not pausing to look around, she continued running until she was again in the dense forest.

Lara kept the same fast gait, oblivious of the strange shortness of her breath, the agony of shoulder and leg. Only when the silhouette of the bridge appeared did she stop.

The reason he wasn't following her became suddenly clear. He had guessed her destination. He would be waiting here for her to cross the bridge.

A sickness struck her stomach, followed by a feeling of weakness that manifested itself in visible shaking. How could she venture into the total exposure of the bridge? In spite of deep promptings that said, "Go on," she remained secluded behind the thick branches. The dryness of her mouth had moved deep into her throat.

Lara remained hidden until the shaking of her limbs

became only a sight trembling. She skimmed the area once more. The bridge had no overhead structure, just an ancient, metal base covered with thick, wooden planks. Lara drew in her breath, climbed up the slope to the road, and with trembling legs began to cross the bridge.

She hadn't realized before that the Quachita River possessed such width. The narrow track seemed to stretch endlessly before her. Only a low, wooden guardrail separated her from the deep water below.

Her hearing from the long, guarded period of waiting had become acute. She detected the sound of a car motor before she saw the vehicle.

The car did not come from the road itself, but from the side of the road as if it had suddenly backed up to turn around—a battered station wagon, white and ghostlike. Mark's death flashed before her mind. Was she to die, too, in exactly in the same way her brother had?

She realized at once that her goal of reaching the other side of the bridge was impossible.

Lights shifted upward as the front tires hit the wooden edges of the bridge floor. Headlights blinded her with their brightness, held her transfixed.

She whirled and ran back the way she had come, her steps made a clacking noise on the loose floorboards. She would never get to the other side! Her only hope was to plunge into dark, concealing water and try to swim to safety! She zigzagged indecisively, then lurched toward the railing, preparing to hurl herself from the bridge into the water.

In the same instant she heard the spinning of tires as the car swerved to a sudden stop.

"Lara! Don't!"

Dane's deep voice, sharp and commanding, brought renewed panic. The railing was higher than she had believed. She struggled to pull herself up, to cross it, but before she could do so, his strong hands caught her and drew her back. Lara fell against him. He tried to hold her, but she pulled herself away as if his very touch were fatal.

Headlights illuminated Dane's features, reflected in his eyes. His pupils, encircled by white, gave his face a dangerous, predatory dimension.

He stepped closer to her, grasping for her shoulders and holding her at arm's length. His turning away from the direct glow of car lights created hollowed shadows at his jawline and around his tense mouth. "What has happened, Lara? Tell me!"

She was trapped! Terror blotted her vision, caused Dane's features to become indistinguishable. She was unable, despite her frantic attempts, to break the fierce grip of his hands.

She tried to speak, but her voice was caught in a sob.

"What's wrong with you, Lara? You must tell me! Who frightened you?"

The tightening of his fingers hurt her injured shoulder. Lara winced, shook her head. "I don't know! All I saw was a dark form. He had a ski mask over his face!"

Without Dane's supporting hands, Lara knew she would not be able to stand. She could hear his deep, calming voice, but she could derive no meaning from his words. It dawned on her ever so slowly that Dane Lanford had no intention of harming her.

Lara felt foolishly exhilarated. She was safe! If Dane had been the one chasing her, he would have killed her by now. He would simply have struck her and thrown her body into the deep Quachita River.

A wonderful sense of relief flowed over her. She had been right all along about trusting Dane!

This shifting of emotions made her extremely verbal. She began to understand what he was saying and to respond. She poured out the details of her flight from Crystal's house.

Dane reacted by drawing closer. She could feel his strong, muscular body so very near hers, and longed for a moment to cling to him, to be comforted by his embrace. But he made no move to take her into his arms. He merely began guiding her toward the station wagon.

"I started to meet you at the cafe as we had planned, but my car wouldn't start."

Whoever killed Crystal had definitely known about their plans to search Crystal's house tonight. How cleverly he had delayed Dane so he could meet her himself in order to . . . kill her.

But why? Was he mad—were they dealing with a serial killer? Dane's arm, solidly around her, made it possible for her to think more clearly. She had faced certain death tonight, yet the murderer must surely know she could prove nothing concerning his crime. Was he so convinced she was going to uncover the truth that he was willing to silence her forever?

"You saved my life," Lara said.

"I knew I had no time to lose. When I called Hallie at the truckstop, she told me you had already left. She had seen you turn toward Crystal's house. I started over here on foot. Luckily," he added grimly, "I met Jim a little while ago on this road."

Because of the glaring headlights, she had not noticed that someone was seated behind the wheel of the station wagon. When she first made out Jim Bearle's dark, slouched form, a new surge of fear swept over her. It couldn't be just a coincidence that he would be driving back to the hotel at the very moment she was being terrorized. When she faced him, noted the sullenness that marked his face, she felt certain he had been the one chasing her. Jim Bearle had guessed that she would flee toward the hotel and had gone back to his car, planning to intercept her as she crossed the bridge. But Dane's showing up had kept him from his deadly purpose!

"Get inside, Lara," Dane said, noting her hesitation. "We'll go back to the house and take a look around."

Lara cast a quick glance back at Dane. As she did, her thoughts did a terrible about-face. It was just as reasonable to suppose that Dane had failed to keep his appointment with her purposely, believing she would drive out to Crystal's house alone. Then Jim Bearle, innocent of Dane's plans, had accidentally run into Dane here. If that were the case, then Jim Bearle's presence had prevented Dane from killing her!

Whatever had happened, one of them, at least, was telling the truth. Their encounter with each other tonight had been purely by chance. It was likely that chance, alone, had saved her life!

Jim's eyes remained locked straight ahead as she slid into the seat beside him. Lara, afraid of both of them, tried desperately to recall the clothing her pursuer had worn. All that came into mind was an impression of darkness. Both of these men were dressed in dark clothing—Dane, in navy trousers and brown shirt, Jim, in jeans and the same black T-shirt he had worn when she had first seen him.

What had Jim Bearle been doing on this old road that almost no one used? She stole a glance at him. In profile, he looked all the more dangerous—the broad forehead, the shaggy hair, the jutting lower lip.

"I didn't know anyone used this bridge anymore," Lara said shakily.

"Jim started taking this road to the hotel," Dane explained, "right after Mark was killed."

"That other road gives me the willies," Jim remarked,

still without looking at her.

"Did you happen to see anyone as you passed Crystal's house?"

Jim's gaze shot from the road to her. The dashboard light caused an eerie light to glow in his eyes. "No."

Dane leaned back against the seat. "I can't imagine what possessed you to come out here alone," he said. "How long were you in the house? Did you find anything?"

They both seemed to be waiting anxiously for her answer. She replied briefly, just as Jim Bearle had to her question. "No."

Once again clouds obscured the moon, making weird darkness engulf the trees along the narrow, dirt road. The old car bounced and swayed as it hit unexpected ruts. Jim's meeting each obstacle with a low curse was all that broke the silence.

Jim recklessly swung his vehicle in close to her car, whistling softly and saying, "Damned if they didn't get all four tires!"

Dane got out and inspected the nearest one. "Slashed," he said. "Jim, you stay out here and keep watch. I'm going inside."

"Wait for me."

"You stay out here with Jim."

"No, I'm going with you," Lara insisted, following after him. She paused on the step.

One of the hinges had broken loose allowing the door to hang askance. On the other side the lock had been ripped away from the wooden frame. Dane propped the damaged door all the way open and crossed the porch which Crystal had used as a workroom. The pieces of broken and unfinished sculptures had been swept up and removed, leaving the area barren and empty. He crossed the open threshold and stood in the center of the kitchen, near where Crystal had been struck down. His face, as he turned back to Lara, was ashen.

His voice because of the distance between them was strangely hollow. "How well did you search the house?"

"I was almost ready to leave when I saw this man outside near my car."

"Why don't you stay right here while I check the place I had in mind?"

"I want to go with you," Lara said with determination.

Dane paused, doubt present in his lingering look. "Then let me make certain there's no one inside."

Lara waited on the step, not wanting to look through the porch into the kitchen nor back to where Jim Bearle stood beside his car. She was aware of his shadowy form, alert, like a paid bodyguard.

Dane returned. He studied her and the deep concern in his eyes made her aware of the streaks of mud upon her jeans and sweater, her aching shoulder. "You've been through enough tonight, Lara," Let us take you home. We'll take care of your car and see that the house is locked."

"You mentioned Crystal's special hiding place. Where was it?"

He hesitated. "Are you sure you want to go back inside?"

"Yes."

Lara felt a moment of panic as she stepped ahead of Dane through the porch. Dane bypassed her and took the lead through the kitchen where Crystal had died. In the hallway he stopped to wait for her. "We have to go upstairs."

As she met Dane's gaze, she had the strong impression that he had already searched every corner of the house, that he had already checked that "special place" that he was about to show her. He was only going through the motions now for her benefit.

"How did you know about her hiding place?"

"She took some money from it one day in my presence," Dane said. "Crystal used to call it 'a poor-man's safe.'"

She knew he was leading her toward Crystal's room. He wouldn't be so familiar with Crystal's house, with Crystal's bedroom, unless—he had lied to her—Crystal and he had been lovers!

Dane reached Crystal's room first. Brilliant light spilled out into the hallway where Lara remained. He was moving directly to the place beneath the oriole window, to the loose paneling she had bent to examine when she had spotted the figure in the yard.

Dane spoke over his shoulder. "This looks as if it's been disturbed."

He took a small knife from his pocket and began very carefully to pry the board from the wall. Even before she had stepped close enough to see the empty shelves, she knew what he would say.

"Someone must have gotten here before we did."

In wooden silence void of expectation, as if he were playacting for her benefit, he completed his examination, replaced the panel, and rose. His black eyes were shadowed, unreadable.

Lara backed from the room and started down the steps. Close behind her she could hear his footsteps solid on the oak stairway.

"Lara." He caught up with her easily, just as he had done on the bridge. Where before his grip had been firm and determined, it was now so very light. With a gentle touch of his hand he lifted her face upward, so she would meet his gaze.

"I can't bear to have you look at me like that," he said, his voice deep and full of passion. "Don't ever doubt me, Lara!"

The great, black depths of his eyes worked, in spite of her

protests, to restore her faltering trust. For a long moment she forgot her brush with death, the fact that she was inside the house where her friend had been murdered. It was as if she were hypnotized. If was as if only Dane existed, and nothing else. And Dane was so close to her, his strong arms finding their way around her, drawing her tight against him. She drew closer to his body, strong, protective, warm.

"Don't ever be afraid of me," he said. "Your trust means everything to me!"

Fingers moved from the small of her back to entwine in her hair, to tilt her head upward. As he held her captive, his lips touched hers ever so softly.

"Let go of her!"

Scott Tyler, Jim Bearle at his heels, strode into the room.

Jim came to a menacing halt. In the full light, his face was darkened by the beginning of a beard—a face, it seemed, from out of a police line-up.

The sheriff glared from Dane to her. "What's going on here?" He made an angry circle and came to a stop in front of Lara. "What's happened to your car? To the porch door?"

Lara, feeling guilty, embarrassed, and once again afraid, managed to tell him. She ended by saying uncertainly, "I was just out here to go through some of Crystal's things."

"A damn-fool thing to do!" Scott barked out. He turned back to the door, "Tom!" A deputy appeared behind Jim Bearle. "Call the office. We'll need to go over this place again!"

"How did you know I was out here?"

"Easily! When you weren't at your house, I traced you to the cafe, and Hallie said you had headed in this direction." Scott's voice became cold and certain. "I'm going to tell you just as plainly as I can. I don't want your interference, Lara. I want you to leave this investigation completely, totally, up to me! Does that in any way get through to you?"

"Lara owns this place," Dane said quietly. "She has a perfect right to be here. And I'm going to ask you not to talk to her in that tone of voice."

Scott had positioned himself so he could see both Jim Bearle, hulking near the doorway, and Dane, who he now addressed with undisguised hostility. "And you just happened to come along, did you?"

Dane with a never-failing poise maintained the upper hand. He refused to become angered by Scott, only dryly annoyed—the stance of a professor toward some exasperatingly stupid pupil. "Lara and I are in total agreement about one thing: Crystal's death and Mark's death are related. If I were you, I would try to find the link between them. I would reopen Mark Radburn's files."

Scott stepped closer. "The answer to Crystal's murder doesn't lie there!" Scornfully his voice raised in volume. "I know exactly where it does lie. I'll tell you what I'm going to do. I'm going to look for the father of Crystal's child!"

Chapter Ten

Scott insisted on driving Lara home. Exhausted, she watched the headlights cut through the darkness. "When I heard you had been to the jail to see Lanford, I just couldn't believe it! And then finding you out there with him! Do you realize what you're doing? You're playing right into his hands! You're working against all I'm trying to accomplish!"

Lara tried to close her mind to his outraged torrent of words.

"Dammit, Lara, why don't you let me handle this? Lanford belongs behind bars. I had good reason to detain him!"

"And I had just as good a reason to want to talk to him." Lara turned from the window to face Scott's unyielding profile. "I know he didn't resist arrest."

His alarmed gaze shifted from the road to her. "That's where you're wrong, Lara. He did try to escape. On the way to town."

"Wearing handcuffs?" Lara questioned with open skepticism.

Her words were countered by a calm explanation. "Even so, he was able to force the back door of the squad car open. Tom and I had no choice but to subdue him."

Lara remained silent. His words planted seeds of doubt. Was it possible Dane had tried to escape as Scott insisted? She continued to stare out at the dark shroud of trees that sheltered the isolated road. The drive into town seemed endless.

"If you don't believe me, ask my deputy."

Lara realized the influence Scott had over him, and suspected Tom would not fail in his loyalty even if that meant supporting Scott in an outright lie. "You have no real evidence to tie Dane to the crime, not even a fingerprint!"

"Whoever murdered Crystal was very careful, very professional. But I'm going to follow every lead! I'm going to find out everything I can about Crystal's past. I'm not going to stop digging until I get to the truth!"

"I believe Crystal might have been killed because she knew something about Mark's accident," Lara confided in a quiet voice.

"That's impossible!"

"You said you were going to follow every lead. Why don't you start there?"

"Mark's death was a simple hit-and-run. Probably a drunken driver. It had nothing at all to do with Crystal."

"Why won't you admit that my brother could have been murdered?"

"Because he wasn't!" Lara saw Scott's clenched hands, knuckles white, upon the steering wheel. For a moment, the look on his face frightened her. "Why do you insist on working against me, Lara?"

The rest of the drive passed in stony silence. Finally, Scott pulled up into the driveway. The sprawling, ultra-modern split-level with its "For Sale" sign staked in the landscaped yard loomed before them, empty and uninviting.

The darkness filled Lara with dread. In spite of herself, she was grateful when Scott stepped out and walked with her to the front door. He waited while she unlocked the door and turned on the lights.

Scott lingered in the doorway long after welcoming light flooded the room, casting its bright, artificial glow over the fine furnishings. "By the way, where is the little girl?" he asked.

"Charles took her to visit his sister in Eureka Springs," Lara answered. "He's bringing her back tomorrow."

Scott took a step toward her and suggested cautiously, "Maybe you should consider putting her in foster care . . .

at least temporarily."

"Karma is safe with me!"

"If you really believe that, why is she with Charles now?"

Lara answered defensively, "Charles is like family. You surely know how much I trust him."

Scott ran fingers through unruly, rust-colored hair. Then, as if wanting to change the subject, he said, "I took the keys from your car. I'll radio a local garage to fix the tires and bring it back here."

Lara found herself responding with cool formality, "I appreciate that."

Although her tone and manner dismissed him, Scott remained, studying her with a solemn expression. "Sooner or later," he said finally, "You're going to find that I'm not the enemy, Lara." His voice sounded hurt and angry. "The time will come when you'll put your trust where it belongs . . . in me."

Charles had dropped Karma off late Sunday night and, exhausted by the long drive home, she had not fully awakened even as Lara had helped her struggle into pajamas and crawl into bed. Early the following morning a sleepy-eyed Karma appeared in the kitchen as Lara finished her toast and coffee.

"Good morning, sweetheart. Are you hungry? Would you like oatmeal?"

Karma nodded. Lara gave her a warm, welcoming hug and was rewarded by a drowsy smile. "I missed you, Lara," she said as she settled in at the table.

Lara kissed the top of her head. "I missed you too, Karma."

Lara buttered more toast, then prepared a package of instant oatmeal and placed it into the microwave. While it cooked, she moved to check the calendar on the wall near the refrigerator. Karma's appointment with the psychiatrist, Dr. Meg Warner was at ten-thirty. She glanced out of the window where her Taurus, tires repaired, waited in the drive, and was momentarily grateful to Scott.

After slipping into a skirt and blouse and fixing her hair in a French braid, Lara went upstairs to help Karma dress. In her absence, Lara had tried to make the room more appealing to a child by adding bright curtains and a matching, quilted spread in rainbow colors. Karma's brown, well-worn teddy, which she had lovingly named Buddy Bear sat in the exact middle of two new, plump pillows.

"Where are we going?" Karma asked.

Lara hesitated. "To visit a nice lady. She wants to ask you some questions."

"Can I wear my new dress?"

"Why don't we save it for a party or something special?"

Her look of disappointment made Lara weaken. Maybe letting her wear the new dress might lift her spirits and in some way prepare her for the visit to the psychiatrist. As Lara helped her into the ruffled pink frock and let her select a matching hair bow, she felt apprehensive, wondering how Karma would react to Dr. Warner.

"You're hair's pretty, Lara," Karma told her. "It looks like sunshine." She admired Lara's French braid. "Can you fix mine just like yours?"

Karma sat perfectly still as Lara brushed the silky strands of black hair and separated it into three sections. When she got a little older, Lara knew the child would become aware of her own beauty and be proud of the glossy charcoal locks and thick, sweeping lashes that put Lara so much in mind of Crystal. With a flourish Lara snapped the bow into place at the end of her braiding. Just as she had finished, she heard the doorbell ring.

"Anyone home?" Joan called, poking her head in as Lara hurried down the stairs. "I just thought I'd stop by on my way to the office," she said as Lara met her at the door. She noticed Lara's white skirt and jacket, the sandwashed silk blouse of deep violet. "Were you on your way out? I don't want to keep you from anything."

"Karma has an appointment with Dr. Warner," Lara explained. "But it's not for another forty-five minutes. Please, come on in. The coffee's still hot."

"No, thanks. Not even noon and already I'm on a caffeine high." Joan's gaze shifted to Karma, who had followed Lara down the stairs. "My, don't you look pretty today!"

Karma giggled and spun around to model the dress for her. Joan turned to Lara with a smile, "Maybe it's my imagination but the kid's beginning to resemble you. I don't see how when she's so dark and you're so fair. It must be that French braid."

"She wanted me to do her hair like mine this morning."

"Kids are so impressionable!"

"I hope I'm being a good influence," Lara said, watching Karma with pride. The pup had wandered in with Joan and now waited for Karma with thumping tail by the doorway.

"Don't get dirty!" Lara called after her as the two of them scampered outside.

"You're beginning to sound like my mother." Joan quipped as they settled into the living room. "Now here's what I came to tell you. Austin has invited me to a big art show in Hot Springs and I've found out some of Mark's paintings are going to be sold. I knew you'd be interested. You could ride along with us," Joan suggested with slight hesitation.

"I do plan to go to the auction." Not wishing to horn in on Joan's date, she added, "Thanks for the offer, but I believe I'll drive up in my own car. That way I can leave early if I like." After a pause, she asked, "Does Austin share your interest in art?"

"Not for art's sake alone." Joan made a wry face. "Paintings are a good investment, you know." Changing the subject, she said, "If I wasn't going myself, I'd offer to baby-sit. Maybe you can get Charles to watch Karma for you."

"I don't want to impose on him too much. I'll just take her along. She's not much trouble."

"I guess I just can't get used to the thought of you, Miss Career Woman, having a kid in tow," Joan remarked. A serious expression crossed her face. "I hope you don't take this the wrong way, but have you really thought this guardianship thing over?"

"What do you mean?"

"All this time I believed you were just taking Karma temporarily, but Whitney tells me different. Now, don't misunderstand me. Karma's a darling child. But a week or two of playing 'Mommy' is a whole lot different from a lifetime of commitment." She sighed. "I guess it's up to me to give you this lecture so later on I can say, 'I told you so.' Lara, you're not even thirty, and single! Are you really sure you're ready to saddle yourself down with the responsibility of raising a child?"

"There's the trust fund Crystal had set up for Karma. It's not much, but it will help."

"It's not money I'm talking about." Joan persisted. "And I think you know that." Taking on her big sister tone, she said, "In case no one's ever told you, kids can be a burden. You haven't been around children much. You don't have any idea how much time and energy they can consume." She shrugged. "Maybe I'm selfish, but if I were in your shoes, I'd think about giving her away to some nice, child-less couple who'd welcome the patter of little feet."

The advice, Lara thought, was just what she might expect of Joan. Although generous, sometimes to the point of extravagance, her friend had a tendency to avoid making personal commitments, especially ones of the kind that caused her inconvenience.

In the stillness Lara could hear the puppy barking just outside the door. "Sometimes I think I'm the selfish one for not wanting to give her up. Maybe she deserves two parents, the kind of normal family life I won't able to give her."

"Then you should find someone to share the responsibility," Joan suggested glibly, as if she had just come up with the perfect solution. "A husband, that's what you need! I keep telling you Scott Tyler's handsome and available." Joan grinned. "And from what I've heard, definitely interested."

"I'm not the least bit interested in him!"

"But you two would make such a perfect couple! In fact, I think I'm going to work on getting the two of you together."

Lara wished she would just let the subject drop. Joan's flippant manner, which Lara usually tolerated, was beginning to grind on her nerves. She was relieved when Joan rose abruptly to her feet, saying, "Well, I must be off! I have eager clients waiting for me." She gave an exaggerated sigh. "Picky, picky, picky. This is the fifth house I've shown the Thompsons' this week!"

Lara walked Joan out to her car. Upon returning to the house, she found Karma sitting forlornly upon the front porch. Noticing her trembling lower lip and downcast eyes, Lara sat down beside her.

"What's wrong, Honey?"

"Spot got my pretty dress all dirty," she said, her eyes filling with tears.

Lara sighed in exasperation at the sight of the muddy

paw prints on a dress that had been clean five minutes ago. "Here, let me see what I can do." Lara rubbed the frilly, pink skirt briskly, glad that most of the mud had dried and dusted easily away. "There," she said, satisfied with her efforts. "Good as new."

"Are . . . are you mad at me, Lara?" Karma looked up at her, eyes wide and anxious in the round, baby face.

"Why, no! Of course I'm not angry." Lara felt pangs of anxiety. What had she done to make her think so? Joan's words had filled her mind with doubts. She really didn't know anything about being a mother. What made her think she was capable of dealing with the day-to-day trials of a small girl?

"I'm glad!" Karma reached out her arms to Lara. She looked so fragile, Lara thought, like a China doll that would easily break. On impulse, she lifted the child into her arms and for a long moment hugged her close.

Dr. Warner's office was not entirely what she had expected, and neither was Dr. Meg Warner. Lara, who had conjured up in her mind images of a female Sigmund Freud was pleasantly surprised to find the psychiatrist plump and unassuming with kind eyes and a cap of short brown curls. Her ordinary appearance seemed incongruous with the formidable array of framed degrees that covered a good portion of the wall behind her desk.

Through the glass window of the private office, Lara could watch Karma who was busy with a large box of toys which sat in the far corner of the spacious waiting room.

"I sent for Karma's files soon after you made the appointment," Dr. Warner said, lifting a tan folder from her desk and quickly reviewing its contents. "According to the police psychologist, Karma was outside playing at the time of her mother's death. It was his opinion that the child didn't witness the actual murder, but wandered up to the house much later. The child experienced trauma when she found her mother's body. The shock of the discovery caused her to run away and hide in the woods."

Dr. Warner paused to jot down notes as Lara told her story of how she had followed the trail of small footprints into the trees behind the house. "I found Karma hiding in the rocks near the river. Ever since that night, she's had these ghastly nightmares." Lara's voice trembled slightly as she spoke of waking to Karma's terrified shrieks, the open window, the marked-up doll. The doctor waited patiently for her to go on.

"The sheriff could find no trace of a prowler. The weather was warm and stuffy, so Karma must have opened the window herself. Scott Tyler believes Karma may have been reenacting through the doll what she saw that night." Lara said in summation what she sincerely hoped was true. "Karma appears to be adjusting. But she's bound to have frightening memories."

"You're very wise to seek professional help. Being able to work through what she saw that night could be very important to her emotional recovery." Rising, she said, "I'll talk to Karma privately for a while now." Dr. Warner called to her, and Karma abandoned the toy chest to join them in the private office.

Later, sitting in the waiting room, Lara's attention wandered to the far corner, where Karma had been sorting playthings. She noticed Karma had divided the ones she liked into piles. Lara winced as she saw the rejected dolls, once a favorite toy, stuffed behind the box as if Karma had tried to hide them from her sight.

Lara had formed a favorable opinion of Dr. Warner and felt reassured that she had made the right decision by bringing Karma here today. Still, time seemed to pass slowly. Waiting made her restless, and Lara crossed a section of the waiting room to study the magazines fanned out upon a glass-topped table. With surprise, she noticed an issue of *City Square* among the rest and brought it back with her to the sofa to read.

The sight of the magazine reminded Lara that soon she would be back in New York. For the first time, she felt actual dread of returning. The publication had recently changed editorship and with it had come a shift in direction. The new editor seemed dull, restrictive, money-oriented. With a voice devoid of warmth or enthusiasm, he had already rejected most of Lara's ideas. Over the phone, he had told her that he was compiling a list of artists for her to interview upon her return.

She had hung up feeling discouraged about his limiting her features to a select few artists of his choice. In fact, she was beginning to question if the goals of the magazine and her own personal goals were still compatible. She entertained elusive thoughts of moving on, of pursuing her dream of starting her own publication.

Lara closed the magazine firmly, as if she were also closing a chapter of her life. Although she had no clear plan for not returning, her work in New York seemed already like something in her distant past, something she had left permanently behind.

Lara's thoughts were interrupted by the sound of an opening door. "How would you like to play out here again while Lara and I have a little chat?" she heard Dr. Warner ask Karma.

As if they had become good friends, Karma nodded and made her way eagerly back to the box of toys. Dr. Warner motioned to Lara and they once more entered the private office.

Dr. Warner showed her pictures Karma had made for

her with crayons, saying, "You indicated that Karma likes to draw, and this is an excellent way for her to express her feelings. She does quite well for someone her age." The first few were happy drawings of dogs and stick figures and houses. Lara recognized among them a picture of Spot and Charles, then one of her and Lara smiling, holding hands.

"This is a very positive sign," Dr. Warner told her. "It means that Karma is bonding to you and her new life. The holding of hands symbolizes that she thinks of the two of you as a family."

Dr. Warner handed Lara a second group of pictures, saying, "After she started to feel comfortable, I began to ask careful questions about the night her mother was killed."

The first drawing Lara recognized as the house where Crystal had been murdered. Karma had colored the sky dark and the windows had eyes that seemed to follow the stick figure of a girl running away.

Lara quickly reached for the next drawing. Her heart caught in her throat as she recognized the small figure huddled in the tiny cave where they had found Karma.

Lara's attention fell to the final drawing. She studied the crude sketch that looked like a man with a lion's face, and felt a chill creep over her.

Visions of the shattered pieces of the broken statue entered Lara's mind. In a flash she understood its significance. "Karma's mother was working on a sculpture of a mountain lion the day she was murdered," Lara said. "She was killed by a blow to the head from that very sculpture."

Dr. Warner added solemnly, "It is obvious that Karma has suffered severe trauma. I sense a lapse in her perception of what happened that night, a subconscious omission of a frame of time. When I questioned Karma, she told me she had been playing in the yard. The next thing she consciously remembers is being found in the woods.

Yet in fragmented terms, she spoke about seeing the body, the blood, the broken lion. She also seems able to discern that someone was in the room with her mother. A dark figure. She called him a "bad man."

Lara felt her mouth go dry. "Could she say anything to identify him?"

Dr. Warner shook her head gravely. " When I asked her what he looked like, she cried and stopped talking. Then she began to describe the lion."

Bewildered, Lara asked, "What can this mean?"

"I believe the shock is making Karma have difficulty interpreting what she saw. Young children are often afraid of animals. She could be transferring her terror of the person she saw kill her mother into the murder weapon. To Karma, the stone lion may be the embodiment of fear itself."

"Do you think it possible she did see the man who killed her mother?"

"Karma was aware of someone in the room. But she may not have seen more than a shadow. Maybe it was too dark for her to get a close look at him. Or his features could have been covered by a cap or stocking, some kind of disguise."

Lara thought of the dark figure in ski mask crouched near her car the night her tires had been slashed. Doubtlessly he had been wearing that very mask the night he had murdered Crystal.

"On the other hand, if she is subconsciously blocking what she saw, she could meet her mother's killer face to face and not be able to recognize him."

The thought that Karma might actually have seen the killer chilled Lara. "If we only knew what she actually saw that night. Is there a chance she will ever be able to remember?"

"Karma may experience flashbacks. Sometimes another

traumatic event can trigger the memory." She studied Lara thoughtfully before adding, "Chances are, she didn't get a good enough look to identify anyone. But if she is suffering from a mental block, hypnosis could be very effective in helping her to remember."

"Hypnosis?" Lara felt dubious, and she found herself almost automatically rejecting the idea. "Do you really think it would work?"

"Children often respond quite well to hypnosis. Unfortunately, I'm not a qualified hypnotist," Dr. Warner continued. "But I could refer you to one of my colleagues. Mason Adler."

Sensing Lara's hesitation, she said, "Take some time to consider my suggestion. In the meanwhile, encourage Karma to express herself through her drawing. Let her talk and confide in you. If she does recall anything significant, call me immediately. But don't expect too much. It could be years before she experiences any significant breakthrough."

That night as Lara read "Rapunzel" from the bedtime story book, she noticed that Karma appeared quiet and subdued. As she tucked her in, the child seemed reluctant for her to go.

"Is something wrong, honey?"

Karma clutched Buddy Bear tightly in her arms. "My tummy hurts."

Believing the visit to the psychiatrist might have upset her, Lara asked, "Do you want me to sit with you a while?"

Karma's large, sad eyes raised to hers. "Will you tell me another story?"

Lara sat back down on the edge of the bed. She began to recount "Sleeping Beauty", but before she was even halfway finished Karma's eyelids started to droop. Smiling, Lara bent to kiss her gently on the forehead, then began to tiptoe out.

"Lara?" Karma asked.

"Yes, darling?" Lara returned to the bedside to find her once again fully awake.

Karma plucked at the fur on her teddy bear. "Are you going to give me away?"

The child's question took her by surprise. "Why, of course not! What ever gave you that idea?"

Taking deep breaths, she stammered forlornly, "Joan said . . . Joan said so." Lara watched tears brim in her eyes. "She said you were going to give me away!"

Lara realized that Karma must have overheard Joan and she talking this morning and had misunderstood.

Stifling a sob, Karma cried, "Lara, I want to stay with you!"

As she looked at her tear-stained face, all of the doubts she had felt earlier about raising a young child seemed to fall away. Lara felt a tug at her heart. Karma needed her! And that was what mattered the most.

"Oh, Sweetheart, don't you know I love you? And I want you with me always!"

Karma peered up at her, eyes growing big and trusting. "Promise?"

"Of course I promise!" Lara said.

Long after Lara had left the room, Karma lay awake in her bed. Her thoughts drifted to the nice lady Lara had taken her to visit. She had liked the lady named Meg with all the toys, but she wished she hadn't asked the questions. They had taken her mind back there again, had made her think about the dark and ugly things she wanted to forget.

Karma had drawn the pictures for her, and the pictures had made her remember.

About the lion.

And the bad man.

A fractured image came to mind, the hunched form in dark jacket and boots bending over her mother's body.

The bad man was real. She was sure of that now. He had come into her room the night she had screamed.

What if he came back for her tonight? What if this faceless, nameless monster came and stole her away?

Or maybe the lion would come instead, the lion with its sharp claws and hungry fangs!

Tears spilled down her cheeks. She missed Mommy. Somehow, she knew she wasn't ever coming back, and that made her feel lonely and afraid.

But she still had Lara. Karma knew that if she cried out, Lara would come, and that thought comforted her.

Karma shivered and snuggled deeper beneath the new blanket Lara had put on the bed, the one with the bright rainbow colors. The soft warmth of it against her cheek felt nice and soothing like the worn fur on Buddy Bear.

Lara wasn't going to give her away, after all! Lara would take care of her. Yes, she had promised. Lara would keep her safe.

With a little shuddering sigh, Karma hugged her teddy close, and curled up, still thinking about Lara, she drifted off to sleep.

Chapter Eleven

Raswell Galleries, one of the oldest and finest establishments the thriving arts community of Hot Springs had to offer, was nestled in the heart of the historic district. Its ornate, turn-of-the-century facade reminded Lara of the Lost Pines Hotel. The bottom story had been modernized with shimmering, glass windows and a curved, red awning, which arched high above the entrance.

Holding Karma's hand, Lara entered a huge, brilliantly lighted room with row after row of plush chairs facing an auctioneer's podium. Paintings, some upon easels, were arrayed in grand and lavish display for this special auction. The buzz of voices drew her attention to the seats, many already occupied, even with more than half an hour to spare before the auction was to begin.

With Karma close by her side, Lara made her way through the milling swarm of people to the front desk where she registered and was assigned a bidding number of 89. She had just started to move away, when she ran into Whitney Jordan.

"Lara! Joan told me you might be here today," Whitney greeted as he tucked his own bidding number neatly into the vest pocket of his jacket. "Did Charles ride along with you?"

"No, he said everything would probably go too high for his tastes. Ordinarily I'd agree with him, but I drove up anyway in the hopes of purchasing Mark's two paintings."

"I had plans to take one of them home myself." Deep lines appeared at the corners of his mouth as Whitney assured her with a smile, "But don't worry. I wouldn't think of bidding against you, Lara. I'll content myself with that still life my wife has her eye on. That is, unless it brings some outrageous price."

"Oh, did Nancy come with you?"

"Yes." Whitney glanced over the rows of chairs. "She's sitting somewhere in the middle."

As Lara tried to locate Whitney's wife, she spotted Joan, whose blonde hair and bright emerald dress made her stand out among the crowd. Beside her, immaculate in dove-gray suit, sat Austin Graham.

Joan waved enthusiastically. As Lara returned her greeting, Whitney also turned his attention to Joan and her escort. "I wish she hadn't brought him along," Whitney commented, his spirits dampening. "Austin Graham will probably outbid us all."

Nancy sat alone a few rows behind Joan and Austin. Her beige sweater made the pale, wisp-like woman blend in with the crowd. Her lank brown hair was pulled back from her thin, pinched face in a loose twist. Lara raised her hand in greeting, but Nancy's eyes remained locked on Whitney. Appearing to ignore Lara, or perhaps not seeing her, Nancy continued to peer anxiously at her husband. Whitney seemed to read into her expression a plea for him to return to her. "I guess I'd better get back to Nan," he said somewhat unwillingly. "Don't wait too long to get a good seat."

Lara glanced around for Karma. In the brief amount of time she had paused to talk to Whitney, the little girl had wandered off. How quickly she had lost herself in the crowd! Lara felt a moment's anxiety before she discovered the small figure in blue jumpsuit gazing up in wonder at a painting of a bright bouquet of flowers.

"The flowers are pretty, Lara!" she said as Lara approached and once more took her hand.

"Which one do you like best?"

"The pink one."

A glance at her watch told Lara they had just time for a quick look at the artwork. Eager to find Mark's paintings, she paused only briefly before the first few displays.

One of Mark's oils suddenly caught Lara's eye, and she crossed the polished oak floor to admire the stark beauty of the scene upon canvas—a storm in the mountains, trees bent and twisted against a bleak, El Greco sky. Mark's style, evident in every brush stroke, created a perpetual sense of sweeping motion that evoked a powerful mood.

Close by, Lara discovered Mark's second painting. Keeping an eye on Karma, who had wandered a short distance ahead, she lingered before the battle between Sioux warriors and cavalrymen. The fight was portrayed in a deceptively capricious mood. Lara studied the leaping figures, the dash and color, death displayed in mocking accent. The satiric and bitter statement that assured the viewer that any glamorous portrayal of war is a farce sobered Lara.

Each of Mark's paintings was so thought provoking. If he had lived, what greatness might he yet have achieved? Lara felt the familiar sting of helplessness and anger. It wasn't fair that some hit-and-run driver had obliterated the answer, had wrenched away his promising life, silenced forever that exceptional talent. Nothing remained of his great visions except the few precious paintings he had left behind.

How Lara would treasure these last works of his! Mark's paintings were her legacy, all she had left of the brother she had loved so dearly.

Lara felt the presence of someone standing beside her. "Mark was a master at evoking mood," commented a deep, familiar voice. Lara turned to find Dane Lanford close beside her. For a moment, he silently studied the canvas, then said, "Notice his method. It's like counterpoint in music, but instead of two instruments working simultaneously, here we have two distinctly different themes working in a kind of distressed harmony."

As he spoke, Lara studied Dane Lanford, impressed by

his eye for detail. In the security of daylight, he looked cultured, sophisticated, anything but dangerous. The perfect fit of dark suit accentuated wide shoulders, the wings of silver at his temples gave him a distinguished bearing, which made him seem part of the refined crowd of professors and art collectors.

"While painting this, Mark was driven to the point of exhaustion." A faint, sad smile crossed his lips. "He didn't sleep for three days."

"Mark always became obsessed by his work," Lara said quietly, taking comfort in the fact that someone else had known and understood him. "He often neglected other areas of his life."

"The bane of the artist! I often tried to tell him that he must take time out to live," Dane mused. "But, of course, he never listened."

"Mark lived for his work. It had to come first with him. But isn't it that way with every artist?"

"The sorry truth is," Dane told her, "my own ambitions have cost me a good deal more than I'd like to admit." He was speaking to her in a special way as if she were one of the few capable of understanding. "Opportunities lost. Years of discipline, loneliness, debt."

The somber mood lifted as they left Mark's display to join Karma, who had wandered to a Picasso-esque painting nearby. Attracted by the bright colors, she stood on tiptoe, attempting to get a better look at the canvas.

The child, wanting to be lifted, raised her hands to Dane. He swung her up in his arms so she could get a clearer view of the picture, saying, "What do you see, Karma?"

Lara and Dane smiled at each other as she pointed to bright, indiscriminate splashes of color, saying with confidence, "There's a bird. And there's a great, big butterfly!" As they strolled together to view the rest of the displays,

Karma ambling along beside them, Lara felt her doubts of
Dane quickly fading. The thought of this cultured man
slashing tires and stalking her through the woods, face
covered by a dark ski mask, seemed totally absurd.
Whoever had followed her that night had been a madman!
She was very fortunate Dane had come to her rescue!

The very last painting on display was a captivating portrait of Francisco Goya. Lara was immediately entranced.
She noticed the intense, brooding eyes, the face half in
light, half in shadow. The haunted countenance of the
painting seemed to capture the soul of every artist. She felt
the deep inner conflict, the passion of the spirit, the beauty
and darkness that must have lived side by side in the man.

Lara's eyes held to the portrait. One bright, clever eye
stared boldly at her from the canvas; the other, more heav-
ily-lidded, more sullied, was so deftly painted that it
appeared blind to the outside world, its focus turned
inward to some black and evil depth.

"This is perfect!" Lara exclaimed. "This is the real Goya,
the man of conflicting passions. He's always been one of
my favorite painters!"

"Then we have something in common," Dane said,
pleased by the fact that she found the portrait of Goya so
deeply moving. "I've always admired his works. Even his
dark side."

Lara thought of the bleak paintings, the howling dogs,
the witches, the grotesques, which Goya had painted in
moods of deep depression. Whoever painted this had captured the very essence of Goya. "It both repels and fasci-
nates," she said, "exactly as the artist, whoever he is,
intends it to do."

An elderly gentleman with a white goatee had paused to
study the painting. Lara heard him tell his two compan-
ions, "Notice the contrast between light and shadow, how

a sense of heroism arises from the grimness of the theme?" He stroked his goatee, saying, "Yes, I'm definitely going to bid on this one!"

"It looks as if I've caught the attention of the critics," Dane said with a modest matter-of-factness.

"You have?" She turned to him in amazement. "You mean you're the one who painted this portrait of Goya?" She should have realized Dane was the artist! As they stood face to face, Dane Lanford seemed suddenly as complex and as full of contrast as the face of Goya that he had created. Was it in some ways not Goya at all, but a self-portrait?

"Ladies and gentlemen, we'll be starting the bidding in a few minutes." The droning voice of the auctioneer continued above the bustle of the well-dressed crowd. "Make sure you obtain a number from the front desk."

Dane's dark eyes with a glow of admiration continued to watch her. She was glad she had worn her favorite summer dress, a soft shade of coral.

"Maybe I'll see you after the auction," Dane said.

"You're not going to stay?" Lara asked, surprised, and strangely disappointed.

"As much as I'd like to see the auction, I have an appointment to keep." Dane paused to say goodbye to Karma. "Don't let Lara spend too much money," he teased.

Lara watched his retreating figure with a sense of regret. The auctioneer, his voice loud over the microphone, began explaining the terms of sale. Lara scanned the seating area. True to Whitney's warning, the chairs had filled up quickly.

"Over here, Larie!" A bold voice called to her over the buzz of voices and commotion. She saw Hallie with a jacket spread over two seats beside her. "Hurry! I'm saving these for you!"

Defiant of convention, Hallie wore faded jeans and a

rumpled white shirt, and her mass of hair loose and frizzled about her face. Hallie retrieved her denim jacket, searched the pockets and offered the child a stick of gum. "Crystal used to bring Karma out to the retreat with her all the time," Hallie explained to Lara. "We're good buddies, aren't we, Kid?"

Just before the auction began, Hallie leaned forward to tell Lara. "Dane's meeting with Dr. Shelton today. He used to be the Dean of Arts in Little Rock, you know. But he's branched out, formed his own private art school on the coast. He wants Dane to move out there and join him this fall." Hallie looked sad. "Dane will probably jump at the offer to teach again. Who can blame him for wanting to go way off to California, somewhere he's appreciated?"

Dane knew of Lara's anxiousness to sell the old hotel. It was only logical that he should begin making plans for his own future. Still, the thought of Dane's actually leaving, of abandoning without a word all of the time and effort he had invested in the artist's retreat, took Lara by surprise. She had been expecting him to appeal to her not to sell the hotel so he could continue with Mark's plans. In the back of her mind, she had intended to say yes for she had wanted him to stay.

"It's a super opportunity for him," Hallie was saying. "He'll make big money. He's wasting his talent with just Jim and me left." Hallie sighed. "I'd feel guilty trying to talk him out of it, wouldn't you?"

"I suppose. He should do whatever he thinks best."

"He wants us to come along. He's so loyal. But Dane says loyalty is our virtue. Jim and I, he means. Anyway, he deserves better than Quachita Springs has given him, that's for sure!"

Maybe Dane had become disillusioned. He had probably grown to regret ever becoming involved in Mark's venture in the first place. Lara had not realized until this moment how much the breakup of the artist's retreat, Mark's dream, would sadden her.

"What will you do, Hallie?"

"Oh, me? I'll get along. I seem to always make a place for myself no matter where I end up. Closing the retreat will be hardest on Jim. He just loves it out there. He gets strange sometimes, you know." Hallie shook her head. "God knows what will become of Jim."

The auctioneer, using a slow, speaking voice instead of a chant, began, "What am I offered for this lovely watercolor?" A hush fell over the crowd as two helpers brought forth a huge seascape. "Everyone knows Jim Matthews, Hot Springs own resident artist. Who will start the bidding? Do I hear one-thousand dollars?"

"Eight-hundred," Austin Graham spoke without hesitation.

Lara was surprised when Whitney raised his bid to eight-fifty. Another man in the crowd bid nine hundred. Tension within the room mounted as the price for the first buy of the day escalated.

The third bidder soon dropped out, leaving only Whitney and Austin. For the first time, Lara noticed the similarity between them, both strong men, vying for control, stubbornly unwilling to back down. Of course, Austin had the advantage, for to him money was no object. She saw Whitney's tense, tight expression as Austin topped each of his bids with a cool, barely perceptible nod of the head. When the price rose far beyond a thousand dollars Whitney's bids became increasingly hesitant. Finally, Whitney shook his head with a look of cold disdain, and Austin Graham triumphed with a smile.

Lara was glad when Austin didn't bid on the next painting, and Whitney was able to secure for a decent sum the still life Nancy had wanted.

Lara felt breathless as Mark's first painting went up on the block and she silently hoped it wouldn't appeal to Austin Graham. "This is one of the finest scenes I've ever had the privilege to offer. And there won't be any more by this talented artist. As everyone knows, Mark Radburn was killed in a car accident not long ago. Who will start the bidding? Do I hear six hundred?"

Immediately, Lara raised her bidding card. Although several others in the crowd bid against her, this particular painting was not as sought after as some of Mark's others, and she was able to purchase the storm scene at a fair price.

But not so with the second, the more well recognized of Mark's paintings. "Now this," the auctioneer began, offering the battle scene of cavalry men and warriors, "is part of his famous Native American Series. And all of you collectors out there know that the value of this particular series is expected to skyrocket." At his words Lara stole a glance at Austin Graham and noticed with sinking heart his sudden interest.

"Who will start the bidding at $1,000?" Lara felt dismayed when Austin Graham raised his hand in haughty confirmation. Determined to have the painting, Lara raised her bidding card once, twice, three times. Austin topped Lara's every bid with a self-important nod. She felt bewildered as the price spiraled upward, far more than she had intended to pay. "Who will bid $2,000? Two thousand five hundred?"

Lara felt the tension in the room as once more she raised her bidding card. Lara knew Austin Graham had the power and the money to defeat her. Yet stubbornly she stayed in the race. As her bid of two thousand five hundred fifty was acknowledged, silence filled the room. Then all eyes in the house turned to Austin. She saw Joan tug at his elbow, noticed his look of annoyance as she interrupted his concentration to whisper something into his ear.

To Lara's amazement, Austin Graham declined with a slight shake of his head and the auctioneer banged his gavel. The painting was hers!

"Good for you, Larie," Hallie exclaimed, clasping her hands in delight, for since Mark's paintings had belonged to her, the extravagant bidding had made her profit beyond her wildest dreams.

Lara did not bid again until Dane's portrait of Goya was offered. Austin, having made many purchases, had lost interest, but the distinguished man with the white goatee she had seen admire the painting earlier gave her tough competition. The price once more was going a little out of her range. On impulse, Lara raised her bidding card one last time, and was almost taken by surprise when hers was accepted as the final bid.

When the auction was over, Lara felt satisfied with her three purchases. She was glad that she had been able to buy Mark's paintings, even though she had spent much more than she had anticipated. And owning one of Dane's works was an additional and unexpected pleasure.

"I'm happy Mark's paintings went to you," Hallie told her sincerely. "That's where they belong."

On the way to pay her bill, Lara encountered Whitney, who had just settled up his account. "I appreciate you're not bidding against me," Lara told him. "Having Mark's paintings mean so much to me."

"Yes, but it looks as if you paid top dollar for them," he said shrewdly. His eyes moved with dislike toward Austin Graham, who was busy writing out a check for his many purchases while Joan looked on, dutifully waiting. "Did you notice how he only bid when the auctioneer mentioned "collector's item"? The shame of it is he's not a bit interested in art, only in lining his pocketbook."

Whitney words trailed off as Joan left Austin's side to breeze over. "Well, well, well, you two gave Austin a little competition today!" she said in a cheery voice. Lara felt grateful toward her, for she knew without Joan's intervention, she would never have been able to outbid Austin Graham.

"Yes, and we could have gotten by a lot cheaper if you had left your boyfriend at home," Whitney remarked a little sourly.

"An auction's an auction," Joan retorted, playfully tapping him on the chest with her bidding card. "If you want the item you have to pay the price."

Joan's smile rapidly faded as Nancy suddenly appeared and in a grim, territorial way stood close beside Whitney. Nancy's huge, lusterless eyes fastened on Joan and conveyed some muted warning. Whitney slipped free of her grasp as if weary of his wife's constant clinging or embarrassed by her obvious jealousy, jealousy that to Lara seemed petty and unwarranted in light of such a harmless flirtation. The air around them seemed suddenly tense and strained.

"Got to get back to Austin," Joan said to Lara and Whitney, acting, as always, as if Nancy were not even present. Nancy continued staring after her as Joan returned to where Austin was discussing his purchases with the man Dane had called an art critic.

To fill in the awkward silence that followed, Lara said with forced cheerfulness, "Karma loves the little squirrel you made her. Ceramics is such an interesting hobby."

"It's just something to keep me busy," Nan responded woodenly. Then she noticed Karma, and for the first time her eyes seemed to brighten, "Such darling little girl!"

Both thin, white hands reached out for Karma. Nancy's self-conscious, unexpected motion caused Karma to shrink away from her. The slender fingers remained out-stretched, seemed frail and helpless.

"Come along, Nan," Whitney said with sudden impatience. "It time to leave. We've got a long drive home."

Lara had just finished settling up her own bill and arranging to have the paintings packaged and delivered to her car when she saw Dane approaching. "Hallie tells me you bought both of Mark's paintings. Good for you! Who would ever think you would battle Austin Graham and come out the winner?"

"He did put up a fight."

"So I heard." An amused twinkle lit his dark eyes. "Every artist dreams of having a high bidder in the crowd. I must admit I was flattered that my own painting brought such a good price."

"I couldn't let Austin Graham go home with everything," Lara said, showing him her receipt.

"You bought Goya?" Dane gave a short, appreciative laugh. "My painting couldn't find a better home."

"This day has been totally successful," she answered. "Are you ready to leave, Karma?"

Dane lingered. "Do you have to leave so soon?" He smiled down at Karma. "I'll bet your little friend is getting hungry. There's an outdoor cafe walking distance from here. Since I made so much money today, I can afford to take you two lovely ladies out to lunch."

"I haven't been to Hot Springs since I was Karma's age," Lara said, enjoying the walk down Central avenue. They paused to look idly into store windows, antique shops filled with porcelain, China and Oriental rugs. Souvenir stores displayed handcrafted wooden goods and dolls with dried-apple faces. The rock shop's window sparkled with jewelry made from Arkansas diamonds.

"My parents used to bring us here on vacation when Mark and I were little," Lara told Dane. In the years when Mark and she had been small, she remembered family outings, happy times, and laughter. Lara had stored such memories of her childhood against the bitter ones, her parents' arguments, the anger, and finally their divorce. "Maybe that's why the city seems so familiar. Or it could be the historic buildings make it resemble Quachita Springs."

"The two old towns are definitely patterned after each other," Dane said. "Except the hot springs here are real, not legendary." They had reached the huge park in the center of town. Here, the similarity to Quachita Springs ended. A steep, winding walkway led upward to bubbling springs and toward a scenic view of the mountain area.

As Dane gazed out at the surrounding mountains Lara thought to herself that he belonged here. She couldn't imagine him living anywhere else. Would the lure of a promising job take him away from here, from the dreams Mark and he had almost attained? "How did your meeting go?" Lara ventured.

"I think," Dane said without looking at her, "that I might soon be moving to California."

Accepting this position would probably be best for Dane's future. She wondered if it were what he really wanted, if he would be happy abandoning the dreams Mark and he had worked so hard to achieve? The exultation she had felt upon purchasing the paintings had suddenly vanished. Dane and she would soon part, no doubt, forever.

Dane caught her arm and they silently watched a line of people fill thermos jugs and cups with fresh mineral water. "The healing water," Dane said under his breath. "Sometimes I do believe these hot springs possess power!"

In the distance Lara could see the stately buildings along Bathhouse Row. "My father was convinced of it," Lara said. "He loved to visit the bathhouses. He said a hot soak in mineral water always made him feel ten years younger."

Near the fountain was an outdoor cafe where they ordered hot dogs and cola. At Dane's suggestion, they hiked for a short way up the trail until they came to a place with a view overlooking the town.

They spread out their lunch beneath a shady tree. The soft wind rustling through the branches felt good after the stuffy air of the auction house.

"There's lots of pretty rocks up here," Dane told Karma after they had eaten. "Why don't you look for some?"

Dane removed his jacket and unbuttoned his white shirt at the throat before leaning back against the sturdy tree trunk. The warm, balmy breeze made Lara feel relaxed and contented, in no hurry to start the long drive home.

Lara smiled as Karma brought a small piece of glittering quartz she had found to show first her, then Dane.

"Hallie told me Crystal used to bring Karma out to the retreat," Lara told him. She watched as Karma wandered a short ways down the trail, collecting more rocks to show them. "That must be why she feels so comfortable around you."

"Karma and I go back even further," Dane said, watching the child with affection. "I was at the hospital with Crystal the night she was born."

Lara felt a tightness in her chest before he hastened to explain, "Crystal was one of my most promising students in Little Rock. When she suddenly quit attending classes, I became worried about her. That's when I found out she was expecting a baby. She refused to say who the father was."

"Was she dating any of your students?"

Dane shook his head. "Not to my knowledge. I offered to assist her in getting financial aid so she could finish and graduate, but she turned down my offer of help. She was a tough one. Always so blasted independent, so set on taking care of herself."

"Did she ever return to your classes?"

"No, but one night, several months later, I received a phone call. It was Crystal. She sounded like a frightened little girl. She told me she was so alone and afraid. So I drove her to the hospital myself." Dane turned dark eyes upon Lara. "You can surely see why Karma is so special to me."

Lara glanced cautiously to where Karma was playing, then inquired, "Didn't Crystal give any clue at all about the baby's father?"

Dane hesitated a moment. She studied his somber profile as he gazed silently down the sloping hillside to the street far below. "No, his identity is as much a mystery to me now as it was then."

Lara knew Crystal well enough not to have questioned the likelihood of Crystal's choosing a free lifestyle over a marriage of convenience. Now she was having second thoughts. Crystal may have had some hidden, sinister reason for refusing to marry Karma's father. Or wasn't the old saying that love and hate sometimes intermingled, true? Scott Tyler might well be correct in thinking Crystal's killer and Karma's father were one in the same.

Dane knew that Scott Tyler was digging around in Crystal's past. It was only a matter of time before Scott discovered that Dane and Crystal knew each other in Little Rock. Did Dane want to plant the seed in Lara's mind that there had been nothing romantic between Crystal and him before Scott turned up with more evidence to the contrary?

The knowledge that Crystal and Dane had known each other in Little Rock at the time of Karma's birth had caused Lara's doubts of Dane to resurface. It wasn't uncommon for professors to be idolized by students. And any woman, Crystal included, would be in danger of falling under the spell of Dane Lanford! As Karma came skipping toward them, dark eyes smiling as she offered her handful of shiny stones, Lara wondered: Had Crystal followed Dane to Quachita Springs because he was the father of her child?

Karma fell asleep curled up beside Lara as she braved the winding Arkansas curves toward home. Even though it was late, she felt an excess of energy. After putting Karma to bed, Lara carefully hung up the three new paintings in the living room. The battle scene looked perfect above the sofa. After much deliberating, she decided the storm in the mountains belonged on the bare space near the doorway. The portrait of Goya she placed over her father's roll-topped desk.

Knowing Dad, he had probably lived at the office, coming home only to change clothing and sleep. Devoid of personal touches, the house had seemed to Lara cold, austere, spartan. Standing back to view her handiwork, Lara thought with pride that the three new paintings added a most welcome dimension.

The dream again. Karma was running, running through the woods. She could sense him in the darkness, moving swiftly, silently, close behind her. She could hear the snap of twigs and branches. Karma could almost feel the lion's hot breath upon her neck, knew that if she dared look behind her she would see sharp fangs and claws gleaming in the moonlight.

Now Karma was huddled in her secret place near the river. But this time Lara had not come to find her. This time it was the lion just outside the narrow stone opening, pacing, waiting.

Karma cried out, and awoke to her own choked sobbing.

She was back in her room at Lara's house, the one with the pretty curtains and blanket. All was warm and quiet. Soft shafts of light filtered in from the doorway. No one was there but her and Buddy Bear. It had all been just a bad dream.

She hugged Buddy Bear closer. Some sixth sense, some part of her beyond sight or sound could feel the danger all around her. He was coming closer and closer. And no one else knew. No one could help her because it was just a feeling, not something she could explain. But she knew. A part of her knew. The Lion was closing in . . . and this time there would be no escape.

Chapter Twelve

The sound of a bulldozer roaring through the vacant tract across the street drew Lara's attention to the office window. Plans for the new mall were underway. A construction crew was hard at work on the large parcel of undeveloped land that had once belonged to her father. Once more, Lara wondered what Dad had done with all the money he had taken in from the sale of this downtown property.

Lara turned to ask Charles, who sat behind the desk in Dad's huge, oak swivel chair, with Karma, becoming his shadow, beside him, drawing pictures while he typed.

"In spite of my advice," Charles answered, his voice edged with an unfamiliar sharpness, "Lawrence continued to turn cash over to your brother. There's no telling how much Mark drained from him to sink into that hideous hotel." He typed a few more sentences, then looked up at her again. "I went out there once just to talk some sense into Mark, but he was twice as hard-headed as your father." Charles looked hurt. "He refused to even discuss it with me."

Disagreements had a way of escalating. Lara thought of the hard feelings Whitney had mentioned. Was Mark and the hotel the source of the trouble that had arisen between her father and Charles?

Dad would surely have been accustomed to Charles' interference into his private concerns. He would have told Charles to mind his own business, but he wouldn't for a minute have believed Charles would do so. Charles took responsibility, even when he expected to derive nothing from the outcome. It was what caused him to remain active in police affairs, even though retired. A sense of responsibility kept him coming to her office now, even though he would rather be free.

"Dad was always so opposed to Mark's 'dream world', as he called it," Lara said. "I can't see why he would turn around and pour cash into what he would consider a hopeless venture."

"Your father's health failed so quickly, Lara." Charles hesitated a moment before he added, "It seemed to me that Mark took advantage . . ."

She did not allow Charles to finish his sentence. "Mark would never have done that!" But Lara had seen the books; the large cash withdrawals made out to Mark just before Father's death. How else could they be explained?

Joan's drifting into the office interrupted her thoughts. Lara noticed she wore the kind of day-to-evening attire she was so fond of. The long, chic white jacket with padded shoulders opened slightly to reveal a glimpse of a skimpy, black satin dress suitable for an after-hours visit to a cocktail lounge. Joan paused in the doorway and pointed a finger toward Lara. "I need your assistance," she said. "You and I are taking Mr. Money out to the hotel! I've talked long and hard and Austin Graham is finally willing to take a look at the place."

Lara's heart sank. She did not want to be a part of flaunting the sale of the hotel in Dane Lanford's face. "Can't you just go without me?"

"No. It's rented, remember? We'll need you to get us admitted. Besides you can help me give the pitch that will bring in the do-ra-me!"

Lara reluctantly stood up. "Come on, Karma."

"Why don't you leave her?" Charles suggested, glancing from his work up to the clock on the wall, which read 4:30. "After I close up here, we'll go catch a hamburger and a movie."

Lara could not help but notice how Karma's eyes lit up at the prospect. "Can I stay, Lara? Please?"

"Sure you can," Charles answered for her.

"You'll bring her back after the show?"

"No," Charles chuckled. "I'll kidnap her."

"Very funny, Charles," Joan remarked as she and Lara left the office. Joan's talk bubbled with enthusiasm as they passed through the sea of glass into the brilliant glare of afternoon sunlight. "Austin's going to make an offer today. I just know it! And I know just how to deal with him, too. Here's what I want you to do. Agree, agree, agree! Take every one of his ideas for that resort of his and exalt them! He has some great plans. All he needs is a sounding-board for them."

"I told you I might not want to sell the hotel."

Joan cast her a sidelong glance. "You tell me one thing; Whitney tells me something else. He says you're so anxious to get back to New York, you'd even be willing to sacrifice the property you have left." With a flip of blonde hair Joan challenged, "Now don't tell me you want to leave a monstrosity like this hotel behind? It's too big to handle. It will end up being a deficit, one that will grow every single year. And buyers for a place like that don't come along like stars at Christmas!"

"I keep thinking about Mark, about how he would feel about my selling it."

"Mark!" Joan's buoyant step slowed. Either it was the glaring sunlight, or she had actually grown pale as she turned to face Lara. Her voice, when she spoke, had lost all trace of exuberance. "Oh, Lara, we can't live in the past! Mark and all of his plans are gone, are buried. I know. I was there. And we're here and we have to go on from here." Like a battered survivor, she straightened slender shoulders. "We're talking cash, Lara! This transaction could put you way ahead financially. And you're going to need all the money you can get with Karma to raise."

Lara didn't feel at all convinced. They fell silent as they

got into Joan's car. Joan turned at the corner, drove around the block, and swung into the circular driveway in front of the Convention Center Hotel. Austin Graham, dressed in an expensive, beige suit left the windowed entrance to the lobby and started toward them.

"I'm going to let on like Whitney Jordan is really interested in purchasing this property," Joan said in a low voice. "Austin's the type of man who needs immediate competition."

"Good afternoon, ladies," Austin said, pausing to wait as the doorman rushed forward and opened the back door of the car for him.

Once inside, he smoothed slick, gray hair that the wind had ruffled, and leaned forward to remark, "Being seen with two gorgeous young women should enhance my reputation."

"And I thought I was the super-salesperson!" Joan said with a rippling laugh.

Austin looked pleased. "You know I'm not thought of as a seller, Joan. I'm a buyer." His pale, alert eyes as they met Joan's backward glance became suggestive, intimate.

Lara, wishing Joan had not become involved with him, turned back to watch the road.

"By the way," Joan said airily, "Whitney Jordan made me an offer on the hotel."

"How much?" Austin grasped the back of the car seat and drew closer. Lara did not see his face, only glimpsed his hand with the neatly clipped nails and the huge ring, that looked like a gold nugget.

"You don't expect me to answer that!" Joan laughed playfully. "That would be like kissing and telling."

"I'm the kind who wants to know just how much kissing is going on," Austin insisted. He settled back against the seat. "When you introduced me to Jordan at the country club last night, he struck me as not having much to offer."

"I wouldn't underestimate him," Lara spoke up, offended by Austin's superior manner. "Whitney has done very well with his law practice."

"So he's a good friend of yours," Austin noted. "My apologies. I shouldn't have been so verbal. I am often accused of making snap judgments. A poor policy, I admit." He added with a satisfied turn of the lips. "Not that it hasn't served me well."

"How would you react if I said I was speaking of above three hundred thousand?"

Austin raised a thin, arched brow. "I would say you are adding on twenty thousand or so. But whatever his offer: I'll guarantee you it's not cash."

They crossed the bridge. "Anyway, we're getting ahead of ourselves. I may very well be willing to let him have it," Austin said. "Look at this narrow bridge. And this road! No one of finer tastes would relish making this miserable drive!"

Many times Lara had weakened in the face of Joan's 'big sisterly' determination. Today she wished sincerely that she had resisted.

She didn't want Dane to see her showing the property to Austin Graham, although surely she wouldn't need to explain to him that selling the hotel to Graham would be only a last resort, in case Dane no longer wanted to rent. She could not, in the event that the rumors of Dane's taking a teaching job on the coast proved true, be expected to ignore her own interests.

When they reached the hotel, Austin was the first one out of the car. He stood, hands in the pockets of his jacket, surveying the aging building with a skeptical eye.

Joan, drawing up beside him, said, "It's a lovely building. It puts you in mind of a castle in the highlands of Scotland."

"Old buildings should be buried with the bones of the dead," Austin said shortly. "I, for one, promote what's modern. I promote today! What I visualize," he continued, with a low sweep of his hand, "is a low, sprawling world of glass, surrounded by a golf course, riding stables, pools, and gyms with the latest equipment."

"You mean you would destroy all of this?" Lara asked, astounded. Though Joan had urged her to meet Austin's plans with enthusiasm, Lara could not bring herself to encourage him. She felt sickened by the vision of demolition crews, heavy machinery battering against rock, tearing down the magnificent building that had endured for so long. She cringed at the thought of the wild, lush surroundings of the hotel being leveled into a golf course.

"Have you seen pictures of the chain of retirement paradises Austin's built?" Joan said to Lara, then to Austin, "This would be a terrific setting for one of your projects. So many people love the Ozarks! Will you just look at this view?"

Lara passed them and started across the flagstone walkway to the entrance. Joan's voice drifted after her. "Back behind the hotel are the cliffs. You won't believe how beautiful they are! After you see the building, we'll take a little stroll back there."

Rays of lowering sun fell across the dark, weathered stone of the hotel. Above, the towers on either side of Lara loomed, watchful and grim.

"I'd say nobody's home," she heard Austin tell Joan. "And hasn't been since the Civil War!"

Why hadn't she stayed back in the office? She felt apprehensive over meeting Dane's dark eyes, filled, as they had been when he had believed she had turned him into the police, with disappointment and hurt. Reluctantly she stepped nearer, wondering if she should knock or, as she had last time, simply go on inside.

With a sudden intake of breath, she halted. A face peered out at her from behind the thick, ancient panel of glass.

She retreated from the hostility of the narrow, glittering eyes. The door was thrust open and Jim Bearle, like an angry watchdog, bounded forth and stood squarely blocking her way.

His face was tight and heavily creased. Unkempt locks of hair straggled across his dingy, paint-spattered T-shirt.

As if trying to recover from Jim's threatening appearance, Austin stepped forward and after an awkward moment, said, "I'm Austin Graham." He started to extend his hand, but in the face of Jim's disdain, let it drop to his side.

"Are you . . . here alone?" Lara asked.

"Yes."

"Joan and I want to show Mr. Graham the hotel. We won't be long."

Jim did not budge. His gaze, narrowing even more, slid from Austin back to her. "No one comes in here but who we invite! So you had best be heading back to town!"

"I'm sorry," Lara said, turning from Jim to Austin, "but there's nothing I can do. I'm afraid I can't show it to you without the renter's permission."

Austin raised an arrogant eyebrow. "I've seen all I want to see of this building, anyway. It would be of no earthy use to me! If I buy this, it will be only for the land."

Jim Bearle with a final, hateful glance toward Lara, turned on his heels and disappeared inside. She was certain he bolted the door behind him.

Denied entrance, the three of them stood in the stifling heat of late afternoon.

"I'm beginning to believe all those stories I hear about Lanford," Austin Graham said finally. "But for the life of me, I don't know how he could get any following."

"Oh, that's wasn't Dane Lanford," Lara said. "Jim Bearle

is one of his students."

"Students of what?" Austin asked haughtily.

"He can't keep us from looking over the grounds," Joan remarked, trying to ease the tension.

"I think I've seen enough," Austin replied stiffly. He removed a handkerchief from his pocket and wiped sweat from his brow.

"Come along, Austin." Joan linked her arm through his. "I'm not driving you back until you have a look at this lovely view! I just know you'll be impressed."

Lara waited for them in the car. The old hotel loomed before her, reminiscent of one of those stately homes along Bathhouse Row in Little Rock. It was a part of the history of the area. It belonged here, along with the surrounding acres of undeveloped timberland, which had been in the Radburn family for generations. How could she ever be a party to its destruction?

Lara wished Dane were here. They needed to talk. She should never have let Joan talk her into showing Austin the hotel without first consulting him.

 Lara felt a shiver creep over her as she saw a curtain move slightly at one of the upstairs windows. She could almost feel Jim Bearle's hostile eyes glaring out at her. She was relieved when Joan and Austin finally returned to the car.

Austin sat in the front seat with Joan on the way back to town, and Joan chatted about the possibility of Quachita County making the needed improvements on the road. "I'm sure they would be very open to the type of project you have in mind," she said. "Especially since it would increase the tourist trade."

"I am impressed with the setting," Austin conceded. "I'll tell you what I'll do, Joan. I'll met you both for dinner tonight at the Convention Center Dining Room." He checked his watch. "At say, six. Then I'll give you girls my one and only offer."

After letting Austin out, Joan drove Lara to her home. "You've got to slip into your very best!" she insisted. "Austin, you know, likes making deals with people who look the part. You could wear that sexy blue dress that I'm always threatening to borrow."

"Do I have to go? Can't you . . ."

"Absolutely not! You don't have to take his offer. But since I went to all this trouble, the least you can do is listen to it."

As Lara slipped into her best dress, she felt once again swept along, pushed by Joan to do something she did not really want to do. But Karma would be with Charles until after the movie, so that meant she would be here alone, eating alone; she might just as well go along with a good grace.

"We're an hour too early," Lara reminded her once they were back in Joan's car.

A mischievous sparkle lit Joan's hazel eyes. Lara recognized that look, which usually meant trouble. "What I'm going to do will take up the slack."

"Joan, what are you up to?"

Instead of answering, Joan, just before reaching the Quachita Springs city limit sign, turned from the highway unto a blacktop road that led into the surrounding hills.

The thickness of trees, the cool air from the open window, the cautious pace of the automobile, caused Lara to relax a little, made her feel closer to Joan, as if they were once again school girls embarking upon some carefree adventure.

"What do you see in Austin?" Lara asked. "He's so much older than you. And he doesn't seem to be your type anyway. He's so . . . self-important."

"My type, as you call it, has changed from the old days." Joan glanced from the tree-lined road to Lara. "Maybe I don't want to grub for a living all of my life!"

Lara met her saucy announcement with a sense of sadness. What had happened to the starry-eyed girl who had worshipped Mark? "And you're the one that told me you would marry only for love!"

"New days," Joan said, "bring new thoughts."

"You are getting so very modern," Lara observed, unable to keep the sarcasm from her voice. "You and Austin Graham, Mr. and Mrs. Today!"

"You can't say Mr. and Mrs.. He hasn't bought. Yet."

"And if you're lucky, he won't!"

Joan pulled the car into a driveway that led to a clearing of trees with a cabin-like house and a huge shed behind it. "Just what are we doing out here?"

Joan didn't answer, but drove around the cabin where Lara saw an old car up on blocks. Extending from beneath it were jeans-clad legs.

Joan pressed the horn.

The lean legs stirred. Scott Tyler struggled to his feet, wiping his hands on a greasy shirt.

"Hi, handsome," Joan said.

Scott bent, looking past Joan to Lara with surprise and a hint of pleasure. "What brings you two out here?"

"I've got a dinner date with Austin Graham. And since Lara's too shy to ask you out, I thought I'd just do it for her."

A smudge of grease on Scott's broad jaw made him look very different. So did the grin. "I accept! Just give me time for a shower."

Lara's heart plunged. She didn't want Scott to think she was chasing him. What on earth was Joan thinking of? She couldn't just back out now without insulting both Joan and him. She would have to endure the evening the best she could.

Scott led them into the small living room—a bachelor's home stacked with books and car parts. "Excuse the mess," he said. "My hobby is cars. I've got a shed full of them. Find a chair. One without grease, if you can. I'll be just a minute."

In his bedroom he switched on the radio and the sound of country music drifted out to them.

"Why did you do something like this?" Lara hissed in a low voice.

"You complain about the dumbest things," Joan sighed, dropping into the recliner that faced a small TV. "I did it because you need to get out and have some fun. Scott is . . . cute! A real hunk, in fact. And he's nice, too."

"Then why don't you date him?"

"I try to do you a favor and what do I get? Complaints!"

A while later Scott's voice boomed, "Shower's over! I won't be long now!"

"Why don't you come out and model your towel?" Joan called over the hum of the blow dryer.

Scott's head appeared from behind the door. His blue eyes looked straight into Lara's. "I think this is sexual harassment!" he said with feigned seriousness.

"Take us to jail, then!" Joan shot back. "That way we could see you every, single day!"

When Scott finally stepped out of the bedroom, he wore light trousers and a camel-colored jacket. His hair was carefully styled and he smelled strongly of spice.

As they walked out to Joan's car, Scott slipped his hand around Lara's waist. "You look great!" he said.

For a long time, with mind far away, Lara listened to Joan and Scott's carefree chatter. At the first lull in the conversation, she said to Scott, "I'm going to need to see Mark's files."

The mention of the crime caused the lightness to leave him entirely. "Don't you ever think of anything else?" he asked a little coldly. "When you want to see them, they're in my office."

The evening wasn't going to go well. What of it? It wasn't Lara's idea, anyway. The very last thing she wanted to do was go to dinner with Scott Tyler!

Once again Joan and Scott struck up their easy banter. Lara sat quietly, miffed at Joan, and feeling ill at ease. How little she knew Joan Sommers anymore! For all of Joan's personal plans concerning Austin, she was more than willing, through false reports concerning Whitney's offer on the hotel, to force Austin Graham into making a high bid. When had she started making a practice of duping people?

"By the way," Scott said, "where are we going?"

"To the Orchid Room. You know, that place Crystal liked so well."

"I didn't think you would . . ." Scott's voice drifted off.

"I can't avoid every place and every person Crystal liked, now can I?" Joan countered. "That would mean I would have to give up Austin Graham! I even introduced him to her, you know, so he could buy one of her sculptures."

Lara tried hard to be polite, to join in their fun, but her talk was forced and she was glad when they reached the Convention Center Hotel.

Austin Graham, prompt and efficient, as always, had arrived early and in an alert and important way, stood looking out into the parking lot.

"Have you met Scott Tyler?" Lara asked, as they stopped before him. "Quachita County's sheriff. Scott, this is Austin Graham."

"Yes, of course." Austin shook hands with Scott and announced, "I've reserved a table for us in the Orchid Room."

They entered a lavish room, whose name was derived from the orchids designing the velvet wallpaper. Candles glowed from tables. That, except for the soft illumination above the piano and dance floor, was the only source of light.

Austin paused to watch the hands of the piano player sweep across the keyboard. He flipped a bill from his billfold and said, "Moonlight and You."

"Before my time," Joan whispered, raising her eyes heavenward.

Not hearing her, Austin said, "You'll like this one, Joan. It's my favorite song. Martin has learned to play it especially for me."

The room had only a scattering of people, mostly couples out for an evening of dinner and dancing. They followed a waiter in formal black toward their reserved table.

The candlelight softened the lines of Austin's sharp-featured face, made him appear much younger and very much the man of the world. He ordered wine, then toyed with the menu and made suggestions. "I'm going to have the filet mignon," he said decisively.

"Sounds like a winner," Scott followed his lead. "How about you, Lara?"

"I would prefer the shrimp."

"Joan?"

Joan looked around nervously. She opened and closed the menu as if she had barely heard Austin.

He asked her again what she wanted.

"I'll have . . . whatever you're having." Joan's face seemed pale as she turned to Lara and spoke abruptly, "Lara, let's go to the little girl's room and wash up."

Once inside the huge, empty lounge area with its white marble sinks, Joan paced in front of the door. She had shed the jacket and her skin against the skimpy black satin dress seemed ghostly white. "I've got the most terrible feeling," she moaned.

Lara, forgetting her annoyance at Joan, exclaimed, "What feeling? What's wrong, Joan?"

"I keep . . . it's eerie, but I keep getting the feeling that we're being watched." As if chilled, she crossed her arms in front of her. "It's just giving me goose bumps. Did you notice it too, Lara? I just had to know. That's why I wanted you to come in here with me!"

"I haven't seen anyone . . . watching us," Lara answered hollowly, remembering the curtain that had moved at the window of the hotel while she had been waiting for Joan and Austin in the car. "When did you first notice it?"

"As we got out of the car in the parking lot. Then again while we were ordering. Do you think someone . . . that weird man that wouldn't let us in your hotel . . . might have followed us here? And if he did, why did he? Lara, I'm scared. He's so creepy! I've never felt quite like this before."

"You might be just imagining things," Lara said. "But we'll both keep a look out. If I see anyone I recognize, I'll let you know."

"Thanks, Lara." She turned to the mirror to apply lipstick and smooth her hair, but the paleness remained. "I feel better already."

During the long dinner, with the laughter and conversation around the table, Lara forgot for a while about what Joan had confided to her. She didn't think of it again, in fact, until Scott and she began to dance.

Scott managed, despite a certain lack of skill, to glide somewhat gracefully around the floor. They had made several turns around the room before Lara was struck by the chilling sensation that eyes were following their every movement.

Noticing her sudden tenseness, Scott's hand tightened against her back. "What's wrong, Lara?"

Her gaze skimmed the dimly lit room. Nothing looked suspicious, and yet there were so many archways and doorways, so many dark recesses from where someone could at this very moment be watching them. She found that she was now fully convinced that Joan had been right. Someone had followed them here! Someone had tracked her, as he had in the dense forest beyond Crystal's house, and now stood hidden from their sight, watching and waiting.

Lara confided her uneasy feeling to Scott.

"I wish this was all over," Scott said with exasperation. "I'm always afraid for you. I have this feeling that you are in danger!"

They continued keeping the beat of the slow music, but neither of them was thinking of the dance.

"I wish I didn't know you so damned well. You see, I know if you uncovered some clue, I would be the very last one you would share it with," Scott said.

Lara looked across his shoulder toward the doorway leading into the parking lot. Had it moved slightly, or was she becoming a little dizzy from Scott's continually swirling her around? "That's not true, Scott."

"I really don't know for sure whether or not you found anything when you searched Crystal's house the other night."

"The only thing I found of any importance were her bank statements. The large deposits she made with such regularity puzzled me. Have you looked into her business affairs?"

"Of course," Scott replied. "Crystal was beginning to sell her work for big money. But she didn't keep a lot of cash on hand. She transferred all of her excess into a trust fund for Karma. But money isn't why she was murdered. As I've indicated to you many times before, we're dealing here with a crime of passion."

"Or with a madman," Lara countered, looking once again around the room, trying to locate the eyes she was so certain were still there, watching.

"Only madmen commit crimes of passion," Scott

insisted.

His grip about her waist tightened as he added, "I've done a little checking into Crystal's background. And guess what I've found out? Crystal and Dane Lanford knew each other in Little Rock. He was her instructor there."

"He told me as much."

"Did he also tell you that he is almost certainly the father of that child?"

"You have no proof of that." Lara stiffened in Scott's arms. "And even if he is Karma's father, that doesn't necessarily mean he's guilty of Crystal's murder."

"He and Crystal go back a long way, Lara. The truth be known, they probably had years and years of stormy relationship behind them." Scott finished with conviction, "Crystal follows Dane here from Little Rock. They reconcile. Then, while he's doing time, she meets someone else. They argue, he loses control . . ."

Lara thought of the generous bank deposits Crystal had made to Karma's trust fund. Had all that money really come from the sale of her sculptures, or had some wealthy man been keeping her?

"If you think Crystal jilted Dane for another lover, why don't you look for the other man?" Lara demanded. "Isn't it just as likely he might have killed her?"

"I have tried. But whoever he is, he's covered his tracks well. Probably a married man, or some prominent citizen who can't afford to have his name drawn into a scandal. He's running scared." Scott shrugged. "But it doesn't matter. He's not the guilty one. It was Dane Lanford who was out there the night of the murder."

Lara was relieved when the dance ended. Lara found herself looking directly across the table into Austin Graham's calculating eyes. He flashed her a special smile, which called forth in Lara the opposite effect from what

was intended. She found herself disliking what she considered his false front, that careful balance of worldliness
and respectability. Men like Austin Graham lived only for
themselves, promoted and protected themselves no matter
who they hurt in the process.

"I promised you an offer on the hotel property," Austin
said confidently. "And I'm ready to make one."

His abrupt statement startled her, forced her to turn her
thoughts back to the business at hand. She noticed how
Austin studied her, as if to size her up before he committed
himself. "Three-hundred thousand dollars."

"But that's less than Whitney . . ." Joan started.

"Ah, but you'll like my offer better than Jordan's,"
Austin said. "For I'll write a check for the full amount the
minute I am supplied with a clear title. And I'm willing to
wager, if you deal with Jordan, you'll have to hold the
papers yourself and take payments from him."

Joan looked uncertainly across the table at Lara. "We'll
just have to discuss this and let you know."

"Take your time." Austin patted her hand. "An offer of
mine, once made, will stand," he paused and added with
a twinkle in his eye, "just as long as I do."

Chapter Thirteen

"I feel jittery," Joan said. "Scott, will you drive?"

Joan, very pale and shaken, huddled in the back seat of her car, not bothering to return Austin's wave as they pulled away from the hotel complex. Lara noticed the way Joan's eyes darted to the black shadows of the parking lot, like a solitary soldier searching for an invisible enemy.

Joan's blithe mood of this afternoon had totally vanished, and its final disintegration unnerved Lara. Her friend's uneasiness was contagious. Had Joan actually seen someone she recognized as they left the restaurant, or had she just once again been gripped by the sensation of being watched?

Lara turned to look at her. She hadn't noticed before that Crystal and Joan resembled one another. They certainly didn't look alike; Joan was as blonde as Crystal was dark, the similarity between them lay in that bubbling, girlish manner. Could it be that Lara herself had placed Joan in danger by bringing her into some maniac's focus?

The thought caused her to shiver inwardly and glance at Scott Tyler beside her. Shouldn't she, for Joan's sake, mention this to him the first time they were alone?

They passed by souvenir shops filled with browsing tourists, then turned down into the older section of town where dark, stone buildings lined either side of the cobbled street.

Scott's eyes strayed again to rear view mirror. Did he, too, wonder about the change in Joan? "What's wrong, old kid?" he teased. "You should be happy! Just think of all that commission rolling in!"

"I guess I'm . . . sick," Joan said tonelessly. "Too much food. And I should have passed on the wine."

"If I had known Graham was picking up the tab," Scott

said, laughing. "Then I'd be sick now, too!"

From the window, Lara caught sight of the old Grand theater. "Isn't that Charles and Karma?" Lara asked. From the scattering crowd leaving the building, she picked out Charles' bulky form. Karma, beside him, was trying to keep up with his long-legged stride. "Let's pick Karma up and save Charles a drive out."

Scott, honking the horn, pulled in close to the curb beneath the bright billboard that advertised the current movie. Karma ran toward them. "Lara! Lara, we saw the best show! Didn't we, Uncle Charles?"

Charles' gray eyes looked heavenward and he touched his forehead in a gesture of pain. "You just wouldn't believe how good it was!" he said. "Mean, little aliens all over the place! Blue ones, no less! What ever happened to good entertainment? Those westerns starring Robert Mitchum and John Wayne?"

Karma, talking excitedly, climbed in between Lara and Scott.

"Karma seemed to enjoy it," Lara said. "Thanks, Charles. I'll see you tomorrow."

"Lara, the spacemen had big eyes. Like this." Small hands made proper reference. "And they could see through anything. They could see through walls!" She stopped abruptly. "Why can't we see through walls, Lara?"

"Scott will explain that to you."

"Because," Scott answered, slanting a smile toward the child, "we have human eyes and they have spacemen eyes."

Karma had never seen Scott wearing civilian clothes. As if she just now recognized him, her face clouded with fear and she shrank closer to Lara. Lara, arm tight around her, tried to turn her attention back to the movie, but to no avail.

"Joan, if you don't feel well, why don't you stay here with us tonight?" Lara asked as they pulled into the driveway.

"Scott could bring your car over tomorrow."

"I've got an appointment early in the morning," she said.

"You could cancel it. I really would like some company."

"I can't, Lara. It's too important." Joan attempted a smile. "Don't worry about me. I'll be all right."

"Joan thought someone was following us tonight," Lara told Scott as he walked with her and Karma up to the door.

"We're all a little uneasy," he said. "But you can be sure of this, Lara. If someone had been lurking around us, I would have spotted them."

"In some ways Joan resembles Crystal. Her appearance is so striking, so noticeable." Lara hesitated. "Crystal's killer could be . . . like a serial killer, after a certain type of woman. What if Joan's attracted the attention of this man . . ."

"You're talking nonsense, Lara," Scott replied calmly.

"Still, Scott, I'm a little afraid for her. Could you try and talk to her? Make sure she locks up!"

"Sure, if it will make you feel better." Scott's sincere blue eyes met hers. "But it's you I'm more worried about, Lara."

"I'll be fine."

Scott drew to a stop at the front door. His quick kiss, over Karma's head, caught Lara unaware. She would have expected, had she had time to consider it, the touch of his lips to revolt her, but they did not—too brief to be exciting, but not in the least, repelling—solid, comforting.

Scott insisted on checking the house before he left.

Lara thought again of Scott's kiss as she helped Karma change into her pajamas. An unwanted kiss—Scott could read nothing into it but that. She had been too taken back to even pull away, and now, this knowledge edged her thoughts with an almost guilty disconcertion.

Damn Joan for tricking her into having dinner with him this evening! And then the kiss! The very last thing she wanted was for Scott to believe that she welcomed his attention!

"Lara, I don't want to be in here alone." Karma's soft voice startled Lara from her thoughts. "Can I sleep with you?"

"Of course, if you want." Lara wondered if the alien movie had frightened her.

Soon Lara lay in bed, worrying about Joan and only half listening to Karma's endless talk about space ships and aliens. The child's sudden silence called back her drifting attention. "What did you just say, Karma? I didn't hear you."

"He had big eyes, too. Big, round eyes!"

"Who did?"

"The man, the bad man that hurt Mommy!"

Lara's heart seemed to stop beating. She attempted to make her voice even, matter-of-fact. "What else do you remember about him, Karma?"

"He had a blue face!" Karma raised her arms. In the moonlight Lara could see the small, dim outline of her fingers, first stretching, then clamping into fists. "And he had blue hands, too!"

Cold chills went through Lara. Karma had seen the killer! But he had concealed his identity with gloves and ski mask.

"He took off his skin, Lara."

Lara's heart froze.

"I saw . . . I saw . . ." Karma covered her face in her hands and began to cry.

After he had struck Crystal, had he pulled up the blue ski mask? Was Karma reliving those terrible moments now—was she seeing in her mind a face?

"What did he look like, Karma? Try hard to remember. Did you see his hair? His nose?"

"No! No! No! He didn't have a nose!" Karma sobbed, "He didn't have a face!"

Lara couldn't keep questioning her; it was too cruel! Lara cuddled the child in her arms. "Don't cry, honey. Don't cry. Let's think about something else now. Someday, soon, you and I might go to New York. I have a big apartment there. From my home you can see the bay."

"What's a bay, Lara?"

"Water. Like the Quachita River, only much, much larger. Would you like that, Karma?"

"No, I don't think so. If we left, Uncle Charles would miss us. He wants to take me to see Donna again. She's going to let me help her with the puppet show when I get bigger."

"Let's just wait and see. But wherever we are, we'll be together. I promise you that."

"You promise." The child quieted. Lara began telling her about Cinderella. It wasn't long until she fell asleep.

But sleep for Lara didn't come as easily. She tossed and turned and wished it were morning. First thing tomorrow she would call Dr. Warner and tell her what Karma had remembered.

Tonight, Karma had experienced a breakthrough. Lara was certain now that she had seen the killer's face. Tomorrow, she would talk to Dr. Warner about the hypnotist. Maybe he could help Karma to remember. Maybe, with hypnosis, Karma could fill in the empty features on that face.

An hour or two passed and finally all thoughts and fears began to fade and she drifted toward the oblivion of sleep.

A slight noise brought her back to full alertness. Lara automatically reached for her robe, then sat, listening. This time she recognized the scraping of a door as it opened or closed. Someone was downstairs! Someone had broken into the house!

Joan had been right! A stalker had followed them to the restaurant, had, blending in with the shadows of the

Orchid Room, watched their every movement! And now he was here! The target hadn't been Joan, but Lara herself!

There was no phone in the upstairs area where the bedrooms were located. The nearest one was down the steps beside the couch in the living room.

Lara's reaction was confused, panicky. She groped for the dresser drawer, her hand closing over the gun Charles had given her. She, backed by the skill of Charles' teaching, loaded it quickly, adeptly. Then she slipped through the darkness to stand beside the door leading into the upstairs hallway.

Did she dare open it? Would the man wearing a ski mask attack the moment she did? Agonizing thoughts whirled in her mind. "You only have a split-second to stop him," Charles had told her more than once during their target practices. "So make your shot count! Remember, if you don't get him, he'll get you!" Would she be able to put in practice Charles' council? Could Lara Radburn shoot to kill?

She brought her left hand up to steady the right one.

Slowly, quietly, she turned the knob and, standing back, pushed the door open.

Lara drew forward and peered into the narrow corridor, the long, black space, like the endless stretch of bridge across the Quachita. Total silence engulfed her. She had no strong sixth sense, as Joan had. She didn't have any idea whether the intruder had fled or whether he remained watching and waiting!

Lara forced herself to step toward the staircase. At the top of it was an electrical switch that would flood the room below with light. She inched her way slowly toward it, gun in both hands; the way Scott had approached Dane that day at the hotel.

The sudden glare of light poured over the empty living room. She remained in this position, able from her vantagepoint to cover all directions where he could be hidden. Her eyes locked on the front door, left wide open. Is that where he had made his hurried exit?

She skimmed the room, sucking in her breath at what she saw. One of Mark's paintings lay on the floor in front of the couch, another on the coffee table. Both had been shredded to bits with a knife!

She must reach the phone! But how? She couldn't leave Karma unguarded upstairs without first making sure he was not hiding up here. Slowly, watchfully, she entered the bedroom next to hers where Karma usually slept. Keeping a lookout on the hallway, she searched it. She threw open the bathroom door and went on into the adjoining guestroom.

If he were still in the house, he was downstairs.

In the same manner Lara entered one first floor room after another. She even checked the basement. When she returned to the living room, keeping her gun in her left hand, she dialed Charles' number. There would be no chance of catching whoever had been here now. Too much time had elapsed. She should have taken a chance and made the call before she had searched the house. Charles' voice answered on the third ring. It was obvious he had not been asleep.

"Someone was in the house tonight! Mark's paintings," Lara's tearful voice caught in her throat, "have been cut to pieces with a knife!"

Charles snapped immediate response, "Go get Karma. Keep her and the gun right with you! I'll be there in no time!"

As Charles had instructed, she went upstairs after Karma. The child half-roused when Lara lifted her. "Where are we going, Lara? Are we going to New York?"

"No, just to the living room."

She descended the stairs slowly, saying to Karma in a low

voice, "Just go back to sleep, honey. Everything's all right."

As she placed Karma on the couch, the little girl's large dark eyes opened, then closed again. Lara stepped away from Karma and groped for the gun she had concealed in the pocket of her robe. Was the intruder gone, or hiding somewhere within the house? Lara tensely raised the weapon once again, in the stance of a guard.

From the wide-open front door, a damp breeze blew into the room, stirring papers on the desk. Lara made no move to close it.

Lara's eyes moved to Mark's painting that lay in front of her on the coffee table. Her fearful gaze traced the ugly rips left by the knife blade. They crisscrossed in angry, jagged slashes, totally destroying the clever, complex battle scene.

Weakness surged over her. This painting in particular was so dear to her. Why would anyone do this? She wanted to lift Mark's canvas, to cry over it, as if it were human.

Lara's attention fell to front door. It, like Dane's painting, had been left unharmed, as if someone had merely turned the knob and walked in. But she had locked it! She remembered checking it after Scott left.

One of her father's keys must be in someone's possession. Or had whoever done this been able to slip her key from her purse and have it duplicated, so he could come and go at will? Maybe neither, she decided. Cat burglars, criminals, men like Jim Bearle, could open any kind of a lock. "We install locks for our own peace of mind," Charles had told her once. "They never keep anyone out that wants in."

Lara returned to the child, covering Karma with a throw that lay on the couch. Why had he been here tonight? Not to kill her or Karma, not to steal. What then, for some insane revenge?

Lara did not change positions. She could see only the edge of Mark's second painting on the floor beyond the coffee table, but she was aware more than ever that the beautiful storm scene had met the same horrible fate.

Only Dane's painting remained intact, hanging undamaged over the desk. Would it, too, have lain in ruin, if she had not interrupted the trespasser?

Time passed slowly. Lara's gaze swept back to the painting, to the eyes that seemed to be watching. She was suddenly frightened of it. In the shadowy darkness Goya's face had become sinister, mocking, the image of evil!

She heard from the open door the distant sirens of the patrol cars drawing steadily closer, rising and falling, like a screeching cry of protest. Charles had, of course, alerted the police. Lara watched the fingers of glaring red lights from the domes of the vehicles as the swung in close to her door.

Scott entered first. Charles followed close behind. "I'll be damned!" Charles exclaimed with disbelief. "Who would want to do anything like this?"

The sheriff took up a position in the center of the room and directed the uniformed men who had just entered. Without wasting a second, they took up assigned tasks, several leaving to search the grounds, a young deputy Lara recognized as Tom, beginning to dust for fingerprints.

Scott, feet apart, chin thrust forward, stood in front of Dane's painting. "What I would like to know is why he didn't get this one, too!" Scott said, his voice sharp and accusing.

Charles responded just as sharply, "Why would anyone would want to break into Lara's house to destroy any painting? It just doesn't make sense."

"Someone is trying to frighten me," Lara said.

Charles seemed in immediate agreement. "I'd say he's trying to scare you into leaving town. You're being here in

Quachita Springs is a threat to someone. Why? Do you have any idea?"

"Surely, it must concern Mark's death."

"You don't know any more about Mark's death than the rest of us," Scott broke in. "You're both on the wrong track. I tell you, evil seeps from that so-called art retreat! It's bound to spread its poison out into the community! It did before, with the Baxter case. It has again!"

Scott, his voice growing more confident as he continued, looked squarely at Lara. "I talked to Joan just as you asked me to. I believe Lanford was at the hotel when you were showing Mr. Graham the property. No doubt he was watching from some upstairs window, mad as hell because you were planning to sell the place out from under him!"

"That's ridiculous. Dane's not the type of person who would stoop to . . . this."

"Lanford certainly would do this!" Scott's voice raised theatrically. "Just to spite you. And don't forget, he's got an eye on you for himself! He probably saw us in the Orchid Room tonight. When he saw you and me together, he just snapped, like he did when he killed Crystal!"

Lara felt a little dizzy as she regarded Dane's painting. The light and dark colors on the canvas ran together, became blurred.

Scott turned back to stare at it, too. "What egotism!" he said in anger. "Lanford's unwillingness to destroy his own work is clear proof of his guilt! That, and the fact that he is so adept at the skills of burglary!"

"Jim Bearle was the only one at the hotel. He was angry because I wanted to let Joan show Austin through the building."

"Did Bearle let them in?"

"No."

"What do you know about this Jim Bearle?" Charles

asked. "It wouldn't be a bad idea to run a check on him. Have you?"

"Not yet," Scott said, and added defensively. "He hasn't been considered a suspect, up to this point. But when I get to the office, I'm going to make a few phone calls and see what I can find out about him."

"You let me know the minute you get any information," Charles said. "I'll be here the rest of the night." He turned to Lara, "Didn't I see a lock around here somewhere?"

"There's one on a shelf in the basement," Lara told him.

"I'm going to have to leave now, Lara." Scott said reluctantly. "As you can see, Charles will take care of everything. You try to get some rest."

Charles trudged down the steps and returned with a package, a hammer and a screwdriver.

"I'm going to call Joan," Lara told him, "and make sure she's all right."

The phone rang again and again before Joan's tired voice said, "Hello. Who is this? Don't you know it's . . . four a.m.?"

"It's Lara and it's important." Lara told her what had happened and ended with the warning, "It wouldn't hurt for you to be on guard."

"I've been on guard," Joan answered. "I haven't slept a wink. And might never again!" A pause. "How did he get in?"

"I guess he picked the lock on the front door. Or Scott believes he might have gotten a key. Charles is already busy installing a deadbolt."

"I'm really scared, Lara!" Joan said. "Would you care if I stayed with you and Karma until they find this creep?"

"If you're not afraid of being in a house where something like this has happened."

"There's strength in numbers, I'm told. Lara, are you

sure you don't care? I'd been thinking of having you two stay over here, but you know how small my place is."

"I'd love to have you here."

"It's almost morning. I'll just wait until daylight and then I'll bring my things over."

"That will be fine," Lara said, relieved. "I think we'll all feel much safer together."

Charles, finished with his chore, sank down in the recliner. Karma still slept soundly on the couch, but Charles did not mention Lara's taking her back upstairs. Although he didn't say so, he seemed to want neither of them out of his sight.

Strangely, he didn't speak about the happenings of tonight. Instead, he talked about Lawrence Radburn. Even as a policeman, Charles had always found time to wander in and out of her father's office. He was now recalling some amusing event involving Whitney and Dad.

His words were cut short by the ringing of the phone. He scooped it up and as he listened, a frown appeared on his face.

"I was afraid of something like that. If I were you I'd contact his doctor, see exactly what sort of a psycho we're dealing with."

He listened again, his frown deepening. "I'll check with you later," he said and dropped the receiver in place.

"What is it?" Lara asked.

"Jim Bearle," he said. "For the past few years he's been in and out of the veteran's hospital in Little Rock. It looks as if we've got a mental case on our hands." Charles lapsed into a deep silence before he spoke again. "Ever since Nam, he's had relapses that have been periodic and violent."

A chill ran though Lara. Little Rock, that's where Dane had met Jim Bearle. Everything about Jim Bearle suggested instability! No wonder he frightened her so much! No telling what hideous crimes he had committed during the war . . . and after!

She met Charles' inquisitive, gray eyes. But she knew that Charles' question was not the same as hers: if Jim Bearle had committed these terrible crimes, was he acting on his own, or was Dane Lanford using him to carry out his own ruthless plans?

Chapter Fourteen

Lara stood staring at Mark's ruined paintings that she had just transported into the basement and propped against the line of empty shelves. She knelt before them, fingers gently exploring the vicious gaps. Restoration was out of the question. Repeated thrusts of the knife's blade had in places shredded the canvas into unrecognizable threads.

She drew her hand back quickly, as if the touch of the ripped material had seared her skin. Remorse over the loss of Mark's work slowly receded, replaced by a strong and certain presence of evil. It seemed certain that the violent force behind the destruction of the paintings was now focused directly upon her.

Still the fact that no one had tried to harm either Karma or her last night puzzled her. That must surely mean that Lara was being threatened for a reason other than the possibility that Karma might be able to identify Crystal's killer. Was someone trying to pressure her into leaving Quachita Springs, knowing that she would sell her holdings here as quickly as she could?

Dane flitted first through her mind, and in the background was the shadowy figure of Jim Bearle. Austin Graham slowly replaced their images. From what she knew about him, he would use any method available to obtain what he wanted. If the sell of the hotel had inspired this act, it seemed perfectly likely that Austin Graham was behind it, either him, or . . . who was this Evergreen Corporation?

Just last night Joan had told her that she had received a very unexpected call from a representative of the Evergreen Corporation saying they were extremely interested in purchasing the hotel property. Lara had recognized the name at once, one she had seen on the contract for the vacant land across from her father's office that Dad had sold shortly before his death.

It might be a good idea to check this potential buyer for the hotel; to find out all she could about this corporation, for it did seem strange to her that they would all of a sudden pop up from nowhere as an eager buyer.

Her eyes returned uncertainly to Mark's paintings. If she were on the wrong track thinking this had to do with the hotel, then she was left with what was infinitely more sinister: a killer afraid of her presence here, afraid of what she might uncover concerning Mark's death and it's link to Crystal's fate.

This ugly threat had only increased her determination to find out what and who was behind it! She vowed to Mark's memory that she would never leave here as long as even a possibility existed that Mark had been murdered and she could uncover his killer!

"Lara, where are you?" Joan's distant voice floated down to her, breaking through her resolve and reminding her that she had not only herself to look after, but Karma as well.

"Be right up!" Lara called.

The living room she passed through was already filled with friendly clutter. Joan's briefcase on the coffee table, her sweater flung over a chair—comforting reminders that Karma and she were no longer alone in the big house.

Early morning had been spent lugging boxes from Joan's apartment to the spare bedroom just beyond Karma's. Karma, totally caught up in the excitement of Joan's moving in, had tagged along, asking a million questions. Lara had been glad that Joan didn't seem to mind. In fact, after all of Joan's remarks about how burdensome children were, she seemed perfectly content and pleased by Karma's attention.

At the threshold of the guestroom, Lara could see Joan preening in front of the mirror, and Karma holding up her dangling earrings with a child's awe.

Joan's eyes met hers in the mirror. "Where have you been for so long?" Her comb had paused in mid-air. "You really look pale, Lara. Why don't you just lock up the house good and get some sleep. I'll take Karma with me. She can keep me company while I work on the closing costs for the Thompson's."

Lara stepped further into the room. Mounds of expensive garments spread across the bed; boxes crammed with make-up, nightgowns, and papers set in disarray on the floor.

"I'll straighten this up later," Joan said, but the inattentive sweep of her hand made Lara doubt her blithe promise.

"Joan, I would like to get in contact with the Evergreen Corporation. You must have handled the sale of Dad's lots to them. Do you know who runs Evergreen? How they could be reached?"

Joan shrugged. "I didn't handle that sale. But now that I am agenting the hotel property for you, I intend to keep in close contact. So anything you want to tell them, just tell me."

"Have you ever met personally with this representative?"

"No, we've only spoken on the phone. But he did give me a number where he could be reached, an easy one to remember. Little Rock: 903-3777."

The moment Joan and Karma left, Lara wrote down the number Joan had given her and tried to place a call. "You have reached the office of John W. Reed," droned a toneless, recorded voice. "I am unable to talk to you at this time. Please leave a message at the beep . . ." With no response Lara replaced the receiver. So many questions needed answers.

She hadn't slept at all last night and felt physical as well as mental exhaustion, but the minute she lay down on the couch, memories of Mark began to haunt her. He had been destroyed and now his finest work lay slashed beyond repair in the basement retreat where he as a boy had labored and dreamed.

In order to escape the intense pain and anger she felt, Lara left the house and drove aimlessly around Quachita Springs. In the end she found herself parked, as she did every morning, just outside her father's office.

She remained in the car listening to the clamor of construction workers across the street and watching the men scurry here and there. Dad's treasured land was fast being turned into a shopping mall; Mark's hotel, into an Austin Graham project. Unless the Evergreen Corporation, whoever they were, outbid him.

Lara wondered a little cynically what their plans were for the land. Surely something commercial intended to make fast money. Noticing a couple of workers sitting in the shade drinking coffee, Lara crossed the street. With curiosity they watched her approach, the younger, a thin man with longish, blonde hair, eyeing her with a playful grin.

"I wonder if you could tell me who's in charge here?"

The older of the two men, bearded and burly, stood up importantly. "I'm the foreman," he said.

"My father used to own this land," Lara told him. "I understand the Evergreen Corporation is doing the building. Do you happen to know any of the officials of the corporation? I am trying to contact them."

"I don't know anything about Evergreen. This job was sub-contracted by Marlin's out of Dallas." He hesitated. "I could give you his number."

"Would you, please."

After jotting down the phone number, Lara left quickly. The blonde man's voice drifted after her. "Why don't you write down my phone number, too? I get off work at five."

Lara took the elevator up to the second floor office,

where she found Charles staring out of the window, sipping coffee and munching a cinnamon roll.

Almost guiltily, Charles turned and set the food down. "Eating on the run. A habit I picked up when I was on the Force." He glanced back out the window. "They're really working overtime across the street. I hear they are planning a grand opening in early September."

She asked him what he knew about the Evergreen Corporation.

"I'm afraid I can't tell you anything about the deals your father made during the last six months of his life," Charles answered somewhat curtly. "As you know, I even quit dropping by the office."

Charles sank down again at the desk and began sorting papers in an abrupt, irritated manner.

Lara watched him in silence for a while, then drew the phone toward her and dialed the number the foreman had given her.

"The job was contracted to us by a John W. Reed from Little Rock," the voice on the other end of the line stated. After some prompting he reluctantly gave her the same number she had received from Joan. After hanging up, she tried this number, but again got the answering service.

Lara looked up to find Charles watching her, his forehead furrowed. "Since last night," he said, "I keep asking myself why anyone would be trying to frighten you."

When Lara didn't attempt a response, Charles continued, his voice slow and grave. "Anyway you figure this, the answer centers around Karma."

"But the intruder didn't try to attack Karma," Lara reminded him.

Again he looked at her closely, gray eyes penetrating. "Maybe Crystal's killer doesn't want to kill the kid unless he is forced to."

"You give him too much credit. You saw what he did to Crystal."

"But he wanted to kill her." Charles' gray eyes narrowed. "But maybe he wouldn't want to kill—for instance, his own child."

Lara looked away from him, reading in the lines of his face, so trusted, so familiar to her, a blunt accusation of Dane.

"I think you're wrong, Charles. I think this act of malice was aimed directly at me."

"Why?"

"I'm not sure. For a reason I don't even know, maybe someone I don't suspect at all." She was speaking haltingly and this seemed to increase his worry, his intensity. "A person who has something to hide. Concerning Mark's death perhaps."

"Mark's death has nothing to do with what happened last night."

"The attack was on his work."

"The attack was on something dear to you. But for whatever reason," Charles said sternly, "what you're being told is perfectly clear. Someone wants you out of the way, out of town."

Silence fell again and this time lasted a long time.

Lara said at last, "I think Karma is experiencing some sort of breakthrough. She is beginning to talk about . . . that night." Once more her talk to him, which usually came so easily, was forced and choppy. "Karma spoke of seeing a man in the house with Crystal. She said he had blue hands and a blue face. That he peeled off his skin. Of course that was the ski mask he was wearing."

Another stillness ensued. Lara shivered as she pictured Karma appearing unexpectedly at the screen door at the exact moment when the killer, thinking he was alone with

Crystal's body, had paused and lifted his mask. To the terrified child in shadowy darkness, the mask's removal looked like the peeling of skin. But how much of his face had she seen? Enough to form a lasting impression, enough to identify him?

"I don't think we'll ever be certain of what Karma saw," Charles said. "Even if she led us to some particular person, we would need more proof than the testimony of a traumatized child."

"We could find out the truth of what happened if we knew who killed Crystal." Again Lara paused. "The psychiatrist she has been seeing recommends that I take Karma to Mason Adler, the hypnotherapist. He is coming to town for a convention Friday after next and has agreed to see Karma while he's here."

"Adler," Charles repeated. "Yes, I know him. But maybe it won't come to that. What I've been thinking of might be even better, much easier for the child. Why don't you let me take Karma back to my sister's in Eureka Springs for the weekend? Donna is so wonderful with children. She might be able to find out something using the puppets."

Before Lara could answer, a deep voice behind them announced, "Lunch time, Charles."

"What?" Charles responded. He nodded toward the half-eaten roll and cup of cold coffee. "I'm still eating breakfast!"

Whitney, dressed in a brown suit that was perfectly tailored to fit his rangy form, stepped into the room.

"I thought you had court today, Whitney," Charles said.

"The hearing was called off. So I've been holed up in my office all morning, working." Solemnly he turned to Lara. "Charles told me about the damaged paintings. I'm so sorry, Lara. I know how much they must have meant to you." His hawk-like features became darkened, as if with anger. "And what a price Austin Graham forced you to pay. I trust they were insured."

"Before I took them from the gallery," Lara responded. "But nothing can replace my loss."

Whitney nodded his head in sympathy.

"I'm just grateful that I still have one of Mark's paintings left. It was hanging upstairs."

Charles suddenly changed the subject by asking, "Whitney, don't you know Mason Adler?"

"The big-time child psychologist?" Whitney answered absently, his mind still on the paintings.

"You surely remember him. He grew up here."

"You could say we were professionally acquainted. Before he got rich and famous and moved to California." He looked curious. "Any particular reason why you're asking?"

"Lara is making arrangements for Karma to see him," Charles explained. "There's a strong chance that under hypnosis Karma may be able to identify the man who murdered Crystal."

"He wants to hypnotize Karma?" Whitney looked skeptical, just as Lara had felt the first time Dr. Warner had mentioned the idea of hypnosis to her.

"He's good," Charles encouraged. "When I was on the force, I remember, we called Adler in once on a case involving a little girl who was abducted by a pedophile. He took her out to a house in the country, did terrible things. Of course, she blocked it all out. We brought her to Alder, and through him we were able to get a positive ID and put the bastard behind bars."

Whitney, still seeming unconvinced, began to move toward the door. "Charles can live on black coffee, but I can't. What about you, Lara?"

Rising, she told Charles, "I left Karma downstairs with Joan. She's probably getting hungry." Whitney waited, hand on the doorknob, as she moved to join him.

As they walked down the corridor, Whitney ventured cautiously, "I don't know much about hypnosis, but I question the wisdom of putting the child through still another trauma. She's been through so much already."

"Hypnosis is perfectly safe," Lara said. But she, too, was filled with doubts. Maybe she would let Charles take Karma to his sister in Eureka Springs again first. Karma seemed happy there, and even though Lara did not believe the child was the target for what had happened last night, it might be wise to get her away from the house.

"After what happened last night, I can't help but be worried about you're safety . . . and the little girl's," Whitney said as they stepped into the small, dimly lit elevator. "I would feel much better if you were back in New York."

"How will I ever be able to leave here not knowing . . ."

"Believe me, there's worse things than not knowing." The absence of bright light hollowed his cheeks, emphasized the sharp planes of his face, his receding chin. "But your leaving here doesn't necessarily mean that. Scott will eventually find out who killed Crystal." He gave a significant pause. "It's beginning to look as if he's been on the right track along, suspecting Dane Lanford."

Because Dane had served time in prison, the close-knit people of Quachita Springs were forming solidly against him. Even men like Whitney, who had managed to escape the small-town mentality, were quickly labeling Dane as guilty.

Or was the opinion building up against Dane, right, and she wrong? Wrong about Dane, wrong about thinking Karma was not the target of last night's violence? Whitney's deep concern or the sudden descent of the elevator brought a woozy feeling to the pit of Lara's stomach.

Whitney placed a steadying hand on her arm. She

recalled other times that he had been there to support her, ready with his sober, intelligent assistance. He never tried to force his advice on her, only guided her, like a dependable, older brother.

As they approached Gino's, Lara was startled to see Scott at one of the tables near the window. Karma sat close beside him, a huge chocolate sundae in front of her.

"Where's Joan?" Lara asked as they entered the crowded room.

"Something important came up, so I volunteered to baby-sit." As Scott's eyes met hers, they widened in admiration, making her wonder if he had been purposefully lingering in the cafe, waiting especially to see her. Since Scott wasn't wearing the usual uniform, but Dockers and a crisp, new shirt, this must not be a business call. Lara hoped Scott hadn't misinterpreted their hasty kiss of last night to mean that she felt for him something beyond what she was able to feel.

Karma, who was happily spooning the last few bites of ice cream and chocolate sauce, smiled shyly at Lara as she sat down beside her. Lara felt a little annoyed at Scott for buying the child so much ice cream before she had even eaten lunch.

Her annoyance vanished in light of his grin. Off duty, Scott's could easily turn his boyish carelessness into a virtue. He winked conspiratorially at Karma, leaned toward Lara and whispered, "I think I've won her over!"

Lara tried, despite the heaviness she felt, to be civil. "A sheriff resorting to bribery. I'm glad I brought my lawyer with me."

Karma took a last spoonful of ice cream and then busily scraped the dish. Lara watched her, hoping all that ice cream wouldn't give her a stomachache.

"I wonder what's keeping Joan," Whitney remarked as

the waitress came around to take their orders.

"It must be really important to keep her tied up this long," Scott said. "Order something for her, Whit."

After the orders were placed, Whitney demanded of Scott, "Why weren't you at the club this morning? You know nobody else can give me any competition on the racquetball court."

"I was busy tuning up the carburetor on that '70 Mustang. You know how I am when I get under the hood of a car. Just lose all track of time. This Mustang's a real cherry, Whit. You'll have to come out so we can test drive soon."

"Ever since I've known him, even when he was a little boy, Scott has been a great car enthusiast," Whitney explained to Lara.

She had never really thought of the two of them as long-time friends. In fact because of the great contrast between them, it was difficult to see how they would have anything in common. Cars would not interest Whitney for very long. She doubted that he would even know how to change oil.

The waitress soon brought platters of sandwiches garnished with pickles and chips. Lara thought of the old junk cars up on blocks she had seen around Scott's yard when Joan had taken her out to his place. "So you fix cars for other people?"

"On a sheriff's salary, you have to moonlight. Usually I fix up old cars and sell them. I've never run across any car I can't make run," Scott boasted.

"He has that big shed in back crammed with old cars," Whitney said. "There must be thirty of them."

"You exaggerate, Whitney! I only have seven cars now. And all together they wouldn't amount to the price of that new Caddy of yours."

"I have to drive a new car," Whitney defended with a

shrug of well-tailored shoulders. "Can't even adjust the carburetor myself."

"That new car of yours doesn't even have a carb," Whitney," Scott said with a gloating look. "That, Ol' Buddy, is how much you know about cars." He added, "That's why I like to work on the older models. Can't get your hands dirty with the new ones. If the fuel injectors go bad, you have no choice but to take it in to a shop."

Through the glass windows, Lara saw Joan approaching. Appearing excited, she interrupted them with a merry greeting. Although there was a vacant chair next to Lara, she slipped into one beside Whitney, saying, "You ordered for me. How sweet!"

Whitney, coming immediately to life by Joan's presence, gave her a sideways glance. "I know that look," he said jokingly. "Tell us what you've been up to, Joan."

"You'll never believe what's happened," Joan began. The dangling earrings faintly jangled as she turned to Lara. "I told you last night the Evergreen Corporation had expressed some interest in your hotel property. Well, listen to this, they out bid Austin by fifty-thousand dollars!"

"You mean they made us an offer . . . sight unseen?" Lara asked. "It sounds too good to be true."

"Not exactly," Joan explained. "One of their representatives, John W. Reed, spotted my ad in the paper and drove around out there himself. He thought the setting was perfect for a group of condominiums. But that's not the best part. Austin is furious! He's not about to be outbid!"

Scott gave a low whistle. "You'd better strike while the iron is hot!"

"I told you, Joan, I'm not sure yet what I will do with that property."

"If you ask me, you'd be well rid of the place," Scott said. "And with that kind of money you could afford to set off and see the world."

"What about you, Whitney? Do you want to raise your bid on the property?"

"Definitely too rich for my blood," Whitney answered. "Now that you have two interested buyers, Lara, I guess that leaves me out in the cold." Far from being disappointed, Whitney looked relieved. Lara knew he had only made an offer on the property in the first place to get her off the hook. She felt a fondness toward him for his willingness to take on a responsibility he didn't really want so that she could return to New York. Lara could see that he was glad that she now had other options.

"Now just a minute," Joan insisted. "Let me tell you the rest. When I talked to Austin on the phone, he was outraged! Deep inside, the man thrives on competition, but you'd never know it. Here's what he tells me. He doesn't want to keep bidding on the place. He wants you to set a firm price and he will make a decision.

"Sounds like Graham's afraid he's met his match," Whitney said with satisfaction. "These big corporations have endless money backing them, while Austin is a single investor. They are bound to outbid him."

They all watched Lara, who remained silent.

Joan arched a brow. "Now, Lara, you can't just willy-nilly around, not when I have not one, but two prospective buyers. I have to know right away, before we lose our opportunities!"

In the face of such competitive bidding, the thought that someone was trying to force her into selling the hotel, now seemed totally absurd. She had failed to recognize that her land had become valuable because of the fast pace of Quachita Spring's expansion. And it was clear that Joan Sommers was actively working for her, would work the bustling market for all it was worth. Then why didn't she feel so reluctant to commit herself?

Faces around the table watched her eagerly. She was aware of them, even though they seemed very vague and distant.

With Dane leaving, selling the hotel did seem logical. Joan would insist she get top money, so really, what could she lose? At best the ancient hotel was what Charles could be counted on to refer to as a white elephant.

Keeping the building was not going to bring Mark back. And she couldn't expect Dane to turn down a high-paying job to try to piece together for her Mark's broken dream. So what choice did she have?

Of course her reluctance to set a final price had to do with loyalty, with sentiment, with all of Mark's grand and elusive plans for an artist's retreat. "I'll have an answer for you soon," Lara promised. Lara knew she had to go back to the place one last time, while it still belonged to her. She would have to make peace with herself about selling before she would be able to relinquish forever Mark's dream.

Chapter Fifteen

Lara stood before her most prized possession—what she had left of Mark, his painting, "The Healing Water." She studied, behind the solitary form of the Indian, the porous limestone cliff, weathered and eroded by time. Directly above his outstretched arms, jutted a cave-like wall of over-hanging rock, mingling eerily with the rising mist. No camera could have captured the scenery with such dexterity— the gaping cracks and crevices, the brittle calcium and dolomite, the pool, emerald green and endlessly deep.

Lara's eyes lingered on the mineral water, believed by medicine men ages ago able to restore and purify. She wished she were really standing in front of the hot spring, and that it was capable of washing away her fears and erasing her grief.

Joan had left for her office early and wanting Karma to meet the children of one of her clients had taken Karma with her. Before Joan had left, she had given Lara a caustic reminder. "Austin wants your decision on the hotel now. I don't know how long I can string him along. You are going to have to make up your mind . . . soon!"

Lara glanced again at Mark's painting. From boyhood Mark had roamed the mountainsides near Quachita Springs. Her brother had been drawn to the towering bluffs, the forested gorges, the miles of rolling hills that surrounded the old hotel. Lara, herself, had never wan-dered far from building, had never even viewed in any real sense the land Joan was pressuring her to sell.

On impulse Lara called Charles, already at the office, and told him she would be late; then, slipping into jeans and a faded cotton blouse, she started out for the hotel. She hoped the solitude of the mountains would instruct her, would overrule her indecision, so she could give Joan a final answer.

With only a glance toward the darkened windows that seemed to be on guard, Lara drove around the circular driveway and cut behind the hotel, following an eroded, dirt road that wound around immense cliffs.

Before she had driven a quarter of a mile, the narrow gorge widened to what at one time must have been a grand picnic area. Some of the tables, half-rotting, remained, as did portions of stone grills. A steep, ridge road, too rough, she thought, for her low car, trailed up the canyon wall.

It would be safer to walk from here. She would climb to the rugged summit for a sweeping panorama of her land and of the entire valley.

She had not noticed the easel until she had started to cut through the picnic area, now overgrown with weeds. She stopped in front of the abandoned canvas, puzzled that the painter was nowhere in sight, puzzled that the painting had no link to the abundant beauty of the mountain scene, but was a portrait of a female figure.

Marks of vivid scarlet in broad strokes outlined the flowing shape of a woman's gown. The face, at present featureless, was encircled by long, flowing tresses of glossy black.

The styling and color of the hair made her think of Crystal.

Lara stiffened. She raised her head, aware of the mossy smell of spring water, and listened intently. She gazed around the primitive picnic area, across a small stream, and far back into oaks, hickories, and shortleaf pines. Had the sound of her car motor caused the artist to abandon his work? Had he hidden himself? Was he watching her now?

Lara, no longer desiring to explore the cliffs, started back to her car. Just as she did, Jim Bearle emerged from around the jagged wall of rocks that lined the base of the bluff. He strode down the road she had just taken, closing the space between them with rapid strides, as if it were his intent to keep her from reaching her vehicle.

A mental case, a psychopath! Lara stared at his thin face, hollowed and darkened with the beginnings of a beard. Today he wore no cap. The sparse hair on the top of his head looked dull and dirty, as did the long, straggly ends that in places touched his sweatshirt. The knowledge that Jim Bearle had a moment ago been working on what surely must be a portrait of Crystal caused her to freeze.

"Why the hell are you sneaking around out here?"

The total contempt he had for her filled her with panic. Lara struggled for control, trying to say matter-of-factly, "I am just looking over my property."

Jim straightened up, as if he were preparing for an attack. Gripped with fear, Lara saw his form darken before her eyes and Lara visualized him, wearing army fatigues, in the midst of a steamy jungle in the heart of Vietnam. Was he so mentally sick, he would not be held responsible for any atrocity he might commit? She had another image of him locked in a whitewashed room in some lonely ward in an army hospital.

Jolted back to present reality, Lara realized that Jim had been speaking to her for some time. "This place is a haven, for trees, for animals, for us! I'm not going to let Austin Graham with his bulldozers and his fancy-pants condos destroy it!"

Jim's thick lower lip protruded from his slack mouth as he fell suddenly silent.

He waited until she made response. "I may not sell to him. I haven't decided what to do."

As if he had not even heard her, Jim Bearle's next words, fueled by his own conclusions, swiftly ignited, "Graham's been sneaking around out here, too! I caught him yesterday evening! You'd better warn him!"

Lara's fears increased. He seemed to be headed toward a total lack of control. She tried desperately to think of some words that would reach him.

"You'd better tell him not to even think of buying this place! I don't want to see you or Austin Graham around here again! Do you understand what I'm telling you?" He was shouting now. "You had better not come out here again!"

"Don't threaten me," Lara said. In spite of her pretense of maintaining composure, she found herself shrinking away from Jim Bearle as he advanced a step toward her.

Once again his features became blotted and obscured with darkness. Lara was filled with the desire to run, just as she had ran from the masked figure that night near the river. She forced herself to remain immobile, facing him.

"Lara doesn't need our consent to show this property." The deep voice from behind her was familiar and filled her with relief.

For the second time Dane had delivered her from Jim Bearle's anger. Lara turned to him gratefully.

"But if she did need my permission," Dane continued, his dark eyes holding steadily to Jim's, "you can be certain that she has it."

Jim said disdainfully to Lara. "You don't know how hard we've labored here! How hard we've tried to make this work! Why can't you just leave us alone?" Irrational eyes slid back to Dane. "You've got to talk her out of letting Graham demolish all we've done!"

Dane regarded him patiently.

"If I have to leave, where will I go? I'm not going back there! I'll never go back there!"

"I've told you before," Dane said gently, "you limit your thoughts. You close yourself in. That's why you become so upset, that's why you experience panic." In the same soothing manner Dane continued, "There's always options, always another choice. Other alternatives can turn out good, too. For instance, you could come with me to California."

"What would I do in California? You'll be stuffed away in some classroom—rotting, like in a prison! Things will never be the same!" Jim spoke with an ominous certainty. "And we'll lose all those years, all those dreams! The things I kept going for you while you were locked up!" His voice rose as if he were once more on the verge of losing control. "Remember what it was like before you left? It can be that way again! Only bigger and better! But we've got to stay here, right here!"

"There's where you go wrong. We can begin again. And we haven't really lost anything by physically changing locations. We can only profit from what success we've had here." Dane during their exchange of words had placed himself between Lara and Jim. He now took Jim's arm in an effort to guide him back toward the hotel. As the two men walked away, Dane's reassuring voice took distance and was soon out of Lara's range.

Lara remained looking after them and wondering if Dane would return. No more than five minutes passed before Dane appeared again from behind the rock wall of cliff, walking briskly toward her. Neither of them spoke until they were standing close together.

"He left his canvas," Lara said. Only after she had spoken, did it occur to her that Jim may not have been the one painting Crystal's portrait.

Dane smiled and firmly closed the car door Lara had just opened. "You came out here to look over the land. Let me accompany you." His dark eyes raised to the cliff.

"Let's hike up there now. It will be easy walking following the road. And it's worth it. The view at the top in early morning is magnificent."

"You mentioned once that you enjoy painting outdoors. Were you working out here this morning?"

"No. As a matter of fact, I was in my room when I saw you driving by the hotel." His eyes sparkled as they returned to hers. "By my own admission, I came out here just to find you."

That meant Jim Bearle was the one working on the canvas, that is, if Dane were telling her the truth. Intentionally she led him by the easel, and watched him as he stepped back to survey it. But she found no change in Dane's expression, no indication that he believed the painting to be a portrait of Crystal Mar.

"You'll want to see this when Jim is finished," he said with a deep, low laugh. "His explosive changes of emotion definitely show up in his work. That's what makes his art daring, avant-garde, in the highest sense of the word."

"Are you ever afraid of him?"

Dane shook his head as if he found her question amusing. "Jim is a modern-day van Gogh. A troubled, tortured soul in need of help. But, then, aren't all artists?" As he stopped to read Lara's expression, another short laugh escaped his lips. "Seriously, working with Jim has been very rewarding. He is immensely dedicated and greatly talented. I wouldn't be surprised if he shows up soon in one of your journals!"

They started up the ridge in silence. The ascent was slow and difficult. In places the slope of road tilted precariously close to the rock-lined edge that dropped in straight descent toward the base of the bluff.

"Have you always wanted to paint?" she asked him.

"I've always searched for answers to questions," Dane

answered. "I suppose that explains my attraction to painting. It's like I am always telling my students: truth is traced though art."

They drew to a stop, already breathless from the climb. As he smiled at her, she felt a strong tie between them, an undeniable affinity.

"Mark told me many times," Dane said, "That you are a very capable painter."

"I love painting," Lara confided, as they walked on, "but more in the art-appreciation sense. I want to study it, to promote it, to enhance others' joy of it. In fact," her enthusiasm increased in light of his interest, "my greatest dream has always been to have my own publication."

He turned to study her. "So what have you done about your dream?"

"Nothing. I probably never will. But it is nice to have a dream. To imagine complete freedom from the narrow-minded criticism of editors and bosses."

"If it's really what you want, then make sure your dream is well-established in your own mind," Dane suggested. "Give this publication of yours a name, make it real in your own thoughts. You will be surprised how fast it will surface."

Lara turned back to smile at him. "Is it really that easy?"

"No, but it's a definite beginning."

At the top the road leveled into a broad plateau spotted with scrubby pines. Just above them a gigantic formation of stone towered, and Dane turned to look straight up. Dangerous rocks, that in places nature had set like steps, led to a narrow, precarious level at the top. Time and wind had eroded it on all sides, making it loom a freestanding mass.

"We're not at the summit until we climb this," he teased.

"I'll watch you from here."

"I call this formation the Devil's Stairway," Dane said.

"Then shouldn't it be leading downward?"

"It does if you happen to be on the top." Lean fingers caught her hand and led her back toward the rim of the canyon. "This is what I wanted you to see." He let go of her hand and drew closer to stand alone near the cliff's edge. "When I was in prison, I had the same vision over and over. Of a place like this, wide and open and full of promise."

Lara gazed with him at the mountainside in the hazy morning mist. Lara breathed deeply of the fresh morning air, perfumed with the scent of plants and flowers. Her eyes rose to the highest peaks with their pitted limestone overlays, and fell to their deep descents into mysterious, hidden places.

"This is where I come when I need inspiration," Dane said.

Lara drew forward to look straight down the sheer wall of stone. As she did, she felt Dane's hand clasp her arm protectively. "Not too close."

"You can see Quachita Springs from here," Lara said excitedly "And just look at that network of water. The river and springs. Isn't it just beautiful? And over there, Dane, isn't that the opening to a little cave?"

"I've found many caves up here, some even large enough to explore. And more are being exposed all the time."

'You mean by erosion?"

"Yes. The water dissolves limestone. So it has hollowed out a great system of underground caverns throughout the area. I wish we could go exploring today," he said, then added teasingly, "Do you happen to have a miner's hat and a flashlight or two with you?"

Lara laughed. "Not today, but someday I'm going to pack a lunch and spend the whole day up here."

"Let me know when that is." Dane eased himself down

on a rock. Once seated, he leaned back against the sloping stone behind him, stretched his legs, and placed his hands behind his head. Lara was aware of his long length, his muscular arms, and the dark tangle of hair that showed from the open collar of his shirt.

He was still gazing at some point in the distance. "You've never experienced any confinement, have you? A barred door that clicks between you and all of your choices? Jim and I have." His face became grim. "There's no feeling in the world like that."

"But that's behind you."

"Freedom." He spoke the words almost bitterly. "I'm free now."

The sadness Lara detected in his voice made her wonder if he were thinking of Mark or Crystal, the free way they lived. Or was he thinking of some foiled dream of his own?

"One seldom finds a friend as good as Dr. Shelton. He's overlooked the smudges in my past and offered me this teaching position at his foundation in LA"

As she looked deeply into his dark eyes, an emptiness filled her. She did not want him to leave. He was a part of Mark's dream . . . and hers! For a moment she felt tinges of desperation and considered asking him to continue renting the hotel. "Will you . . . like California?" she ventured, sitting down beside him.

What did he want? If only she knew! If only she could bring herself to ask him. She could not expect him to lose a golden opportunity for what little he had going for him here. And would he, if she did ask him? She did not want to meddle in his life or experience his rejection.

"California is where the job is. It's a job I know well, one that changes very little." He paused. "I can make more money out there in six months than I have made in Arkansas during the last five years."

So this job was what he wanted. He had not received fair treatment here in Quachita Springs. If he stayed, he would experience more of the same. She couldn't blame him for leaving.

As if his mind were fully made up concerning his departure, he went on, "What I worry most about is Jim."

"He is not your responsibility."

"He's probably the best friend I've ever had." Dane hesitated. "Jim can't handle change. Or any stress, for that matter. During our first art show here, none of his paintings sold. I had to look for him for three days and found him in a one of those caves along the river."

"You can't make someone sane that isn't."

Dane laughed. "He's not insane, even though he's been through enough to drive him there." The look of sympathy relaxed his features and made Lara feel strongly drawn to him. "Jim had a wife and baby in Vietnam. He was driving and they hit a mine that killed them both and placed him in a series of hospitals." He paused. "Jim is idealistic, sensitive—one of the few among us who really care. Unfortunately these kinds of people often in one way or another destroy themselves. They always experience the most pain."

"What about Hallie?"

"Hallie . . . is not like that at all. If she can't paint, then she will do what she can. Hallie will get along."

The breeze that tousled her hair made her feel cool and comfortable. She cast another glance at Dane's lean form, so relaxed. A wonderful sense of intimacy, of closeness to him stole over her.

"So, why don't you start your publication here in Quachita Springs? Art is rampant here in the Ozarks. You don't need to be at the top of some skyscraper in New York City."

Lara's eyes left his face to scan the perfection of the mountainside. "Because it's only a dream," she answered quietly.

"But dreams are what form reality," he said.

She was aware of his stirring, of the wondrous silence as he drew himself up to sit close beside her. She did not look at him, but could feel his dark eyes and was conscious of the breeze tugging at his shirt and rippling though his black hair.

Lara waited breathlessly for Dane to draw her close against him. When he did, she clung to him unresistingly. She closed her eyes and saw more beauty than she had ever beheld before as his lips claimed hers. His lips, warm, gentle, exploring, left her trembling. Slowly Dane's kiss became more demanding, and Lara felt swept away, possessed with a glorious passion.

Chapter Sixteen

Charles, who always liked to get an early start, had picked Karma up before dawn for the weekend trip to Eureka Springs. The child had risen early, filled with enthusiasm about another visit to Donna and her puppet show. Unlike the first time she had left with Charles, she this time had shown no reluctance to leave Lara. Karma was gradually becoming less dependent upon her. As Lara had watched her scamper away with Charles, she had felt happy, but a little empty, too, the way mothers must feel when they send their child off to that first day of school.

The house seemed unusually quiet after Karma's bright chatter. Lara had just begun to start the morning coffee when Joan, clad in an elegant satin robe, appeared at the entrance to the kitchen. She ran polished nails through straight, blonde hair and said, "Make it super strong, Lara."

"Too many nights out with Austin Graham!" Lara teased, heaping in an extra spoonful of coffee grounds. She had expected Joan to sleep late, for she didn't open the real estate office until noon on Saturdays.

"He had to break our date last night, if you'll remember," Joan reminded her. But to make up for it . . . breakfast at Luccerman's. Actually, he's making a speech this morning before the Chamber of Commerce, so he's invited me to join him." She sighed. "At least there won't be anything stronger than orange juice on this buffet!"

"You've been seeing a lot of Austin lately," Lara said, unable to keep her words from sounding like a censure.

"So what's it to you?" Lara would have thought Joan had taken offense if not for the carefree smile. "I happen to find his bulging credit cards immensely impressive!"

"Credit cards should not be the basis for a lifetime

relationship," Lara cautioned.

"I've tried love," Joan sing-songed. "Now I'm trying money!"

The perking of the coffee sounded loud in the silence that followed. "It's not just Austin's wealth that attracts me," Joan explained more seriously. "I've never met anyone before so strong, so dynamic." In the grip of enthusiasm she had lost her look of haughty worldliness. She seemed again a high school girl, immersed in dates with Mark and the senior prom. Joan poured herself some coffee before the cycle had finished and sank down at the table. "Be happy for me, Lara. This time I think things are going to work out."

By the time Austin Graham arrived, looking as if he were ready to appear before a TV audience, Joan like an eager teenager was hovering in the vicinity of the front door. She had changed into high heels and a cream-colored dress. How could anyone, Lara thought, look so glamorous before ten a.m.? No one could say that Joan wasn't a perfect match for Austin Graham's polished lifestyle.

"Good morning, Joan, Lara," Graham said as he stepped into the room.

"I won't be a minute," Joan told him. "I need to get something from upstairs."

Joan had not forgotten anything; she never did. Lara knew Joan was only giving them an opportunity to talk. "Won't you sit down, Austin," Lara invited.

Austin selected the recliner, managing, even in repose, to look active, impatient. "I'm getting anxious to begin the Graham Manors project," he told her. Austin paused and smiled somewhat pompously. "Don't wait too long to accept my offer. A number of fine opportunities are lost by people who wait too long, who procrastinate."

"I have to find out for sure what my present tenant

intends to do."

"Dane Lanford?" Austin's arched brows made his pale eyes seem sharply inquisitive. "Didn't he just get released from the state prison? I doubt he would have the cash on hand to buy."

"Still, I would like him to be a part of this decision. I am satisfied to keep leasing the hotel for as long as he wants to continue renting."

Austin's laugh was brittle and somewhat cold. "I've got connections. If that's what's holding you back, I'll help your tenant find another place."

"If Dane leaves here, I understand he'll be moving to California."

"I've made up my mind to have that land." With conviction Austin added, "I'm sure Lanford can be persuaded to relocate a little early. I just might drive out there and talk to him myself."

Lara wondered if he intended to offer Dane money, to try to bribe him into leaving. "That won't be necessary," she replied rather coolly. "If I decide to accept your offer on the property, I'll have Joan contact you."

Lara had the feeling that Joan had been listening behind her door at the top of the stairs. Because of the gathering silence, Joan now breezed down the steps, saying, "Austin, we'd better hurry." Then to Lara, over her shoulder, "I don't know why Austin always has to be the first speaker." She waved happily. "Goodbye, Lara. See you later!"

With Karma gone for the weekend, Lara was determined to begin her investigation of Mark's death. She would start by getting the files on the accident Scott had promised her. Wondering if Scott would be working on a Saturday, Lara called the sheriff's office.

"Hello? Is this Scott Tyler?"

A voice she recognized as the deputy's answered, "I'm sorry. Scott isn't in. It's his day off."

When Lara asked if she could drop by for the files, Tom told her grudgingly, "They aren't here. Scott took them home with him yesterday."

Lara felt disturbed by his announcement. Did the fact that Scott had been reviewing the files again mean that he was once more seriously looking into the case? Another possibility entered Lara's mind—that he had taken them home purposefully to prevent her from seeing them.

Later that morning, Lara decided to pay Scott a visit. She turned down the blacktop Joan had taken that wound into the hills toward his cabin. Lara drove slowly, searching for some familiar sign or landmark that would tell her she was nearing his place, which, she remembered, was hidden from the road because of the trees.

Lara noticed a clearing in the woods that seemed vaguely familiar. She turned down a long, unpaved drive overgrown on either side with uncut weeds. The sight of several rusted car bodies hiding in the grass told her that she had found the right place. As she drew nearer, she spotted the cabin. True to her expectations, she found Scott near the big shed to the side of the house, working on his Mustang.

Scott glanced up from beneath the hood of a battered yellow convertible, seeming startled, but pleased to see her. He was tanned from working shirtless in the sun, and when he smiled at her the skin about his blue eyes crinkled. "Lara. I was just going to take a break."

Scott reached to wipe oil from his hands on what she thought was an old rag, then recognized as the new shirt he had worn to Gino's. You can tell he's a bachelor, Lara thought to herself as he tossed it carelessly aside. He cast her a boyish grin, saying, "Come on, let's go inside where it's cool."

Scott led her through the cluttered living room into the

kitchen where he pushed dishes aside to make room for her at the small, wooden table. "If I had known you were coming I would have . . . what do they say? . . . baked a cake." In good spirits, he wandered to the refrigerator, took out a beer, and offered her one. It was obvious that he thought this was a social call.

Lara declined with a shake of her head. To set him straight, she explained, "I just drove out here to see if I could have a look at the files concerning my brother's accident. Tom said they were here."

Mention of the files made the smile drain rapidly from Scott's face. Looking disappointed, he said, "Lara, I've told you before, I really wish you wouldn't get mixed up in this."

"You promised to let me see them."

He studied her for a long moment. As if sensing her determination, he said finally, "O.K. You win." Scott disappeared into the adjoining room and returned a short time later with the files. "You'll have to look at them here," he said gruffly as he tossed the papers down on the table before her. "I can't release them to you."

Lara was aware of Scott's watching her as she started to read. His close scrutiny made her increasingly nervous. The thought crossed her mind that he seemed worried, anxious. Was there something in the files that he didn't want her to see?

Lara continued to scan the contents of the police records while Scott grimly sipped his beer. She studied the sheriff's report, which told of Scott's coming upon the scene, the position of Mark's body, the measurement of the skid marks. Scott's watchfulness made it difficult to concentrate as Lara searched for some detail he might have missed, something that might lead to Mark's killer.

Lara's gaze wandered to the handwritten notes that accompanied the official report. Suddenly, a familiar name glared out at her. Lara quickly read the brief notation that followed. Hallie Parker had noticed a strange car speeding quickly past the truck stop and turning on the bridge road shortly before the accident. Color: dark blue or black. License number or make of car unknown.

Had Hallie seen the car that had struck down her brother that night? Even before she glanced up, Lara felt Scott's eyes upon her. "I didn't know you had questioned Hallie Parker."

Scott's face was totally expressionless. "She saw a car turn down the road toward the bridge. But there's no real proof it was the car that struck Mark." Scott shrugged. "Even if it was the right car, Hallie didn't get a close enough look at it for her statement to be of any use."

Even though what Scott pointed out was doubtlessly true, Lara nevertheless felt encouraged. Hallie might be able to recall some detail not written in the report that would help her trace the driver of the vehicle. She would talk to her as soon as she could.

"Lara." As if reading her mind, Scott warned, "Don't go around asking a lot of questions. That's my job." His voice, terse and urgent, forced her attention to him. All traces of boyish charm had vanished, leaving an expression in his eyes, blue and narrowed, that chilled her. "I'm looking into this again only because of you, in the hope that I can find some way to link the driver of that car to Dane Lanford."

His words startled Lara. "Dane and Mark were friends. Dane would have no reason to kill him."

"If Mark's death wasn't an accident, then he's involved. And he would have motive. Money would be behind it . . . and that retreat. Your brother chose the wrong person to trust. If you ask me, he went into business with a con-man."

"But Dane didn't get what he wanted. He would have had a better hold on the retreat if Mark were still alive."

Her simple statement made Scott react with impatient

exasperation. "I don't know why you always defend him, Lara! At the very least, he's guilty of murdering Crystal. Everything is linked to him. I would think those paintings of yours he slashed would be a clear enough warning to you."

At the office Lara called the Last Stop Cafe and found out that Hallie would not be on her shift until evening. That would be the best time to talk to her, she decided, rising from her desk. The sight of Joan's white car parked directly below her window told her that Joan had returned from her brunch with Austin Graham. Reading about Mark's death had depressed her and she found herself looking forward to seeing Joan, who was always so cheery.

"Hi, Joan," she said as she stepped through the door of the real estate office. "I want to hear all about that breakfast date."

Joan attempted a smile, but her face remained pale and drawn. Lara noticed traces of puffiness about her eye as if she had been crying.

"Damn allergies," Joan remarked suddenly. She bit her lower lip and reached for a tissue.

Since when had Joan ever suffered from allergies? Lara sensed that something had gone terribly wrong. She sank into the plush chair across the desk and sat quietly for a moment. "What's happened?"

In answer Joan thrust the morning paper toward Lara. Silently Lara studied the debonair image of Austin Graham, his arm around a smiling, dark-haired, young woman in an expensive, low-cut gown.

"That's why he broke our date last night. The rat," Joan said with venom. "He's been seeing her on the sly!"

Joan snatched the paper from Lara and glared at the photograph. "I'll bet he didn't count on this being in the newspaper. You should have seen him this morning, acting the perfect gentleman, and all the while he's been two-timing me!"

Austin Graham, when confronted, would be prepared to justify the presence of the lady in the picture. He would try his best to hold on to Joan, even though Lara was sure he would never make any commitment to her.

"The liar!" Joan stifled a bitter, little sob. "He led me to believe I was the only one." Wide, hazel eyes brimmed with tears. "I don't just sleep around. I thought he really cared about me, Lara!"

Joan sounded so totally surprised, so totally disillusioned over Austin. Poor Joan. She had been so happy this morning, so bubbly, so filled with hopes and dreams. Despite her pretense of sophistication, Joan was just a small-town girl, who had been hearing wedding bells. "I'm so sorry, Joan."

"You're a pal," Joan said, "not even a single 'I told you so'. God, I wish I had listened to you." Joan dabbed angrily at the tears overflowing in trails across her cheeks. The hurt that fueled her anger sounded in Joan's shrill words, "I've let him make a damned fool of me."

Nothing Lara could say was likely to soften Joan's heartbreak. She maintained a sympathetic silence.

"I'll get even with him!" Joan raged. "Just you wait."

A little ripple of alarm raced through Lara as Joan suddenly grasped the paper between long fingernails and ripped the smiling couple vengefully in two.

"I'll make him pay! Nobody makes an idiot out of Joan Sommers and gets away with it."

A yellow sliver of quarter moon appeared in the night sky as Lara drove down the highway toward the Last Stop Cafe. If Karma were here, Lara thought with a smile, she would call it a "banana moon." Funny, how much she missed her. She wondered what Karma was doing now, and hoped that the child would fulfill Charles' expectations and be able to talk freely to Donna.

Lara felt a sudden pang of loneliness. The stretch of winding highway was deserted this time of night except for an occasional trucker. The hazy peaks of mountains, that seemed to go on forever, formed a jagged purplish barrier against the dark sky. Lara felt suddenly anxious to reach the noise and bustle of the all-night cafe.

Hallie called a greeting as she entered. Because there were few customers, she was able to join Lara quickly at one of the booths that lined the wall near the front windows. After they had talked a while over hamburgers and cokes, Lara brought up the subject of the car that had killed her brother.

Hallie seemed willing, even eager, to talk about what she had seen that night. "It was late, close to midnight. We weren't very busy. In fact I was standing by this very booth looking out the window. That's how I happened to catch a glimpse of that car. I probably wouldn't have paid much attention if it hadn't been going so fast, then all of a sudden slowed and turned down the road toward the bridge."

Hallie paused for effect. "Now, there's a fair bit of traffic on this main road by the truck stop, but not many cars turn off on that old road. Of course, at the time I didn't know anything about the accident. But I had to wonder whose car was turning down that way, toward the retreat, so late at night. And, as I said before, he was driving like he had a definite purpose."

"Did you see the driver?"

"No. But I felt he was . . . sort of evil. You know what I mean? I get these vibes."

"Can you remember anything at all about the car?"

Hallie brought a hand up to twist frizzled, yellowish

curls. "It was so dark, but I know the car was either blue or black. And big, but not a family car." Again she looked thoughtful. "Sort of sporty, but not like the hot rods they make these days. It was one of those old cars, you know, the kind with the souped-up engines. The noise when it revved up, that's what first caught my attention."

"Do you know anyone who drives a car like that?"

"Not anymore. But it sort of put me in mind of this old Chevy my boyfriend in high school used to drive me around in." She smiled a little, as if in fond remembrance, "I can't tell you what year that was, can I? That would be giving away my age." Hallie gave a girlish laugh, then sobered as if remembering the reason behind Lara's questions. "That car, Joe's, was a 1960-something model."

"Can you recall anything else about the car?"

Hallie gave a sudden little snap of her fingers. "I do remember something, but it may not be of any help. I got a real good look at the back of the car when it turned. That's when I noticed it had those unusual taillights, three round little lights on either side."

"Did you mention this to the sheriff?"

Hallie nodded. "I'm sure I did, because I remember him telling me that he wished I had gotten a look at the license plate instead." Hallie looked hurt. "Cars can't be traced except through their numbers, he told me. But I couldn't remember a thing about those tags!"

"Did the car you saw ever come back to the main road?"

Hallie shook her head. "It must have went on past the retreat and out that old dirt road that winds through the woods and hooks up with that main road a ways from the hotel."

If someone who knew his way around the area had driven the car, then it was highly possible that the driver was a local person and that the car might still be in the vicinity.

And even though there might be an old Chevy parked in hundreds of yards, there would not be one with the unusual taillights Hallie had described. Here was the clue she had been looking for—but surely Scott had checked this out.

In any event, Lara would do some checking on her own. A car that old, unless it was a classic, was likely to be abandoned or sold to a junkyard for scrap. The murderer could have purchased such a car solely for the purpose of killing Mark, then immediately gotten rid of it. She would start by inquiring at the junkyards.

"You know, I still have nightmares about that car." Hallie's hollow voice intruded into her thoughts. "I got the strangest feeling when it passed by. I get them, you know, clear messages of some fated happening." Hallie suddenly looked wise and knowing, like a woman on one of those telephone psychic ads that claim to have a link to other worlds. "That's why I'm so certain the car that passed by the truck stop that night was the same one that ran Mark down."

Hallie's gaze slid to the window. Lara, too, stared past the blue lights of the cafe's sign toward the empty highway. She visioned the shadowy outline of a speeding car. How quickly it had come into view and disappeared. Would there ever be any tracing it?

She rose, suddenly dreading the drive home. "Thank you, Hallie. You've been a big help."

"I wish I could have told you more, kid," Hallie called in parting. "I want you to know I spent hours looking for that car myself. I want nothing more than justice to be done."

Outside clouds had passed across the faint, quarter moon, leaving an eerie darkness. Once on the highway Lara glanced in her rear-view mirror. A car emerging from a side-road caught her attention. She had not seen any vehicle approaching. Had he been parked there and had just now switched on his headlights?

On the narrow strip of highway, the car behind her seemed an intruder. No doubt it was just Hallie's influence that made her feel for a moment the effects of some evil presence.

Nervousness gripped her. But as Hallie had said, this road was always well traveled, even late at night, with truckers and tourists who considered Quachita Springs a sleepover between larger towns and home. Still, Lara's foot pressed down slightly upon the gas, trying to put distance between herself and that other, lone vehicle.

Lara's fingers tensed upon the wheel as the car behind her also picked up speed. Was that just a coincidence? Who would be following her? Only Scott would know she was going to contact Hallie, but she did not think it was Scott behind her.

Feeling frightened now, Lara picked up speed. She could see the car's headlights in her rearview mirror as it kept pace with her. Glaring beams prevented her from identifying the vehicle, but in her mind she pictured the same, heavy, dark car that had struck Mark.

Her view momentarily disappeared as the road curved. She could not risk going home. She would drive directly to Charles' apartment. She was speeding now through the last stretch of darkness toward the city limits. Her heart pounded as she glanced behind her, half-expecting the sinister car to still be tailing her.

To her amazement the other car flicked its turn signals and without further incident cut into a side road. No one had been following her! Lara felt weak with relief. Just another driver with a heavy foot on the gas, anxious to get home.

She must not let her nerves and an overwrought imagination rule her.

Lara was glad to arrive home and to see the brightly lit house. Before going in she sat a moment and thought about the death car Hallie had described. However vague and sketchy, she now had some kind of real description—a dark, heavy-framed car with a powerful engine, possibly an older Chevy. She could imagine its dark shape blending with the night, the thud of impact as it struck an unsuspecting Mark, the glowing taillights speeding away through the darkness. Although she might never be able to locate it, the ghost car that had killed her dear brother was gradually taking shape, forming substance in her mind.

Chapter Seventeen

The morning sun cast a blinding reflection upon the windshield of the Taurus, preventing Lara from recognizing until she had reached the car what lay pressed against the window. When her gaze locked upon the small, dark object pinned by the wiper blades, she recoiled, staggered back, and stifled a scream.

A dead bird, grotesquely limp, dangled beneath the blades. One broken wing drooped pitifully from the ruffled feathers, pointing downward to huge, blood-like letters: ACCIDENTS HAPPEN.

Accidents! Lara sucked in her breath. Mark's accident! A similar accident happening to her! The ripped paintings had borne the same threat, but not so boldly, not so clearly spelled out as in these hastily drawn streaks so like blood.

Why hadn't Joan seen this glaring warning when she had left for work? Lara turned, her gaze wandering around the yard. For a moment she was certain, just as she had been last night, that someone was watching.

Her gaze fell again to the sparrow. She fought for control, managing somehow to take slow, even steps back toward the front door.

"Stop pursuing your investigation of Mark's death." The meaning of the message was as clear as if those very words had been scrawled across the windshield. A car really had been following her last night, and the driver of it had left this warning for her! Lara's hand poised above the phone. Without doubt this incident was linked to her visit with Hallie. And who knew about that visit but the sheriff himself?

She hesitated again, then lifted the receiver. Even though she dreaded the thought of facing Scott, she must have a police report in order to force a reopening of Mark's hit-and-run case.

Tom, the young deputy answered the phone. "Scott Tyler isn't in the office right now." After she explained what had happened, he promised to send him over as soon as possible.

Lara stood at the window, the pathetic, broken body of the sparrow remaining before her eyes as she watched the highway.

All the time she had believed the killer's fears concerned Karma, that the child might in time be able to point him out. Now she knew that she herself was the one the killer feared. He had killed Mark and her presence here unsettled him. So he had been keeping close watch on her, stalking her, waiting and fearing.

Soon she spotted the sheriff's car speeding toward her house. It swung recklessly into her driveway. As she stepped out to meet him, the sight of his sturdy, brown-clad form, the gun at his belt, gave her a momentary sense of security.

Horror again flooded over her as she walked with Scott and Tom to her vehicle. What a ghastly sight! She was suddenly thankful Karma wasn't here to see this.

Scott bent closer to study the lettering. "Lipstick," he said. "One of those dark, smeary types." He turned to her. "Damned maniac wanted it to look like blood!" He seemed to grow angrier as he continued speaking. "We're going to heed his warning this time! I'm taking you and Karma into protective custody!"

That would be doing just what the killer wanted—getting her out of his way. "No," Lara said definitely. "I'm not going to hide from him!"

Ignoring her protest, Scott began to question her concerning the details surrounding this morning and last night. Tom copied some of her answers onto a form. "You might just as well wait in the house," Scott said finally. "We're going to take samples of the lipstick and dust the windshield for prints."

On shaky knees, Lara followed his advice. She sank down upon the recliner. If she did not stop investigating Mark's death, the murderer would kill her, too—just as he had killed the poor, dead bird upon the windshield—just as he had killed Mark.

She wished Charles were here. He was the only one she trusted completely. She wanted to tell him all about the car that had been following her, even about the way Scott had reacted when she had wanted to look at Mark's files.

Lara glanced up to see Scott standing in the doorway, and drew in a quick breath. He entered, seated himself on the couch close to her and pronounced grimly, "Tom's still dusting for prints. But my guess is he's left no more clue than we had with the slashed paintings." His voice grew thickly bitter. "He is no novice where crime is concerned. Probably picked up more skills when I did manage to get him locked up!"

"I don't believe Dane did this."

"Why did I know you would say that? Tell me more about last night."

"I waited until about nine o'clock when Hallie comes on for her night shift, then I drove to the "Last Stop Cafe" to talk to her."

"You know I've already questioned Hallie."

"I'm sure someone followed me there."

Scott's reaction, impatience that she had gone against his advice to stay out of his investigation, made her suspicion of him waver. "I thought you were probably doing something like that. Joan told me you were gone when she got back from work."

"When did you see Joan?"

"At the annual Chamber of Commerce dinner last night. She was with Whitney and Nancy."

"How long did that last?" He stared at her as if she had openly accused him, then he answered grudgingly. "All evening. You know how those things drag out. Everyone and his cousin makes a speech. Did you get a description of the car that followed you?"

"No. Do you think Hallie is in danger, too?"

"Hallie doesn't know enough to pose a threat to anyone." With skepticism Scott added, "I suppose she told you the same story she told me. About seeing an old car with those odd taillights. Lara, I have to remind you there's absolutely no proof the car she saw that night was the same one that hit your brother."

"Did you ever try to find the car that Hallie saw?"

"Of course I did," Scott assured her. "The car Hallie described sounded like an old 60's sports coupe, big and fast, with a powerful engine. Because of the three round taillights, I figured it for an early-model Impala. Off the record, I ran a check on every old car in the area even remotely fitting that description."

"Did you find any?"

He laughed dryly. "A few. In back yards, up on blocks, without engines." He added thoughtfully, "I did find two or three still running. These "muscle cars" are popular with the kids because of their powerful engines. Restored, they are a pretty hot item."

"Could one of them . . . ?"

"Have you ever seen a car after it's hit a deer or some large animal?"

Lara shuddered.

"The impact of hitting a person is pretty much the same. None of these cars showed that kind of damage."

"Cars can be repaired. Quickly and easily."

"I talked to all the local shops. Nothing there."

"Maybe the killer made the repairs himself."

"I figure the car must have been from out of town or even out of state. With no number to check, I reached a dead end."

"This car . . . and Mark's killer are still around."

Scott gave her a tolerant look. "Be sensible. It's been some time since the accident. The first thing a hit and run driver would do is ditch the car. This happening after your talk with Hallie is probably nothing more than coincidence." Scott's blue eyes darkened with worry. "I think we both know who's doing this . . . and why. If you refuse what protection I can offer you, then you should at least take that little girl and get out of town as soon as possible."

His words, intentionally planned to turn her thoughts to Karma, made Lara shiver. But Karma wasn't the target of these threats! Accidents happen . . . that was a sinister, personal warning meant for her alone.

When Lara reached the Ozark Realty office, intending to tell Joan about the threat, the sign on the darkened window with its hand at twelve told her that Joan had been there and left. She was probably out showing a house. Disappointed, Lara turned away from the locked door, feeling a desperate need to talk to someone.

The solitary elevator ride up to the second floor increased her aloneness; the silence amplified the frightening thoughts gathering in her mind.

She had been warned. If she continued, her investigating of Mark's death might very well lead to her own. In a way, Lara was relieved that the threats were aimed at her. She was more able to cope with the fact that she was in danger instead of Karma. But if harm did come to her, then what would happen to the child Crystal had placed in her care?

It might be a good idea to talk to Whitney and secure Karma's future. Since the adoption hadn't been completed, the child would receive absolutely nothing of her estate in the event of . . . an accident. ACCIDENTS HAPPEN. If Lara were killed, how long would the trust fund Crystal set up for Karma last? Not long. She must take care of the child and the best way to do that would be simply to make out a will.

When Lara reached the second floor, she found herself dreading the dark emptiness of her father's office. It always seemed so vacant without Charles. She wished he were back now. As Lara stopped in the corridor to find her keys, she noticed the door to Whitney's office was ajar. Her thoughts of Karma and her loneliness drew her toward it. She heard voices from inside.

"You stay away from home more and more often!" Nancy spoke vehemently. "Even when you are home, you never even talk to me! What's happening to us?"

Whitney's answer was razor-sharp. "What's happening to you? You don't even make sense anymore!"

"I don't make sense!" Nancy expelled a horrified little gasp. "I should have had more sense than to marry you! Daddy said you never loved me. He told me you were just using me so you could become his partner. No, I didn't have the sense to listen!"

"I'm not going to put up with your damned childishness, not here in my office! Go home and work on your ceramics!"

The door Lara had started to push open now moved a little as she stepped back.

Whitney, alert to her presence, spoke, his tone of voice becoming immediately sober and professional. "Come in."

Either the interruption had incensed Nancy or the fact that Whitney's visitor was a woman. Above the puffy, pale skin, Nancy's eyes burned with spite—or was it jealousy? But, surely, she wouldn't be jealous of Lara.

"Why don't I come back later," Lara said.

"Nancy was just leaving." Whitney did not look at his wife again, but reached for his rimless glasses and drew before him a stack of papers. "I've been wanting to talk to you, Lara."

Lara's gaze followed the exit of his wife, who like an apparition seemed just to fade away and blend with the silence of the hallway.

"I still haven't been able to get a satisfactory court date," Whitney said with an apologetic smile. "I know how badly you want to hurry this adoption, but there is a great backlog of cases. It would take a miracle-worker to cut in line. And that," he said tiredly, "I am not."

"How long will it take?"

"It looks as if we'll have to go with the date I originally scheduled. That's a month from Wednesday." He removed the glasses, rubbed a hand across his eyes, and said with a certain lack of interest. "This doesn't have to delay your leaving. Since the Evergreen Corporation has made such a good offer on the property, Joan can handle the sale for you. And between Charles and I, we can manage to close out the rest of your father's business." He finished with a wave of his hand, "So you could go on to New York and plan on flying back with Karma later for the court appointment."

"I've decided to postpone my return to New York indefinitely," Lara told him.

"Oh? What has caused your change of mind?"

Alertness returned to Whitney's features, entwining with an expression of brotherly concern, which caused her to appreciate more than ever his enduring friendship. She began to pour out to him the events of last night and this morning.

Lara finished by telling him, "At first I thought someone was trying to harm Karma. But now I'm convinced that someone is trying to frighten me away so I won't find out what happened to Mark."

"Then you must not even think about staying here!" Whitney insisted. "You can't take such a chance with your life!"

"I've made up my mind," Lara said. "I would never take a risk with Karma's safety, but since I am convinced these threats are meant for me, I will not be intimidated." Lara's expression darkened, "But there is something I want you to take care of for me. Since Karma still is not legally my daughter, I want to make provisions for her future . . ."

"You want me to draw up a will?"

"Since I have no living relatives, I've never given the matter much thought until I took on the responsibility of raising Karma." Nervously, she added, "I was thinking of appointing Charles as executor."

"Charles would be a good choice," Whitney agreed, as if resigning himself to the fact that Lara would not be dissuaded. He hesitated, tapping pen upon the desktop, then suggested carefully, "But, of course, he's getting along in years. Someone more your own age . . . Joan, for example . . ."

"Of course. Joan," Lara said, anxious to get the task over with. "I'm sure she'll have no objections."

After she had gone over the explicit provisions for her will, Whitney leaned back in his chair. Deep in thought, Whitney looked very capable, very sharp and attractive. Lara could understand why Nancy was jealous of him.

"Lara, l wish there was some way I could convince you to go back to New York. You'll be much safer there."

"The risk is all mine." Lara told him with quiet emphasis, "I'm not leaving until I find Mark's killer."

*   *   *

When Lara returned to Joan's real estate office, Joan was seated at her desk. The pale yellow, three-piece suit blended with her hair and made her face look ghostly pale. Careful makeup concealed the faint dark circles about her eyes. Only someone who knew her as well as Lara did would recognize that she wasn't quite herself. Lara felt a little sorry about not having consoled her more about the breakup with Austin Graham. Soon, she promised herself, she would have a heart-to-heart talk with her.

But it was Joan who thought Lara was in need of solace. "Scott called and told me what happened," she said. "It's just terrible! Who could be doing this?"

"I don't know," Lara replied. "But, Joan, if you would feel safer back at your own apartment . . ."

"If you're not leaving," she said, with a lift of her chin, "neither am I!"

"I just came from Whitney's office. I was talking to him about writing a will to protect Karma's interests in case something should happen to me."

"You're really scaring me!" Joan exclaimed.

"I told him to put you down as executrix, if that's all right with you."

Joan was silent for a long time, then she said, "I'd be happy to be your executrix." She smiled faintly. "Happy doesn't seem to be the right word, does it?"

A sound from the hallway made both of them glance toward the entrance. Through the glass windows of the office, Lara could see Austin Graham striding confidently toward them.

"Oh, great. Just what I need," Joan murmured under her breath.

Austin stepped inside. "I've decided to top this Evergreen Corporation's bid," he announced with the assurance of someone accustomed to having his own way. "By the way, Joan, have you found out for me who the head of this outfit is?"

Joan regarded him coolly. "All I know is that they have money behind them. Big money."

"I'm used to fighting the big boys," he said with a false smile. "My mind is made up. I want that property."

Joan's pretty face seemed immobile, expressionless as wood. Lara hoped she was beginning to see Austin Graham for what he really was, pompous, overbearing, self-serving to the core.

"I still may decide not to sell," Lara said, taking Joan's side even though she disliked being caught up in their personal feud.

"I'm sure we can come to an agreement, Lara." Austin gave her a sly, knowing smile. Lara sensed that he believed Joan and she were in on the game of playing one potential buyer against the other, and that she and was holding out for the highest profit.

"In the meantime, I'm going to find out who the head of this Evergreen Corporation is and speak to him in person. I like to look my competition square in the eye."

Charles and Karma pulled into the yard with the first shadows of evening. Lara, who had been watching for them, stepped out on the porch. Karma jumped from the car, ran to Lara, and hugged her.

"She had a good time," Charles said, coming up more slowly behind Karma.

"Next time, Lara, will you come, too?"

Karma's request made her feel a slight pang of guilt. She hoped the child didn't think she had sent her away because she didn't want her around. "Yes. I would love to meet Donna and see the puppets."

While Karma scampered off to find Spot, Lara turned her attention solely to Charles. She could tell by his sober expression that he was deeply upset. His mood must concern Karma, she decided with sinking heart. Charles wouldn't have had time if they were just now returning from Eureka Springs to have heard about the threatening message left on her car.

"Did Karma talk to you?" Lara asked. "Were you and Donna able to find out anything?"

"Nothing," Charles answered briefly, as if he were willing to push aside the entire reason for his trip as if it were no longer important to him.

So he had heard. Stillness settled around them.

"I talked to Scott a while ago," he said gloomily. "Now I'm totally baffled. This isn't just some damned scare tactic. It is a direct threat on your life!"

Lara told Charles everything that had happened.

"Someone did kill Mark," he said. "And you're getting too close to the truth."

"I must have been on the right trail by talking to Hallie. I can't help but think she might be in danger because of me."

Charles seemed to question that. "If Hallie knew enough to be a threat to anyone, she probably wouldn't still be alive. No, Hallie only saw a glimpse of an old car. And I checked on that car myself. What other questions have you been asking and to whom?"

Lara shook her head.

"There's always clues. We've got clues right under our noses. We've only got to recognize them. I want you to think about everything you've said and done since you arrived at Quachita Springs."

They stood side by side on the porch. Lara watched Karma romping with the dog.

"There's some things that puzzle me," Charles said.

"For instance, whenever I think of Mark, I keep thinking about that woman I told you about who used to call the office and ask for him." Charles frowned as if trying hard to recall every detail. "Whoever she was, she made an attempt to conceal her natural voice. It always sounded low, a little above a whisper, and sort of husky. Even at the time, I thought that was strange, that and the fact that she never would give her name or leave any message."

"She could have been an old girlfriend . . . someone Mark dated."

"One time I was in Whitney's office and I answered his phone. I was really surprised when this same woman spoke and asked for Whitney."

"Did Whitney talk to her?"

Charles nodded.

"Did you ask Whitney who she was?"

"He didn't know. He said it was just some inquiry about divorce proceedings."

"Was that before Mark died?"

"Come to think of it, it was a few weeks after." Charles stopped short, then added, "But mysterious callers always get my attention."

Karma's laughter and the puppy's exited barking broke into their talk, but did not lift their spirit of heaviness. "He used a certain shade of lipstick to write the warning," Lara said, her voice hollow and far away. "He chose it because it looked like blood."

A muscle tightened in Charles' jaw. "Maybe you should be saying she. She chose it. We've been assuming this person is a man. But we don't know for sure. All we have is a hooded figure wearing a ski mask. And now leaving messages with lipstick."

Lara recalled the dark form that had chased her though the woods. She had no actual reason for believing her pursuer was a man. It had not crossed her mind before, but now she had to admit that Charles was right. Whoever murdered Mark and Crystal could just as easily have been a woman.

The idea somehow compounded her fears.

Chapter Eighteen

Still drowsy from a deep sleep, Lara shifted positions, burrowing the side of her face contentedly into the soft pillow.

Reality and unreality floated in indistinguishable patterns. The dreams of sleep tugged her back and she resumed walking with Dane. His hand—she adored the lean, strong fingers, an artist's hand—interlocked with hers.

The two of them descended steep rocks that led to a bubbling hot spring and Lara felt the warm mist rising from the water. Dane faced her, handsome in the shaded light of overhead cliff, and his lips, warm and exciting, sought hers.

"You must stay with me, my love," he insisted, holding her close. "We will keep the retreat and together we will make Mark's dreams come true!"

Lara heard, as if from far away, her own response, "Someday, I must return to my career, to New York."

She imagined Dane's eyes, dark and intent, upon her. "This is your chance to break away, to start the art journal you've always dreamed about. We could work together at the retreat, help each other . . ."

"It will never be, Dane" she said wistfully. "The art journal is only a dream."

"You could make it a reality!"

Restlessly, Lara turned, pulling the pillow with her, eyes still closed. Hazy, free-floating thoughts began gathering like clouds, drawing up in her mind's eye a vision of the journal. Why, she could even begin to see pages filled with beautiful artwork, the brilliant cover. And from somewhere deep within her a name burst forth, Sacred Springs Gallery."

Lara saw first, when she opened her eyes, Mark's painting.

For a moment it seemed that she were actually still there with Dane, standing under the jutting edge of overhanging limestone and feeling the steam billowing around her. The dim light from the heavy drapes set a unique, smoky cast across the man's painted features, which changed slowly from Dane's to the Indian's.

The alarm had not yet sounded. Lara clicked it off and rose, ideas for the art journal still drifting through her mind. Lara did like the name—Sacred Springs Gallery. Ever since confiding in Dane about her dream, ideas for the magazine must have been presenting themselves to her subconscious. The plans for her magazine lingered as she showered and dressed.

One thing was certain: the workings of the mind were totally unpredictable. Impressions and memories surfaced at strange times in strange ways, often when least expected.

Doubtlessly it would be that way with Karma and her flashbacks to the killer of her mother. Charles believed Karma was on the verge of remembering. If only Lara could think of some way to help Karma break through the barrier, to put aside all fear and see again each detail of that night. Lara knew she should not attempt to force Karma to remember, but perhaps she should create activity that might in subtle ways help her to recall.

Three busy days had passed since Karma had returned from her trip to Eureka Springs. Lara wanted to spend some time with the child. She glanced out of the window to a bright, sunny sky and decided to declare a holiday and let Charles manage the office. This entire day she was going to devote to Karma.

"We've got all day to spend together," Lara told Karma when she came downstairs for breakfast. Joan had left minutes ago, bearing the message to Charles that Lara would not be in until tomorrow. "Where do you want to go? We'll do anything you want to do."

Karma's large, dark eyes widened. "Really, Lara? Anything?"

Lara laughed. "Within reason. We could go to the park, the zoo . . ."

"I want to go to the mountains! Lara, we can pack a lunch. We can have a picnic. And then we'll walk. And you can tell me about the flowers, like Mommy used to do."

Sadness gripped Lara, but she managed to respond brightly. "What do you want to pack for lunch? You're going to have to help me fix it."

"I want . . . peanut butter sandwiches. And cookies. And Lara, can we take some pop?"

"Of course."

Karma scampered about the kitchen, opening cabinets. She soon began smearing peanut butter and jelly on bread. Lara waited with sandwich bags.

"Can we take Spot?" Karma asked with growing excitement. Lara noticed lately that Karma was beginning to open up, to talk more. "I'll fix him a sandwich, too."

"He might not like peanut butter. Let's take him," Lara held up a package of dry dog food, "some of this."

"Yes, he'll like that. I know a nice place where we can go, Lara. Mommy always took me to the stream and we'd wade. Can we go there today?"

Lara hesitated. Hallie had said that Crystal had often taken Karma around the hotel. That was one place Lara did not want to go, not with Karma. "Where is it?"

"You go over the bridge. But you don't turn to the big, rock house on the hill. You go way on farther. I can show you!" Karma said with confidence.

This favorite spot of Crystal and Karma's sounded as if it would be a long way past the hotel. It might be exactly the right setting, placing Karma back in a familiar scene where she had once been very happy. Lara must put aside her doubts for today and let Karma take the lead.

No harm would come of it. Lara would make certain they were not followed. No one could possibly know where they were then, so nothing could possibly happen that would place Karma in any danger. In fact, they would be much safer out on the mountainside than they would be here, where everyone would expect to find them.

Ever sinse they made the turn leaving the highway toward the bridge, Lara had watched the empty road behind her through the rear-view mirror. Spot, ears straight up, perched in the window directly behind Karma's seat.

Karma leaned forward as far as her seat belt would allow. "Not this road," she said. The car passed the turn-off to the hotel and they traveled several miles before Karma yelled, "Here! Here! Turn here!"

With another glance in the rear-view mirror, Lara swung the car unto a dirt road that sloped through pine-forested hills toward high country. Karma watched, wide-eyed and silent.

"I'm surprised you remembered exactly where to turn."

"Mommy and I came out here all the time. It was our secret place."

Karma had assumed a tense pose at the window, trying to locate, Lara thought, the stream where she and Crystal had waded.

The road began to twist and then angled sharply back in the direction where they had come. The forest had given way to a place of high rocks with gaping cracks and crevices.

She had driven on about a mile when the sight of the

tall pinnacle of the rock Dane had called the Devil's Stairway helped her get her bearings. Lara realized she was now back on her own land, land that lay directly behind the hotel.

Just ahead loomed the opposite side of the cliff that Dane and she had climbed—where he had kissed her. The dirt road she and Karma were on began winding up that very bluff. The condition of the road on this side looked good, entirely passable. Once at the top, she could turn around and come back down the same way and not have to use the rut-filled road that led down into the picnic area on the other side.

"Stop here!" Karma cried out.

"This doesn't look like a good place for a picnic," Lara said. She barely had room to pull off the road. Around them loomed high cliffs.

"We have to walk from here."

Feeling an ever-growing apprehension, Lara lifted the lunch sack and a blanket she had thrown in. She locked the car as Karma ran on ahead.

"Through here!" Karma said.

"I might not be able to make it through there," Lara answered, gazing doubtfully at the narrow slit between looming rocks.

"Sure you can! Mommy did! Come on. I'll help you."

Karma slipped through the cleft in the cliff's wall and Spot romped after her.

"OK. Take this," Lara squeezed the bulging lunch sack through to Karma and edged herself between the ledges of stone into an opening of valley. Just as Karma had said, a small, shallow stream cut through the center of it. Lara paused to look up at the surrounding grandeur of the cliffs. For an instant fear crept into the scene and made the landscape seem desolate, places of shadows and dark abysses.

As Karma and the dog bounded off toward the stream, Lara slowly followed and spread the blanket close to where Karma had busied herself looking at small stones.

"Here's a pretty one!" the child said, doubling back to Lara and holding up an ordinary-looking stone for Lara's inspection.

"You gather the ones you like best and we'll add them to your collection," she said.

Karma raced back to the stream, where Spot awaited, bouncing around her playfully. As Lara watched them, she began to feel less ill at ease.

She soon began setting out the lunch. The air around her felt hot and humid. She called to Karma to join her. What a lunch—dry peanut butter, crumbled cookies, and pop that had already grown warm.

"Isn't this fun?" Karma exclaimed, holding part of her sandwich toward Spot, who snatched it and gulped it down.

Lara opened his package of dog food, which lasted only a few seconds, after which he barked and watched expectantly for another of Karma's generous offerings.

As soon as lunch was over, Karma asked, "Can we wade now?"

The little girl headed back to the stream. She sat on the ground to remove her shoes and socks and shrieked at the coldness of the mountain creek. Lara gathered up the lunch. Spot remained beside her, still hopeful of receiving further treats. When Karma called to him, he shot toward her. Reaching the child, he jumped up. The unexpected impact threw Karma off balance.

With a splash she fell into the shallow water. Lara rushed anxiously toward her, getting her shoes wet as she hurried forward to catch the child's arm and lift her back on her feet. Spot, becoming excited, began jumping around and around, sloshing the cold water over Lara's slacks. Karma and Lara, both wet and laughing, ran from the frisky puppy back to the blanket.

"Now we have to lay in the sun and get dry," Lara said.

They stretched out on the blanket. Spot loped, shaggy fur dripping with water, toward them, encircling the blanket again and again. As he did, Karma laughed. Lara had not seen the child so happy. Even with Crystal, Karma had seemed somewhat isolated, always lonely.

The sun bore down on them. Layers of hot, pine-scented air soothed Lara. She closed her eyes and listened to the rippling of the water.

It had been a long time since she had relaxed. She was glad to be here this afternoon, in this beautiful mountainside—her mountainside. Everything she saw belonged to her. If only she could manage to keep it forever! For a moment, the pleasant dream returned to her, of she and Dane working together at the retreat, she starting her art journal. Hastily, she pushed the thoughts from her mind, forced herself to separate dream from reality. Dane was leaving. Even if she decided to stay in Quachita Springs, it would be neither practical nor possible for her to keep the hotel.

"Are there animals out here, Lara?" Karma, copying Lara's exact position, gazed up at the cliffs with her hands behind her head.

"Of course. Raccoons and opossums and even bobcats. But they only come out at night."

Karma's eyes widened and her mouth formed a round little circle. "It would be scary at night, Lara."

"You would hear strange noises," Lara explained calmly. "But they would be nature's sounds. Like the ones hoot owls make."

"How do they sound?"

Lara laughingly gave an example. Karma did an imitation.

After they had sunned for a while, Lara sat up and gazed toward the rugged cliffs. With hand shading her eyes, Lara traced the rough ledges that protruded from the wall of the bluff.

"Let's go exploring," Lara suggested, rising to her feet.

Karma lagged behind stuffing stones into her already crammed pockets. They waded the shallow steam and worked their way through cedars, pines, and oaks, until they were surrounded by masses of rocks at the base of the towering cliffs.

"Be very careful," Lara warned, catching Karma's hand. They begin an easy ascent, winding through rocks and over them. Karma, who Lara had placed in front of her, stopped, "Look!"

The child was pointing at a small cave; much like the one Karma had hidden in the night of Crystal's murder. She held her breath, half-expecting Karma's features to cloud with terror, but she only stepped closer. "Can we go inside?"

"It isn't big enough for both of us," Lara said.

"Let's find a big cave!" The child started off again. The climb became more rugged as they continued. When they finally reached a small plateau of smooth limestone, they stopped to rest. "We should go back," Lara said, realizing how far they had ventured. They had wandered deep into the heart of the cliffs into isolated areas where few feet had ever traveled.

"Why?" Karma asked, looking disappointed. "I'm not tired."

Enjoying the view, Lara looked straight down from the plateau to the sunken rocks far below her. Her gaze moved past a jutting overhang of rock, then returned to it. The odd, mushroom shape of the formation looked familiar to her, exactly like one in Mark's painting, "The Healing Water".

"What is it, Lara? What do you see?"

"Let's go down there, as close to the cliff as we can get."

"OK."

Their slow climb downward led them past gaping hollows of caves.

"Can we go in a cave?" Karma asked.

"These aren't big enough to explore," Lara said.

Their descent became more rugged as they continued, until they reached another small plateau of solid limestone.

They were approaching the huge, overhanging rock. Lara became filled with excitement. She knew this was the identical rock Mark had used as a model for his painting in "The Healing Water".

Karma, distracted by Spot's attempt to play, fell behind. Lara drew closer to the ledge. The entire expanse of cliff was marked with many such protruding formations. If she hadn't recognized the shape of this particular one, she would not have bothered to stop for a closer look.

Because of the great extension of rock above her, she had expected to find beneath it the opening of a huge cave. Instead she faced two, gigantic and solid masses of stone that supported the extended roof of rock. A narrow opening, which might be large enough to pass through set between them, but was blocked by chunks of limestone.

The rocks that blocked her view were of a size she could easily lift. Wanting to see what lay beyond, Lara began lifting the rocks and placing them on the ground.

"What are you doing, Lara?"

Lara peered through the opening she had made. All she could see was that the opening angled to the left. If she were able to follow it, would it dead-end into another wall of stone, or would she have discovered one of the many caves Dane had told her existed here?

"Can we go in?" Karma asked excitedly.

Lara spoke doubtfully, "We'd have to leave Spot out here."

"Why? Spot likes to explore." Karma reached down to quiet the waggling puppy.

"I guess it won't hurt to go a little way." Lara helped child and puppy squeeze through the narrow gap. Once inside, she cautioned, "Karma, you stay close behind me."

In the semi-darkness within Lara could see that the opening in the rocks continued. How far back did it go? Curiosity made her press on, wanting to at least look around the bend and see if they had discovered a cave of any size. Around the first turn the passage unexpectedly widened until they could almost stand upright.

Lara paused to assist Karma over the pathway of rough stones that sloped gradually downward.

The dim light from above grew fainter. Ahead of them was a much lower, narrower passageway. Lara hesitated. She did not want to risk getting lost, not with a small child along and no flashlight. "Right now we're getting light though the rocks overhead. That may soon stop. I think we had better go back."

"Where's Spot? We can't leave Spot!"

The dog, smaller and more agile, must have loped on ahead. Lara called to him. A bark echoed back to them from further down the passage. Unless they wanted to leave him behind, they had no choice but to continue.

The opening now closed in again, the stone walls narrow and suffocatingly close. Lara on hands and knees inched her way forward. She could see just ahead that the slope jutted downward to what appeared to be a smooth and level surface. To her relief, the light from overhead, rather than fading out, grew a little stronger.

"This is fun, isn't it?" Karma said.

Lara eased herself downward and turned back to lift Karma to the smooth solid base of rock where she stood.

Light filtered from above them through crevices that didn't quiet meet. To Lara's amazement the small passage-way had opened into a huge chamber. She looked for Spot and saw him standing near the edge of a vast body of water, barking with confused excitement. Lara approached the dog and the pool. The emerald-green water bubbled from an unfathomable depth. Steam flowed upward, defusing from slits at the top of the cave.

The hot air around her was pungent with the slightly unpleasant smell of sulfur. Trails of water from the great pool overflowed, spilling over rocks crusted, white, brown, and yellow.

Happily, Karma shot forward.

"No!" Lara said. "That water is boiling hot!"

Karma stopped abruptly and retraced her steps. She slipped a chubby hand into Lara's. "Why is it hot, Lara?"

Lara stared at the bubbling hot springs that was part of her hotel property. She had stumbled into finding a very huge hot springs—large enough to be of great commercial value! No wonder Austin Graham was so anxious to close the deal on this land!

Graham had been, as Jim Bearle told her, sneaking around her property. Without doubt he knew of the exis-tence of the spring and saw it as a financial gold-strike. That's what his pushing her to close the deal was all about—he would be able to tap the thermal energy and set up his own mineral baths and pools and attract vast numbers of tourists.

"Lara," Karma was tugging at her hand. "Why is it hot?"

"It's supposed to be hot," Lara answered, then kneeling beside the child, she said, "This is our place. Our secret place. I want you to promise not to tell anyone else about it."

Even though Lara had sworn Karma to secrecy concerning this unexpected and baffling find, Lara felt a strong compulsion to talk to someone about it herself. Her first impulse was to share the discovery of the hot springs with Joan. Joan, active and able, would know or find out the impact the spring would have on the Quachita Springs area, already being commercialized. Joan would glory in the new, inflated value and calculate it to Lara's advantage.

Before she arrived home, however, she decided to postpone involving Joan in this. Too many unanswered questions swirled in her mind. Because of "The Healing Water," Lara believed Mark must also have stumbled upon the hidden hot spring, which had inspired him to create the painting. Could he have told someone else about it, Crystal, perhaps? And who would Crystal have told? Lara knew Joan had introduced Crystal to Austin Graham as he had mentioned purchasing some of her sculptures, but exactly how well did they know each other?

Lara must first talk to someone who believed as she did concerning Mark's death. Her trust of Dane, which had never wavered, prompted Lara to drive back alone to the hotel later that evening. In her mind and heart she did see him as a confidant. She would share with him her important discovery. Maybe together, they could figure out if the hot springs had played some role in her brother's death.

Lara knocked lightly upon the lobby door, then opened it to a cozy scene. Dane, in a chair near the marble fireplace, was reading aloud. Jim Bearle sat on a stool behind the lobby desk writing in a small tablet. Hallie, seated beside Dane in one of the scattered easy chairs, tilted her head slightly as she listened to the rise and fall of Dane's deep and resonant voice.

When Dane saw Lara, he rose, placing aside the art history. His distinguished features lit in an engaging smile. "Hello, Lara, come in and join us."

"If I'm interrupting . . ."

"We're just having a little study group," he said. "One of many. And we are in need of a break."

"It's my turn to get the refreshments," Hallie announced. She cheerfully scurried from her chair to an area where a coffee maker set.

"You want coffee, Larie? Or I could make you some instant tea."

"Coffee will be fine."

Lara hesitantly drew forward and slipped into a chair beside the one Hallie had vacated.

Dane turned to Lara, his smile lingering. She was aware of his dark, serious eyes, the lean, handsome face, the waves of coal black hair touched with silver. His gaze following Hallie, he said, "Everyone here works, or they did, when everyone was here. We used to have classes, but since there are so few of us now, we have evening discussions instead. Tonight we are studying the rise of Neoclassism."

"Your dedication is impressive," Lara said, thinking how interesting it would be to join them sometime.

"When trouble started, only these two remained." Dane's voice, without affectation, empowered his words of praise. "They deserve the best I have to offer."

Lara glanced from Jim to Hallie. She realized that she was beginning to understand, even grow fond of these loyal students; Jim, with his intensity and great talent, Hallie with her girlish enthusiasm. Still, they were little more than drifters—and Dane far out-distanced them.

"We've got sugar donuts," Hallie called, eager to please.

"Sounds good to me," Dane responded, then to Lara, "Jim keeps the books. He must be a good manager, for we have continued to pay the bills month after month. And Hallie." He turned his dazzling gaze upon the simple girl who paused to bask in his praise. "She is our promoter. Without Hallie I doubt that a single sale would ever be made!"

Lara studied Dane, and felt the first slight stirring of doubt. What made his comments seem timed and planned tonight, like purposeful flattery?

Lara glanced from Jim, stonily silent, to Hallie, who handed her coffee and a jelly donut on a small plate.

Once more she regarded Dane, so convincing in appearance. The warnings she had heard about him echoed in her mind. Was Dane Lanford really who he appeared to be?

"By the way," Dane said, "just yesterday Hallie sold the painting she was working on the day I was showing you the hotel." Lara remembered the slightly grotesque painted head, which was reminiscent of primitive art.

"To a collector from Baton Rouge!" Hallie broke in, giddy with excitement. "Gosh, was I surprised when he pulled out his check book at my first price! Two thousand big ones!"

Lara ate and drank in silence, watchful now, guarded. Dane's faithful ones: Jim, so very much aware of evil; Hallie so childishly unaware—but both pitifully vulnerable. It would be so easy for a powerful man like Dane, with his arresting charisma, to take advantage. How far would his followers go in serving Dane's goals? Lara's eyes strayed back to Dane, who continued to watch her with that special intensity. What, for that matter, were Dane's goals?

All along, Lara had felt compelled to trust him. She had come out here intending to confide in him about the spring, but something now made her hesitate. He seemed so different today—or had only her perception of him changed?

"Dane makes us sound so loyal and all," Hallie said, "But he's the strong one! And Jim and I are so indebted to him. He practically saved our lives, isn't that right, Jim?"

Jim gave a dry, silent nod, but did not look up from his notebook.

Hallie replaced her coffee on the stand beside her and eagerly leaned closer to Lara. "Do you know what we're going to do, Larie?"

Lara shook her head.

"Jim and I are going to help Dane come up with a down payment for this hotel! All three of us are going to sell every painting we have on hand!" She settled back in the chair, looking smug and self-satisfied. "All we need from you is the amount you will take for a down payment."

Lara could feel the blood rising to her face. Dane already knew about the hot springs! All three of them did! And they were plotting together to cheat her! The room became unbearably warm, as if the last sip of coffee had given her a fever.

She stole a glance at Dane, whose eyes shot a warning at Hallie. The way he looked now, the dark pupils expanding, becoming opaque, sent a chill through her. "Hallie," he said with reproach, "you know why I've never made Lara an offer on the property. You see, we can't expect Lara to accept a contract for payments when she has a cash offer. It's not even right to discuss it with her."

"We've got to take some action," Jim Bearle spoke for the first time since Lara had entered the room. "If we don't, Austin Graham will buy the place out from under us."

"If he does, we'll think of something. Since I've decided not to take the job in California, we might all go back to

Little Rock. Lara," his dark eyes became imploring, "I don't expect or want you to feel any obligation toward us." A proud, weary smile touched his mouth. "We'll manage, regardless. We three are survivors."

Survivors, Lara thought. *By what means?* Now Lara knew his intentions. It became clear to her that Dane had never intended to take the job in California; he did not plan now to relocate. No doubt he expected her to accept without hesitation their offer to buy the hotel and the land they knew was so valuable. Feeling stunned, betrayed, she rose abruptly and set aside her unfinished refreshments. She could not stay in their company a minute longer.

She could hear Dane's footsteps behind her as she hurried out to the car. "I'm sorry if Hallie upset you. I had no idea what she and Jim were planning." He paused convincingly. "I certainly do not expect you to give their offer any serious consideration."

Lara started to get into her car, but his hand on her arm detained her. Dane gave her a long, questioning look. "Lara, was there something special you wanted to talk to me about?"

As she regarded him, waves of suspicion, distrust, washed over her. She answered with one, brief word, "No."

Chapter Nineteen

The shrill ringing of the telephone sounded above the blare of the TV set. Joan, totally engrossed in her show, barely glanced up from the screen as Lara said, "Hello."

Lara did not recognize the male voice with its clipped, vaguely British accent. "May I speak to Lara Radburn?"

"This is Lara," she replied, carrying the extension into the kitchen.

"John Silverman from the Clark Creek Gallery." After a slight pause, he continued. "I was so sorry to hear about Crystal Mar's death." The speaker cleared his throat, then added, "I've talked to Crystal's lawyer and he advised me to contact you. You see, I have one of Crystal Mar's sculptures on consignment."

"You have one of Crystal's works?" Lara echoed in surprise. "I'm so glad! I've been wishing I had more of Crystal's art to save for her daughter."

After getting directions to the gallery, which was several miles outside of town, Lara called to Joan, "I'm going out for a little while. Would it be all right if Karma stays here with you?"

"Sure," Joan responded, "I intend to stay right here on this couch until The Young and the Restless is over." Bored and listless since her breakup with Austin Graham, Joan was dangerously close to becoming addicted to soap operas.

"Where are you going, Lara?" Karma, comfortably curled up at Joan's side, looked up at her and smiled. She had dressed herself this morning in flowered top, navy pull-on pants, and bright pink sneakers. The barrette, the same neon color as the shoes, was clipped too high on her scalp, making the dark pony tail stick up like "Pebbles" on the Flintstones.

"Just to town for a little while." Lara returned the wide, dimple-cheeked smile. "Be back soon," she promised.

"Oh, wait a second, Lara." Joan's eyes remained locked on the TV as she groped for her purse, rummaged through it, and drew out a list. "While you're in town, would you mind picking up a few little things for me?"

Lara glanced at the mile-long list and grimaced. But since Joan had offered to baby-sit, she could hardly refuse.

Lara passed the outskirts of town and drove several miles beyond. Around a sharp curve in the road, she sighted the small, modern looking gallery, which rested in the crook of a sloping hill. She understood why it had been located it here, some distance from town, for the impressive view of the mountains on either side served as a natural tourist stop.

The faint tinkle of wind chimes announced her arrival.

Most of the displays were paintings of colorful mountain scenes. Behind the counter glass shelves were lined with sculptures, most of them of marble, wood, and granite. Lara's gaze fell at once to a magnificent doe and fawn cast in bronze. Even if she hadn't seen it before, she could have told by the slightly elongated lines and the minute detail, that this was one of Crystal Mar's creations.

The appearance of a neat, side-burned man, who came from a back room to greet her, matched completely the slightly British voice she had heard on the phone. "You must be Lara Radburn."

At her nod, he lifted the doe and fawn Lara had already identified. She remembered when this sculpture had adorned the living room of Crystal's house.

"Such a tragedy about her death," the gallery owner said as he gazed sadly at the perfectly sculptured work. "She had a great talent!" He quickly glanced away and the effort he made to compose himself told Lara he must have been a personal friend. "I have made out a check for two other sculptures which sold the same week she brought them in. That was shortly before she died."

"I will deposit the check to her daughter's trust fund," Lara said, regretting that she was getting money instead of Crystal's work. She wanted to save as many sculptures as she could for someday they would mean as much to Karma as Mark's work did to her. "Do you happen to recall who bought them?"

"A collector from the north, a Dan Bennett." He shook his head. "I'll give you his phone number, but I don't think there's any chance of his parting with them."

"Did you ever handle any of Mark Radburn's work? He was my brother."

"Only one painting. I sold that one to Bennett, too."

"Do you think there may be more of Mark or Crystal's work consigned to other galleries?"

"Not as far as I know. I understand Mark sold most of his paintings himself or at auction. And as for Crystal, she brought almost everything to me. I had no trouble selling for her. There is probably very little of her work still available."

His statement made Lara remember the sculptures still at the house, the bronze stag's head above the stairway and the unique terra cotta bird upon the mantel. Although she wished there were more, she was grateful that she had these three to save as a keepsake for Karma.

"I'm sorry the check isn't for more," he said, "but you know what they say about artists starving. Crystal was just beginning to make a name for herself."

John Silverman walked with her to her car and set the sculpture he had carefully wrapped inside. "Crystal brought her daughter out here a number of times," he said. "Such a beautiful little girl! Crystal's death is a terrible loss to everyone, especially to her."

As Lara drove back from the gallery, she was so

immersed in thought, she barely noticed the breathtaking scenery, so very much like the paintings in the Clark Creek Gallery. Lara had once believed that some of Crystal's sculptures had been missing, had even wondered if their absence might have had something to do with her death. But the bronze doe and fawn and the two sculptures Silverman had sold would account for what she had remembered seeing around Crystal's house. The lost had been found . . . the sculptures had been consigned to the gallery all this time.

Lara's thoughts turned to the sizable cash deposits she had discovered when sorting through bank statements at Crystal's house. They couldn't have been from the sale of her artwork. John Silverman had given her only a very modest check. Crystal's artwork, however exquisite, simply had not been selling for that kind of money. All the cash Crystal had deposited with such regularity had come from another source.

As Lara reached the edge of town, she remembered with disconcertion the errands she had promised to run for Joan. The list of a "few things" consisted of going to three different stores.

Finished at last, Lara started for home. She glanced at her watch, startled to discover that it was almost 3:30. She had not intended to be gone for so long, but since most of the time had been spent finding a store that carried Joan's favorite brand of pantyhose, her friend really couldn't complain if she were a little late.

Lara, surprised to find Joan rushing out to meet her, pulled into the driveway. At first sight of Joan, a creeping fear slowly engulfed Lara, draining away all satisfaction she had felt over obtaining Crystal's sculpture.

Lara bounded from her car and met Joan as she came

down the front steps. Joan's eyes were filled with tears, and her lower lip, moist and bright with lip gloss, trembled.

Karma, Lara thought, drawing in her breath. Something has happened to Karma! "What's wrong, Joan?"

"Karma's gone!"

"Gone? How could she be gone?" Lara's breath stopped, leaving an ache in her throat.

"I dozed off," Joan sobbed, "and when I woke up, she wasn't there!"

Lara stared at Joan with disbelief. She clearly understood what Joan was telling her, would have known if Joan had not spoken the words. But mercifully, all shock and pain, began to take distance, and she felt the real Lara Radburn replaced by some logical stranger who said, "She must be somewhere in the house."

"I've searched every single room! Oh, God, Lara! I should have been watching her!"

"Go into the house and call Charles and Scott. I'll take a look around the yard." Even as Lara spoke, she whirled and searched the cluster of evergreens and high shrubs that bordered the lawn. If Karma had wandered outside, she might have crawled into the shade, as she often did, to play with her bear, which she almost always substituted for the dolls she had once loved so much.

Finding nothing, Lara rounded the south brick wall and confronted the empty area of the garage and patio deck. "Karma!" she yelled, then again, "Karma!"

Spot scampered from the doorway of the small shed Charles and Karma had converted into a doghouse. He ran in circles around her, bidding her to play, and barking, the way he did when Karma called to him.

Fear came alive again. If Karma were outside, Spot would be with her. Someone, Mark's killer, must have spied an opportunity and taken her away! A faintness darkened Lara's vision. She struggled for control. She must stay calm. She would be of no help to Karma if she allowed herself to give in to her emotions.

Anyway, she was jumping to conclusions. It was sensible to suppose that Karma had merely grown restless when Joan fell asleep and had gone outside. She might have wandered off into the woods to gather rocks for the little collection she kept in a box under her dresser.

Karma couldn't have been gone long. She couldn't be far. The thought, though not convincing her, did serve to steady Lara.

She bent and patted the puppy's head. "Where is Karma?" she said. "Go find her, Spot."

The dog jumped up at her, then bounded away toward a pathway leading through thick trees.

Lara stared at the slope, shadowed with pines and oaks. Eventually, across an endless stretch of forested hills, her land would join the bank of the Quachita River. The thought of the deep, fast-moving water sent a weakness throughout her body. She thought of Karma innocently playing the night Crystal was killed, of Karma, filled with terror, running, running, running!

As she ventured deeper into the woods, the clouds drifting across the sun darkened her way. She kept her eyes on the ground, which no longer reflected the patches of sunlight filtering through branches. She detected no footsteps, no shiny rock carelessly dropped, nothing to indicate that the child had been this way.

Way ahead of her, Spot had stopped and was sniffing the ground excitedly; as if he was following a trail that only he could sense. Knowing that animals have a keener intuition, Lara let him lead her onward. Every once in a while she would yell Karma's name or shout encouragement to the puppy, "Find Karma, Spot."

Karma could have ventured out here and lost her way. The thought of the child out here alone with storm and darkness caused her to increase her speed. Spot disappeared from her view, then returned as if waiting for her. Lara cautioned herself not to get her hopes up. Spot was probably on the trail of one of the many animals that inhabited the forests. Still she followed him for a long, weary time.

Disappointment filled her when she finally realized that the pup had taken her in a wide circle that was leading directly back to her house.

At the edge of the yard, the dog stopped again, sniffed the ground, and waggled off toward where the circular driveway joined with the highway. He stood for a moment, ears pricked, beside the rural mailbox still lettered Lawrence Radburn.

Lara gazed in the direction he looked, down the endlessly empty road that curved past fields and growths of trees until it in the distance wound along the crest of the hill.

Losing interest, Spot began sniffing the ground again, straying from the mailbox toward the growth of weeds just to the side of it.

Suddenly he stopped. He drew closer to the weeds, then backed away, barking furiously.

Lara's heart caught in her throat as she stepped closer. Not a child, but a shaggy, stuffed bear lay abandoned, face down, in the undergrowth. With numb fingers Lara reached for it, turned it toward her. Glassy, unknowing eyes stared up at her.

At that moment Lara realized that what she had feared from the beginning had actually happened. Karma would never toss aside her prized toy, would not leave it out here along the road—unless . . . unless someone had forcefully parted them.

Lara clutched the bear close to her. She could see in her mind Karma opening the brightly colored birthday package, hear once again Karma's squeal of delight, her baby's voice declaring, "Buddy Bear! I'm going to call him Buddy Bear!"

Chapter Twenty

"We still have several hours of daylight," Scott said with unfailing conviction. "I've got a search party combing every inch of those woods and along the bank of the Quachita." His steady blue eyes met hers. "Believe me, Lara, we are going to find her!"

"Searching the woods won't do any good," Lara insisted. The image of Karma's teddy bear lying abandoned near the edge of the driveway struck terror into her heart. Once more panic threatened to break through the total numbness of shock. "Someone has abducted her! They must have pulled her into a passing car."

Right now, that's only an assumption, Lara. We have to begin with what is most logical," Scott maintained in that inflexible tone so familiar to her. "Karma may have simply wandered away."

Someone had kidnapped Karma and they were losing precious time. Why didn't Scott realize this? Surely he must understand how important every minute was to finding her! "After all that's happened, you can't really believe that!"

"Children do wander off. All the time." His careful words were meant to reassure, but his blue eyes clouded with an unsettling look of doubt.

In Lara's despair she thought of Dane. Her distrust of him had faded, replaced by an urgency to call him. Dane loved the child, as she did. He would believe her when she told him that Karma had been kidnapped. She was certain Dane would do all he could to help her find Karma!

Scott's gaze moved from her to Joan, who had just appeared, pale as a ghost, in the kitchen doorway. "Have you been able to get hold of Charles?"

"No," Joan answered, wringing her hands nervously. "Where do you think he could be?"

"Keep trying to contact him. And Joan," Scott said, as if trying to steady her. "Will you do me a favor and put on some coffee?" He added before he went outside, "Make it good and strong."

Lara could hear the nervous bustle of Joan in the kitchen. She lifted the phone and dialed the hotel. The phone rang four times, five. Lara closed her eyes and willed Dane to come to the phone. If she ever needed help, she needed it now! Please, please, answer! The phone continued to ring hollowly again and again. Accepting defeat, Lara replaced the receiver.

She would take this opportunity with Scott and the deputies out of the house to leave, to search for Karma herself. "I'm taking the car out," she called to Joan.

Her words summoned Joan again to the threshold of the room. "Do you think you should, Lara? Scott won't like . . ."

"I can't just sit here," Lara replied, her voice edged with desperation. "I have to look for her myself."

"Then I'll go with you."

"No, you're needed here, Joan. Stay close by the phone and keep trying to reach Charles."

Time seemed both to crawl and race at the same time as Lara pursued a vague and aimless search. She had no neighbors on her left, but one house sat across an acre of timber toward town. She found the elderly couple, fond of gardening, working in their flowerbed. She was not surprised that they had noticed no car near her house today, or had no glimpse of Karma playing in the yard. Trying not to react with despair to their shocked words of consolation, Lara pulled away, backtracked by her own house.

As she did Lara thought of the way the child had looked

as Lara had left this morning. She remembered distinctly and had related to Scott that Karma had been wearing a flowered top, blue pants, and bright pink sneakers. She could see the straight, baby-fine black hair escaping its pink barrette, the trusting eyes, the dimples at the corners of her cheeks as she had smiled and waved goodbye. Would that image, the last one she would have of Karma, haunt her as long as she lived?

Pictures flashed through her mind of vanished children, lost faces, smiling out from black and white posters and on the backs of milk cartons. A warning pierced her heart—it was likely she would never see Karma again.

Biting back the tears that threatened to choke her, Lara drove blindly down the old highway. She felt over-whelmed by fear and grief. And guilt. For if Karma had been abducted, then Lara had been seriously mistaken about the warnings being tied in some way with Mark's death. The threats hadn't been for her after all, but for the innocent child. Karma had seen the killer's face. And the monster who had murdered Crystal had finally gotten his hands on her! That surely meant that Karma . . . no, she must not think of that!

Karma was still alive, she told herself savagely. And she could not allow herself to break down, not when Karma needed her! Lara was going to find her!

Thinking Hallie might know where Dane was, Lara checked the truck stop, but the waitress had not yet come on duty. Lara decided to drive out to the hotel. It would be comforting, Lara thought, to enlist Hallie's help, even if Dane were not there. Selecting the back road, she swung down the dirt road away from the metal bridge. Many times Lara had driven this very same road to visit Crystal and Karma. She strained her eyes for a glimpse of the weathered, white house, as if it were a beacon of light at the end of a long tunnel.

A shroud of overhanging branches cast shadows in the early afternoon sunlight. Lara's hands tensed on the steering wheel as she reached a clearing and the house appeared in full view. It now bore the look of total abandonment—the silent yard, forlorn windows that gaped vacantly at her slow approach.

Instead of passing by it on the old road leading to the hotel she on impulse swung into the drive and followed it all the way around to the back of the house.

Lara's gaze fell to the path Karma had taken the night of Crystal's death, then returned to the back entrance of the house. With shock she saw that the door was slightly ajar. She leaned closer for a better look and noted the broken wood around the latch. Someone had been inside since the sheriff had secured the door after her last visit here.

Or were they inside now?

She cut off the engine and quickly stillness surrounded her. With dread Lara approached the door to the porch where Crystal had done her sculpting. She gave it a push and it swung open in a haunted, creaking way.

Nerves screaming, Lara halted and scanned the shadowy shelves lined with nameless, faceless animals, Crystal's aborted, half-finished projects. From here she could see the kitchen. Faint, barely perceptible traces of chalk marking still smudged the yellow tile, outlining the exact spot where Crystal had died. A trick of light, an illusion, made Lara see once again Crystal's dark hair splayed out across the tile, the dark stains spreading on the floor.

Wavering, she edged backward. It would be wise to go back and tell Scott about the break-in. She remained undecided for a moment. Had the intruder found what he wanted? Had he discovered within the house and destroyed whatever Crystal had intended the night of her death to share with Dane?

Steeling herself, Lara hurried through the kitchen, down the hallway, and into the huge living room. A musty odor permeated the house, which had been closed up for so long. Muted light filtered from the heavy, drawn drapes.

From the fireplace mantel the round, pebble eyes of one of Crystal's last finished sculptures, a long-beaked bird in a cage, watched her with unblinking stare.

As she hurried upstairs she found herself reliving her last visit to this house. She heard again the sound of splintering wood, her footsteps, running, fleeing into the cover of trees.

A vision of the masked intruder filled her mind, the dark, empty face with its gaping hollows for eyes and mouth. Had that blank and featureless face been the last thing Crystal had seen? Was it the last thing Karma had seen?

At the doorway to Crystal's room she allowed herself time. Only barely imperceptible differences could be noted, slight details of disarrangement. Still, traces had been left of a deadly, methodical presence. The room had been searched with unrelenting thoroughness. The lack of disordered rage chilled her, seemed at the moment infinitely more savage.

Whoever had been here had discovered the panel that Dane had removed from beneath the oriole window. She could tell by the slight protrusion of an upper edge, that it had been precisely replaced. Why, she didn't know. From the way the latch had been sprung open, no thought could have been given to concealing the fact that he had been here.

How foolish it was to believe she would find Karma alive.

Frightened, Lara ran back downstairs as if a force of evil moved with her.

She stopped at the foot of the steps and once again the

round, inquiring eyes of Crystal's terra cotta bird on the mantel caught her eye. This sculpture was one she had planned to save for Karma. Tearfully, almost as if it beckoned to her, Lara approached the statue and reached out for it.

Lara gave a startled cry as the sculpture slipped from her grasp and clattered on the oak floor just beyond the marble hearth.

Lara leaned over the fallen sculpture. At first she believed the valuable work had broken. Upon closer inspection she saw that the caged bird had only separated from the wooden base.

With nervous fingers she lifted it and in an attempt to put it back together, noted what had been stuffed inside the hollow base.

Photos. Three of them. Two were clear photographs of an old, dark car with a crushed fender and dented hood. She felt ill as she rose. These must be pictures of the car that had killed Mark! Snapshots, taken with a Polaroid camera. Already they had started to fade and discolor. They were not focused very well, taken in haste, from some elevated area. Where? The place where the license plate should be was blank. In the first two photos, only one side, the driver's side of the car, was shown and revealed details of the damage. In the next one Lara could see the exact shade of the car, a dark blue, and the unusual taillights, three in a row. This was without doubt the car Hallie had described.

Lara had suspected that whatever Crystal had concealed within the house had been behind the panel in Crystal's room. It had even flitted through her mind that Dane had secretly removed whatever had been hidden there before he had looked behind the panel when she was with him.

She had been wrong. The man in the ski mask was still

looking for these photos. Lara clearly understood now the reason behind Crystal's murder. She had known the identity of the hit-and-run driver who had killed Mark!

Lara recalled the bank deposits, the evidence of steady money being deposited into Crystal's account and realized that Crystal must have been blackmailing Mark's killer. Crystal must have been afraid of the man she was blackmailing. Because she was frightened of him, Crystal had intended to share the killer's identity with Dane. Perhaps the killer was someone Dane also knew.

The threats, then, had been meant for her, warnings for Lara to quit her investigation of Mark's death. She clung to the desperate hope that Karma's kidnapping was another such warning. He might be hiding the child somewhere to frighten Lara. If he hadn't allowed Karma to see his face, he might intend to let her go unharmed.

Lara peered closely at the photos, now hoping to recognize something within them that might lead her to the identity of the kidnapper or provide a clue to where the child might have been taken.

The backgrounds in the pictures were dark, barely discernible. The car appeared to be housed in a garage or shed of some kind, and the snapshots possibly taken from a high window. The background was little more than a blur of indistinguishable shapes, nothing that could be positively identified. In one of the photos, beyond the car Lara could faintly make out what looked like a square-shaped, iron object, possibly a wood-burning stove.

Crystal had called Dane to the house that night to show him these photographs. That meant Lara no longer had any reason to doubt Dane. She would find Dane now and trust him to help her find Karma. From the photographs he might be able to identify the owner of the car or the place where the photos were taken. These photographs could lead them directly to Mark's killer. And to Karma!

* * *

Hallie greeted her cheerfully. "Hi, Larie," she said, opening the door to the hotel wide and saying, "Come on in. I've just finished a painting. Would you like to see it?"

Woodenly Lara told her she was looking for Dane and that Karma was missing.

The smile died from Hallie's face. "I don't know where Dane is, but Jim and I will help you. We'll look for her! Do you think she's out here somewhere?"

"The sheriff is searching the woods near my house." Lara pressed her lips together to keep them from trembling. "But, Hallie, she's not there. She's not lost. Someone has kidnapped her!"

"Oh, my God! Poor little girl." Hallie whirled around, yelling at the top of her voice. "Jim! Jim! Do you have any idea where Dane is?"

Jim, sullen and hostile, as he had looked on their first meeting, quickly responded to the call. He strode into the lobby from the hallway, saying, "I think he went to Hot Springs."

"Can you call around and find him?"

Jim shrugged.

"This is important, Jim. Life or death. You know how much he thinks of that little girl!"

"I don't even know what's going on! Why do you want me to find Dane?"

"Because of Karma! She's been kidnapped! You find Dane and I'm going to get us some more help." Hallie swung back to Lara. "We'll take care of this area, Larie. We'll search from here back to the truck stop."

For the next hour Lara remained close to the hotel. While waiting for Dane, she drove slowly along the back roads for some sign of tracks, some evidence that whoever had taken Karma might have gone this way. In the picnic area, she stopped at the base of the cliff and looked up, seeing at the top of the bluff the formation Dane had called the Devil's Stairway. From that high cliff near that formation, Dane and she had an overview of the entire area. That's what she needed now.

The road leading up the bluff on this side was so badly eroded that she decided to go around and approach it from the other side. She drove back past the hotel and joined the main road until she found the turn-off Karma and she had taken the day of their picnic, the day she had found the hot springs. It now seemed so long ago.

The scattering darkness made it difficult to see the twists and curves as Lara began to wind her way up the cliff road. She parked her car at the top of the bluff and stood beneath the looming tower of the Devil's Stairway.

Silently, observantly, she studied the entire area. The semi-darkness cast a haze over the cliffs and shadowed valleys below, and the encroaching nightfall made unsuccessful her view. To the left of her, the road she had been afraid to take leveled off and joined the one she had taken. Dane and she had stood in this very spot, among rocks and trees, the day they had walked up here. As she moved closer to the cliff's edge, to where rocks jutted down sharply, Dane's warning once more echoed in her thoughts, "Don't get too close."

She could barely make out the weeds and scrubby trees so far below at the cliff's base. Her gaze strayed, then returned directly below her. She caught a glimmer of blue and her heart caught in her throat. Was it cloth? Something—a human form—lay half-concealed in the high weeds!

Lara had never known such fear. It froze her limbs, making it impossible for a moment for her to cry out or even move. She must be looking down at Karma's body, lying so prone and still.

When motion returned, Lara scrambled blindly down

the steep road, running, sliding, stumbling. Once at the bottom, heart pounding fearfully, breath coming in uncertain gasps, she stopped and attempted to orient herself.

She had just begun to leave the road and scramble over the rocks and underbrush that lined the bottom of the cliff when the sight of approaching headlights pierced the night.

Realizing it must be Dane, she cried out to him.

The dark form, at first too obscure to identify, hurried through the shadowy darkness in her direction.

"Dane . . ." she gasped. "There's a . . . body . . . ."

Total blackness blotted her vision. If Dane hadn't caught her, she would have fallen.

"Jim! Over here. Bring a light!" She could tell by the choked, distant sound of his voice that he believed they had arrived way too late. Karma was dead! Jim, as if a soldier on some silent jungle mission appeared, quickly, silently.

"You wait here!" Dane said firmly to Lara. He took the flashlight from Jim and wound close to the cliff's edge. She could see Dane's tall form, and Jim, slouching with quick and silent step, close behind him. She could not let them get out of sight. Lara, too horrified to wait, too horrified to confront what lay just in front of them, followed.

All of a sudden the light stopped skimming through the darkness and settled. Dane, handing the flashlight to Jim, knelt, then rose quickly, bypassing Jim, and catching her shoulders.

"You don't want to see . . ." he said.

Steeling herself, she looked around Dane. Jim was holding the light steadily on a motionless form. But the prone body did not belong to a child. Austin Graham's finely cut features were frozen in an expression of terror. Lara buried her face against Dane's shoulder. He was dead. She didn't need Jim's words to inform her.

"Must have been snooping around and fell," Jim said,

flashing the light up the rock wall. It lighted only a small area, but Lara could feel the imposing presence beyond, of sheer cliff and at the top the towering of Devil's Stairway into the dark sky.

Lara felt grateful for the support of Dane's strong arm locked solidly around her. "Jim, I'm going to let you off at the hotel so you can call the sheriff," Dane said. "But give me enough time to take Lara back to her house."

"What about her car?"

"You and Hallie can bring it in later."

"I don't suppose you want him to know the two of you were out here," Jim said.

"That doesn't matter." They had started back toward the old station wagon. "Tyler won't be able to find me by then." Dane directed his next words to Lara, in calm explanation. "If I stay here, the sheriff will take me in for questioning. And I can't afford that. Not with Karma missing."

Chapter Twenty-one

After he let Jim out, Dane swung the station wagon around and chose the fastest route to town, the back road that would lead across the old wooden bridge and past Crystal's house. His rigidness, his silence, the way his hands clenched the steering wheel, renewed Lara's sense of panic. It was clear that Dane was thinking the same thing she was thinking—that Karma, too, was dead!

The shock of finding Austin's body had caused a shaking in her limbs, which now became worse. She knew Austin Graham's death had not been an accident. He had been cold-bloodedly pushed from the cliff.

Austin Graham's body, twisted and limp, and his face, frozen in terror, remained before her eyes. It would always be there, stamped as indelibly as Crystal's. But why would anyone want to kill Austin Graham? How could there be any connection between Austin's alarming and unexpected death and Karma's kidnapping?

Confusion added to her desperation. "I want to stay with you. I want to keep looking for Karma."

"Lara." Dane cast a quick, worried glance toward her. "You've had a bad shock. In fact, more than one. You are in no shape to keep on searching. I am going to take you home."

"No!" Tears choked her voice. "We don't have any time to waste. Every minute counts!"

"You have my word, Lara, I will keep searching for Karma until she is found!"

The determination evident in Dane's vow offered no comfort. She had never known such anguish, such total weakness. Physically she would not be able to hold up much longer. Something hot to drink, a little rest, then . . .

Then, what? Again she felt the impact of disaster hovering close to her heart.

Clouds passed in front of the moon intensifying the darkness. Poor Karma! Poor baby! If she were alive—what a dim hope—how terrified she would be!

In a limbo of stillness Lara straightened up in the seat. She struggled to control herself, to restrain the threatening tears.

Tires bounced as they crossed the uneven planks of the old bridge. Headlights tossed reflections of light across the wooden side-rails. The blackness beyond prevented her from seeing the water, but from the open window she could hear it ripple around boulders and branches.

Depth. Darkness. Terror.

An image of the child's uplifted face, smooth and plump, like a baby's, appeared to her. She could feel Karma's great, dark eyes, eyes that looked to her for protection, for safety.

She brought an unsteady hand to her forehead. "Whatever has happened to Karma, I'm to blame. I put myself and my own interests first. I should have put Karma first."

Dane pulled the car to a stop, his deep voice protesting, "No, no, Lara! It was you alone who cared for her, who accepted responsibility for her!"

"But look what happened! She would have been better off if I had placed her in a foster home. I should have followed everyone's advice and left her alone!" For the first time violent tears broke through her stoic pain.

Dane drew her against him, strong hands holding her as tightly as a moment ago he had held the steering wheel. She clung to him, her head pressed against his shoulder until her sobbing ceased.

"You did exactly what I would have done," he said at

last, a lean hand smoothing her hair. "You were only being loyal to Mark and to Crystal."

Why was everything so complicated? How could loyalty work both good and evil? She spoke dully, "But I should have been loyal to Karma. I should have let the whole thing go, for her sake."

"You couldn't have just left here. And you couldn't have just handed her over to strangers. You know you're not the type of person to do that." Dane's eyes in the light of the dash smoldered. "If you were able to turn your responsibilities over to someone else so easily, I would not love you so very much!"

Again Lara clung to him, feeling his lips against her hair, against her mouth.

She had never been in love before, but for a moment, despite the irrational timing, the irrational situation, she was certain that she loved him. Although she had every reason to distrust him, she had from the first believed in him. Was she as wrong about that as she had been about what was best for Karma?

Lara freed herself from the circle of his arms. "Dane, when I was in Crystal's house, I found something." She reached into her pocket and drew out the photos that in the shock of finding Austin's body she had until now totally forgotten. She told him where and how she had found them.

Dane took the photos, switched on the dome light, and studied them.

"Crystal knew who murdered Mark. I'm certain this was what she intended to show you. Do you recognize the place in these pictures?"

Dane gave a troubled frown. "No," he said. He slipped the photos into his breast pocket, adding, "But I'll do some checking."

Now grim and silent, Dane started the engine and

pulled the car back on the road.

"Let's stop at Crystal's house again." She thought of the trails along the river that led to the cave-like rocks where Karma had hidden the night of Crystal's murder. "Maybe he has hidden her somewhere. We should check the old boathouse."

Without glancing at her, Dane said, "I'll take a look around that area after I take you home."

"I want to go with you!"

Despite her continued protests, he drove her directly to her house.

Joan, her face white and pinched, met them at the doorway. "I just heard the news about Austin. Scott's over there now. He thinks Austin was out looking at the land and fell from the cliff. It's all my fault," Joan wailed. "I kept goading him into making a higher offer!" Straight, blonde hair fell forward across her face and the hands that tightly covered it.

Dane stood uncertainly in the doorway. "I'm going to leave now, Lara. I'll have Hallie and Jim bring your car over later. Please try to get some rest."

The moment Dane left, Joan suggested they go into the kitchen. The cup after cup of black coffee braced them, as did the ham sandwiches Joan insisted on making.

"Did you get Charles?"

Joan shook her head. "I don't know where he could be."

Afterwards Joan lay on the couch near the phone, and Lara, seated in the recliner, listened to her steady flow of talk. Lara was thankful that Joan did not speak of Karma or of Austin. She talked instead of Mark. She spoke on and on, but Lara heard only isolated sentences, which spasmodically broke into the frozen depths of her own thoughts.

"Remember when we were kids and we used to swim in the Quachita? . . . that time Mark dared me to jump

off that old wooden bridge. Damned near drowned. . . .
I was so scared, but you know me, always rallying to a
challenge! God, we were happy then! Where did those
days go, anyway?"

Lara could not even force a response, but in spite of
this, Joan's words flowed on and on, remembering Mark,
reliving events from her treasured past.

The food, the rest, was slowly renewing Lara's strength.
Soon she would be able to look for Karma again. She
couldn't help but feel she had been close to Karma tonight
when she was near Crystal's house and around the area of
the hotel. Her gaze moved to the clock. It would soon be
dawn. It might be a good idea to wait now for daylight to
break before she started her search again.

Joan's sudden question broke into Lara's thoughts. "Life
doesn't make any sense, does it? Why should I still be alive?
What do I add to the world compared to Mark, or Crystal
Mar, or an important man like Austin Graham? I've never
done anything for anyone." She began to cry. "Why did I
have to fall asleep? Karma would still be here, safe!"

Lara realized that Joan shared the burden of her guilt.
"Joan, don't think that way. Look at me now, what would
I do without you?"

Joan slumped back in silence, her eyes closed. After a
while she sat upright. Her voice sounded choked and distant. "Mark, Crystal, Austin . . . they were all killed by the
same person, weren't they? By some demented madman!"

"I'm afraid they were all murdered," Lara answered sincerely. "But it doesn't have to be by a maniac. They could
have been killed by someone with a very logical motive."

"What motive?"

"Money, probably lots of it," Lara said, thinking of the
hot springs beneath the cliffs on her property. Lara had
intended to tell Joan all about her discovery, but now was

not the time.

Joan watched her, her face a mask of fear. "He kills so freely. Why didn't he just kill her right away? We both know he could have at any time."

"He might not want to kill her. He could have kidnapped her just to frighten me into leaving here. If he is convinced she can not identify him, he may let her go unharmed."

"That's crazy. A demon like that, he will think nothing about killing her, even if she is just a little child. She's been missing for a long time now." Joan's voice faded into a low moan. "It's beginning to look as if Karma is already dead! Lara, you had better prepare yourself for that."

Lara finally contacted Charles. Hours later just as dawn was breaking, he appeared at the door. His clothes were wrinkled, his gray hair disheveled. He sank wearily into the chair Lara had vacated and did not speak. When he looked up, his eyes reflected her own pain.

"I can't wait here any longer," Lara said miserably. "I've found a good photograph of Karma. I'm going to talk to all of the people who live in this area. Maybe someone got a glimpse of her. Or saw a car."

"I've already done that," Charles said. "I think I've showed her picture to half the people in this town. Without even a clue. But I haven't given up," he added, his voice devoid of its usual confidence.

Joan brought him some coffee and a sandwich. "I'm going to work on the home front," she said, trying hard to give her voice an encouraging brightness. "And this soldier looks as if he could use some bracing up."

Charles accepted the tray and began eating mechanically, as if too absorbed in his own thoughts to put forth protest.

When Charles finally rose to leave, Lara said, "I'm going

with you."

Early morning mist fell across the fields, obliterated the distant peaks. They drove aimlessly. Charles stopped to talk to the scattering of early risers at the "Last Stop Cafe". Lara watched through the window as he showed Karma's photo to a thin boy, who stood behind the counter, and she wondered when Hallie would arrive.

Charles shook his head as he slipped back into the car. He did not turn at the bridge, but continued on the highway, driving far too fast for the narrow, winding road.

"I thought I'd drive over to Riley. Put some pressure on the local boys there. They're responsible for all this rural area just across the county line."

At Riley, Charles went into the police station, while Lara talked to the townspeople, mostly to the attendants of service stations. Charles and she met at the car an hour later. "Let's go back to Quachita."

Once there Charles drove up and down side streets. So many motels, so many doorways. If the child had been abducted, she could be hidden anywhere! By now she could be in another state, even another country. But, most likely, Joan was right.

She was fully aware of child's chances, but Lara knew nothing would ever prepare her for Karma's death. She brought her hands to her eyes as if to blot out the vision she had of the sweet, innocent child, still and dead.

Charles rounded a corner, steered the car left and pulled to a sudden stop in front of the Convention Center Hotel. "It looks as if Scott's here inspecting Austin Graham's room. Let's go see if he has found out anything."

The huge, lobby had the smell and look of newness. Charles crossed the pale blue carpet and spoke to a man at the desk, then they took an elevator up to the forth floor.

Charles, a few steps ahead of Lara, entered Austin

Graham's room first. Lara could hear the murmur of voices, Charles' louder than the others.

Lara's steps lagged.

Charles' voice became clear to her. "By God, we've got to be doing more!"

Lara stopped in the doorway, her gaze locked on the sheriff's face. As his eyes slid from Charles to her, she saw them become shaded and distant, the same way she had remembered them when she had tried to discuss with him Mark's death. She felt the tugs of old hostility, fired by the knowledge that Scott was handling Karma's disappearance in exactly the same way he had handled Mark's investigation.

Feeling a trembling in her body, she gripped the doorway for support and managed to say, "Have you any leads to follow? Have you talked to anyone who thinks they might have seen her?"

Scott turned back to his task at hand, stacking papers from the top drawer of a chest into Austin Graham's briefcase. "Not yet. But I have to take care of this, too."

"You can get a . . . janitor to do this!" Charles reprimanded. "It's been almost seventeen hours! God, that isn't good!"

"We're doing everything we can," Scott replied, his tone matching Charles' for sharpness. "The minute twenty-four hours has passed, we'll be able to file a missing persons report. That will make the search for Karma nationwide."

"You know yourself if they're not found . . ."

After a period of silence, Scott's voice took on an appeasing gentleness. "Graham's a prominent citizen. That's why I had to stop by here myself. I've got to be sure we've notified everyone that should know of his death before it makes the six o'clock news." Scott looked weary, as if overwhelmed by the demands upon him. "It's beginning to look more and more like we have another murder on our hands."

"Do you think this is likely to be connected to Karma's disappearance?"

"It's possible." Scott turned to Lara, saying, "Joan told me Dane Lanford brought you home last night. No one has seen him since. Do you know where he might be?"

"No."

"I intend to bring him in for questioning."

"Instead of wasting your time on Dane, why don't you look for Karma?" Lara demanded. The outrage in her voice made the two deputies that had been busy sorting through Austin's personal effects look up in surprise.

"Because Lanford has a tie to Karma. If anyone knows where that child is, he does."

Lara silently turned to stare out the window. She had learned from past experience the uselessness of pursuing any argument with him.

Dark clouds had formed, hanging low over the mountains. They forewarned a thunderstorm, which was likely to further delay their search for Karma. It was hopeless. She had lost Karma, too, just as she had lost Mark.

Charles and Scott had continued their discussion, but the meaning of their words had become lost to her. She could not bring herself to face Scott again. She could not bear being in this room any longer.

"I'm going back downstairs," she told Charles as she started to the door. As she walked past Austin's bed, her eyes fell to the stand next to it. A pad beside the phone was filed with lines and doodles, as if Austin's last conversation had been a long one. At the bottom of the paper, he had scratched in the same broad strokes the word, "Evergreen Corporation," and beside it, "See Jordan."

She knew that Whitney, because of some personal dislike, did not want Austin Graham to buy her property.

Was it possible that Whitney had recently talked to representatives of the Evergreen Corporation and was helping them secure the land? It seemed quite natural that they might seek the services of a prominent, local lawyer.

Lara could have walked across the street to Whitney's office, but she decided instead to call him from the lobby.

Whitney's distinctive voice answered on the first ring. After a few minutes of talking about Karma, she told him about the note and asked him if he were representing the Evergreen Corporation.

"I've had no dealings with them whatsoever. I don't even know who they are. You know, of course, that Austin looked on me as competition, even though I was long ago outbid. He was probably just analyzing his competitors. He struck me as a man who sat up late at night trying to beat out everyone else."

"I would like to know more about this corporation," Lara said. "I've tried to find out about them, but I keep running into dead ends."

"Let me see what I can do," Whitney answered. "I'll pull a few strings and find out everything I can about this Evergreen Corporation." He paused. "If you really think you need to know, that is. Joan tells me they just called a few hours ago and withdrew their bid on the property."

Charles stepped out of the elevator looking even more agitated. "Law enforcement isn't what it used to be," he muttered.

Was he reacting to the tiredness so clearly etched in his face or was he expressing some deep disappointment over Scott?

Charles' mood, like the overhanging clouds, grew heavier and darker throughout the afternoon.

Somber thoughts always brought him back to the subject

of her father. He was talking now about the rift that had separated them.

More to take her mind off Karma than because she wanted to know, she asked, "What caused your disagreement? I never thought dad and you would ever fight."

"Maybe he was sick and I laid too much blame on him," Charles said, "but he started acting as if I were . . . his enemy. He began to shut me out. It was almost as if he didn't trust me." Charles slanted a glance at her, sorrow and worry making tight lines around his eyes and mouth. "You'll never know how much that hurt me, Lara. I know now what they mean when they say the people you care about the most are the ones that hurt you the most."

"I'm so sorry, Charles. You did so much for him. I can't believe he would ever turn against you. Did you try to talk to him?"

"I wasn't smart enough for that. Instead I reacted with anger. I started staying away from him. I shouldn't have, Lara. I did realize how ill he was, but I just couldn't understand or accept the change in him."

Everyone made mistakes, Lara thought, Dad included. He should never have betrayed the solid, wonderful friendship that had existed between the two of them for so many years.

They had made a wide circle and were nearing the house again. "Do you want to rest a while?"

Lara shook her head. "Let's keep looking."

They took the highway to the other side of town from where she lived and searched country roads, mostly to the south of Quachita Springs. Lara maintained constant vigil from the open window, so thick with moisture.

"What I'm hoping," Charles said, "is that Karma was kidnapped for the purpose of frightening you. If that's the case, he may have just dumped her out somewhere. And if we keep on looking, we'll find her."

His words, though not spoken convincingly, filled Lara with hope. For endless miles past tree-covered slopes, Lara kept avid watch. The land became rougher. The canyons, so vast and unpopulated, made finding a lone, little girl seem an impossible task.

For a late supper Charles bought hamburgers at a drive-in, and they continued their vain searching, neither of them willing to give up.

The storm, which had threatened all day, finally broke. Charles passed her house, passed the Last Stop Cafe and turned toward the metal bridge, whose dim outline could barely be seen through the darkness and sheets of rain.

"Damn!" Charles said above the sweep-sweep of wind-shield wipers. "This is all we need!"

Thunder rumbled, followed by torrents of rain that almost blocked visibility. Charles drove cautiously so he would not miss the turn-off to the hotel. "We probably should go home," he said, "at least until this lets up."

"Let's drive around the hotel," Lara answered, "then take the shortcut back to Quachita Springs, across the old wooden bridge and by Crystal's house."

Through the storm-swept night Lara made out the stone building, the towers that rose on either end of the hotel. Here and there a light gleamed from a window, still it looked unoccupied, like some evil, deteriorating structure from out of the works of Edgar Allan Poe.

Charles slowed the car. He had begun to circle the building, but when he saw the narrow road that twisted its way toward the Devil's Stairway, he turned off. Wind whipped at the low, over-hanging branches. Above the pounding of the rain, Lara could hear them scraping against the car.

"Maybe we shouldn't go back here tonight," Lara said.

Charles made no reply. His face had become hard. His wide shoulders were hunched, big hands locked on the wheel, which he guided skillfully through gullies filled with mud and water.

"I hope we don't get stuck back here," Lara said, feeling a rush of fear. They would soon be approaching the very spot where she had found Austin Graham's body, lying so still at the base of the cliff.

Charles stopped the car. Through pouring rain the outline of the cliff loomed over them like a black shadow. Directly above them, rising from the top of the cliff, would be the pinnacle Dane had called the Devil's Stairway. Lara could make out the base of it, but the top was lost in stormy obscurity.

Charles rolled down his window. Rain and wind pelted against him, but he didn't seem aware of it. He glanced around, trying to locate a safe place to leave the road and turn back.

"What was that noise?" Lara asked, sucking in her breath. "Charles, did you hear that sound?"

Charles, wet from the rain, stopped to listen. The noise sounded again—a wavering, pitiful shriek, as if the ghost of Austin Graham had risen and was hovering far above the spot where he had fallen.

Chapter Twenty-two

"The cry is coming from the cliff," Charles said, pointing to the towering rock formation that projected from the flat top of the bluff directly above them.

As he spoke, he began to drive, stepping down hard on the gas to meet the eroded incline that rose straight up, then wound precariously around the steep slope.

Lara held her breath as the car labored upward. From her first sight of it, she had thought the road much too dangerous to drive, even without considering the conditions of night and storm. At first she felt only the impact of tires against stones, but when they reached the first water-washed twist, the tires spun and the car began to slide. Charles expertly swung the wheels away from the drop-off and skidded to a stop at the very edge.

"We can't make it much further," he said, reaching over her to the glove compartment and taking out a flashlight and a small, holstered gun. "I'm going up on foot."

Lara watched the beam from the flashlight diffusing into the pouring rain. She felt a sense of panic as Charles' form, bent against the wind, became more and more faint. She could not just stay here and wait for him. She groped for the door handle, jumped out into the cold, pelting rain, hurried after him.

The road, because Dane and she had walked it before, had about it a familiarity that made her journey easier. Still the blackness and the uncertainty of her footing caused her to slow her steps. She called out to Charles, but he, now far ahead, did not hear. It was as if her voice had blown away from him, echoing into the downward hollows of the valley.

She struggled on, totally drenched, questioning now if

what Charles and she had heard had been only the product of the storm, perhaps the howling of wind through the tree branches.

After a long, tiring climb, Charles' form and the beam of light her eyes had held to for a sense of comfort and direction was abruptly lost to her. The fury of the rain had increased. She could see almost nothing, but knew she had reached the summit of the cliff because the ground beneath her had leveled.

She halted, feeling isolated and afraid, and tried again to locate Charles.

At last with great relief she spotted a flash of light and headed toward it. "Charles!"

The figure halted, turned, playing the light toward her. Even with the lack of visibility she realized the form was too tall, too lean to be Charles. Again she stopped, this time in the grip of fear.

"Lara?"

She recognized the deep voice. Wind gusted around Dane, whipped at his hair and clothes and at the scrubby trees behind him. He lowered the light and drew forward. His arm went around her, as if to shelter her from the angry storm. "I have been covering this entire area looking for Karma!" he said.

"Have you seen Charles?" She caught her breath. "We were down below and heard . . ." Again she had the impression of her words blowing away from him.

"I heard it, too. That's what brought me out here. The crying. It has to be Karma! But where? I haven't been able to find her!"

"I think I know where she is." Charles appeared from behind the high rock turret to join them. Lara hadn't realized how close they were to the towering stones of the Devil's Stairway. Now she could make out the base, slippery, crumbling rocks, wet and streaming with rain. They led upward to a height she could not decipher.

"The kidnapper brought her up here. Somehow she must have gotten away from him!" Charles said, his voice almost a shout. "She has climbed up those rocks!"

Lara thought of Karma's chubby legs and hands, her motions, still immature and awkward. She would be certain to fall . . . to her death! Strength drained from Lara's body. She was grateful that Dane's arm still supported her.

"Karma's up there? What . . ."

Lara's words were cut off by a piercing scream of total terror. It died, then sounded again, louder, filled now more with agony and pain. Was she hurt? Even if she wasn't, how much longer could she hang on?

The thought of Karma clinging to those rocks so far above them prompted Lara to break free of Dane's grasp and rush forward. Dane caught up with her, gripping her shoulders with both hands. "Lara! You can't go up there. It's too dangerous!"

Charles had moved toward the base of the formation, shouting, "Karma! This is Charles. You stay right where you are! You hang on tight, you hear me? I'm coming up after you!"

Dane released Lara and turned to Charles. "I'll go instead," he told him firmly.

Charles, breathing heavily, as if he knew he were too heavy, too out-of-shape for such a task, stepped back in silent consent. His hand clamped Dane's shoulder. "Be careful. I'll be here. When you get close enough, hand her down to me."

Dane gripped jagged stones above him. Lara could see his drenched white shirt, the straining muscles, as he pulled himself upward. "Talk to her, Lara," he called, glancing back down. "Your voice will calm her."

"Karma! Lara is here!"

No answer.

"Karma, can you hear me?" Lara's voice to her own ears sounded futilely small and uncertain. She attempted again and again to project enough volume to rise upward though the wind and rain. She continued yelling until she felt hoarse from the effort.

The storm increased in fury. Lara, momentarily falling silent, watched with bated breath Dane's slow progress. Lara gasped as his foot slid. She was certain he would fall, but Dane skillfully caught his balance and began again the same tedious ascent.

His shape soon became an obscure shadow, which finally blended into darkness and storm. The upward climb with both hands free would be simple compared to the descent with the frightened child in his arms. She began to pray. Please bring Karma back to me. And Dane—she loved them both!

"Karma! Karma, please answer me!"

Once again the wailing sounded, this time less fearful, more of an anguished moan.

The cry would surely help Dane locate her.

"Karma! Dane is going to help you! Charles and I are here waiting for you! You must stay right where you are!"

Charles, face uplifted and wet, said, "I think he's found her! It won't be long now."

Time inched by. The rain Lara had hoped would slacken continued in the same relentless manner.

"Why haven't they returned?" Lara stepped closer to the rising pinnacle of rock.

"Wait. I think I see them." Charles watched intently for some movement from above. Finally, alert and tense, he spoke again, "There!"

Lara caught sight of Dane's legs, the slow, cautious

placement of his feet upon rain-washed stone. He had one hand free, the other tight around Karma's small, clinging body. In the raging storm, they looked so far away, so vulnerable. Lara's heart seemed to stop beating.

Dane stepped uncertainly downward. Once again his free hand lost its solid hold. She saw them slide and heard herself cry out, "Dane! Be careful!"

Dane managed to clutch another outcropping of rock in his path. He found a place to stand. There, he stopped, shifting Karma's weight. He hesitated, as if still unsure of his balance, then began lowering himself again.

Charles climbed upward to meet them. Lara waited at the bottom so the child could be passed from one to the other.

"Hand her down to me, Dane!" Charles called.

Lara could not hear what Dane was saying to Karma, but the child, cooperating, her hand in Dane's, allowed herself to be dangled downward toward Charles.

Charles caught her, slowly easing her on to Lara. Karma looked so pathetic, soaked to the skin, with torn top and wet hair plastered against her head.

"Lara, Lara!"

Lara hugged the little girl close to her, crying from relief and joy.

Soon Dane's arms surrounded them both. From the beam of Charles' flashlight, she could see his face, the wet hair falling across his forehead, the warmth in his eyes. How proud she was of him for risking his own life to save Karma!

The storm had spent its rage; only a light drizzle remained. Gently breaking free from them, Dane said, "I'm going to have a look around." With his flashlight he took a wide swing around the area as if looking for clues the kidnapper might have left behind. He soon vanished from their sight.

Charles stepped closer, said soothingly to Karma,

"There, everything's all right!" Then to Lara, "I'm going to start down now. I imagine you'll want to wait for Dane."

Charles moved down the slope away from them. Lara glanced around, trying to locate Dane, but he still had not reappeared. Now that the rain had cleared, she could see his car half-obscured by the rocks, not far away from the spot where Charles had abandoned his.

Karma remained silent and clinging, her head buried against Lara's shoulder. Lara noticed blood from a scrape on her forehead and becoming anxious, started at once toward the dark outline of Dane's car.

The dead weight of the silent child caused an aching in Lara's arms. She thought ahead of the warmth and comfort waiting for them at home.

Lara opened the car door, which, caught by the wind, broke free of her grasp. Lara started to put Karma inside, but recoiled, jerking Karma back out of the car and holding her in a frenzied grip. The light, which had gone on with the doors' opening, glared down upon an object beside Dane's seat—a crumpled, knit cap. Her eyes traced the ugly outline of two, gaping eyeholes. She shrank back, pressing Karma's face against her so the child would not be able to see what she saw—what Crystal's killer had worn to conceal his identity—lying there so plainly before them—a drenched, dark blue ski-mask!

Chapter Twenty-three

Charles must have sensed her fear for he was beside her immediately. The car light made silvery streaks in his gray hair as he leaned over to inspect the ski mask. His lips compressed and his jaw set in a hard line that remained when he turned to face her. They stared at each other in unspoken horror.

They did not see Dane approach. All of a sudden he materialized from blankets of heavy mist.

Charles reacted by bringing his hand to the butt of the gun concealed beneath his thin jacket.

Dane's eyes locked on the ski mask. "Someone planted it there," he said steadily. The deep, reassuring voice, confident in the face of indictment, had served before to sway her. This time Lara could not believe him.

"That means the kidnapper was on hand while we were trying to rescue Karma," Dane said.

Did he expect them to accept the notion that another car had been up here and had crept back down the cliff without any of them being aware of it?

Charles, his hand remaining on the gun, sounded just as calm as Dane. "How did you get here? You couldn't have taken the same road or we would have seen you."

"I drove up from the other side. The road is rough, but passable."

"Did you see anyone?"

"No, but there are many places a car could turn off into the rocks or trees. Whoever brought Karma up here might have pulled off somewhere when he saw headlights approaching. I could have been very close to another car and not seen it in that blinding rain."

Although Charles' tone failed to reveal his accusations,

his expression remained grim and frozen. Still keeping a hand on the gun and a wary eye on Dane, he wandered to the edge of the road. Lara watched the beam from his flashlight flitting across pools of water, across the graveled slope that Dane had recently traveled.

Would Charles find other tracks? Lara hugged Karma tighter, glad that the rain had stopped. Even though soaked to the skin, Lara realized the child could not have survived out in the open the entire length of time she had been gone. The abductor had been keeping her somewhere, probably at the hotel. The kidnapper had brought Karma up here from the hotel to kill her. That man had to be Dane.

The child must have slipped away from him and in panic climbed up into the rocks to get away from him. Dane had tossed aside his ski mask and chased after her, but Charles and she had interrupted him before he had caught up with her.

Lara found herself staring at Dane. To face her he braved the impact of wind, though he seemed unmindful of it. It swept his hair and fluttered angrily at his clothing. Confusion filled her. A short time ago Dane had inspired in her such honor and love; now she was convinced he himself had kidnapped Karma. If they had not arrived just in time, the precious little girl would be lying dead. By daylight she would have been found, just as Austin Graham had been, sprawled on the ground at the bottom of the cliff.

Lara began to feel anxious and turned again to look for Charles. He was moving back toward them, still flashing the light here and there through the storm-swept darkness. He stepped directly to the open car door, reached in, and carefully lifted the ski mask. "I'll take this in to the sheriff's office," Charles said, and placed it inside his jacket. "You'll be amazed at the evidence they can find on something like this. A stray hair, a bit of saliva, and we've got the man who wore it!"

Again Lara's gaze was drawn to Dane. Charles' words, with their under-current of threat, evoked no change in him.

Lara did not look back as they moved away from Dane. Was he watching them? Would he try to stop them before they reached the car?

Even though the child had grown heavy, Lara declined Charles' offer to carry her. They walked rapidly, slipping and sliding in the mud. Lara was relieved to arrive at Charles' car and to place Karma safely inside.

"Now, to get out of here," Charles said under his breath. He rolled down the window and kept his head out so he could see the sharp drop-off so dangerously close to them. The car inched backward. He stopped several times to straighten the wheels, pull forward, and edge back again. The tenseness left him a little when they were back in the picnic area and driving toward the hotel.

"Where have you been, Karma?" Charles asked gently.

Karma said nothing, just drew closer to Lara. "Maybe we shouldn't try to talk to her tonight."

Charles paid no attention. "Karma, listen to me. Do you know who took you away, who pulled you into his car?"

"No," the little girl's voice was weak and distant. "He . . ." She covered her face with her hands. "He . . . I couldn't see him."

"Why not?"

"He put something over my head."

"Where did he take you?"

"To a room!" Karma wailed. "It smelled funny. He left the water running." Karma leaned limply against Lara, sobbing. "I want to go home!"

"It's all over now Karma," Lara said, protectively drawing her closer. "He can't hurt you. Soon we will be home with Joan and Spot. Everyone's missed you so."

"It's not a good idea to take her back to the house,"

Charles advised. "Let's take her to my place tonight instead. We'll call the sheriff from there. It's not so easy to get into my security apartment," Charles added.

"Maybe that would be best," Lara agreed wearily. "I should have listened before. If I would have protected her better, this would never have happened."

"No one can get into my high-rise without being admitted by the doorman. Not unless they can fly. It's safer than Fort Knox." He turned his gaze toward Lara, saying, "In fact, I think you should both stay with me until this madman is captured."

The rain started again as they crossed the metal bridge. Charles leaned forward in his seat. Rain streamed across the windshield so forcefully the wipers did little good. A semi-truck had pulled off the highway to wait out the storm. Charles kept going.

"Do you think Dane will be arrested?"

A silence followed. "It depends on what they find on the mask." When Charles glanced at her, he frowned as if he were perplexed or in doubt. "Lara, I found several sets of tracks on the road. And some clear ones in the mud cutting back into those trees along the east side."

"If Scott gets out there soon enough," Lara said hopefully, "maybe he can take impressions of the tracks."

"In a little while with this flooding downpour there will be no tracks," Charles said.

"But you saw them."

He gave a weary sigh. "That's what I'll testify to, if it comes to that."

"Then you believe Dane may have been telling the truth?" Lara asked hopefully.

"I don't know, but I think it's possible someone else besides Dane was up there tonight." She could see, by the reflection of the headlights, the deep, heavy lines that cut between Charles' eyes. "In fact, I'm beginning to suspect the man may have been railroaded before, and someone is trying to do the same thing to him again."

Charles had tried his hardest to persuade Lara to remain with Karma in the security apartment, but in the end, after bringing Karma's clothes over and seeing her safely asleep, Lara went back to stay with Joan.

She was awakened early by the sound of the doorbell. Pulling on a robe, she quickly went downstairs, pausing to look out the window at the sheriff's car in her driveway. The moment she unbolted the door, Scott pushed his way into the room.

"I've been up all night," he said gruffly. "I personally bounced the lab man out of bed and stayed with him for the findings on that ski mask."

"What were they?"

"No hair, no saliva, nothing we can use as evidence." Scott looked frustrated. "And now Charles is telling me he's going to throw a monkey-wrench into my case with those damned tire tracks he thinks he saw."

"Charles will tell the truth as he sees it."

"Or as he wants to see it. Even if it means letting a murderer slip right though our fingers. Even if it means more deaths! God!" Scott sank down on the recliner. "Some people have a damned strange sense of ethics."

"Someone could have tossed that ski-mask into Dane's car. It may not have even been the same one the killer wore."

"There you go again. What does it take to convince you?" Scott ran a hand through his rumpled hair. "How the hell am I ever going to protect you, Lara?"

Lara turned away. At the same time Scott rose. She could feel his presence close beside her, yet he made no attempt to touch her or to take her in his arms.

"You're getting to be all I think about," he said.

She might have even grown a little fond of him, she decided, as she turned and looked squarely into his eyes. Fond, but nothing more. She didn't want him to go on speaking of his feelings for her, but she could tell by the determined narrowness of his gaze that he intended to do so.

"You know, the election is coming up, and I've been thinking seriously about not running again for sheriff."

"I never thought you would want to give up your job," Lara responded. Trying to switch the subject away from what she knew he had in mind, she asked, "What other type of work interests you?"

"Who's talking about work?" he grinned. "I've saved a bit of money. I could go back to New York City with you."

"I may never go back there."

"Then, hell, we could pull up stakes and just travel." His smile widened and totally erased his look of tiredness. "We could take a trip around the world. Who knows? Maybe more than one! Lara, take me seriously. Please!"

"Even if I did want to go," Lara said thoughtfully, "I couldn't. Karma will soon be in school."

"We could put her in boarding school somewhere until we got back." Scott paused again. "I am doing my best to try to propose to you, Lara. Would you like me to get on my knees?"

"I'm not in love with you, Scott."

Her announcement did not seem to hurt him. He shrugged. "I'll settle for that. And I'm willing to raise Karma. As long as we have children of our own. What more can you expect?"

Even if she had considered Scott's offer, he made it so clear to her that he didn't really love Karma, or even want her around. What else could she expect? Perhaps his question had been well put. She knew in her heart she had always expected way too much of him. Falling in love, like seeking justice, might indeed take time.

Chapter Twenty-four

Lara gazed down at the sleeping child. She reached out to touch Karma's forehead, relieved to find her skin cool. Gratefully she detected no sign of fever from the time she had spent out in the chilling rain.

Lara smoothed the disarray of black hair. The small form cuddled around the stuffed bear looked so innocent and so vulnerable. Their safety seemed only a temporary reprieve, a strange eerie quietness forewarning some final disaster.

For the first time Lara was willing to abandon her search for Mark's killer and flee with Karma from Quachita Springs. But as Charles had reminded her last night, that action might serve only to make them a more open target.

Her only hope lay with the hypnotherapist. Dr. Adler had arrived in town and Charles had already contacted him. If the doctor was successful, then what Karma told him might lead them directly to the murderer. To Lara, it seemed an overwhelming impossibility.

Her gaze returned to Karma, whose dark eyes, fully open now, lit when they met hers. "Lara, can we go home?"

Pangs of helpless anguish gripped Lara. Home to the child had become Lara's late father's big, sprawling house, the cheery room that Lara had decorated especially for her.

"You must stay here with Charles for a while," she answered hesitantly.

"Why, Lara? I want to go with you!"

Lara waited by Karma's bed until the child drifted off to sleep again, then she returned to the living room looking for Charles. The room, so neat it seemed barely lived in, was furnished with only simple necessities. A faded Afghan and white, crocheted dust covers, no doubt crafted by his wife, made up the only homey touches. On a stand beside the television set a smiling picture of the long dead Alice. How lonely, she thought, how bare and lonely.

The image of loneliness intensified when she found Charles seated at the kitchen table. He wore a faded brown robe and sat before an open newspaper that he gloomily disregarded. When he looked up, Lara noticed the lines of weariness in his face.

"I've spoken with Dr. Adler again," Charles said. "He has appointments with several people while he's here, so I told him he was welcome to use the vacant office next to ours."

"Fine," Lara said sinking down into the chair across from him.

"I talked him into moving his appointment with Karma to today, right before dinner—11:30."

"Good."

Charles ran his fingers though rumpled gray hair. "All the investigating we've done and we still don't have a solid clue. Everything hinges on what Karma is able to tell us."

"Did Karma tell you anything last night?"

"Donna and I had quite a time with her. She kept waking up. She kept muttering about being in a dark room with the water running."

In Charles' gray eyes tiredness mingled with pain. "From what I could gather Karma was kept bound and blindfolded until she was taken to the cliff, and then the kidnapper wore that ski mask. I'm afraid that's all the doctor is going to get out of her."

"Unless she can give information about where she was held."

"It could have been . . . in a basement, maybe. If Karma actually heard running water and it wasn't just in a dream, she could have been close to some sewer or water line." He continued as if he were just exploring possibilities without any hope of an answer. "Or she might have mistaken the sound of water for other noises, like the gurgling of an old furnace or hot water heater."

Charles slow-spoken words caused an image to spring to Lara's mind of the huge, partially renovated hotel. Could Karma have been hidden somewhere in those vast rooms and finally led out to the cliffs to meet her death?

The image began to merge with the rain-soaked ski mask in Dane's car.

The quiet of the room was jarred by the loud sound of a buzzer.

"Who could that be this early?" Charles said, getting heavily to his feet.

She could see Charles though the huge, arched opening that separated the kitchen from the living room. He pressed a button. "Yes."

Lara recognized Dane's deep voice on the intercom and drew in her breath.

"Is Lara there? I need to talk to her."

Charles, frowning, glanced toward her. "It's Lanford. Do you want to see him?"

Lara's throat tightened. Her voice sounded strained as she answered, "We should probably see what he wants. Do I need to go downstairs and let him in?"

"It's all computerized. Through the security guard at the entrance." Charles pressed another button. "It's, OK, Jack. Have him sign in and come on up."

From deep inside a hope revived: Karma's kidnapper had not been Dane. Charles had found other car tracks on the cliff. The killer, who Dane must have accidentally come across while he was searching for Karma, had intended to dispose of Karma in the same way he had killed Austin Graham. The killer wanted her body to be found near the hotel to make Dane look guilty. Then he had tossed the ski mask in Dane's car, convinced that this act would frame Dane, just as he had successfully done in the past.

Even though Charles tended to believe this, it was a dangerous theory to accept. She felt a thudding in her heart.

When Charles opened the door and Lara glimpsed Dane's tall form, the lingering picture of the ski mask became replaced with the image of Dane clinging to Karma as he made slow, treacherous descent down rain-drenched rocks.

Dane stepped inside. Trust and distrust alternated in crazy patterns as her eyes remained locked on him. His features, like Charles', were taut and strained.

"How's Karma?" His dark eyes, as concerned as if the child were his own, regarded Lara.

Waves of fear and alarm receded, replaced momentarily by a strong sense of trust. "She's sleeping," Lara answered. "She's all right."

At that very moment a long, plaintive cry came from the upstairs bedroom.

"Karma did that all last night," Charles said, starting toward the stairway. "I'll just go on up."

Lara watched Charles' broad back, clad in worn robe, disappear into a door at the top of the stairway. She started to follow him, but Dane's voice stopped her.

"There's something I've found, Lara. Something you need to see."

Dane reached into the breast pocket of his white shirt and extended a paper. He had drawn forward to stand close beside her, and his closeness made her uneasy. Lara began to carefully unfold the sheet of beige stationary, for it was fragile and deeply creased.

"I found this in one of Mark's art books. This may come as quite a surprise to you. It did to me."

Lara gazed down at the flowing handwriting knowing, as she did, that it was written by Crystal, or at least by someone who could expertly copy her writing.

Dear Mark,

Maybe I was wrong not to tell you about the baby. But I know how you have always felt about marriage, and not wanting to be tied down. And of course I've always felt the same. I believed that both of us were meant to be free, to live for our art's sake alone. I wanted our love to remain like that beautiful place in "The Healing Water", secret and unspoiled. That is why I chose not to intrude in your life, but to keep Karma's birth a secret. But now I realize I was being unfair to you for when I look at that lovely child of ours, I know that she is our best creation.

All my love,

Crystal

"Karma . . ." Lara gasped. "Mark's child!"

She gazed up at Dane. His dark eyes glowed warmly.

"Crystal had a valid reason to name you as guardian," he said gently. "Now that Mark's gone, Karma really does belong to you."

"I should have guessed."

"I'm the one who should have known, but I didn't. I never even knew the two of them had been acquainted then. Mark had graduated and left Little Rock before Karma was born."

As the reality of the revelation began to reach her, Lara

wiped at her eyes. Karma was Mark's daughter! In his daughter Lara would always have a part of him to love and cherish.

Dane was watching her intently, and she felt a sudden need to explain to him. "Our parents had such an unhappy marriage. Their divorce hurt both of us so much, Mark vowed he'd never make the same mistake. But Crystal should have told Mark from the beginning. He would never have rejected the child and he would have made such a wonderful father

"After Mark found out," Dane said, "he probably pressed for marriage. No doubt they would have married if he had lived."

"I wonder why Crystal didn't confide in me that Karma is my niece?"

"She may have intended to . . . eventually. I imagine the guardianship was a safety measure in case something happened to her. She knew she was in serious trouble. Which leads us to this." Dane drew the photos of the death car Lara had given him from his jacket pocket and handed them to her. "These prove that Crystal was blackmailing Mark's killer. I believe it was her way of revenging Mark's death, tormenting the killer, getting money from him to secure Karma's future, before she turned him in."

"Were you able to find anything out about the photos?"

Dane shook his head. "I showed them to Jim and Hallie. Hallie thinks it is the same car she saw, but neither of them could identify the place where the pictures were taken."

He placed the photos on the coffee table.

Lara reread the letter, taking note of Crystal's reference to the "The Healing Water". Lara recalled how the backing of that painting had seemed disturbed. She suspected Mark had once kept the letter from Crystal there and had removed it when he had decided to sell all of his paintings.

"Did you know, Dane, that the hot spring in Mark's

painting, "The Healing Water," really does exist?"

"Exists," Dane said, "where?"

"On the hotel property. It is well hidden within the caves. Because our family has privately owned the land for many years, no one has ever found it. Mark must have discovered it by accident when he was looking for a setting for his painting."

Lara watched Dane for some reaction. His features remained immobile, unchanged. If Mark had known, it made sense that Dane would also know about the hot spring. She couldn't even be sure that this letter she was holding was authentic. It could have been easily manufactured by Dane to remove her suspicions of him, to restore her faith in him, faith that had suffered a severe blow at the sight of the ski mask.

"I've walked all over that land," Dane was saying with disbelief.

Lara explained to him the exact location of the spring and how she had found it because of the unusual boulder in Mark's painting.

"I've passed by that very place," Dane said. "So that solves yet another mystery—why Austin Graham was killed. Either someone had told him about it or he had snooped around the area and found it himself."

"Do you think Crystal could have told him?"

"That's not likely," Dane answered promptly. "She was a private person, who confided in few people." He paused. "The hot spring must have been a very special place to them. Of course, Mark would have realized its great commercial value. But it would have been like him to want it to remain natural and undisturbed."

"But someone else must have known about it," Lara insisted. "Whoever killed Austin Graham."

"Who else was interested in the property?"

She thought of Dane and his loyal followers, Jim and Hallie, but said, "The Evergreen Corporation was trying to outbid Austin on the land." Then, she hastily added, "But if purchasing the land because of the spring was behind all this, why would the corporation have all of a sudden canceled their bid just after Austin's death?"

"Who heads this corporation?"

"I don't know. Joan has never talked to any of the representatives in person."

"I'm going to find out all I can about this mysterious corporation," Dane spoke with determination.

His words sparked a wary note in Lara's mind. "I'll get you some numbers to call. But, Dane, be careful! That is what Austin was trying to do before he was killed."

"So Karma is Mark's child. I never once suspected . . . and yet it all seems to fit, doesn't it?" Charles returned the letter to Lara, then lifted the photos of the damaged car and gave them careful scrutiny. "Why didn't you show these to me, Lara?"

She didn't answer.

"Has Scott seen these?" he asked finally.

"No."

Her directness seemed to exasperate him. "That's where people go wrong, not trusting the officers in charge. If people would only come forward and tell what they know . . ." He seemed very disappointed in her.

"I thought I could find out on my own."

"No, Lara, you can't. And even if you could, you'd be a fool to play solo. You must take this evidence to Scott immediately." Charles' voice sharpened in an unfamiliar way. "You just can't withhold important information. I'm not going to let you do that."

"That never was my intention," she said in weak reply.

"Then give him these photographs right away. At once!"

Lara wavered. She had always taken such stock in Charles' opinions. And right now she couldn't afford to make any more mistakes. Anyway so many people already knew about the photos that sharing the information with Scott could do no harm.

She should tell Charles and Scott everything, even about the hot spring. She remained silent for a while longer, still undecided.

Charles checked his watch. "You can take these over to Scott now. You have plenty of time before Karma's appointment."

Photos in hand, Lara left the high-rise apartment complex. Once outside she looked up to locate Charles' window and saw him standing, drapes pulled back, watching her.

The sky, overcast and heavy, added to her reluctance to face Scott Tyler and his inevitable questions about why she hadn't come to him with the photos in the first place. She stopped at the sheriff's office, but found only the deputy, Tom.

"I haven't seen Scott since early morning. He was up all night so guess he went back home. Is there anything I can do for you?"

"No, I must talk to him in person."

After following the blacktop out of town for several miles, she found the turn-off and from it soon pulled into the weed-tangled driveway. The yellow Mustang, hood up, rested in front of Scott's house, but the vehicle marked Quachita County Sheriff was nowhere in sight. Doubting that he was home, she left the car and knocked at the door.

The sound rang hollowly within. She felt a sense of relief to find Scott gone. She shouldn't have allowed Charles to pressure her. She needed more time to sort out her thoughts.

Lara checked her watch. The stop at the sheriff's office had delayed her. She had no time to locate Scott before Karma's appointment, so this task would have to wait. She started back to her car and stood facing the huge shed that set a short distance from Scott's cabin.

Even though the roof was flat, it reminded her of a converted barn, with aged, unpainted boards and makeshift garage doors, left carelessly half-raised.

Perhaps Scott was inside. She called to him as she drew closer. She tugged at the frayed rope and the door creaked further upward. She could hear plainly the sound of a radio playing, but her second call elicited no answer.

Daylight filtered from gaps in the roof and in places the dirt floor was moist from the recent rains. She entered cautiously, bypassing mud and stacks of old car parts. Along the wall on pegs hung an assortment of keys; shelves beneath were cluttered with tools. She passed an old Ford, which set on rims, an ancient red truck that looked long past restoration, a motorcycle minus a back wheel. Propped on the motorcycle seat she found a battered radio blaring country music.

Lara switched it off. Silence settled around her, as heavy and thick as the grease and oil that covered everything.

"Scott!" This time she knew no one would answer. A sense of total aloneness caused a tightening of the muscles in her body. She had an urge to flee from the dim shed toward her car, toward the activity of Quachita Springs.

She steadied herself and continued walking toward the back of the shed, where yet another vehicle loomed, partially covered by an age-darkened canvas. She was surprised by the weight of the recently wet canvas as she worked to draw it back.

Lara gasped at the sight of three, small, round taillights. For a moment shock immobilized her. She quickly uncovered the entire car, a dark blue Impala Chevy, perhaps a 1965 model—the exact image of the car in the photographs she carried.

Scott must be insane! He had kept the car he had used to run down Mark! Maybe it wasn't insanity, but cleverness. After all, he was the investigating officer—the only description of the vehicle had been the vague one Hallie had given and even that had been deleted from the sheriff's report.

She examined the front of the car, but could detect no visible signs of bodywork. She was convinced, nevertheless, that Scott had repaired this car himself.

But why had Scott Tyler killed Mark?

With trembling fingers Lara carefully replaced the canvas and raced toward her car. Thoughts swirled madly in her mind. Why had Scott killed Mark? Animosity because of a common girl friend, Crystal? A business deal gone sour? Or had it actually been an accident?

Lara sped toward town. Charles wouldn't think of arriving at an appointment late. He and Karma would be preparing now to leave for the meeting with Dr. Adler. She must call Charles and tell him she would meet them there.

Lara swung her car to a stop beside a phone booth at the quick-shop. She tried to calm herself, to think clearly and logically. The vehicle she had found in Scott's shed might not be the same car, she tried to tell herself. Collecting old cars was Scott's hobby. He had avoided mentioning to her that he had owned an old Chevy like Hallie had described for fear she would jump to conclusions, exactly the way she was doing now.

She drew the photographs from her purse and studied them intently. The car was identical to the one she had found, but the pictures had not been taken in Scott's shed. The photos revealed a modern garage with high windows and with that dark, barely discernible object that looked like a wood-burning stove. Scott's shed had no windows and no stoves.

Lara quickly dialed Charles' number. She made an effort to keep the edge of panic from her voice. "Charles?"

"Lara. You just missed Scott!"

Lara's heart sank at the sound of Scott's name. She must not blurt out to Charles what she had just found. It would be better not to alarm him, but to talk to Scott first and make certain she was right about the car. "Where did he go? I must talk to him right away. Could you take Karma to her appointment? I will meet you as soon as I can."

"She's on her way there now," Charles answered cheerfully. "It was getting so late, I let Scott take Karma with him."

Lara could hear a pounding in her ears, like the roar of the ocean through a seashell. "You mean Karma left with Scott?"

"I know I promised to take her," Charles said, sounding amused. "But with the sheriff for an escort, I figured she couldn't be much safer."

Chapter Twenty-five

It was happening again—that scary thing that was almost a dream. No! Karma fought against the swirls of images that surged through her brain, trying to push them back into darkness. But this time they wouldn't go away.

She was back there again, staring through the screen door. And she could see Mommy, lying so still, her long hair wet with blood. A shadowy figure bent over her, the one Karma had seen so many times in her nightmares. But this time was different. This time she watched in horror as the head slowly lifted. The darkness was ripped away and she clearly saw a face.

That face!

The Lion smiled and reached out a hand to her, pulling her inside with him.

A scream rose thick in Karma's throat, remained frozen just as it had that night as the elevator door slammed shut behind them.

Karma felt a sinking feeling in the pit of her stomach. This was no dream. It was real. She was trapped inside with the Lion all alone.

Lara rushed to the spare office that Dr. Adler had taken for the session with Karma. As she hurried down the corridor, she prayed desperately that she would find the child waiting safely within.

The psychiatrist, a tall, lank man with a full, black beard, gazed from the window as if he had been waiting a very long time. He turned with an expectant smile. "You must be Lara Radburn," he said. "Where is the child?"

Lara's greatest fear became a reality: Scott had not delivered Karma to her appointment. Icy fingers clutched at her heart. "Scott Tyler was supposed to have brought her here at eleven -thirty."

"I was about twenty-minutes late getting here today," Dr. Adler responded with an apologetic smile. "I was detained at the hotel by an unexpected call. Perhaps they have come and gone. I tried to call Mr. Cade a while ago, but there was no answer."

Why hadn't Lara told Charles her suspicions about Scott Tyler? She needed Charles here with her now.

Dr. Adler studied her a moment then reached for the phone and dialed again. "Still no answer," he said finally, looking puzzled. "Do you think there may have been some misunderstanding about the time?"

A panicky feeling swept over Lara. "Will you keep trying to reach Charles?" She backed toward the door, her eyes still holding to Dr. Adler's face, now tense with worry. "I'm going to look for them."

Outside the office her gaze fell to the door marked, "Whitney Jordan, Attorney at Law". Not bothering to knock, she turned the knob and found Whitney's office solidly locked.

Where could Whitney be?

Where was Charles? Perhaps he was driving down here now. Poor Charles. How confidently he had turned Karma over to Mark's killer.

She passed the stairwell to the elevator. Crystal had been blackmailing Scott and he had killed her to avoid exposure. Now, afraid that Karma under hypnosis would be able to identify him, he was going to kill her, too! It had been Scott who had ripped the paintings, written the threatening note across her car window, kidnapped Karma and let her go—all to frighten Lara into taking Karma and leaving town. He had given Lara every chance to save the child, chances Lara had not heeded. Now it was too late.

Where had Scott taken her?

In contrast to the quiet upper floor, the lower level was a bustle of noon-hour confusion. Lara peered anxiously through the glass window of Gino's, seeing only unfamiliar faces. A memory of Scott indulging Karma in an ice cream sundae flashed momentarily through her mind. Could it all have been a pretense? Was Scott really evil enough to be willing to kill a helpless child?

Fighting back tears, Lara turned toward Joan's office. Joan, sitting at her desk, flipped through a mail-order fashion catalog. "Do you think I'd look good in this?" she asked, holding up a picture of a svelte model in red-sequined dress.

"Joan, have you seen Scott and Karma? The psychiatrist is here and Karma is late for her appointment."

The urgency in Lara's voice made Joan place the catalog down, the sequined evening dress forgotten. "They were in Gino's earlier. In fact, Scott was looking for you. Whitney and I were having an early lunch when they came in," she explained. "I remember Scott was complaining about that shrink not showing up on time."

"Did they leave the building? Do you know where they went?"

Joan shook her head. "I couldn't stay. Whit and I had just gotten our orders when guess who else comes in? Nancy! Made me so nervous I couldn't eat a bite. Just sits there smiling that jealous smile of hers and shooting daggers at me with her eyes. Can you believe it? The way she acts you'd think Whit and I were having an affair or something. Well, anyway, I made my excuses and slipped out."

"Then the Jordans were the last ones to see Scott and Karma?"

"You know how impatient Scott is. He kept saying he had business to see to. He might have left Karma with

Whit and Nancy. Did you check Whitney's office?"

"I just came from there. It's locked." Lara failed to keep the rising panic from her voice. "Joan, we've got to find Karma!"

Joan rose from the chair. Her face had grown pale, her eyes wide and frightened, as if she were remembering the afternoon when Karma had disappeared from the house. "Oh, God. It's happening again, isn't it? Someone's taken her!"

"Please, Joan. Help me. See if they are anywhere in the building. I'm going to drive out to Whitney's house."

Lara drove, fingers tense on the wheel, toward the north side of town where the Jordans lived. Through a haze of fear, she thought about what Joan had told her. If Scott had intended to abduct Karma, it didn't make sense that he would have shown up at the office complex and looked for the psychiatrist.

Was it possible that Scott had, as Joan suggested, left the child with the Jordans? But if that were the case, then why hadn't one of them brought her in time for the appointment? Her need to find answers to her questions, to be certain about Karma's safety, made Lara press her foot down harder upon the accelerator.

Whitney's house was on a wooded knoll near the country club. Lara turned off into a well-kept drive lined with impressive, executive-style homes. Lara had been past Whitney's house enough times to easily recognize the sprawling Spanish-style home with its glowing white walls and red-tiled roof at the very crest of the hill.

No car was parked in the circular driveway. Lara hurried to the arched doorway and rang the bell. The sun had come out and the air was hot and sultry. Summer flowers in pots upon the patio looked faded and dusty in the late August sun. Lara rang the bell again. A tinkling sound once more chimed from within, remained unanswered. Yet as she stood there, she got the eerie sensation that someone was inside.

Lara moved along the terraced walkway to the double garage in back of the house. As she peered through one of the small, high windows, the red Toyota parked within gave away the fact that someone was home. Since Whitney drove a dark Cadillac, the car must belong to Nancy. Was she hiding within the house, refusing to answer the door?

Lara started to step away, when a vague feeling of recognition made her turn back and stare once more through one of the garage windows. In the far corner of the garage was a kiln for making pottery. Lara gaped at it, momentarily stunned. She was staring at the same dark shape that had appeared in the photos she had found in Crystal's house!

Lara's gaze moved from the dark kiln to the three high, square-shaped windows. Suddenly, she knew without a doubt that Crystal had taken the photos from the very same spot where she was now standing. The night of Mark's death, the hit-and-run car that had killed him had set in the exact place the red Toyota now occupied.

The sharp banging of a door made Lara whirl around. Nancy Jordan's high voice, becoming shriller as she quickly approached, demanded, "What are you doing? You have no business back here."

"I'm looking for Whitney."

Nancy had dressed up, no doubt because she had intended to surprise her husband and meet him for dinner. The shapeless gray dress accentuated her thin arms and gaunt face, making her look pathetic rather than attractive. Strands of limp, brown hair dangled down across her high, pale forehead.

"Do you know where Whitney is?"

Her lips were moist and quivered a little. "He's not here."

Lara's other questions died in her throat. Her eyes remained fixed on Nancy's lips—the same brilliant shade of red as the lipstick that had slashed the warning note across the windshield of her car.

Chapter Twenty-six

"I'm looking for Karma." Lara tried to keep her voice calm as she explained, "Joan said she might be with you or your husband."

"I don't know where she is." Nancy clasped her hands together nervously. "She was still in Gino's when I left."

"With Whitney?"

Lara's eyes once again drew to Nancy's lips. The artificial redness seemed to have faded slightly. The lipstick—was it an exact match or just a similar shade? "Scott was there, too," Nancy said. They were talking about the psychiatrist."

"Karma never arrived at her appointment. Nancy, if you know anything at all, you must tell me."

Nan's eyes widened. A frightened, bewildered look crossed her face. "I told you I don't know where she is. I can't help you." With these final words, Nancy whirled back through the doorway and disappeared into the house.

Lara heard the click of a lock and knew she would never be able to persuade Nancy to open the door. Still, Lara sensed that Nancy had been telling the truth. Karma was not with her.

Lara's desperate gaze shifted back to the garage that had once hidden the old Chevy that had struck down Mark. She was convinced it was neither of the Jordans she had to fear.

The car that had run down her brother belonged to Scott. It made sense that it had been in the Jordan's garage because Scott had told them that he had accidentally killed her brother and had turned to them for help. One, or possibly both of them, had been protecting him, had helped Scott make arrangements to get the car repaired and cover up his crime.

A chill, dark terror encompassed Lara as she staggered

back to her car. She knew Mark's death was no accident. Why hadn't she told Charles her suspicions of Scott when she had the chance? Where was Charles now? At this very moment Karma was in the hands of an enemy posing as friend, a madman, a killer. She had no clue to where Karma had been taken.

Shaken, Lara turned the car toward the hotel . . . and Dane. How could she have ever believed that he had been involved? She should have suspected the night of Crystal's murder that Scott was behind this.

The hills and river passed by her in a rapid blur as Lara sped past the old iron bridge and turned down the dirt road. Lara understood now that Crystal had called Dane out that evening because she had become frightened. She must have intended to tell Dane everything, but he had arrived too late.

Would she be too late to save Karma?

A dark room. Water running. Karma's vague description of where she had been held, probably blindfolded, when she was last kidnapped echoed in Lara's brain. He had gotten by with it once, had he taken her to that very same place again?

Thoughts swirled in her fear-gripped mind. It all began to make sense now. The tire tracks Charles had seen— Scott must have hidden Karma somewhere near the hotel the night of the rainstorm. Under the cover of the rain he had released her and planted the ski mask to make Dane look guilty, just as he had framed Dane by placing the stolen paintings in the back of his car.

Lara swerved to avoid a curve she had come dangerously close to missing. She drove instinctively, for her panic-stricken thoughts made it impossible to concentrate upon the sharp turns and twists of the road.

Mark's death was connected in some way to Radburn Investments . . . and the Evergreen Corporation. She was certain of that. Those who knew most about her father's business, she had always trusted—Charles, Joan, and of course Whitney Jordan. But would Scott have been close enough to her father to have known about his business investments? No. Not unless someone had been working with him.

Lara's fingers tightened around the steering wheel. The missing money in her father's business accounts pointed to the fact that her father had been robbed, taken advantage of during his long, final illness.

The contract for the city property entered her mind. And suddenly, she realized exactly what Mark had found out.

Someone, under the guise of the Evergreen Corporation, had cheated her father out of the valuable land. Property Dad had never intended to sell.

Lara approached the turn-off. Like a haven of safety the ancient hotel loomed just ahead of her. She longed desperately for Dane's strength, for his calmness. Lara started to turn down the winding drive when a sudden thought made her slam on the brakes. The same mysterious buyer whose name appeared on the contract for her father's city property had also made an offer on the hotel. That was what this was all about.

Whether Scott was working alone, or with someone, whoever was behind the Evergreen Corporation knew about the hot spring on this land.

Then the sound of running water Karma had heard had been the constant gurgle of the spring. All the time Karma had been missing she had been hidden within the cave.

Lara had not a moment to lose. If she were right, she would find Karma in the most isolated place imaginable . . . a cave no one knew about. Last time the child had been taken only to frighten Lara. This time her life was at stake! Without hesitation Lara passed the turn-off to the hotel and sped toward the cliffs.

Her mind whirled as quickly as the wheels of her car, fitting together all of the scattered clues. Finally, she knew beyond doubt exactly who had murdered Mark.

Before leaving the car, Lara unlocked the glove box and slipped Charles' gun into her pocket. Following the course of the stream, she raced blindly in the direction of the cave.

When Lara reached the towering mass of stone below which she and Karma had hiked, she began a rugged descent, not stopping until she reached the flat plateau of limestone.

Breathlessly she gazed downward. Just below her was the overhanging shelf of rock that Mark had used for a model for "The Healing Water". Lara tensed. The entrance to the cave had been disturbed. Chunks of limestone had been set aside, exposing a narrow, gaping hole. Although she had not seen another car anywhere on the bluff, she knew without a doubt that someone was within.

Lara dropped down the rocks to the cave's entrance. Darkness immediately enveloped her as she slipped through the narrow opening. A chill crept down her spine as she felt her way along clammy rock until her eyes gradually adjusted to the dimness.

The light grew even fainter. The passage curved snake-like to the right and then to the left, sloping sharply downward as Lara wound further and further into the heart of the cave. She was aware of a deathly stillness all around her.

The solid, massive walls of stone grew tighter, seemed to be closing in on her as Lara entered the narrowest part of the cave.

Cries . . . were they sobs of fear or pain . . . echoed through the eerie stillness toward her. Lara felt her throat close up, an unbearable tightness in her chest. Karma!

She felt a jolt of pain as her knee struck a sharp, protruding rock. Impeded by the closeness of the surrounding stone, she made slow and agonizing progress as she crept toward the heart-wrenching sound.

At the end of the passage, the darkness slightly lifted. The air felt warmer here, heavy, thick with the burning match-smell of sulfur. From just beyond she could hear the faint sound of running water from the still-hidden spring.

The cries sounded again, closer this time. Fingers tense upon the gun, Lara crouched to her knees and peered warily into the large chamber where Karma and she had found Spot the day he had leapt on ahead of them. Would the killer still be in the cave with the child? Lara glanced down at the gun in her trembling hand and prayed that, if necessary, she would have the strength to use it.

The trapped, steaming mist made everything surreal, hazy. Huge rock formations thrust up from the cavern floor, obstructing her vision.

And then she saw her. Karma, arms and legs bound with rope, huddled back against an outcropping of rock, perilously close to the hot, bubbling pool.

Lara's heart cried out to the frightened child. She fought against a desire to rush forward and cradle her in her arms. Instead, she forced herself to remain still and silent.

For what seemed an eternity, she waited. No sound but Karma's wrenching sobs, the hissing of steam, the steady gurgling of water.

Was Karma alone? Had she simply been left down here to die, where no one would ever hear her cries for help? Unable to bear the sobbing any longer, Lara inched cautiously forward, shrinking back against the shelter of stone, toward Karma.

The moment she left the passage, a shadow sprang out at her. She did not even have time to react before the gun was wrenched from her hand. However stealthily she had entered, she had somehow alerted the killer to her approach. He had been lying in wait for her, pressed flat against the rock wall near the entrance to the chamber.

"Whitney!"

In one quick, cat-like movement Whitney aimed the gun at her. "Get over there," he ordered, his voice coldly professional. "By the girl."

Lara took faltering steps toward the frightened child that she had intended to save. Karma looked up at her with wide, pleading eyes. But she was powerless to comfort her. Now, they were both at the mercy of this stranger who had once masqueraded as friend.

Even though she had figured out Whitney must be involved, she still felt the impact of his betrayal. Bewilderment mingled with chilling disbelief, the shock of deception. Whitney looked the same as he always had. The neat suit, the polished leather shoes. Only the deep blue eyes seemed different . . . cold, glittering, narrowed.

Lara's lips formed the question, "Why?"

A muscle worked in his jaw as he moved toward her, away from the emerald pool that formed a misty background directly behind them. Lara instinctively recoiled from him, until she could feel the cool dampness of stone against her back. "I had no choice. Mark found out about the contract I had forged on your father's city property."

"Property that was sold to the Evergreen Corporation."

Whitney nodded soberly. Lara was appalled by the greed so clearly evident in his hawk-like features. Her father had trusted him, this friend. She thought with horror of the many times she herself had leaned on him, as her father must have done, seeking out his solid logic and advice. It seemed Lara had thought of Whitney her entire life as supporter and confidant. And yet she had never really known him.

"When Mark was at his office one night, I fixed his car so it wouldn't make the complete drive to the hotel. I borrowed one of Scott's spare cars from the shed while he was still on duty." A faint smile crossed his lips. "Convenient of him to leave his keys lying about. I had the car repaired and returned before he ever knew it was missing. A murder committed with the sheriff's own car. The perfect crime."

Scott, then, had never been involved in Whitney's plot. Whitney, alone, was responsible for all that had happened.

"I hadn't considered that Mark might have told someone about his suspicions. When Crystal heard of the accident, she knew Mark had been murdered and the same night photographed the car in my garage. I soon got the phone calls demanding money for her silence."

Crystal was the woman who had been calling first Mark at the office, and later Whitney. "At the time you cheated my father out of the city property you must not have known about this spring."

"I didn't find out about it until recently. I only made an offer on the old hotel to encourage you to leave town." He gave a hollow laugh. "When Austin Graham bid on the land, I knew it must be worth far more than I had imagined. It turned out I had passed up the best deal of all."

"You killed Austin after he discovered the spring."

"And because he had found out the truth . . . that I am the sole member of the Evergreen Corporation." As he spoke, Whitney paced along the rocks. His alertness, his gauntness, had become more pronounced. The lean, rangy form in the well-cut suit seemed the total embodiment of evil.

Lara's breath caught in her throat as Whitney turned his attention from Lara to the helpless child. "I tried to give you warning. I was even going to spare the child. If only you had sold out and left as I had planned. You made all this necessary by involving that psychiatrist. Today in the restaurant, she kept staring at me."

Lara shuddered as his pitiless eyes remained locked on Karma.

"I couldn't take the chance. When I killed Crystal, I

didn't know the child was anywhere around. I lifted the ski mask for just an instant. But I know she saw me. Hypnotized, Karma might be able to identify me as the man she had glimpsed."

Karma sobbed and cried out for Lara. Poor, innocent Karma, barely able to comprehend what was going on. How frightened she must be. "Everyone saw you with Karma this afternoon," Lara said, trying to divert his attention back to her. "Scott knows you volunteered to take her up to the psychiatrist."

"Scott, the wonder-sheriff! I'm sure he'll figure out everything." He gave a brittle laugh. "I'll tell him that someone wearing a ski mask forced me at gun-point from the elevator and out of the building through the stairwell." Calmly, he rehearsed his well-planned explanation. "This madman let me out in a deserted forest area where I spent hours trying to find a phone. I'll claim I don't know what this maniac did with the little girl, but there was absolutely nothing I could do to save her."

"Scott will know," Lara spoke up, the unsureness sounding in her voice.

Whitney's bold gaze met hers with steady defiance. "Scott will be overcome with guilt about leaving the child with me and placing us in such danger. There won't be anything to tie me to the crime. All the evidence is going to point to Dane Lanford." He paused. "When Lanford first began investigating Mark's death, I placed those stolen paintings in his car, just as I planted the ski mask. Now I intend for the sheriff to find evidence that will frame him for your deaths. Lanford will spend the rest of his life in prison." He took a menacing step toward her. "Until I find some proper way to tie him to your deaths, I'll leave your bodies here, a place unknown about for a centuries."

His restlessness took him near the edge of the spring.

When he turned back toward her, Lara felt a chill of horror. He was clever enough to get away with this. Karma and she were going to die.

The narrowed eyes and cruel turn to his lips made him look predatory, savage, like a lion ready to pounce. He finished with a cruel smile, "Now that Austin Graham and the Evergreen Corporation have been eliminated, I'll reluctantly resubmit my original bid on the land. Joan, my friend, who you yourself made your executrix, will be more than happy to sell to me." A deadly light shone in his eyes. "And I'll be even richer than I am now! I'll end up with everything."

A faint sound, like the sliding of a stone, echoed far above them. Whitney must have heard it, too, for his eyes momentarily shifted from Lara.

Out of desperation Lara made a lunge toward him. Caught off guard, Whitney staggered backward, dangerously close to the edge of the spring. As he struggled for balance, the gun slipped from his grasp and splashed over the ledge of rock into the deep, bubbling-hot water.

As Whitney tried to regain his footing, Lara realized he held something in his hand. With a rage-filled cry, arm upraised, he hurled a jagged rock at her. Lara felt the jarring impact and the exploding pain in her temple.

Everything seemed hazy like the mist rising from the bubbling cauldron of the spring. Stunned, slumping to the ground unable to stand, Lara saw Whitney turn from her to the helpless child.

"No!" She felt her lips moving, but no sound came out. Lara desperately battled the threatening darkness, but she was slowly sinking into a dark, empty void. In total helplessness, she was able to make out Whitney's dark form reaching for Karma. As blackness blotted her vision, she saw Whitney lift the child high above the scalding water.

Chapter Twenty-seven

When Lara's eyes fluttered open, they focused first upon Dane, who was gazing tenderly down at her. She stirred, and as consciousness returned, struggled in his arms and cried out, "Karma!"

"She's all right." Dane said soothingly. "When I saw what was happening, I tackled Whitney and forced them both backward, away from the water."

Lara felt small arms go around her, hugging her tightly. "That sound we heard in the cave . . . must have been you, Dane. But how did you ever find us?"

"The psychiatrist contacted Charles and told him Karma hadn't shown up for her appointment. Charles then called me and asked if I had seen you. When I told him I had found out that Whitney was the head of the Evergreen Corporation, he expressed his own suspicions of Jordan. Together, we figured out this all had to do with the hidden spring. I told him about the cave and its location. Charles went to find the sheriff and I went looking for you. When I saw your car parked up on the bluff, I knew you must be in the cave."

Lara turned to see Whitney, bound by the same ropes he had used on Karma, slumped against the rocks.

The sound of sirens pierced the air. "That must be the sheriff now," Dane said.

"Did you ever notice," Lara said weakly, "how Scott has a knack for turning up when it's all over?"

The grand opening and art show had been advertised in the first issue of "Sacred Springs Gallery". Lara, in simple black evening dress, wandered through the flowing crowd, pleased by the attendance.

Renovations upon the hotel were finally complete, and all of their hard work had paid off. The lobby gleamed with polished woodwork. Soft light from hanging chandeliers cast a warming glow upon the many paintings on display.

Hallie was happily showing a group of new students her latest painting. Jim, shunning the attention, had stayed up in his room, but several of his works were also on display . . . one of them the likeness of a woman with glossy black hair who bore a haunting resemblance to Crystal.

Lara's gaze lifted to Mark's painting, "The Healing Water", which hung in its permanent place upon the wall of the lobby opposite the fireplace. Someday, she and Dane would develop the spring as part of the artist's retreat. Somehow, she knew her brother would approve of their plan.

At the entrance Lara spotted Joan, wearing the red, off-the-shoulders evening dress she had been admiring in the fashion catalog. "You look wonderful," Lara exclaimed as Joan spun around. Lara's gaze turned from Joan to her escort. "And so do you, Scott." Lara noticed how happy her friend seemed since she and the sheriff had started dating. And what an attractive couple they made.

"I finally got him to put on a suit and tie," Joan said.

Scott grinned, looking embarrassed. "And you can be sure it's going to be for the last time."

Lara wandered through the open doors out to the patio. She leaned against the high stone wall and stood gazing out at the distant hills bathed in twilight. For the first time since she had returned to Quachita Springs, she felt a sense of peace. Lost in thought, she did not at first realize that someone had come out to join her.

As she turned, Dane's black eyes met hers. He looked handsome in dark suit jacket and white shirt slightly open at the throat. The wind blew back dark hair touched with silver as he moved closer to her, saying, "I think our evening is a success." As Dane drew her into his arms, Lara closed her eyes, waiting for his kiss.

Their embrace was interrupted by the sound of childish laughter.

"Where did you come from?" Dane asked, pretending to be annoyed. "Isn't Charles supposed to be watching you?"

Karma, all smiles in her pretty new dress trimmed with bright pink ribbon, only giggled in response.

Dane took one of Karma's hands and Lara took the other. As the little family walked back into the lighted building, Lara felt a sense of harmony, as if she had some-how been meant to return to Quachita Springs, to find Dane and Mark's child who needed her. Crystal would have called that feeling "fate."

– THE END –